New

Other titles in this series

New Zealand Short Stories First Series
Selected with an Introduction by D. M. Davin

New Zealand Short Stories Second Series
Selected with an Introduction by C. K. Stead

New Zealand Short Stories Fourth Series
Selected with an Introduction by Lydia Wevers

New Zealand Short Stories
Third Series

Edited by
Vincent O'Sullivan

Auckland
OXFORD UNIVERSITY PRESS
Melbourne   Oxford   New York

Oxford University Press

Oxford   New York   Toronto
Petaling Jaya   Singapore   Hong Kong   Tokyo
Delhi   Bombay   Calcutta   Madras   Karachi
Nairobi   Dar Es Salaam   Cape Town
Melbourne   Auckland
and associates in
Beirut   Berlin   Ibadan   Nicosia

First published 1975, reprinted 1980, 1986
Introduction and selection © Oxford University Press 1975

ISBN 0 19 558001 X

Printed in Hong Kong
Published by Oxford University Press,
5 Ramsgate Street, Ellerslie, Auckland, New Zealand

Acknowledgements

Acknowledgements are due to the following periodicals and publishers, and to the authors, for their permission to reprint the stories in this volume: THE CAXTON PRESS for 'An Appetite for Flowers' (*O'Leary's Orchard and other Stories, 1970*); to THE CAXTON PRESS as publisher of LANDFALL, *A NEW ZEALAND QUAR-TERLY* for 'Bluff Retrospect' (*Vol. 21, No. 2, June 1967*), 'The Bath' (*Vol. 19, No. 3, September 1965*), 'The Mace' (*Vol. 22, No. 1, March 1968*), 'Corrective Training' (*Vol. 27, No. 1, March 1973*), 'The Room' (*Vol. 16, No. 3, September 1962*), 'A Retired Life' (*Vol. 23, No. 2, June 1969*), 'A Way of Love' and 'In It' (*Vol. 21, No. 1, March 1967*), 'Summer Story' (*Vol. 15, No. 1, March 1961*), 'A Way of Talking' (*Vol. 26, No. 2, June 1972*), and 'Mavvy Phoenix' (*Vol. 25, No. 1, March 1971*); FABER AND FABER for 'The Healing Springs' (*Introduction 3: Stories by New Writers, 1967*); ISLANDS, *A NEW ZEALAND QUARTERLY OF ART AND LETTERS* for 'Right-hand Man' (*Vol. 1, No. 3, Autumn 1973*), 'Between Earth and Sky' (*Vol. 3, No. 1, Autumn 1974*), 'Freedom's Ramparts' (*Vol. 1, No. 1, Spring 1972*), 'The Dead Bush' (*Vol. 1, No. 4, Winter 1973*), and 'A Servant of the People' (*Vol. 1, No. 2, Summer 1972*); WILLIAM HEINEMANN LTD., for 'A Game of Cards' (*Pounamu, Pounamu, 1972*) ; LONGMAN PAUL LTD., for 'A Final Cure' (*The Stories of Frank Sargeson, 1973*); ARENA for 'Another Kind of Life' (*No. 75, July 1971*); CORNHILL MAGAZINE for 'Winter Garden' (*Spring 1970*); SQUARE AND CIRCLE for 'The Loners' (*The Loners, 1972*) and 'Killers' (*World Short Stories, BBC 1967*); LONDON MAGA-ZINE for 'Wet Season' (*June 1969*); the New Zealand LISTENER for 'The Silk' (*5 March 1965*). Acknowledgement is also made to Barry Mitcalfe for permission to print his story 'Black Cat' which is to appear in a forthcoming collection.

Contents

		Page
Frank Sargeson (b. 1903)	A FINAL CURE	1
Dan Davin (b. 1913)	BLUFF RETROSPECT	10
Roderick Finlayson (b. 1904)	ANOTHER KIND OF LIFE	15
Maurice Duggan (1922-75)	AN APPETITE FOR FLOWERS	19
Janet Frame (b. 1924)	THE BATH	44
	WINTER GARDEN	51
O. E. Middleton (b. 1925)	THE LONERS	55
	KILLERS	67
Philip Mincher (b. 1930)	THE MACE	71
Noel Hilliard (b. 1929)	CORRECTIVE TRAINING	81
Maurice Shadbolt (b. 1932)	THE ROOM	89
Maurice Gee (b. 1931)	A RETIRED LIFE	107
	RIGHT-HAND MAN	121
Barry Mitcalfe (b. 1930)	BLACK CAT	138
Owen Leeming (b. 1930)	WET SEASON	143
Warren Dibble (b. 1935)	A WAY OF LOVE	150
	IN IT	152
Alexander Guyan (b. 1933)	SUMMER STORY	157
Joy Cowley (b. 1936)	THE SILK	178
Patricia Grace (b. 1937)	A WAY OF TALKING	185
	BETWEEN EARTH AND SKY	190
Vincent O'Sullivan (b. 1937)	MAVVY PHOENIX	193
Michael Henderson (b. 1942)	FREEDOM'S RAMPARTS	205
	THE DEAD BUSH	211
Margaret Sutherland (b. 1941)	A SERVANT OF THE PEOPLE	217
Rachel Bush (b. 1941)	THE HEALING SPRINGS	221
Witi Ihimaera (b. 1944)	A GAME OF CARDS	231

Introduction

This is the third collection of New Zealand stories to be published by Oxford in a little over twenty years. The first volume, edited by Dan Davin, drew on stories published before 1952, a period of beginnings and hesitancies, but also the years which included the rich maturity of Katherine Mansfield, and the promise, as well as the fulfilment, of Frank Sargeson. C. K. Stead's sequel to Davin covered the ground of only thirteen more years, but added almost twenty new writers. At least two of these, Janet Frame and Maurice Duggan, were talents so much finer than anything to be expected simply in the march of a new generation. What is offered in this third collection is the work of ten authors from that volume of nine years ago, and eleven 'new' voices. All but two of the stories collected here are works published in the last decade. The stories by Alexander Guyan and Maurice Shadbolt had not appeared in anthologies, and for their sakes I have taken a slight liberty with the notional span of this volume, 1965 to mid-1974.

The present state of the New Zealand short story is at least statistically sound. There are more stories appearing now than at any time, and the conditions for appearance have never been more kindly—twenty-odd publications, and over seven hundred pieces of prose which, for purposes of library cataloguing, are defined as short stories, in under ten years.

I suppose it is impossible for any editor to make his preferences clear without his being charged, and reasonably charged, with presuming to offer his contemporaries some kind of map. The friendly may accept this in the spirit of a guide, or the unfriendly reject it as an imposition on a landscape where there are no right roads, but a network of perspectives, the central point being wherever one happens to stand. Signposts, it might be argued, may be essential for writing from the past. To select the work of very recent years may well be construed as an attempt at nothing more durable than affixing the kind of stars or stamps with which dental nurses repay a certain manageable behaviour.

My assumption is that while these stories may interest readers outside this country, the majority of those who take up this book will be New Zealanders. To know what is being done at this moment, by one's own countrymen, in a form which in the past sixty years has embodied as much of worth in these islands as any form, is to measure the nation's pulse. Where these stories take one, after all, is where some of the country's most perceptive minds have already been, or are currently alert. And they do this in a language which must draw always from shared common life, if they are to create those patterns of fiction which finally clarify to ourselves the kind of tribe we are.

II

Although this collection contains stories by our three major talents, since 1965 both Sargeson and Janet Frame have directed most of their energies to other genres than the short story, and Maurice Duggan has published sparsely.

In 'A Final Cure' Frank Sargeson gives us our own community distilled through his lonely, frequently bizarre, figures. It seems to me that his work offers, among other things, a fine balance where character and society are equally vivid, their mutual dependence and opposition the poles between which his actions are elaborated. That tension too is where sympathy, tolerance, a sharp way with cant, flesh out social commentary with the substance of fiction. And if I may go beyond the story which represents him here, and speak of the body of his work, it is that weight of life behind the specific incident which earns him the authority of our senior talent.

Janet Frame's fiction takes one to a very much more private country, to the 'familiar hopelessness' which overwhelms Mr Paget in her 'Winter Garden'. It is difficult to see where happiness or value may exist for this writer, except in the possibilities of language, in the depiction of a world which offers nothing to delight or endure so much as that very tracing of its emptiness. With sensitivity and command over tone and image, she refuses what most would regard as worth or normality; with an ardour almost endlessly inventive, she asserts that here in words, in the inflections of shapes which only language commands, and in the rare souls who bear its talisman, does life become illuminated or tolerable. The greater part of her prose is a variation on this two-fold theme—the shallowness of life for all but a few, the pre-eminence of language and imagination among the chosen.

The moment when the reader is most struck, in 'Winter Garden', is not at the end, with neighbours uncomprehending as the bereaved husband rests his cheek against the earth. Rather it is at that brilliant image where the red berries at the dying woman's bedside are seen 'surging in their glass like tiny bubbles of blood'. It is not in any event or sentiment that value primarily resides, but in that simile which is set against the grave where 'there was no sun, no shadow, touching of hands, washing of body.' I offer it not as an academic point, but as a tribute to Janet Frame, when I note that her gift for images is not unlike that of certain Jacobean playwrights, for whom confusion and distress were not resolved in action, but whose finest imagery held the appearance of fixity, of illumination, until life again moved on in its chaotic flow.

Maurice Duggan's gift, so much smaller in volume than Janet Frame's, is perhaps broader in its commitment to enduring and unspectacular values, to where people like Hilda and her son in 'An Appetite for Flowers' are bound in the ambience of 'gas and flowers'. And no comment on Duggan will take one far without the concession that he is this country's writer who stands most surely in that strong European tradition in which style is also a moral touchstone; where the stamp of a writer's engagement is found primarily in a language which is self-conscious, elaborate, closer to the intricate grain of living than more subdued styles usually permit.

III

In concluding his review of the last Oxford collection of stories, Terry Sturm wrote in *Landfall*: 'The characteristic New Zealand short story is humanistically centred; the values it affirms are social values.' This is still so. Yet where the short story is now, and perhaps more clearly so than ten years ago, is that while writers continue to be prompted by 'humanistic' convictions, and to examine a society through the divagations of particular minds, there is now a more frequent sharpness in observing how life in these islands does not measure up. Of course one may counter that this always has been so, that Mansfield at times, and then Sargeson frequently, delineated broad areas in our lives where the spirit, to say the least, was meagrely nourished. There is as well that robust tradition of the 'man alone', stories of men in a society which often is hostile and crude. We run to numerous stories where the loner, the underdog, the drop-out, the foreigner, come to terms with life and themselves, and perhaps establish a kind of dignity, in spite of whatever it may be that militates against them. Frequently this is the short story where the most trenchant political implications are to be found. In this volume, O. E. Middleton's 'The Loners' is yet another of his gifts to that tradition. But in saying I detect a new sharpness, I mean that while many of the stories in this book set the individual against the group, there is now less certainty that the individual himself adds up. How many of these stories (and dozens each year) move about characters who variously are trivial, insincere, insensitive, obtuse?

It may be premature to claim that there is occurring in New Zealand a shift of sensibility, a redirection of various myths or attitudes which have sustained the short story in this country. The dream of the egalitarian society, the ethos of the back country, the myth of mateship and the good bloke, the levels of feeling beneath the taciturn exterior (and how often one returns to Mulgan's *Man Alone* as the finest repository, as well as the most probing questioning, of these)—all these remain. But the emphases, I suspect, have shifted ground. There is now more acceptance that there are kinds of national shallowness which are not as redeemable as we once believed. Again it could be said that this is nothing new. One feels it in Michael Henderson, say, at the present, but one might name stories where it was detectable forty years ago. What I claim as more apparent now, is a diminishing faith in the individual's asserting his own integrity. There are now larger areas of shadow than are consistent with a decent national life. If one has in mind Noel Hilliard's fine story of the girls in the reformatory, one must then look hard to find earlier stories of quite such impoverishment. There are pressures in that story which limit the chances of reasonable life so utterly, that 'fate' may serve as appropriately as any other word. Or one may point to those harsh but accurate anecdotes of Warren Dibble and Barry Mitcalfe, and concede yes, this is convincingly one level of the New Zealand mind, and one which we will now acknowledge as more permanently with us than at any other time.

It is not a fruitless exercise to place for a moment Mitcalfe's story with what strikes me as, if not quite its literary forebears, at least as earlier stories which evoke comparison—Sargeson's 'Sale Day', published in 1939, and Mansfield's 'Ole Underwood', written in 1912, but not collected until 1924. Mansfield's cat killer is an insane and persecuted old man; Sargeson's character, before he shoves a cat into a burning stove, has traced a course of frustration and sexual jealousy. Where I find Mitcalfe's story so much more disturbing is that his narrator is, for all social purposes, a normal young man. His emotional fog, where cats and men are virtually interchangeable, will remain a private viciousness. And the strong implication that only through a slowly conceded awareness about animals can this member of a human society come to a vague moral view is both a good deal more depressing, and a good deal more sentimental, than anything in the Mansfield or the Sargeson.

If, in one direction, we may look in our fiction to the increasing appearance of violent acts or violent feelings, in another we face a softness which, if not new in kind, presents itself in a more marketable guise. I refer here to the paradox that from an interest, or even an immersion, in the rich Polynesian life in this country, there derives some of our most perceptive writing, but also our flabbiest slogans, our most superficial prose. (This is an observation, need I say, on a large number of stories *not* in this anthology.)

It is now almost forty years since Roderick Finlayson's sober style, and his meticulous grasp of the English spoken by Maoris, cleared the tracks for later writers. Noel Hilliard and O. E. Middleton have followed him. They have brought to their work that sense of life which one accepts not merely because of the justness of their perception, but because these writers at their best have realised that however genuine or informed one's commitment may be, art elects its own salience. More recently, Patricia Grace has combined Finlayson's restraint with an equally attentive ear. Such writers are seldom touched by the modish; they are also a minority in an area where sentimentality and journalese produce the broad strokes of caricature, or where goodwill too often stunts critical appraisal. If I may be permitted to speculate on the current proliferation of stories, pictorial books, and dramatisations of Maori life and legends, it is partly as if the vision of childhood, and the myth of mateship—these staples for so long in much of our prose—have been subsumed to the immediate, but also easily falsified, area of Polynesian life. And would it be so extravagant to claim that here, by a large irony of history, is the last of our European dreams of the Pacific, the hopeful quest to shore up our imperfections with the values of a people whom a hundred and thirty years of ambiguous official effort has failed to debilitate?

IV

A critic of the second Oxford collection noted that several of its stories reached a sophistication not apparent in its predecessor. One would not so confidently claim for this volume any comparable advance on that score. At the present time there is, if not a deliberate movement away from the sophisticated, at least a tendency to favour the direct and the obvious, the intellectually unsubtle and the emotionally 'straight', as what by nature, as it were, New Zealanders want. This may well be so, and it does not preclude good writing of a kind. What it may also do is to encourage neglect of such rare skills as those which make a story like Joy Cowley's 'The Silk' precisely what it is. Many current attitudes to both prose and poetry in New Zealand fall far short, for example, of that intelligent but by no means restrictive standard established almost as a national norm by the late Charles Brasch, in his twenty years as editor of *Landfall*.

A social critic might point to many pressures which continue to work against writers moving beyond our particular limitations. He might observe to what extent most New Zealanders are deprived by not having what could be called a folk or ethnic tradition, and the corresponding threat of too stridently emphasising our obligations to a limited literary one. (To what extent does convention already prevent the appearance in fiction of, shall we say, an attractive capitalist, a depraved Polynesian?) Again, he might select the indifference of the press and most journals to offer anything like a serious cultural forum, or point to a shift in education which seems likely to deny even more New Zealanders those wider areas of subtlety and concern where civilised minds are frequently engaged. Such observations would keep before our eyes a few of the complexities which must modify comment on this country's writing. Yet one hopes there would be enough in this collection to suggest that whatever generalisations carry *some* truth, there are writers who stake out experience in a way which is something more than simply the well-recorded, something larger than would be possible without the individual talent, that unpredictable and ultimate in any assessment. For finally in good writing, allegiances or boundaries between what is socially impor- tant, what is artistically just, merge one into the other. Our society, like any other, becomes a different thing once writers of the quality of Maurice Gee or Maurice Duggan, Frank Sargeson or Janet Frame, have seen it in a particular way, have written stories which are *their* way of remarking, in James Joyce's phrase, 'the grave and constant' in what is commonly shared.

August, 1974

FRANK SARGESON   # A Final Cure

When he had at last put his name to the separation agreement his
wife refused to help him find suitable lodgings. It was her excuse
that she was exhausted by the worry of his irresponsible behaviour,
and the more especially his bad influence upon the younger
children.

It was fortunate for him that he had the affection of his eldest
son Roger, who rang up advertised numbers and went looking for
likely rooms. The boy wished when he had finished school to
follow his father and become a doctor. Stubbornly sure of himself,
determined about what he wanted, he in most other matters
resembled his mother: he resembled what she had once been in
being fond of his father.

When he was confident that he had found the right room
Roger assured his father a preliminary inspection wasn't necessary.

We've only got to pack up your things dad, he said, then I can
run you over.

There was nothing to be done. There were no patients to speak
of any more, he had signed the document and must get off his
wife's premises. And they were indeed hers—she had married him
with property and money of her own. It was fortunate for the boy
and his career, and for the younger children—upon whose account
she had pressed for the separation. Since he would be living in
lodgings paid for by a wife-in-name it was also his own good
fortune.

And he agreed with Roger that the room would serve. Ground-
floor, a large front room with wide windows, with a couch, a table
and an easy chair, all was run-down and faded though not yet
frayed and torn; and the sheets on the bed were clean. And he
was reassured about having to prepare his own meals when he
inspected the kitchen—also run-down, but spacious, with a row of
gas stoves to suggest that any serious jockeying for position among
lodgers must surely be unlikely.

I'll manage, my boy, he said. In any case, people. I want to
keep in touch.

His approval of Roger's judgment was clinched by an air of
spaciousness about the entire double-storeyed run-down house, an
elaborate wooden structure which dated from beyond the begin-

ning of the century. It was miraculous that a house with a balcony
of wooden fretwork and a slate roof nicely pitched had survived
among all the factories and warehouses. And he decided that the
best of its indoor attractions was the staircase, which descended
in a progressively widening, pleasing curve.

Dignity, my boy, he said. Most attractive.

Roger mentioned that he had inquired, and actually (he hoped
dad wouldn't mind if he said so), the house had been in the old
days the home of a doctor. There was what remained of a stable
at the end of the backyard.

Ah! his father said. Style! In those days a professional man
would never be a moment in doubt how he stood.

According to his self-diagnosis, it was his recognition of the
human need to know exactly how one stood that had been at the
bottom of his domestic trouble. He could recognise this unsatisfied
need in his patients—people who suffered (he remembered his
Latin): they were diseased (and it should always be stressed that
the word was more properly dis-eased) by their isolation. 'Patients'
was just another word for humanity.

Long years ago he had begun to practise as a conventional
bottle-doctor—and moved with the times until the writing of a
prescription began to prompt him to pause over some curious
thoughts. Shouldn't he by rights recommend a chemist who was
certified to be neither colour-blind nor unable to count? And
before very long he had begun to exhibit the unusual characteristic
of moving according to his own time. Disease—it was isolation—
being out of touch, with all the uncertainty of not knowing how
one stood. Why prescribe when the physician was himself, or
should be, the cure?—*not* the modern substance, sometimes
unstable, and probably always poisonous, which was concealed in
the pretty technicoloured capsule. The time he devoted to his
consultations was much increased. People who suffered were not
to be rapidly got rid of with the pseudo-magic formula illegibly
scribbled. And once he had decided that time was of no importance in matters of such urgency (he repeated to himself the
illuminating words and relished the contradiction), nobody saw
much of him any more except his patients. Some of these unfortunate people might well deserve from him an entire day. And
when not closely engaged with his consultations many hours were
consumed by a footling correspondence with the Department. The
subsidy was most inadequate—he was providing what amounted to
a specialist service and should be subsidized accordingly. No? But

surely the sum he saved the Department in chemists' bills should be taken into account? No? Very well then, was it the Department's policy to coerce him into again becoming a bottle-cum-capsule doctor.

But a doctor who never wrote a prescription! It was talked about around the suburb. Apart from a handful of eccentrics (and that included prolonged daily visits from a deaf old lady), nobody could be bothered with him any more. And the crisis came soon after his wife had decided that since he had ceased to earn enough to keep the house in cats' meat he must certainly be mad. She was not comforted when he begged for understanding *please!*

My dear, it's a truism—the more we *have* the less we can *be*.

His wife also suspected some kind of impropriety, and irritated him by her sudden and frequent incursions to suggest a cup of tea—including one for the patient (usually the old lady), with whom he had been secluded for so many hours. She was inclined to be convinced that he was being as bad as he was mad when she discovered the disturbing nature and number of the doodles daily discarded in his wastepaper basket.

To be alone in his lodgings was at first a delight, the kind of quiet holiday he had never enjoyed over so many overworked years. Disengaged from every demand of daily obligation, and free to occupy his mind as he wished he read no newspapers—time was now much too precious to waste on appearances that were so absurdly contingent; and he vowed that he would not be deflected from his purpose of dedicating himself wholly to what was permanent. It was a surprise to apply himself so readily to the books he had put off reading for a lifetime—and he relaxed by relishing his opportunity for an attempt at recapturing a little of his thirty-year-old and now somewhat rusty promise for playing the 'cello. He avoided too the mistake of rushing headlong and heedlessly at establishing his contacts. In the kitchen he spoke the greetings appropriate for the time of day and left it at that. If the response came he would respond. The core of it all was his sure conviction that the permanent stuff of human nature was something neither he nor anyone else could ever get past. In one of his books he discovered the forgotten formula: nothing human is to me alien— and he began to believe that all government in the world had so far failed because human nature had never been properly discovered and understood. It was without question what you started off with—wonderful things might follow, but they must be surely grounded on the permanent truths of human necessity. All had changed in wordly affairs since Galileo had put his eye to that fatal telescope: it was not a man-centred universe—on the contrary, humanity was right out on a limb. And that was why all things human would always demand every scrap of humble reverence which every sane man would always and naturally want to muster.

But in the kitchen signs of response were not encouraging. He was smiling and benign, but when he one morning inquired, And what might your name be? from the tired and taciturn hotel night-porter (a part-time worker crippled by age and arthritis, he occupied the outdoor room in the backyard beyond the wash-house), he was answered by a look that surprised by being as contemptuous as it was sour. His landlady was polite and mentioned the weather—but she also remarked about that fiddle he played. What a pity it didn't sound a bit more cheerful! He would understand she was speaking in the interests of her lodgers in asking him not to play of an evening later than eight o'clock. But he failed to register her request since he had already begun to say:

How very right you are, Mrs Hinchinghorn! A sombre instrument indeed!

It touched him that in her room off the kitchen she that same day began to compete with him by thumping out tunes on her untuned piano.

A tall Dutchman spoke only (although frequently) to say he intended to see the landlady and lodge a complaint; and there were the two Miss Cooneys, not young, red-haired and perhaps twins (that was to say, if they were sisters at all), who occupied a room together and smiled but never spoke (he did not know that they had lately retired from the telephone exchange—and after forty years of listening without any right of participation were not much interested in participating now). His one cheerful and promising kitchen companion was a freezing-works chain slaughter-man (with appropriate gestures he explained about his job as a brisket-puncher), who watched the clock while he scurried about the kitchen, and belched over the food he bolted standing immediately it was removed from the stove.

And then, late one evening when the doctor was making himself toast, the kitchen door was booted open by a very large Maori in a torn jersey and bursting trousers, his arms enclosing two large and bursting bags of mussels: the ukulele slung around his neck was made to look like a child's toy by the size of the vast old iron pot which was likewise suspended. He politely greeted the doctor, and made his excuses as he departed for his room upstairs after putting mussels and water to heat. The sound and thought of gumboots stamping up the stairway made the doctor smile—but soon after he had taken the toast to his room he was frowning instead. The chords strummed overhead and the voice that accompanied them were interrupted by the rumpus which had developed in the kitchen. It was no doubt the persuasive odour of cooking mussels which had brought there the landlady and the Misses Cooney. Unpleasant words were loudly and unpleasantly repeated. A Miss Cooney was heard to threaten, If you don't get rid of him this instant! . . .

The doctor never saw the Maori again.

But although troubled, he was not all that much discouraged by these unfavourable manifestations of human nature. People were to be taken as you found them. It was all genuine and valuable experience—and he reminded himself that it had for many years been his habit to evade much experience taken for granted in his student days: a busy doctor could rely too much on the laboratory to handle many a raw and disagreeable task. One day entering the bathroom, he was sharply reminded how seriously he had slipped. Answering the phone, his landlady had apparently been interrupted while her false teeth were removed—and the sight of two unpalat-able-looking plates would not normally have disturbed him, but the occasion had unfortunately been improved upon by a bluebottle and a gang of houseflies. It surprised him to be affected by nausea; and he was afterwards tempted to suppose that he had only to announce himself a qualified practitioner, and his chances of being distressed over encountering any such human contact would immediately be reduced. He resisted the temptation, which suc-cumbed to would have branded him a cheat. Contacts between individuals were two-way working: he hoped he might be accepted upon his naked merits as a human being even as he hoped to accept.

But there were many bad days when he was so much troubled by his doubts that he would emerge from his room only very briefly to satisfy animal necessities: feeling keenly his own isolation, he consumed the hours by relaxing over his doodles, drawing cornucopias which proliferated over sheet after sheet of scrap paper —integrated satisfying patterns of unimaginable yet meticulously detailed fruits, all of them tumbling out from curling goats' horns in a various and bewildering profusion: some, and some of the horns too, were so oddly shaped (what his wife had thought of as to 'suggestive'), that others too might have had their doubts about his sanity and moral health.

It was Roger who called one afternoon when his father was out

buying his provisions, and without thinking inquired the whereabouts of Doctor Dudley. Soon after he had returned there came
the first knock on his door; it was the night-porter, introducing
himself as Clarrie.

Rheumatism! Well Clarrie, we know next to nothing about that
one—in fact you could say nothing at all. He laid his hand on the
man's shoulder. I think it helps, Clarrie, if each man will learn to
live with his mortality—it's a shame we don't make that the first
lesson we teach our schoolchildren.

Clarrie would have again mentioned his pain, but the doctor
continued.

Yes, yes, I know—but we're all of us nagged by our aches and
pains, Clarrie. Here! He took the man's hand and pressed it against
his own side. Feel! There—that's it. Where I've had a pain for the
last eighteen months. I wake up in the night—in a father of a
fright, Clarrie. I say to myself—Doctor Dudley, you've had it!

Clarrie looked worried. All was a mistake—a doctor who told
you he had a pain!

What about bee stings, doctor? Do you recken it's worth a try?

The doctor smiled and put his hand in his pocket.

Buy yourself a new hot-water bottle, Clarrie. I know something
about you people—you make do with some old thing worn out and
leaking.

Bewildered and suspicious Clarrie backed out. He had *meant* to
to leave ten shillings in silver on the doctor's table. He was not
ungrateful, but he disapproved. It was no way for a doctor to
behave.

There were other knockings on the doctor's door—although a
Miss Cooney smiled on him in the kitchen and apologized: If you
will excuse us, doctor—it has long been our custom to consult a
lady physician.

But although he welcomed each visitor into his room he con-
trived to evade any admission that he was available for formal
consultations. Mrs Hinchinghorn wanted a prescription for aspirin,
and he could fortunately 'tide her over' from a supply discovered
among the odds and ends that Roger had packed. And in the same
way he obliged with alkaline tablets sought by the Dutchman and
also the slaughter-man.

Samples, my friend. You're welcome—I don't imagine they can
do you any great amount of harm.

There were however several lodgers never seen in the kitchen,
who even more mysteriously appeared only very seldom to have
any use for the house's other conveniences. Across from the doctor's

room there lived a little old man who with his head down appeared
to be greeting the ground with a smile of affection, whenever he
might be seen getting off smartly along the street on short chubby
legs and a pair of little round feet. It had become the doctor's
practice never to lower his blind or hide behind his curtain (he
had read about the humanists of the Renaissance who hoped for
self-protection and a quiet life by consistently allowing their private
lives to be publicly inspected), so he was in no doubt that his little
neighbour's disregard for the kitchen was explained by the regular
midday arrival of a lady social worker in a shining car loaded with
meals on wheels. But this service was limited to five days a week.
On Saturdays and Sundays the little man seemed never to emerge
from behind his closed door—although it was clear from the
sounds of a broom that he swept his floor: occasionally he would
lean from his window to shake his square of carpet. It was therefore perhaps a little contradictory that during one entire weekend
when the doctor could not afterwards recollect hearing any sounds
at all, he should also fail to notice that his neighbour's door had
remained consistently not quite shut. Afterwards too, it was a Miss
Cooney who was quick to claim that *she* had noticed. Yes, several
times! Nor had it escaped her that on the last occasion several large
blowflies had been in one great buzzing hurry to enter through the
doorway. It was nonetheless the social worker who discovered that
the doctor's neighbour was dead when she delivered his Monday
meal on wheels. Fully dressed and face down, he lay on his square
of carpet with his hands clasped in advance of his head. It was
as though the ground on which he had smiled for so long had at
last consented to an embrace.

There was immediately a gathering—the two Miss Cooneys, Mrs
Hinchinghorn, the slaughter-man who was on strike that day. The
last to join in was the doctor, and it was upon him that all eyes
focused. Could something marvellous be expected?—the newspapers were these days reporting many instances of 'the kiss of life'.
But the doctor simply looked as they did, and had nothing to say
except, He's dead, you must ring the police. There was silence. The
simple functional words were somehow offensive. The slaughter-
man withdrew—he was very familiar with death, but this was no
occasion for brisket-punching. Nor did the doctor stay—after he
had invited more disapproval. He did nothing, but it was judged
from his use of his handkerchief that he was affected. A display
of feeling was hardly the sort of thing anyone would expect from a
man in his profession.

The news item included the usual announcement, 'no suspicious

circumstances'. But that view of the matter did not wholly satisfy
the plainclothes men who made some formal inquiries after taking
over from the uniformed branch. What the devil was a properly
qualified although it seemed non-practising doctor up to living in
such a place? What was the story? But the answers were nothing
unusual: some kind of emotional trauma—you could say a bit
dopey: yes, a crank but quite probably harmless: no prosecutions:
no history of drink, drugs or violence: abortions no, not thought to
be likely: not a pervert: his wife had money—that could be the
story.

The doctor was not required to appear at the inquest, but Mrs
Hinchinghorn's mention of him as a lodger was reported—with the
unfortunate result that several of his former patients were enabled
to discover his whereabouts. And he was soon so much occupied
with familiar re-visitings that it virtually escaped his attention
there were no more knockings on his door from his landlady and
her lodgers. (His failure to notice his deceased neighbour's unclosed
door over an entire weekend had been much discussed and held to
be against him—after all, you would suppose a properly qualified
doctor to be trained to notice things it might be important to
notice; and in any case, what was one to think of a doctor who had
for several days repeatedly passed up and down within a few yards
of a dead body and never had an inkling! Who could have faith
in a doctor without a nose for the very thing it was the whole aim
and purpose of his profession to prevent?) A regular arrival each
morning was the deaf old lady, and she would remain until he sent
her home in the taxi he paid for; but it was one of his elderly
eccentrics who arrived with a disturbing story. The man insisted
that his health was much improved now that he had begun the
practice of smoking reefer cigarettes, and he wished for the doctor's
co-operation in buying up a large supply which was in danger of
failing as police suspicions were thought to be growing uncom-
fortably warm.

Now the doctor was aware that the use of this drug was in itself
agreeable and harmless: it could however prompt one into becoming addicted to the really dangerous drugs and was in any case
forbidden by the law. He was shocked by his patient's cynicism
and his indifference to the chances of corruption—and the more so
as he was a man with a background of education who had at one
time been prominent as a Church of England clergyman. It became
his long and delicate task to induce his patient to admit the light of
reason, and one that was successfully completed at last only by the
use of a stratagem. Yes, he would assist in buying up the supply of

cigarettes (by an ancillary stratagem his wife was persuaded into financing the transaction), but only so long as it was clearly understood that he was aiming at bringing that particular supply of the drug under proper control: that was to say, the reefers would be surrendered to the doctor, and his patient would be rationed and reduced until he ceased to make any more use of the drug.

The plainclothes men had in the meantime decided after much chewing matters over that a try-out on abortion was as good a tack as any; and the doctor was one evening called upon by a handsome well-set-up and powerfully-built young woman, a member of the uniformed branch clad at the moment in off duty-clothes (which only by an abuse of language could have been described as plain). After a competent show of hesitation and embarrassment, together with a plea that her confidence would be respected, she explained the purpose of her visit, intimating that she could immediately put down a five pound note as a pledge of her good faith. And then she began to feel herself genuinely embarrassed, because despite his appearance of sympathetic interest the doctor made no move to lower his blinds (although the circumstance was in fact no disadvantage, ensuring as it did that all transactions could be readily viewed by her male colleagues stationed on the far side of the street with night-glasses). There were however no transactions of any kind, and the doctor although he remained sympathetic appeared rapidly to lose interest.

My dear young woman, he said, my advice to you is that you have your baby—and may it be your blessing and happiness to bring healthy new life into our sick and sorry world.

As he reached for the doorhandle he withdrew from his pocket a pound note which he pressed upon his caller.

It's nothing, he said, simply a little something to help you with your baby.

A handy Justice of the Peace was located after the two plainclothes men had received their colleague's report; and provided with their warrant they were soon at the doctor's door. Through the night-glasses they had seen the doctor provide their young woman with money—without much doubt intending to assist her to achieve an illegal aim.. But there was a good deal more to it than that—the young policewoman, trained to notice what might be important, had informed them about the many rude drawings which lay about the doctor's table, yes, very rude, definitely! It was satisfactory to search a cupboard and discover stacks of pencilled filth—but a very great satisfaction indeed to uncover what they had all along more than half suspected, a large haul of reefers, all neatly packed in cigar-boxes.

The publicity was all very painful and bad for his innocent wife and children: poor Roger was obliged to begin his professional career under a cloud. But there *was* the compensation that his professional colleagues most generously rallied round. You could say, to a man: there were some very eminent names among those who testified. Doctor Dudley readily agreed to retire to an approved Rest Home—but after some years there is still no prospect that he would want to emerge out into the world again. It had all cost his wife a large slice out of her fortune. On most days he prefers to remain in bed—and yet when his health is inquired about he consistently replies that he is confident of moving steadily towards a final cure.

DAN DAVIN   Bluff Retrospect

It was a stiffish climb to the top of Bluff Hill but he took it pretty fast, remembering how steep they had found it as kids when they had come to the Bluff for Regatta Day and the rows they used to get into when they finally came down again and found the family with the picnic things all packed and his mother and aunts and the girls all sitting round having a last cup of tea and wondering where on earth all those boys could have got to.

He sat on the top and looked out over Foveaux Strait. Three miles away he could see Dog Island with its black and white lighthouse, tallest on the coast. Then Centre Island away to the west, an old burial place of the Maoris. He could barely make out Ruapuke Island which used to be Bloody Jack's hideout and could only guess where the Orepuki Cliffs must be, Papakihau was the Maori name, 'slapped by the wind'.

How strange that a few years should have made the difference between what he was now and the kid he used to be. The preparations for those picnics. His mother making fruit cake, sponge cake and marble cake days beforehand, and deciding how many tomato sandwiches, ham sandwiches, tongue sandwiches, corned beef sandwiches, chicken sandwiches were going to be needed. The packing of tins, and baskets, the search for bathing suits and sandshoes. Julia putting a statue of Saint Joseph on the front doorstep the night before, to make sure the weather was fine. The alarum loud through the house in the early morning and the rush to the window to see whether it was going to rain. The last minute panics about what had been forgotten, the ceremony of closing all the windows and locking the doors, and the despairing look in Roy's eyes at the front gate, hoping to the last, though he knew better from the sorrowful way they spoke to him. His anguished yelp when the front gate closed with a click and he was left behind. Then they all trooped down the street to the early tram and waited listening for its whining throb to turn into action, his mother already worrying whether she'd forgotten anything and whether they would be late for the train.

Then the gathering of the clan at the station, his mother greeting sisters from Makarewa and Woodlands; the girl cousins at once making friends again and comparing dresses and whispering and giggling; the boys looking at one another more suspiciously before merging and boasting about what they had got for Christmas and how good their ferrets were and how they had a new Winchester .22. The wild struggle for seats on the train; the mothers worrying about boys hanging halfway out the windows; the mud of the Invercargill estuary as the train went south through Clyde Street and Clifton. Then, as Greenhills approached, there was the warning to look out for old Auntie Wyatt and this time the children could have only corners of the windows while the full bosoms of the mothers were framed in them, handkerchiefs waving. And there she was, sure enough, at the gate set in the middle of the tall macrocarpa hedge, her eyes as keen as ever for all her eighty years and her spotless white handkerchief waving as the family went by. She was the one who had sent his father the fare to bring him across the world out of Galway which she had herself left twenty years before that.

They would settle back into their seats again, his mother's handkerchief a ball now and dabbing at her eyes, as she thought if it hadn't been for old Auntie Wyatt's money long ago she would never have met her man, and poor Auntie an old woman now with

not long to go, the Lord have mercy on her. But soon it was Ocean
Beach, the sea mysteriously on their left now instead of the right
where there were only the ugly meat works you didn't like to think
about. The women were beginning to stuff things back into baskets,
the napkins that had been changed, the sandwiches that had been
sampled, the thermos flask that go-ahead Uncle Jack had bought
as a Christmas present for Auntie Nellie. And now they were
coming alongside the Bluff platform and everyone was getting up to
disembark and his mother was calling to them to be careful and
not to get out before the train stopped.

Out on the platform the boys always made a vain attempt to
escape without carrying baskets but were always caught and the
family convoy went at a snail's pace through the barrier and out
into the hot sunlight of the street and the smell of the sea. As they
trooped untidily along the street, the boys up and down the outside
gutter like sheepdogs, the men dropped quietly out of the column
and disappeared. His mother would look significantly at Aunt
Nellie and the older girls would solemnly imitate the clicking of
their tongues. From the open doors of the pubs you could hear the
glasses clinking against the clatter of talk.

In Argyle Park the women spread blankets and rugs while the
older boys were sent off to get hot water from the big coppers with
fires under them that lined one side of the paddock. At least one
boy usually escaped while the tea was being made and search
parties would be sent out in case he got himself drowned in the
Devil's Pool. Then there would be a mighty lunch and the men
would arrive back in the middle of it smelling of beer and looking
sheepish but in better tempers than they had been since they started
out that morning.

Afterwards, the grown-ups would sit up against the old oyster
sheds and chat and go to sleep, the men meaning to make off again
as soon as things got quiet. And sometimes, if the sparkle of the
sun on the sea was especially tempting, husbands and wives would
go down to the beach. The women would take off their shoes and
stockings and go paddling, giving little screams at the onset of a
wave or the coldness or their own daring. And the men, after
watching and scoffing for a while, would be jealous at being left
out and would roll up their trousers and follow. And the children
looked shyly at them and then looked away, embarrassed because
their parents had become somehow like them, only their flesh was a
pallid white, and the men's legs hairy and on some of the women's
there were varicose veins which they themselves would never get.
The girls and boys would break up. The younger kids would be off

paddling and looking for crabs or spending their pocket money on a trip around the harbour in the *Skylark* or the *Waterlily*. The girls would go looking at the shops or if they were old enough would set off in twos and threes round the Point, telling one another secrets and throwing their chins up and shaking their plaits when strange boys whistled at them. The older boys went off into the bush to cut supplejacks and throw down stones at the sea. It was there that Martin and his brothers first learnt to look at girls, though they never got much further than looking at likely pairs and following them in the vague hope that something would happen. Only it always seemed that the girls of their own age were too old for them and the younger ones too young.

And sometimes, if there was time, they would climb Bluff Hill to where he was now and speculate about Bloody Jack and the Maoris and tell one another they could see Slope Point, the point of the South Island nearest to the Pole. And they would dream of themselves as whalers and castaways and explorers and prisoners of the Maoris who became tohungas and chieftains because of their bravery and wisdom.

There was the time, too, when his mother and Aunt Nora and the rest really had missed the first train. By the time they got to the picnic place it was too full. They had gone on a bit further and found a nice dry place under some stunted pine trees. They had stretched the rugs over the pine-needles and were just settling down when a gaunt old Maori woman, with blue tattoo markings on her chin and lower lip, came up and began to harangue them fiercely in Maori. No-one could make out what she was saying except that she was obviously furious with them for being there. Neither his mother nor Aunt Nora, especially Aunt Nora who was no mean scold herself and had a very strong sense of her rights, was the sort of person to be easily persuaded to budge once established. But there was something about this old woman that carried passion and authority.

Sheepishly but angrily they gathered up their things and moved back into the crowded paddock, the kids trailing after them, feeling miserable and defeated and somehow guilty. The old Maori, hands at her sides and head up, watched them go, dark eyes still fierce. When they had settled again she disappeared through the trees.

An old man in a fisherman's jersey and wearing a peaked cap had been standing by the road and laughing to himself.

'What was she making all that palaver about?' Aunt Nora asked him. 'Anyone'd think she owned the place.'

'She does in a way,' the old fellow said. 'That's an old Maori cemetery you picked on. There's always hell to pay if she catches anyone there. She's even after the loving couples at night if they curl up there for a canoodle on their way home from the dance.'

'Poor old thing,' said Martin's mother. 'I can imagine what she feels. Only she ought to have seen we wouldn't have gone there if we'd known.'

'Ah, well, she's a funny old stick,' the man said. 'She'd be a chief if she had her rights, they say. But it's all old stuff now and who knows or cares about chiefs any more, or Maori cemeteries for that matter. Half the Maoris themselves, even, don't know what they are.' He went on his way, chuckling.

Martin had felt guilty and terribly embarrassed. He hated his mother and his aunt for not getting away quickly. And he hated the old man for laughing at them, and at the old woman. Now, coming back to it, he still found himself blushing. Only now it seemed worse that it should have been his family, Irish people who were in this country because life in their own had been made impossible, their priests proscribed, their chiefs dispersed and their graves forgotten, who had even innocently violated the soil of another conquered race, especially that part of it which was sacred to the dead. By now, probably, the old woman herself was dead and buried, as like as not in the Anglican or Methodist or Presbyterian churchyard instead of in the burial place of her ancestors. It wouldn't be long before the cemetery without its guardian, its *tapu* forgotten, was grabbed up by the new people, its memory as dead as those who lay under it. In fact, now he came to think of it, he could not remember seeing that patch of the pine trees on the right of the road as you went towards Tom's place, though that was where it used to be.

He remembered how his father had merely laughed when they told him and said it was time for the Maoris to forget about all that old stuff, now that they were Christians anyway even if few enough of them were Catholics. Would his father feel any differently about it now, the older man who had replaced the laughing black-haired active man of those days? Probably not. Time that had caught up on the Maoris was catching up on him. Martin thought of his father as an object for a moment, a man outside himself. He saw him sitting across the table at Tom's, so like himself, so different. The same hands as his own, except that his father's were stronger, more worn, the veins on them heavy, the fingernails seamed and black at the ends. The same shoulders, wide and square, the same set of the chest, the same strong neck and heavy head. Only his father's neck was tanned a deep red, with grooves along the lines of the muscles, and a sort of greenish stain from the times when he wore a collar and the stud pressed. The same nose and the same blue eyes, coming down to them through Heaven only knew how many forgotten generations, generations which the Maoris would have remembered and named, and the Irish also, until the confusion of a new language, and the scattering of Cromwell, and slavery to the desperate business of keeping alive compelled them to forget.

But, from his mother perhaps or from the luxury of not having to use all his energies in keeping body and soul together here in an easier country, he, the son, had managed to develop a new sensibility, both a weakness and a strength. To his father, the Maoris were just a poor shiftless lot, who wouldn't do a decent day's work, were rotten with consumption, and spent any money they had buying booze or flash clothes. For himself, they were a persecuted people, robbed of their country and wasters from despair. And the English had seen the Irish in both these ways.

His father would have shrugged if he had said this to him. And rightly. For there was something false in it. Maori and pakeha alike had been driven to what they did and were by forces beyond the mastery of any individual. It was life that had been at work. It was all very well to be 'enlightened'. What was he going to do about it other than indulge the sort of regret that had lain behind their own dreams of being chieftains long ago? There was nothing he would do about it. Nothing whatever. King Arthur never came back.

RODERICK FINLAYSON

Another Kind of Life

Let me tell you about going down to the old people's place at Waiari to look up some of the family, especially Uncle Tu. You remember, he was one of old Hone Tawa's grandsons who was living there at Waiari just before Hemi died in that motor accident. When he was up in Auckland for the Queen's Birthday races he talked a lot to me about his young days. 'Charlie,' he said, 'you should come down where you people belong. You young fellars don't keep in touch with the old folk.' But you know how it is with a job like driving the buses, you don't get anywhere.

This stopwork in the city give me the chance, so I think now's the time to go and visit uncle and auntie at Waiari. But it was all wrong from the kick-off. I say to the wife: 'The long distance buses are still running and one takes off down the coast early. Grab the baby and let's go.' Well you know, she says there's the two school kids she can't leave and she promised help with the school lunches this week and so on and so on. She's half a Pakeha in more ways than one, if you see what I mean.

In the end I'm so mad I go alone. That's not the Maori way where you take the family too. But that the way it goes now. I got down to Waiari pretty early in the day. Nice sunny morning and the sea looked good and I began wondering about the chance of a load of pipis and mussels; it was a great place for those. But when I tried to get my bearings, golly, it all looked somehow different. I nearly forget where people live because last time I was down there was Grandpa's tangi, old Hone Tawa's youngest son, and I was only a bit of a kid then. Lots of places seemed to have gone and there were a lot of new places like Pakehas live there. Looked like someone was trying to turn it into a holiday place. All used to be Maori land round the old marae.

At last I see on the little hill above the beach the old place I remember where Uncle lived. Only now when I look at it it's somehow different too, newer looking, and I see that it's a newer place with a bit of a garden around it. Anyway, up I go and there's a two or three year old playing on the door-step and he says hullo, and then he calls out, 'Mummy, there's a man to see you.' And this young woman comes to the door.

Now as for me I can't speak Maori, can't even understand what they say, the old people. But there was me in the old home kainga, in the middle of Maori country, and there was this young woman that looked real Maori, so the words just came out naturally. 'Tenaa koe, e hine,' I said to her. I do know that greeting and a few of the old words, you see, not that I'd ever come at old Maori greetings to anyone anywhere in Auckland. But there at Waiari, my people's kainga, it just came natural. And what do you think that young woman said, eh?

She looked puzzled. 'Pardon, what did you say?' she asked, a real Kiwi accent, too, not a trace of Maori. But she looked more Maori than me, and I think she don't know one word of Maori. There was me, I look near enough Maori allowing for one or two

Pakeha ancestors, and I know how to say tenaa koe and so on. She surely must have heard those Maori words sometime. It got me wondering. Anyhow, I quickly kept to good old plain English from then on.

She turns out to be the girl young nephew Henare married. She wouldn't know me, of course. But where was Uncle Tu, I asked. Didn't he live there anymore? Oh yes, she says, except when he was away at his cousins' place in Rotorua. But today he was away at work.

'Not the work on the farm here, eh?'

'No,' she says, 'the bus comes every morning at six-thirty and take the men to the Metal Industries factory in Pinewood.' He wouldn't be home till late—overtime.

I looked around and think well, well, well! 'Tu must be getting on in years now,' I say. 'Getting a bit old for hard work, eh?' 'He'll get the pension next year,' she tells me, 'but now he's got no land or anything—well, he does what he can.' I remember when I was a kid, uncle talking about his farm, I could think of him happy on the land, his own boss, eh. It's turned out a bit tough for him.

Was I staying? Well, things weren't the same with uncle not there, and one thing and another. 'I better get back to Auckland tonight,' I said. 'The stopwork's over tomorrow and I might lose my job.'

'Oh, yes,' she said, 'the job. What do you do in Auckland?'

'Oh, I drive the city bus.'

'Oh,' she says, 'lots of Islanders, aren't there, driving the buses in Auckland? Lots of Islanders. The Islanders might grab your job.'

'Yes, the stopwork ends tomorrow, I better get back.'

'It's last year since Tu had a stopwork. He might have been here to meet you if only he had a stopwork now. But he goes to work every day.'

So I just had a few more words before I go, about how things changed.

'The Pakehas want to get the seaside places,' she tells me, as I noticed. 'And the Government people took Tu's land for the big tourist hotels sometime. It isn't the same here anymore.'

Ae, it isn't the same anymore.

So at last I said so long, maybe see you some more. And the kid shouted goodbye as I go out the yard.

Maybe I should never go back. I felt sort of sad and lonely. Down in the settlement by the beach I wondered where the old people were. Not a soul! Surely not all at factory work, or shut up in the house like Pakehas? But I see a big sprawling new motor

camp where the old-timers used to sit in the sun and yarn. A cool
breeze sprang up, south-east right off the sea and the sun disappeared behind clouds. There was the meeting-house where I
remembered being taken at the time of grandpa's tangi, but of
course it was shut up now, and it looked a bit more dilapidated. I
felt quite cold. There was time before the bus back to Auckland
so I think I'll have a drink or two to warm me and cheer me up.

The old wooden pub's gone and there's this new fancy brick
place for the tourist. Anyway, I go in the public bar and get me
a beer. There was two middle-age Maori men at the far end of the
bar and I hear them talking in Maori, but I don't try that trick and
make me feel a fool again. And there's one or two Pakehas
together. But anyway, I don't feel much like talking to anyone.
And that beer don't cheer me or warm me. I knock back a whiskey
or two. But I still feel chilled and sickly. Not sick, mind you, just
sickly, like I might have got on the wrong side of a tapu or something like that. But cut that out, I say to myself, don't you go
getting like the old people. And anyway, a bloody lot you know
about tapu.

I listen to the Maori voices of the two men at the other end of
the bar and try to make out what they say. But it's no use, I
understand only one or two words here and there. What it is, the
sad beer or something, I don't know, but it makes me mad when
I cannot understand. In Auckland, in the big city, I never get mad
when a few times I hear some man speak Maori, but here in my
own home kainga, in this Maori place, in all this Maori country
I am shamed that I cannot speak my people's language; that I
cannot even understand—and it makes me mad. It is because of
what the Pakeha did to my father, and to all the other kids' fathers,
when they were youngsters. My father told me the teacher strapped
him when he was a little boy going to school the first time and
how could he know better? The teacher strapped him, a little Maori
boy, for speaking Maori—and then he made him wash out his
mouth with soap and water, wash the dirty Maori off his tongue.
So my father stopped speaking the Maori. And I never learn.

Golly, that cold pub give me the shivers. I stretch my nerves to
understand the words of the two Maori men at the other end of
the bar. What the heck! Their words flowed around and about them
with a big warm friendly sound. The men looked into each other's
eyes and they laugh a bit and they put an arm around the other's
shoulder. You can tell they're never alone and cold there in that
place where the words warm the heart.

Then I think of the bus load of young Maoris I drive up to a marae way up north to talk about the Treaty of Waitangi—was it for good or the saddest day ever? And I begin to see what they mean. One time I never had much patience with such people, but I begin to see. They're mad because of what they've lost, everyone pushing them around to turn them Pakeha, and they wake up to find what they've lost. And they get mad. Some things you lose, you can find them again, but other things you lose you know it's for ever, and you mourn, you tangi. And for them that's Waitangi. And for me, the day of Uncle Tu and the things dear to his heart, all lost. What the use me coming back to my people that I cannot speak to? And the young woman and her husband and kids lead another kind of life in that old place, something I don't know of. But their talk is what I hope I'd left behind—the stopwork, the factory shift, overtime, the sack.

I wished the Auckland bus comes soon. It was all wrong the way I came down to see Uncle. It was because of the stopwork, a Pakeha thing. When a man goes back to his people's old kainga it ought to be because of a Maori thing, he mea Maori, if those the right words—you see, somewhere in the back of my head or my heart the old words kind of whisper; they keep coming up trying to get out, and give me no peace. Anyway, coming back should be because of a Maori happening—such as a tangi. Ae, a tangi for one of us departed, like Grandpa when I was a little kid. Maybe it's only death that can bring us city horis back to the heart of our people now.

Then the bus comes. I know I never see my Uncle Tu again.

MAURICE DUGGAN

An Appetite for Flowers

Hilda trod the high and holy street. A Salvation Army group was meagre at the corner. The wind blew grit and papers and beyond the cathedral spire the sky was green. Traffic checked her briefly then she crossed, walking in the black spaces between the stripes,

as the words of salvation were blown away. She kept to the inside
of the pavement. Men looked quickly into her face, then at her
legs, then in quick appraisal. She felt rather than saw this, as she
identified objects in shop windows without glancing directly in.
There were not many people in the street. She walked with her
head down into the gritty wind. Her shopping bag dragged and the
coloured paper round the bunch of chrysanthemums—flowers from
Mr Rowbotham—crackled and tore. The lion-faced flowers spread
their yellow manes.

North of the cathedral the shops thinned out and she turned west
and climbed the Jacob's ladder to the terrace street. Here it was
darkening and her heels were loud and she held her face gratefully
to the clear breeze. She lingered as usual by the camellia branch,
blossomless now, and walked on to enter the gate.

She disliked this dense patch of shadow before the door, although
she couldn't have said why. Even in summer the entry remained
damp and the stones grew mould. And the tree which caused it
wasn't worth the keeping; although she could be grateful for
greenness. The cat, as usual, she spurned away—a nameless, mangy
thing for which she felt no sympathy. She supposed it smelled the
meat.

Some nights the stairwell depressed her: tonight she could have
sprinted to the highest doorway.

The butcher, a man of forty with at least four children, had
asked her to run away with him; as he stood in the meaty sawdust.
Hilda had laughed, but not unkindly. Why did he say that, out of
the blue, and mean it? But he gave her excellent meat and did not
repeat the proposal. She kept clear of thick fingers and palms and
watched the blade open marbled flesh.

Now she unlocked her door and entered the wan room, where
the last light was dying in a smell of gas and flowers. A letter had
been poked under the door. She stooped, keeping a straight back in
a movement rather like a deep curtsy, and felt a stocking go. The
letter was from Ben, her ex: she put it on the table by the
telephone. It could wait; as what couldn't, from him? The stocking
was ruined, of course.

What she would like most, she thought, drawing curtains and
switching on lamps, would be to sit for a moment in this amber
dusk and to drink something cool and delicious, an absolutely
foreign drink, exotic. But although there was nothing to prevent at
least a pause, or because of that, she took off her jacket and began
to unpack the shopping bag, while the kettle boiled and the
telephone rang.

'Hilda?'

'Who else?' She raked her fingers through her hair in a practical manner, after the wind. It was his time for phoning, to the minute. A precise man who had been angry at the butcher's proposal, when she told him: a man with children and no runaway thoughts.

'Shall I come round?'

'Now? I'm just about to get my dinner.' They'd quarrelled: she was shaking him off. The silence awaited an invitation she did not extend.

'You're still cross, then?' He seemed to be speaking right into the mouthpiece: there was a hollowness of breathed sounds. A surreptitious phone call, while his wife fed the kids.

'I'm tired,' Hilda said. 'Phone me tomorrow, why don't you?' Or don't phone me at all. Put in a long distance call to your wife, in the next room.

Hilda reached out, full stretch, and could just reach the plug as the kettle rattled and spilled.

'What about later?'

'I told you, Anthony: I'm tired. I want an early night.' Because his days were leisurely he would never believe such a thing.

'Ten minutes, surely?' He was reasonable, and sure of winning. 'I'll phone you back in an hour or so. I must dash.'

Perhaps, thought Hilda, Anthony junior has choked on his raw carrot. It was a familiar story: he must rush. And it could incite her resentment—all the rushing being in one direction. She'd wait if she felt like it. Did she feel like waiting? Better still, she'd be out. Yes, she would be out. Disenchantment was as distinct as indigestion. She would have liked someone to come, simply, with roses and kind hands, to this simple room and her rose simplicities. But it seemed unlikely; and the pan was hot.

On the radio she found fanfares and a long exudation of violin notes to which she paid no attention, wanting only something in the background. She sprinkled salt into the pan and cooked her perfect steak with complete concentration. She ate with it a single slice of fresh white bread, liberally buttered, while she read the evening paper. Ben's unread letter nagged distastefully at the back of her mind; but Mr Rowbotham's chrysanthemums were a consolation on the corner bookcase, an acceptable yellow above the shelves of paper-back detective stories. The sad Mr Rowbotham whose hands would not make fists or talons, whose gentle lusting she did not pity, understanding its inconsequence.

She was Libra : she read : —

A difficult time for your domestic affairs, particularly if you have a Cancer partner. Wisest advice is to take angry scenes with a smile and refuse to be drawn into any arguments. Remember that it takes two to make a quarrel. Take a tip from the stars and do not place any reliance on impractical relationships that may hurt you. Significant shade is tangerine. Best number: one.

To the best of her knowledge she had no Cancer partner, and little in the way of domestic affairs. And tangerine would make her look livid. She hummed to herself over her few dishes, as the coffee jubilantly bubbled. Best number: one.

*   *   *

Perhaps it was what she'd expected of the patch of intense shadow; this man naked and paltry under his spread top-coat, in the tiring wind pathetically exposed. As if suspicion or uneasy imagination bred such things: as if she imagined it. But the man grossly moved and Hilda turned back indoors. She would have had to pass close to gain the street; and refused the indignity of running, in her present shoes. He was a short wraith of a creature: she could have walked up to him and given him a buffet for his silliness.

The pay phone in the hall raised questions: was this an emergency? Hilda doubted it and began to climb. She felt she might as easily have opened the door again and cried 'shoo', flapping her hands.

The sounds were brief and not loud: a scuffling, a thud, a short cry. The door opened and Anthony stood in the porchlight, breathing with a victor's satisfaction. Hilda felt guilty, caught on the stairs, neither ascending nor stepping down, while Anthony rubbed his fist in brute rumination.

'A nice neighbourhood,' Anthony said. 'Was it your butcher friend?'

'I was going for a breath of air. Of course it wasn't. What happened? Poor crazy creature.'

'Pah.'

Anthony picked up the phone and dropped pennies: he was prepared for all emergencies, until they asked him his name. Discretion was a question. They wanted his name, first; it was presumably the immutable order, to start at the beginning and work through the form—name, time, date of call, address of caller. Hilda kept her hip against the banister. Anthony hung up with a bang and pressed button B, just in case.

'I thought I'd just pop round,' Anthony said. 'Good thing I did. Did he accost you?'

Accost? Hilda shook her head and turned and began to climb the stairs. She felt the heaviness in her calf, her buttocks; and two hours earlier she could have run. While Anthony climbed in his own time, adjusting his tie and cuffs. To free herself of this dragging, Hilda leaped the last flight, without daunting him. She hated to be followed on the stairs: the backs of her knees felt naked, her heels strained. Impractical relationships may hurt, she remembered without amusement.

'Ten minutes you said, Anthony. I'm tired.'

'You were going out, nevertheless.'

'A walk before going to bed. You forget, I don't have a great garden.'

'Courting trouble.' He rubbed his knuckles again.

'Nonsense,' Hilda said. 'That sick old man?'

When he had gone, his ten minutes expanded to an hour—the time it took for reconciliation and further recrimination, love of a kind and anger of a kind—Hilda ran herself a bath in the steamy bathroom. She creamed her face and used pink tissues: her hair was tied up in a knot of cloth. Gratefully she descended into the hot, scented water.

This time it was final, and she welcomed it. It was what he had come to say. But took his time, not being one to miss opportunities or leave a body lie about unused. He made his quarrel without her assistance; and his love; and was angry. Remembering her indifference she was pleased, as if she'd won mastery over a habit like smoking or drinking or drugs. She could hardly wait for him to go, to be gone. From on high, even, she heard the roar of his going, the unnecessary fierceness of the engine, the wince of rubber on the road. And she would bruise where he had clenched her arm; but only there. She began to wash, enjoying the generous lather. Anthony, or the poor man in the shadows, or the unopened letter from her ex—she wouldn't embark on comparisons. It was midnight and she yearned for sleep, in the warm water. She definitely needed eight hours, not a minute less. Best number: one.

She might regret it, after all. She'd see.

*   *   *

Roses in season to your love, anywhere in the world. Except

the iron curtain, Mr Rowbotham said. Try the pet shop next door, for doves.

But love was always away, if she could believe the messages they wrote on the cards; and the things they said to her, Hilda Preeble (Mrs).

In silver and bronze distinction Mr Anthony Silversteen was buying flowers, for his wife and their fifth.

'You're Hilda Preeble, aren't you? We met once at a Guy Fawkes' party. Years ago, if you remember? I did some business with your husband. Ben, was it? He was in cars. How is he these days?'

'As always, I imagine,' Hilda said. 'Are we to send these for you?' It was obvious from the note.

'If you would.' He peeled money. 'Is this by any chance your own venture?'

Hilda puzzled as she wrapped.

'Your own business, I mean?'

'Heavens no. I work here, that's all.'

'For the gentleman over there?'

'No. Hilda smiled at the thought. 'That's our Mr Rowbotham. He's a dear. And he has a wonderful way with chrysanthemums.' (Who touched me once, in solemn praise, upon my breast.)

Anthony's wife was named Martha. She was inundated with flowers which Anthony chose but only Hilda might wrap and send. There was some doubt in Hilda's mind as to who was being ransomed, or won, with this profusion. Anthony confessed to being on various boards which precluded frequent visits to the nursing home; and for a moment, remembering a phrase, Hilda took him to be an actor—though it seemed unlikely. She thought a theatrical person would have been less formal, less wealthy. 'Company director' was a disappointment when he took her out to dinner; but he was eager to please, if a little dull. And more eager, driving her home, while she discouraged. After all, as she pointed out, they had so recently met.

If she now remembered beginnings, briefly, running a little extra hot, it was not because she wished to explore the nature of her relationship with Anthony. That was not her way. It was just that it had always pleased her to think of that positive avalanche of blossom, that tornado of flowers in which his wife was whirled, as the prelude to his finally ascending to her flat, where he was eager and dull. He remained that way. For the brief time of their affair he was too unbending a man to command surrender or engender tenderness: his dignity approached pomposity. He was, also, too possessive in his wealth of which she wanted nothing. It was inconceivable to Anthony that Hilda could be happy in the flower shop and content in these small, neat and rather dowdy rooms. He wanted to change her: she wanted him to let her be, in however friendly a way. His plans were too grand for the small future she allowed herself; and he was so married. She simply enjoyed his company, in a limited way, and that was that. He couldn't excite her; there was nothing she could conceivably do for him; and nothing she could permit him to do for her.

Roses in season to your love, anywhere in the world.

Hilda dried herself vigorously on the huge soft towel.

*   *   *

The days were bleak. Mr Rowbotham sat among the pale blooms and wrote poetry in a school exercise-book, in exquisite handwriting. He said it was doggerel, really; but the beautiful writing seemed to redeem. He was a sad-looking jowly man, after all, but he had a deeply poetic nature; and he liked to stand close if Hilda would allow. He coughed persistently and his vivid white handkerchiefs smelled of eau-de-Cologne.

He spoke of Persephone, a goddess of whom Hilda had never heard, going now into the earth. It was strange, as she listened to his gentle voice. Mr Rowbotham was known to be a deep reader.

'She will eat poppy seed and sleep in the earth with her dark king, Hades of the black chariot.'

Was this Mr Rowbotham's poetry? Hilda smelled the richness of his breath: he took frequent nips, in private at the back of the shop, hiding the sherry bottle behind empty flower pots.

'Winter, you see,' Mr Rowbotham said. 'I suppose I'm boring you.' His smile was thin and, she thought, rather bitter. He fixed his eyes on her chest. 'An owl cries', he said, 'and Persephone goes down.'

Hilda was impatient with his sadness, in the warm shop among the flowers. She would not try to understand such an eerie story: she moved away from the timid hands. After all, Mr Rowbotham was not that old and poppy seed or not, or poetry, he was a man like the others—even if his case seemed special.

Now she did not linger before the camellia branch and hurried through the patch of shadow by the door. And no one sent her roses. She kept the kerosene heater burning night and day and her flat was snug; though the nights seemed cold. She had gone past

regret of Anthony: she would not have welcomed him; but she was
piqued that the telephone did not ring. A stinging finality of tone
had been rehearsed.

In the evenings she read detective stories, washed her hair,
ironed clothes or cleaned the flat, while the old rooming house
slept in gusty age. The butcher sold her eye-steaks and milk-fed
veal. Time passed, and she was glad not to be a goddess—in cold
earth.

*   *   *

She was late and tired. Friday was late shopping night and after
the shop had closed there was still a great deal to be done. Mr
Rowbotham was in no condition to assist, at that hour: he was,
even, something of a nuisance, flushed and emboldened, and had
frequently to be sent home in a taxi. Home to Mrs Rowbotham
who had once sung, for Hilda, her one flower song.

> *The foxglove bells with lolling tongue*
> *Will not reveal what peals were rung*
> *In Faery, in Faery, a thousand ages gone.*

Surprisingly, Mrs Rowbotham sang superbly, from a deep globy
bosom. She accompanied herself on the piano; and Mr Rowbotham
kept time with a waving hand, proud of his wife.

And now Hilda hummed it, as well as she could remember, as
she climbed the stairs—to find Adam seated on the floor by her
doorway. In the company of a grim suitcase. He was half-asleep,
but passed her the note, without speaking. Hilda broke open the
envelope and read:

Hilda old thing I have to be off on urgent business. Plans
don't allow for Adam and I thought that seeing you were once
mad keen for custody and all that you'd be happy to take him
in. I may not be able to get in touch for some time. Your X Ben.

Adam was watching her as she read, in the dim light of the
landing. With that curtsy she dropped to him but ventured no
embrace. He was wary; and he looked chill, in a thin jacket.

'How long have you been waiting, Adam?'

He exposed an expensive watch. She thought it typical of Ben:
the boy would have the best, or at least the ostentatious, while she
was dunned for sums of money exactly calculated to distress
without bankrupting her outright.

'Since half-past six.'

'You poor dear, you're frozen.' She couldn't touch him: he gave off such waves. She unlocked the door and they entered awkwardly. 'I had absolutely no warning. Why didn't you come to the shop? He could have said. He could have given me time to prepare.'

'There wasn't time. He was in an awful hurry.'

It looked, somehow, wretched—the small room in its neatness and emptiness—as she tried to see it through his eyes. She snatched up under-garments and stockings drying by the heater: the intimacy shocked her, suggesting a sordid abandon, as she stood in her neat dark dress.

'You haven't eaten, I suppose?'

'Yes. It doesn't matter. I'm not hungry, anyway.' He simply stood.

'Bring in your bag, and close the door. It won't take a minute to get you something.'

She could have wept at the vast unfairness. It was what she most wanted to do—collapse in a chair and weep buckets, or floods. But tears had never come easily. So she drew the curtains and turned on the lights—an unvarying routine of quick, precise movements—and unpacked the shopping bag. After all the flat was warm, even if a little fumy.

Adam stood by his suitcase, waiting; waiting for anything or everything. Fourteen this month, she remembered; and over three years since she had seen him. Just an occasional post-card, because her ex had been 'moving about a bit, old thing'.

'Look, love,' Hilda said. 'We'll have to do better. I fancy we're both a bit shy. We'll think of something.'

And then, for the first time in weeks, the telephone rang. She was sure it was Anthony: things never came singly.

'Hilda?'

'Who else?'

'Can we talk?'

'No.'

'Please. Are you alone?'

'No.'

'I see. Anyone I know?' His displeasure was rewarding.

'Adam has come on a visit.' Hilda smiled at her son.

'Adam? Might I ask. . . ? No, it doesn't matter.'

Against her first decision, she relented. He may have hurt but hadn't harmed her. He wasn't Ben. 'Adam, my son,' Hilda said.

'Your son? You never mentioned you had a son. I find that strange, Hilda.'

'Do you?' Hilda said. 'I must go.' She smiled again, to involve Adam.

'Shall I phone again?' Anthony's tone was neutral, even official. Hilda wanted the conversation finished: Adam was so embarrassingly unpractised in not seeming to listen.

'Well, we'll see,' Hilda said. It wasn't intended as an answer. 'Goodbye for now.' She wouldn't bolt doors quite tight, in her situation, at her age. She replaced the receiver.

'Am I in the way?' Adam expressed his feeling of being everywhere out of place. Like a fork in the knife drawer, Hilda thought.

'In the way?' She only feigned incomprehension.

'He said not to get under your feet all the time.'

'Your father?'

'Yes.'

Hilda soberly made herself a stiff drink from Anthony's bottle which had lain untouched all this time. She sat down.

'Please sit down, Adam. Over there.' She drank. 'Can I make one thing perfectly plain, Adam? You aren't in the way: you won't be. There's simply no question. Will you take my word for that? You couldn't, you know, be more welcome.' Wondering what else Ben might have said: he was never a reticent man. Meantime the gin assisted.

'If you'll tell me where things are, I'll cook something,' Adam said. 'I'd quite like to.' Wanting perhaps to be out of view.

'You can cook? No, there's no need.' She began to get up from her chair.

'I'm housebroken. He said to tell you that, too.' It was a wry grin of more than fourteen years. He pulled off his jacket and went into the kitchen, where closed cupboards were daunting.

Hilda was decisive: she finished her drink and put away the bottle. 'The best thing you can do, Adam, is to prepare your room. In here.'

She swept aside curtains on the glass balcony. It wasn't promising: the view was of lighted windows and the backs of tall houses. But by day there would be a compensation of green, the slope of a hill, a few dark trees.

'Just throw everything out,' Hilda said. 'Except the bed.' Quite suddenly her good temper returned.

'Out where?'

'Pile it up on the landing. Tomorrow's Saturday: we'll take it down. There's a basement of sorts, and it's only junk, anyway. And open the windows; it may be musty.'

'Where's north?' Adam said, when he had the space cleared.

'Sorry love: I didn't catch?' Hilda had moved to the kitchen: the distance between was not great.

'I wondered where north was.'

It surprised her. 'Well, you get the morning sun so it must be. . . .' Hilda turned so that the balcony was on her right. 'Why?'

'It's all right.' For the first time he smiled—not a grin, a smile. 'I've worked it out. I don't know why: I just like to know.'

The boyishness reassured her, a little. There was no mystery: but the distance between did not immediately diminish, and the years had not helped. She sensed the intractable, an intransigence: right or wrong, only so far would he go. She hoped she was mistaken; it was Ben's way.

'Fruit-juice?' Hilda said. 'And tea or coffee? Or do you usually have a cooked breakfast? I suppose you should have. It won't take a minute.' Growing boys were said to need a lot, she thought.

'What do you have?'

'Fruit-juice and coffee. Did you sleep?' The balcony looked uninviting.

'Yes. I'd like the same, if I may.'

'Then you use the bathroom first. I'll get things ready.' The constraint had gathered again, in the hours of darkness.

He had made his bed and there was nothing of his lying about. His suitcase was closed. It's probably locked, too, she thought. And when she used the bathroom she found no trace of him except steam, and a towel. She had provided the towel, and it hung neatly folded. She felt intimidated, and nervous of the days ahead. She wondered how long it would be before he emerged, left his mark, let things lie. He was a neat camper and a stranger, for all the blood they shared. And how heavily she had carried him, at the last, braced back to counterbalance the great burden, while Ben disparaged: she remembered that. She remembered too that she had woken half-expecting to find him gone; and determined, now, to take up the challenge and to make things work. He was hers: there was that fact; and she was quite old enough to be his mother.

'Mr Rowbotham, this is my son, Adam. Adam, Mr Rowbotham.'

'A pleasure.' Mr Rowbotham extended a shy hand. 'And a surprise, if I may say. Brother and sister I could conceive, but . . . .'

Hilda laughed: the gallantry wearied her. 'I'm flattered, Mr Rowbotham. Adam has come to stay. We must do some shopping, if you can cope.'

'Monday morning, if you remember, seems not to promote an appetite for flowers. But there are the usual wreaths. Yes, of course I can manage.'

Adam examined the small shop and the figure of Mr Rowbotham.

'Oh, well,' Mr Rowbotham murmured an apology. 'You should see it in the spring. Persephone, as I was explaining to—to your mother—Persephone has left us. Temporarily, of course.'

'Persephone?' Adam looked about, as for a junior assistant.

Mr Rowbotham chuckled, but Adam's puzzlement was brief.

'You mean the goddess, or whatever she was?' Adam was noticeably pleased to have unravelled the clue.

Mr Rowbotham was delighted. 'I congratulate you,' he said to Hilda. 'A well-taught boy. I fancy there aren't many.'

Hilda too was impressed, not least with Adam's awkwardness under the compliment. She would ask him to tell.

That day they bought, second-hand, a chest of drawers, a folding card-table and a small bookcase. They bought, new, an adjustable desk-lamp, a piece of bright carpet and a bright blanket. Hilda thought she was all right for sheets, in the meantime.

When, in the afternoon, Adam was enrolled at high school, he had to be fitted out in school uniform. He did not wish her to accompany him: he would prefer to manage it alone. He was away a long time but returned, before the shop closed, through the vigorous turbulence of air, all wind blown and ruffled, and handed Hilda the docket and the change. Hilda gasped at how little change there was from so many large notes, but said nothing; and wondered was the boy still growing fast? And Mr Rowbotham, under his fuzz of white hair, spoke of a classical education.

Adam had remained reserved. He had given practical assistance with each purchase, rejecting one chest of drawers as too large and another, to Hilda's relief, as too grand; but apart from that he stood to one side. He appeared to have no curiosity. When Hilda remarked on something he attended, without comment. The city was strange to him but she had very strongly the impression that he would make his own appraisal in his own time, and fix his own landmarks.

She learned very quickly that she was not a woman who could help him, in deeper ways; that help was what he least wanted. He had been removed from her when he was seven; and Ben had taken care that only the bare letter of the agreement should be met. She had seen Adam only briefly over the last seven years, and only rarely alone. He was a stranger, and her son. Yet she could remember summers, faultless vault, unmarked cerulean; but turned from too painful an invasion by the past. To shrug things off; that had always to be her strength. She decided that Adam was naturally shy: she forgot how little choice he had.

She saw that he had found independence of a kind in this shyness, this silence and deep reserve: emotion, she supposed, lay deep. He fitted in with her routine and carefully kept from spilling over into her life—where was no mystery. He seemed impelled to tidy himself away. But, finally, she realized that she could only trust him to deal with his own life, and with a woman he called Hilda; as he searched for his north.

Because these were not things she was good at.

* * *

'Don't you go out, or anything?' Adam said.

'I suppose I don't,' Hilda said, struck with it.

It had only been a matter of months: she tried to remember how she had filled her time before he came. She read detective stories. And there had been Anthony; and now there wasn't. And Adam's tastes, or his mountains of homework, did not encourage the former background of the radio.

'Do you mean you'd like to go out? To a film, or something?'

'No. Not particularly. I only wondered. You don't seem to see many people.'

'Oh, all day,' Hilda said. 'That's enough, surely?' And knew it wasn't. 'I'm lazy. I like to sit.'

She'd left her friends in other places; or they'd grown apart. For a while husbands came, just passing through, with a bottle of something for the gay divorcée alone in her convenient flat: for a year or two after the divorce. But she couldn't accommodate so many impingements of another world; and was slow to respond, hinting at strong emotional attachments and hoping the message would go back. To Ben.

'Adam. If you mean you'd like to have friends in.' Why hadn't she thought of it? 'I'd be quite happy to clear the decks.' It was an expression of Ben's: Clear the decks old thing, we've got a mob descending. She hated it. 'I mean, don't think I'd be forced out into the snow.' She hoped he would see the hilarity of that.

'Have you always lived here? Since . . . .'

'Since our divorce? Yes. I like it; and it's handy.' To what she did not ask, but would have supposed she meant her job. 'I suppose it's not ideal, for you.'

'Oh, I like it,' Adam said, and sounded genuine. 'No. I didn't mean I wanted friends in. Not yet, anyway.' He went back to his homework.

Seeing him absorbed again in his books, Hilda was disappointed. She had thought he might be going to open out, to tell her things— even to ask her things. She glanced at him from time to time: she watched him, fearing to find Ben in him and, she abruptly realized, fearing only a little less to find himself. For some time she had thought of her son as this simple amalgam; until she realized that Adam at fourteen already contained his own mystery and was resolved to be himself, seeming even to know what this could be. No urgency of expression revealed it: Hilda had to search for signs. As Adam studied (Why was there so much?) she witnessed a concentration, a slow passionate attention that neither she nor Ben could ever have commanded; and she thought it a blessing that she could not help.

Faultless vault, unmarked cerulean: remembrance of a time when she had been mother, wife and housewife was not a way through to Adam. She could not insist that he share her memory: for him time past seemed to bear no charge. She had tried it, conjuring up one picture that had stayed bright for her.

The bonfires burned like beacons along the spine of hills. Shots rang in the gully: rockets rose to release a slow bright fall of stars: the rose smoke drifted and the air smelled of gunpowder. Small warriors, Adam among them, held out, against the burning night and the encroach of darkness, with a few hoarded shots, a last hushing rocket. While Ben—she would not recall this for Adam— was somewhere in the darkness with her old school friend, Marie Boyd, and Ben's father was sympathetic and touched her elbow and said it was all coming to an end, and one last Catherine wheel blazed. So she agreed, out of revenge, to meet Andrew Mason, Ben's partner, and Ben came into the house hours later and said Marie Boyd was a bloody understanding woman and she had said: 'She must be: you're wearing her lipstick'. And Adam was crying from the smallest burn, and it was over—never having begun.

But how could she make that blaze for Adam? Or feel other than stupid for having tried—the guilty party with uneasy recollections?

Adam arranged a Saturday morning job for himself, for pocket money. He wanted his own and would accept only the minimum from Hilda, giving as reason his supposition that she didn't have so much. He worked from seven in the morning until two in the afternoon at the petrol pumps of a garage in town. And on Saturday evenings, sometimes, they made a small ritual of a bottle of wine, with Hilda's special tender cuts. (Her butcher definitely let her down during the first few weeks of Adam's stay. A standing order of 'enough for two' was not welcome; until Adam was introduced. Then tenderness came back, without a word.)

They were cramped in the small flat. Hilda thought of looking for something larger but rents were against it and convenience favoured the present arrangement. The initial embarrassment faded and was replaced with a formal friendliness. Adam was interested in her day: they laughed together over Mr Rowbotham; and there were always flowers for brightness, while Persephone visited.

Persephone. It caused Hilda to wonder at the magnitude of what she did not know, and at all irrelevance. She simply couldn't conceive of herself swapping fairy stories about goddesses. Mr Rowbotham was definitely weird at times, when she came to think of it. Winter was winter, as if that weren't enough, without any need of dark kings. Really!

Hilda, in fine impatience, flashed the gleaming iron along a seam.

*   *   *

Adam had been with her almost a year when Ben called, without phoning beforehand, on a weekday evening. Hilda had recently taken up knitting again and sat near the heater with a knitting pattern open on her lap. She asked Adam to go to the door.

'Hello, son. Long time no see. You've grown. Hello, Hilda.' He gave Adam a friendly punch.

Dad plays Humphrey Bogart, Hilda thought. She recognized as of old his condition of equipoise between being sober and being drunk—a condition potentially dangerous to the point of violence.

'Going to ask me in?'

Hilda had not yet spoken. Ben came into the room with his hand on Adam's shoulder and slammed the door carelessly. That too Hilda remembered. Unmindful of the intricacies of her ambitious pattern she continued to knit.

'Must say you're a bit cooped here, aren't you?' His inventory was brief. 'I'd fancied it bigger. Going to offer me hospitality? A reviver after the stairs?'

'There's coffee,' Hilda said. 'That's all, I'm afraid.' She felt her face hardening, the flesh tightening. She remembered all too clearly

Adam's expression, that first evening, as she'd poured herself a
drink: she'd remembered Ben then, and understood. Adam couldn't
draw that sort of distinction; and Hilda wouldn't ask him to. So
the occasional bottle of wine they shared represented, as much as
anything, her reasoning on the matter, and her reassurance.

Adam was standing about with his thumbs hooked in his side
pockets. 'I'll make coffee,' he said.

'Forget it.' Ben took Adam's chair, before the folding table
spread with books and papers. 'Your ma help you with this lot?'

'Well. . . .' A hunching of the shoulders expressed difficulties.

'Of course I don't.' Hilda was downright. 'As if I could.'

'How's it going, then, Adam? I hear you're doing a stint on the
bowsers, Saturday. Helping your ma, is it?'

'It's pocket money,' Adam said. 'I quite like it, really.' He
sounded surprised, as if he'd just recognized his enjoyment.

Hilda felt herself being brought into the line of fire, as she
steadily knitted rows that would have to be pulled down. It would
never be plain, with Ben.

'How's old Anthony, then?' Ben figured a set square, a triangle,
one of whose points he used to scrape a finger-nail.

'I haven't seen him in months,' Hilda said.

'I suppose not.' Ben looked from the day bed to Adam's cubby.
'Cramping,' he said.

'You've hardly come for small talk,' Hilda said.

Ben held the perspex triangle against the light and squinted along
an edge. 'I've come to get Adam. He can come back now.'

She'd expected it; she'd been expecting it every day for the last
month. She registered the evasion, the refusal to look her in the
face, the toying with things. She glanced up at Adam, for comparison. Was the boy then like his father? It was urgent that she
should know. But she could not tell. Adam's mouth (or did she
need to invent it?) had a suggestion of Ben's father. Adam was
taller, with his shoulders against the wall: his dark rather closed-in
face, his good eyes, gave no hint of what he might be thinking: his
expression was a refusal.

'Just like that, Ben?' She hated using his name. 'Out of the blue,
with no warning?'

'Ah well, I got through my bit of business earlier than expected.
And I've set up in a decent place again, even if it's a bit out of
town. You can get the train into school, Adam. That's no hard-
ship, is it?'

'He's all right here you know, Ben.' How hard would she fight,
she wondered? Certainly she would not permit Adam to be, again,

rope for this tug-of-war. But what did Adam want? To know that she would have to know what he felt for Ben; and he'd never told her. Would Adam be better off with his father? She couldn't believe it: she simply refused to. She had noticed over the last few months a greater ease in Adam. Oh, no great flowering, no burst of expansiveness and confidence—just a small advance of boundaries he set himself, so that books and an occasional garment lay about.

'I mean he's welcome here,' Hilda said, in the silence. 'He knows that, I hope. And we do manage.' Her neutral tone was not helping; and she was afraid to try more. Adam evaded her smile.

'Sure you're a skinner? Not a drop in the place, I mean?'

Hilda remembered Anthony's gin. 'Look in the cupboard, Adam. I don't know. . . .'

'Holding out on your ex, eh?' Ben greeted the bottle. 'Not that there's much.'

For another it would have been too much: for Ben it would make two drinks, with flat tonic water.

'I took it your note meant you were going away.' Hilda was being cautious.

'For good? No, just a business trip. Adam wouldn't have enjoyed it. And there's the education caper.'

Hilda's knitting ceased to occupy her. 'You do see me, don't you Ben, as someone without rights of any kind? Not even the ordinary politeness applies.'

Ben emptied the bottle. 'You're forgetting the circumstances, old thing.'

'No. I'm not forgetting any circumstances, past or present. Not mine and not yours. Perhaps Adam can decide.'

'You can't have too much gear,' Ben said to Adam. 'I've got a car: there's no need to pack.'

'Ben, that's absurd.' Hilda tried to control her shrillness. 'It's almost ten, and he's got school tomorrow.'

'He can't be doing too well if missing a day makes all that difference.' Ben stared at his manicure. 'Get cracking, old son.'

'I'd rather leave it.' It cost Adam an effort, visibly.

'Weekend suit you better, eh? O.K. I'll go along with that.'

'I mean I'd rather leave it, altogether.'

'Not sure I follow son. Not come at all, you mean?' Ben looked dangerous.

It was a small triumph, whatever it meant; but she knew better than to show it and took little confidence from it. The knitting pattern fell to the floor. Hilda rose and went out to the kitchen and drank a glass of water. The silence was long, while the wind shook a loose latch on the window above the sink. She returned to her chair but let her knitting lie.

'I can come and see you. I'd like that.' Adam looked at his father—an oblique, quick glance.

Ben was thinking, with a tight, grimacing smile. 'You think you might appeal, is that it?' He turned to Hilda.

She met the blue wild stare. A delusive mist of possibilities whirled through her, as Ben downed his drink and waited with cruel patience. Ben had been in trouble; that much she knew. And that she might appeal, yes, she knew that too. She'd taken the trouble to find out where Ben had been: the answer had not been hard to come by.

'No.' Hilda shook her head. 'I've been content to have him here. I'd like Adam to stay, if that were possible. He'd see you: you could help him.'

'With money you mean? I suppose your little flower shop doesn't pay you so much.'

He could always manage contempt, she remembered, for what he called 'the toiling bloody sheep'; and poverty, true poverty, enraged him. His view had nothing to do with injustice.

'I wasn't thinking of money,' Hilda said.

Ben was pensive over his empty glass—a small man with a strained small face. His suit was new. He had married her because she was pregnant; or so she'd believed. Now she thought there might have been other and less obvious reasons. Adam continued to stand, leaning against the wall by the door to the landing.

'Give us five minutes, there's a lad.' Ben ducked his head sideways towards the door.

'There's nothing Adam can't hear,' Hilda said.

But Adam had already let himself out. Ben followed and called down the stairs.

'The blue Chevvy, the new one—look her over why don't you?' He returned to tilt the empty bottle, pulling a pug's face. 'Turned the clucky ma all of a sudden, haven't you? You forget: I'm the one that's brought him up. You don't see him for years and then it's out with the bloody apron strings. There's a great bloody heap he can't hear, it seems to me.'

'How much I saw of Adam was exactly how much you would allow. It's no use pretending otherwise. I begged hard enough. There's no point in going into that. There's nothing against his staying here: you can both see as much of each other as you want.'

'I can come here, do you mean?' He knew this wasn't the suggestion.

'Wherever you have your decent place,' Hilda said. Her smile exhibited no trace of amusement. 'I won't interfere.'

Ben looked his ex-wife up and down. 'Not as young as you were, Hilda. What happened to the boy friend? You get too demanding? A married man with a rich wife and a packet of kids—Christ, do you ever play the long shots. I checked him out.'

'Then we've both been checking.'

'On Anthony?'

'On each other.'

'Ah.' It was not a sigh but a fierce, explosive grunt as though she had winded him.

She thought he would strike her then. His hands made fists and the muscles in his throat went stringy. He stared and trembled.

'So that's it, eh? Now we come to it. That's to be the play.'

Hilda dared to move closer; it cost her an effort. She was not a brave woman; but it forced him to meet her eye.

'No, Ben,' she said. 'There's no play, as you call it. There aren't any threats, any hints. And I don't tell tales: you can be reassured on that point. If you absolutely won't see that Adam counts in this, then I give him up. I'm not going to drag him over all this dead ground between us, with you pulling one way and me another.' Her reasonableness wasn't up to it: she blazed. 'Ben, I'm not.'

'I suppose you're doing it in the backs of cars these days? Now your tidy little prostitute's flat has lost its privacy. Or on the stairs, maybe? You were always hot for it.' He'd found a tone for his anger—a hiss.

'You've always had a perfectly foul mind, Ben.'

'I suppose you wouldn't consider . . .?'

'If you touch me once more I swear I'll kill you, Ben.' Hilda even looked wildly about and seized a knitting needle, with which she would have been pleased then to inflict a blinding injury.

'Keep your shirt on, old thing.' Ben backed away. 'Let's be reasonable. Sure you haven't got another bottle?'

Hilda returned to her chair, and slumped. 'Reasonable? My God, do you have the faintest idea of what you're saying: do you have any idea of what it means? Have you ever in your whole life done one reasonable thing?' She was closer to exhaustion than to tears.

Had he ever meant to take Adam away—to take him away for

more than the time needed to work his vicious little act of
revenge? Hilda couldn't know. He had divorced her: he would
not, therefore, forget. His memory was as tightly tailored as his
clothes: no one could share it.

In the end it was a common 'touch', a piece of petty blackmail
which, degrading them both, degraded Hilda more. Business, in
fact, had been lousy; it was as much as he would say on that
score. He hadn't been what you'd call active. It was his only
concession to what she knew and neither would speak of. Hilda
was quite right: the boy was better off where he was, in the
meantime. The point was that if he, Ben, could just get out, get
away, right out of the country altogether—he'd thought Australia
where the pickings were better, especially if a man had a bit over
and above the fare—well, Hilda was in business: she'd understand
the old capitalist argument, *caveat emptor* and that sort of thing.

It was a phrase he had picked up somewhere early in his
activities, called by him his career. *Caveat emptor*; it was the
pennant at the mast of his pirate craft; and he spelled it various
ways. She didn't dwell on it now, nor ask what he might mean
by 'the time being.' But the car, she questioned, surely he had
some capital in that?

'Not a razoo, old thing. Borrowed.' He grinned, happily.
Couldn't let Adam think his old man was reduced to walking.
Make it out to cash; it's simpler all round. Don't worry, I'll pay
you back. That's a promise. Just give us six months and I'll buy
up your hat-box of a flower shop—lock, stock and barrel.'

Hilda held out the cheque. 'I wouldn't do that, Ben,' she said.
'You wouldn't like it. All the roses have thorns. That's something
you'd never be able to remember.' She thought of Mr Rowbotham.

'Well, of course, old Anthony is loaded anyway, eh?'

'I told you: I don't see him.'

'Pity, old thing. But,' and he impudently walked round her,
'you're still sitting on a gold mine, I'd say. Which is a compliment.'

'I prefer to think of it as an obscenity.' As she moved towards
the door.

At this moment she didn't even care that the cheque represented
almost exactly the sum of her balance in the bank. She hoped, but
was not confident, that it would be the last demand. It had bought
what she wanted; and she could think the price a light one, the
more so if the transaction were now complete.

'Please go,' she said.

They heard him lingering on the lower landing. Ben leaned
over the rail.

'Adam?' he called down, softly.

'Yes.'

'Hold it, son. I'm coming down.'

'If you could make it seem like your decision.' Hilda wondered whose face she was trying to save—Ben's, her own, or Adam's? 'If you could invent some story,' she said. A known talent she had not expected to invoke.

'Goodbye, old thing. It's all right: you're on your own from now. I'll write the lad. Don't give me a bad name with him, if you can avoid it.'

Her silence was all she would offer: victory could borrow too much of the vanquished's sense of defeat. The exchange had soiled them both. He went down, too dapper and wearing an unsuitable tie. The flower he had taken for his buttonhole was incongruous, a seedy flirtation. She turned back into the room and closed the door before he had gone out of sight, while he was looking up to wave.

When Adam returned Hilda was pulling down her knitting. The knitted wool was kinked.

'He said I could stay. He said you'd talked it over.'

'It was a matter of what seemed best,' Hilda said. 'And of what you seemed to want. It needn't be unalterable, you know.'

That motherly tone: because it was involuntary was it therefore natural? She almost looked into her lap for broad stretches of cloth—as though her hips had hugely broadened: she could all but feel her bosom dragging. A single child seemed insufficient reason for turning into a pudding. Tomorrow she would reconsider the butcher's offer, or run off with Mr Rowbotham to grow chrys-anths—lion-faced Mr Rowbotham whose long inert hand had lain on her bosom like a pale ornament. She could smile for Mr Rowbotham now, as she picked up stitches; Mrs Rowbotham, in faery, was clearly a more suitable partner, in contralto brown with spanning hands.

Adam had taken the chair before the folding table. He fidgeted there, his silence drumming.

'It's too late,' Hilda said. 'You can't go on with that now.'

'He's in trouble, isn't he? He wanted money.'

'In trouble?' Hilda spread her knitting over her fingers, stretching it to examine the pattern: she was some distance yet from bedrock.

'There was a man down there.'

'A man? Down where?'

'By the door: by the old tree. Waiting.'

Now, thought Hilda, she would phone. It was too much: he'd
had his chance. She prepared to leap, in righteousness.

'A policeman,' Adam said. 'I could see his boots, and the
trousers without cuffs.'

'What on earth would a policeman be doing, hiding like that?'

'He wasn't really hiding. He was waiting, by the car?'

Her look was startled: she put down her knitting very slowly.
So much from one patch of shadow? Absurd.

'It's all right,' Adam said. 'I told him. That's why I came up.
I warned him. I didn't go near the car, after all.'

'There aren't any parking restrictions.' Hilda tried for com-
posure, with her heart banging. 'He'd probably forgotten to leave
his parking lights on.'

'He went out the back way, through the yard. I could hear him
running down the hill.'

Adam put his books into a pile, a neat pyramid with the set-
square on top.

Hilda wrapped her knitting in a white cloth and put it away.
Ben's empty glass was still on the table. A Cancer partner? When
was his birthday, ever? She'd forgotten.

'I expect it was some mistake,' Hilda said, and hoped to
dismiss it. 'Will you use the bathroom first, please, Adam? It's
late. I have to be at the shop early to make a wreath.' She wished
she could show more authority, and ease.

'He is in trouble,' Adam said. 'I knew something was wrong
as soon as I opened the door. How much did he want?'

'That sort of tone doesn't suit you, Adam.' It was her first
outright rebuke, and a strong one. 'We all get into hot water
sometimes, if that's what it is.'

'Can I ask you a question, then?'

'Of course.' She gathered herself tight for it, summoning from
remote perimeters her full reserves, wishing for breathing space.

'Do you hate him? Did you? You know.'

It should have been laughably over-dramatic: but she felt only
relief at the simplicity. 'Adam, don't be absurd. It's too long ago.'

'He's asked you for money before. I know that.'

She looked at the dark scowl and knew that anything less than
her full seriousness, her fullest concentration, would be a danger.
'You forget we were married, Adam. There aren't so many places
one can turn to, for help. When you really need it.'

'I don't forget. But he hates you.'

Hilda denied it: she was confident. 'He never really mastered
his habits,' she said carefully. I'm a sort of habit, and not a

very satisfactory one, either. We're too different: he's always wanted to scoop things up, in great handfuls. He can't forgive the pebble-gatherers. It's what he used to call me, a hoarder of pebbles. He keeps me in view for that—to remind him of how much he hates it. And it cuts another great piece out of his pride every time he comes a cropper, every time he finds he's just got a handful of rubble.'

'You mean every time he asks you for help?' He wanted to be clear. He turned the set-square in his hands; it caught gleams of light, quickly.

'Well, that's perhaps when he does hate me; because it makes him hate himself. But it doesn't last long, Adam, don't you see?'

'He hates you because you help him?'

'That's usual,' Hilda said. 'Only I don't help, not really. He couldn't get by on that. You don't help people like him any more than you help a child. He has all the rights; it's not his fault. I suppose it's the way he's made. Children don't have to say thank you to survive, even to thrive.'

'He's not a child.'

'And neither are you, Adam. Otherwise why would I try to explain, or why would you ask? That's too simple. Oh, just look at the time.' She wailed at the clock and hurried out of her chair, and stood. 'You may know him better, after all: he brought you up. I could be wrong: I'm hardly unbiased.'

Adam waited. It wasn't finished yet; and he looked determined.

'Look, love.' Hilda ploughed into strange waters. 'It's just that there aren't any rules for him, except the ones he feels like using sometimes, the ones he can make use of. Only pebble-gatherers have rules. But you can't hate him for that. He strikes out and it's his own knuckles that are broken.'

'Are there rules for me?'

In the face of these sullen looks she found explanation difficult; but she would try. In the face of this insolence.

'Women are sentimental, Adam. It takes a very strong one not to ruin a man with mothering, or perhaps it takes a weakness that's like strength. I think I wanted to do that, once—to live through Ben, to make him see the rules and to make him keep them. Of course I lost. If he does hate me it's for that, for trying to change him. For most women the man they marry isn't enough: they can't let him be that, for long.'

It surprised her: she would have sworn she had never given it a thought; but it was, after all, the truth as she had seen it—or was as near as she could come.

'We never understood each other,' she said almost fiercely. 'We married and lived together and were divorced, all for the wrong reasons—whatever the right ones might be. I don't think it matters who is to blame. I can't hate him, can I?'

'Why not?'

'Because I have to live too, in my own way. Because pebble-gatherers do have rights. Because there have to be rules, for you.'

She took up the empty glass and the empty bottle and put them through on the bench and stood there, before the sink, hearing running feet and wondering what rights or rules she was thinking of. 'Least of all should you hate him,' she called. 'He did his best, there.'

'I didn't say I hated him.' Adam had moved to the kitchen doorway. 'I don't. I was just trying to understand, that's all.'

Not unthinkingly Hilda chose vagueness and a straightening of cushions. She thought she felt his eyes on her, but when she looked up he had gone and the bathroom door was closed. There was the boomy explosion of the califont and the usual drift of gas. Adam was whistling through his teeth; it didn't amount to a tune. Hilda put away the stack of books. She was cross with herself: that was the trap of words—you didn't say what you wanted to say. Between Ben and herself the dialogue would never be concluded; it was something like that.

This was what you surrendered, finally—the luxuries; the feelings of whatever kind you'd come to depend on. Of course she hated him: of course he hated her. It was the strongest tie. It was what had kept them together those few years; it was what kept him nipping at her heels; it was the reason she scribbled out the requested relief. From the very beginning it had been there, only waiting the extinction of that brief infatuation; and it had loomed full height when she had told him she was pregnant. That was the point at which they both began their long search for revenge, began to nurture the strongest feeling either of them had known—unclouded by affection. It had been the reason for passionless Anthony; and for what else she could not know.

But tonight was an excess; and again she heard running feet. Adam had chosen neither, rejected neither, and she suspected contempt in him for them both; depths, as she hoped it would not be, of a new treachery. Tonight Ben had needed help in a different way; and tonight she too might have benefited from some undefined assistance. And Ben was fleeing down dark streets while she, as urgently and as pointlessly, fluffed out cushions and removed flowers in vases to the kitchen bench. That's what it came to, she thought, listening for steps on the stairs.

Take a tip from the stars.

'It's an illusion.'

Hilda jumped, as if an absolute privacy had been invaded, as if she had been speaking aloud. Adam stood damp and wrapped in the bathroom doorway where steam billowed.

'It's an illusion that people need eight hours of sleep,' Adam said. 'That's twenty-five years in bed out of seventy-five, did you know that?'

'What a luxury,' Hilda cried, in some relief. 'Oh what a luxury. I'd settle for the lot, all in a lump, right now. I'm just the right age for illusions, Adam: I positively need them.'

These were the words; but this was not what they were saying: they both knew that. Hilda felt that her nerves had, finally, gone: strings were breaking, snapping in a darkness she could feel. Adam's smile was a laceration: she wished for spears and locks. She wondered what was happening to her: she remembered that tomorrow was Monday.

'Goodnight, Hilda.'

'Goodnight, Adam.' A pause. 'Adam?'

'Yes?' As he turned back.

'No, it doesn't matter. Goodnight.'

'Goodnight.'

*   *   *

Had there ever been anyone in the shade, the shadows? People, women, were known to invent; and her world, she felt, was an unknown one tonight. Tears and smiles conflicted as she rattled the milk tokens and the cat kept its calculated distance with its flag of tail. Had there been, ever, blossoms on the blossomless camellia? Really?

Pssst!

She took her time, now, dawdling under the mere vault of stars. She set the milk bottle in its rack: she smelled autumn earth. The wind was flurrying in the terrace street, quite strangely, pell-mell from every direction, and chill. Beyond the spire, lights contracted or pulsed. Over there would be north, where lights climbed; and she was sad to think of anyone's running in such a mildness of weather.

Pssst!

Had there? Ever?

As a goddess dragged past with a transistor ear-muff and, Hilda imagined, gooseflesh and blue knees.

Hilda spurned the cat: her anger had gathered in her throat.

They would kill the life in you, she thought; and she could have believed someone spoke, from the shadows. And she thought of tomorrow's wreath. Have you a Cancer partner? It takes two to make a quarrel, remember.

Pssst!

And trod again the high and difficult stairs, hoping Adam was asleep.

And Ben, from running.

And Anthony.

And Mr Rowbotham enfolded in globy places, folded in faery and song—if that was what he wanted, most.

Because tonight it was a long way to climb.

But she was, nevertheless, humming softly beneath it all and grateful to think she was not being followed on the stairs.

Because she hated that.

JANET FRAME   # The Bath

On Friday afternoon she bought cut flowers—daffodils, anemones, a few twigs of a red-leaved shrub, wrapped in mauve waxed paper, for Saturday was the seventeenth anniversary of her husband's death and she planned to visit his grave, as she did each year, to weed it and put fresh flowers in the two jam jars standing one on each side of the tombstone. Her visit this year occupied her thoughts more than usual. She had bought the flowers to force herself to make the journey that each year became more hazardous, from the walk to the bus stop, the change of buses at the Octagon, to the bitterness of the winds blowing from the open sea across almost unsheltered rows of tombstones; and the tiredness that overcame her when it was time to return home when she longed to find a place beside the graves, in the soft grass, and fall asleep.

That evening she filled the coal bucket, stoked the fire. Her movements were slow and arduous, her back and shoulder gave her so much pain. She cooked her tea—liver and bacon—set her knife and fork on the teatowel she used as a tablecloth, turned up the volume of the polished red radio to listen to the Weather Report and the News, ate her tea, washed her dishes, then sat drowsing in the rocking chair by the fire, waiting for the water to get hot enough for a bath. Visits to the cemetery, the doctor, and to relatives, to stay, always demanded a bath. When she was sure that the water was hot enough (and her tea had been digested) she ventured from the kitchen through the cold passageway to the colder bathroom. She paused in the doorway to get used to the chill of the air then she walked slowly, feeling with each step the pain in her back, across to the bath, and though she knew that she was gradually losing the power in her hands she managed to wrench on the stiff cold and hot taps and half-fill the bath with warm water. How wasteful, she thought, that with the kitchen fire always burning during the past month of frost, and the water almost always hot, getting in and out of a bath had become such an effort that it was not possible to bath every night nor even every week!

She found a big towel, laid it ready over a chair, arranged the chair so that should difficulty arise as it had last time she bathed she would have some way of rescuing herself; then with her nightclothes warming on a page of newspaper inside the coal oven and her dressing-gown across the chair to be put on the instant she stepped from the bath, she undressed and pausing first to get her breath and clinging tightly to the slippery yellow-stained rim that now seemed more like the edge of a cliff with a deep drop below into the sea, slowly and painfully she climbed into the bath. -I'll put on my nightie the instant I get out, she thought. The instant she got out indeed! She knew it would be more than a matter of instants yet she tried to think of it calmly, without dread, telling herself that when the time came she would be very careful, taking the process step by step, surprising her bad back and shoulder and her powerless wrists into performing feats they might usually rebel against, but the key to controlling them would be the surprise, the slow stealing up on them. With care, with thought. . . .

Sitting upright, not daring to lean back or lie down, she soaped herself, washing away the dirt of the past fortnight, seeing with

satisfaction how it drifted about on the water as a sign that she
was clean again. Then when her washing was completed she found
herself looking for excuses not to try yet to climb out. Those old
woman's finger nails, cracked and dry, where germs could lodge,
would need to be scrubbed again; the skin of her heels, too, growing so hard that her feet might have been turning to stone; behind
her ears where a thread of dirt lay in the rim; after all, she did
not often have the luxury of a bath, did she? How warm it was!
She drowsed a moment. If only she could fall asleep then wake
to find herself in her nightdress in bed for the night! Slowly she
rewashed her body, and when she knew she could no longer
deceive herself into thinking she was not clean she reluctantly
replaced the soap, brush and flannel in the groove at the side of
the bath, feeling as she loosened her grip on them that all strength
and support were ebbing from her. Quickly she seized the nail-
brush again, but its magic had been used and was gone; it would
not adopt the role she tried to urge upon it. The flannel too, and
the soap, were frail flotsam to cling to in the hope of being borne
to safety.

She was alone now. For a few moments she sat swilling the
water against her skin, perhaps as a means of buoying up her
courage. Then resolutely she pulled out the plug, sat feeling the
tide swirl and scrape at her skin and flesh, trying to draw her
down, down into the earth; then the bathwater was gone in a
soapy gurge and she was naked and shivering and had not yet
made the attempt to get out of the bath.

How slippery the surface had become! In future she would not
clean it with kerosene, she would use the paste cleaner that, left
on overnight, gave the enamel rough patches that could be gripped
with the skin.

She leaned forward, feeling the pain in her back and shoulder.
She grasped the rim of the bath but her fingers slithered from it
almost at once. She would not panic, she told herself; she would
try gradually, carefully, to get out. Again she leaned forward; again
her grip loosened as if iron hands had deliberately uncurled her
stiffened blue fingers from their trembling hold. Her heart began
to beat faster, her breath came more quickly, her mouth was dry.
She moistened her lips. If I shout for help, she thought, no-one
will hear me. No-one in the world will hear me. No-one will know
I'm in the bath and can't get out.

She listened. She could hear only the drip-drip of the cold water
tap of the wash-basin, and a corresponding whisper and gurgle of
her heart, as if it were beating under water. All else was silent.

Where were the people, the traffic? Then she had a strange feeling of being under the earth, of a throbbing in her head like wheels going over the earth above her.

Then she told herself sternly that she must have no nonsense, that she had really not tried to get out of the bath. She had forgotten the strong solid chair and the grip she could get on it. If she made the effort quickly she could first take hold of both sides of the bath, pull herself up, then transfer her hold to the chair and thus pull herself out.

She tried to do this; she just failed to make the final effort. Pale now, gasping for breath, she sank back into the bath. She began to call out but as she had predicted there was no answer. No-one had heard her, no-one in the houses or the street or Dunedin or the world knew that she was imprisoned. Loneliness welled in her. If John were here, she thought, if we were sharing our old age, helping each other, this would never have happened. She made another effort to get out. Again she failed. Faintness overcoming her she closed her eyes, trying to rest, then recovering and trying again and failing, she panicked and began to cry and strike the sides of the bath; it made a hollow sound like a wild drum-beat.

Then she stopped striking with her fists; she struggled again to get out; and for over half an hour she stayed alternately struggling and resting until at last she did succeed in climbing out and making her escape into the kitchen. She thought, I'll never take another bath in this house or anywhere. I never want to see that bath again. This is the end or the beginning of it. In future a district nurse will have to come to attend me. Submitting to that will be the first humiliation. There will be others, and others.

In bed at last she lay exhausted and lonely thinking that perhaps it might be better for her to die at once. The slow progression of difficulties was a kind of torture. There were her shoes that had to be made specially in a special shape or she could not walk. There were the times she had to call in a neighbour to fetch a pot of jam from the top shelf of her cupboard when it had been only a year ago that she herself had made the jam and put it on the shelf. Sometimes a niece came to fill the coal-bucket or mow the lawn. Every week there was the washing to be hung on the line— this required a special technique for she could not raise her arms without at the same time finding some support in the dizziness that overcame her. She remembered with a sense of the world narrowing and growing darker, like a tunnel, the incredulous almost despising look on the face of her niece when in answer to the comment

-How beautiful the clouds are in Dunedin! These big billowing
white and grey clouds—don't you think, Auntie?
she had said, her disappointment at the misery of things putting a
sharpness in her voice,
-I never look at the clouds!

She wondered how long ago it was since she had been able to
look up at the sky without reeling with dizziness. Now she did
not dare look up. There was enough to attend to down and
around—the cracks and hollows in the footpath, the patches of
frost and ice and the pot-holes in the roads; the approaching cars
and motorcycles; and now, after all the outside menaces, the inner
menace of her own body. She had to be guardian now over her
arms and legs, force them to do as she wanted when how easily
and dutifully they had walked, moved and grasped, in the old
days! They were the enemy now. It had been her body that
showed treachery when she tried to get out of the bath. If she ever
wanted to bath again—how strange it seemed!—she would have
to ask another human being to help her to guard and control her
own body. Was this so fearful? she wondered. Even if it were
not, it seemed so.

She thought of the frost slowly hardening outside on the fences,
roofs, windows and streets. She thought again of the terror of not
being able to escape from the bath. She remembered her dead
husband and the flowers she had bought to put on his grave. Then
thinking again of the frost, its whiteness, white like a new bath, of
the anemones and daffodils and the twigs of the red-leaved shrub,
of John dead seventeen years, she fell asleep while outside, within
two hours, the frost began to melt with the warmth of a sudden
wind blowing from the north, and the night grew warm, like a
spring night, and in the morning the light came early, the sky was
pale blue, the same warm wind as gentle as a mere breath, was
blowing, and a narcissus had burst its bud in the front garden.

In all her years of visiting the cemetery she had never known the
wind so mild. On an arm of the peninsula exposed to the winds
from two stretches of sea, the cemetery had always been a place to
crouch shivering in overcoat and scarf while the flowers were set
on the grave and the narrow garden cleared of weeds. Today,
everything was different. After all the frosts of the past month
there was no trace of chill in the air. The mildness and warmth
were scarcely to be believed. The sea lay, violet-coloured, hush-
hushing, turning and heaving, not breaking into foamy waves, it

was one sinuous ripple from shore to horizon and its sound was the muted sound of distant forests of peace.

Picking up the rusted garden fork that she knew lay always in the grass of the next grave, long neglected, she set to work to clear away the twitch and other weeds, exposing the first bunch of dark blue primroses with yellow centres, a clump of autumn lilies, and the shoots, six inches high, of daffodils. Then removing the green-slimed jam jars from their grooves on each side of the tombstone she walked slowly, stiff from her crouching, to the ever-dripping tap at the end of the lawn path where, filling the jars with pebbles and water she rattled them up and down to try to clean them of slime. Then she ran the sparkling ice-cold water into the jars and balancing them carefully one in each hand she walked back to the grave where she shook the daffodils, anemones, red leaves from their waxed paper and dividing them put half in one jar, half in the other. The dark blue of the anemones swelled with a sea-colour as their heads rested against the red leaves. The daffodils were short-stemmed with big ragged rather than delicate trumpets—the type for blowing; and their scent was strong.

Finally, remembering the winds that raged from the sea she stuffed small pieces of the screwed-up waxed paper into the top of each jar so the flowers would not be carried away by the wind. Then with a feeling of satisfaction—I look after my husband's grave after seventeen years. The tombstone is not cracked or blown over, the garden has not sunk into a pool of clay. I look after my husband's grave—she began to walk away, between the rows of graves, noting which were and were not cared for. Her father and mother had been buried here. She stood now before their grave. It was a roomy grave made in the days when there was space for the dead and for the dead with money, like her parents, extra space should they need it. Their tombstone was elaborate though the writing was now faded; in death they kept the elaborate station of their life. There were no flowers on the grave, only the feathery sea-grass soft to the touch, lit with gold in the sun. There was no sound but the sound of the sea and the one row of fir trees on the brow of the hill. She felt the peace inside her; the nightmare of the evening before seemed far away, seemed not to have happened; the senseless terrifying struggle to get out of a bath!

She sat on the concrete edge of her parents' grave. She did not want to go home. She felt content to sit here quietly with the warm soft wind flowing around her and the sigh of the sea rising to mingle with the sighing of the firs and the whisper of the thin gold grass. She was grateful for the money, the time and the forethought

that had made her parents' grave so much bigger than the others
near by. Her husband, cremated, had been allowed only a narrow
eighteen inches by two feet, room only for the flecked grey tombstone In Memory of My Husband John Edward Harraway died
August 6th 1948, and the narrow garden of spring flowers, whereas
her parents' grave was so wide, and its concrete wall was a foot
high; it was, in death, the equivalent of a quarter-acre section
before there were too many people in the world. Why when the
world was wider and wider was there no space left?

Or was the world narrower?

She did not know; she could not think; she knew only that she
did not want to go home, she wanted to sit here on the edge of the
grave, never catching any more buses, crossing streets, walking on
icy footpaths, turning mattresses, trying to reach jam from the top
shelf of the cupboard, filling coal buckets, getting in and out of
the bath. Only to get in somewhere and stay in; to get out and
stay out; to stay now, always, in one place.

Ten minutes later she was waiting at the bus stop; anxiously
studying the destination of each bus as it passed, clutching her
money since concession tickets were not allowed in the weekend,
thinking of the cup of tea she would make when she got home, of
her evening meal—the remainder of the liver and bacon—, of her
nephew in Christchurch who was coming with his wife and children
for the school holidays, of her niece in the home expecting her
third baby. Cars and buses surged by, horns tooted, a plane
droned, near and far, near and far, children cried out, dogs barked;
the sea, in competition, made a harsher sound as if its waves were
now breaking in foam.

For a moment, confused after the peace of the cemetery, she
shut her eyes, trying to recapture the image of her husband's grave,
now bright with spring flowers, and her parents' grave, wide,
spacious, with room should the dead desire it to turn and sigh
and move in dreams as if the two slept together in a big soft grass
double-bed.

She waited, trying to capture the image of peace. She saw only
her husband's grave, made narrower, the spring garden whittled
to a thin strip; then it vanished and she was left with the image
of the bathroom, of the narrow confining bath grass-yellow as old
baths are, not frost-white, waiting, waiting, for one moment of
inattention, weakness, pain, to claim her for ever.

JANET FRAME # Winter Garden

Mr Paget's wife had been in a coma for two months. Every day he visited her in the hospital, sitting by her bed, not speaking except to say, 'Miriam, it's me, Alec, I'm here with you,' while she lay unresponsive, not moving, her eyes closed, her face pale. Usually Mr Paget stayed half an hour to an hour; then he would kiss his wife, return her hand that he'd withdrawn and held to her side under the bedclothes, pat the clothes into their position, and then, conscious of his own privileged freedom and movement in the afternoon or evening light, he would go home to the corner brick house in the hill suburb, where he would prepare and eat a meal before going outside to work in the garden. Every day in all seasons he found work to do in the garden. His time was divided between visiting the hospital and tending his flowers, lawn, and olearia hedge. When the neighbours saw him digging, clipping, or mowing they said, 'Poor Mr Paget. His garden must be a comfort to him.' Later in the evening, when the violet-coloured glare showed through the drawn curtains of the sitting-room as Mr Paget watched television, the neighbours said, 'Poor Mr Paget. The television must be a comfort to him.' Often in the evening he would phone for news of his wife and the answer would be, always, Her condition shows no change. No change, no change. He had learned to accept the words without question. He knew what they meant—that she was no nearer living or dying, that the scarcely perceptible fluctuations he noted in his daily visits were ripples only, this way and that, as the opposing winds blew, but were no indication of the surge of the tide. No change. How intently he watched her face! Sometimes he stroked it; even her eyelids did not blink; they were shut and white like lamp shells.

Mr Paget's garden was admired in the street. His roses were perfect, untouched by blight or greenfly. His lawn shone like fur in the sun. Laid between his lawn and the street his hedge looked like a long smooth plump slice of yellow cake—except that it moved; in the wind it crackled its curly dented leaves with a kindling sound as if small fires were being started; in the morning light it was varnished a glossy green; in the evening it became pale lemon, appearing under the mass of houseshadow as lawns do sometimes, seen beneath dark trees at sundown.

In the corner of the garden overhanging the street a rowan tree grew that was Mr Paget's pride. It was now, in autumn, thick with berries suspended from beneath the protecting leaves of each twig like clusters of glistening beads. Everyone admired the rowan tree, and its berries cheered Mr Paget as he trimmed, mowed, staked, planted. In the early days of his wife's illness, depressed by the funereal association of flowers, he made up his mind not to take them to the hospital; but one day, impulsively, he picked a cluster of rowan berries.

He arrived early, before visiting time. He found on his wife's bedside so many instruments, tubes, needles—all the tools neces-sary to care for an apparently lifeless body—that at first there did not seem to be room for the berries. Hesitating, he put them on the locker next to a brick-coloured gaping-throated tube. Perhaps his wife, lying in the strange secret garden where those instruments tended her, would notice the berries.

A nurse came into the room. 'Oh, Mr Paget, you're early. I'll remove this tray and put these berries in water. Aren't they from your garden?'

Mr Paget nodded.

The nurse leaned over his wife, tucking in the bedclothes as if to arrange a blanket defence against the living, speaking creature who had invaded her vegetable peace. Then taking her silver tray of tools and the twig of berries she went from the room, and only when she had gone did Mr Paget say, 'Miriam, it's me, Alec,' taking her hand in his. He could feel a faint pulse like a memory gone out of reach, not able to be reclaimed. He stroked the fingers. He was overwhelmed by the familiar hopelessness. What was the use? Would she not be better dead than lying silent, unknowing in a world where he could not reach her?

The nurse came back. She put the berries on the windowsill, where they made a splash of colour. The slim skeleton-shaped leaves soared, like spears, against the glass.

'With winter coming and the leaves turning, there'll soon be only the late berries.'

'Yes,' Mr Paget said.

The nurse looked at him, answering his unspoken question, her face warm with sympathy. 'There's been no change, Mr Paget. But she's not suffering at all.'

'No,' Mr Paget said.

He waited for the nurse to say what everyone was saying to him now, beating the words about his ears until he wanted to cry out for mercy, "It will be a happy release for her when it comes."

The nurse did not say it and he was glad. She smiled and left the room, and he sat watching the narrow ribbon of afternoon light that had bound itself across the windowpane and the sill and the berries, surging in their glass like tiny bubbles of blood. Mr Paget shivered. He began to feel afraid. What will it be like, he wondered, when death comes and I am with her?

He looked again at his wife's hand, at the wrinkled soft skin; new skin. He stroked her fingers and his heart quickened and a warmth of joy spread through him as he realised her skin was new; and of course her fingernails had been cut; and if they had been cut they had also been growing; her hair, too. Her hair had been cut. Quickly he leaned to touch her damp mouse-coloured hair. It had grown and been cut. They had cut her hair! Then the wild joy began to ebb as he remembered that even after death the hair and fingernails may grow and need to be cut. Was this growth then more a sign of death than of life?

'Oh no, oh no,' Mr Paget said aloud.

For while his wife lay in a coma, again and again they would need to cut her fingernails and hair, to bathe her, to take from her each day the waste of the food they had given her, and each day was different, had been different all the weeks she had been ill; and he had not dreamed, they had not told him, he thought bitterly. They had said, 'No change, no change,' when each day one speck more or less of dust had to be washed away, one ounce more or less of food was stored, rejected; and one day the wide blade of sunlight pressed burning and sharp upon her face while another day she lay in cool dark shade. She was alive, in the light. In the grave there was no sun, no shadow, touching of hands, washing of body.

When Mr Paget smiled happily as he said goodbye to his wife, the nurse looked startled. Poor Mr Paget, she said to herself.

That evening, Mr Paget took special care in trimming the hedge, stepping back to admire its evenness, putting the clippings into a neat pile. He felt quite frivolous as he ran the old-fashioned mower over the lawn; chatter-chatter it gossiped throatily, spewing out the green minus-marks of grass. Then, before he went inside to phone the hospital and watch television, in a spurt of extravagant joy he picked two clusters of rowan berries, and as he was springing back the branch the neighbour passed on her way home.

She saw Mr Paget. Her face assumed the appropriate expression of sympathy. 'And how is Mrs Paget?'

Mr Paget's accustomed answer flowed from him. 'There's been no change.'

He heard the despair in his voice as he spoke. Then, sympathetically, he asked, 'And how's Mr Bambury?'

The neighbour's husband had been ill. She released her news. 'They're stripping his arteries tomorrow.'

There was a jubilant consciousness of action in Mrs Bambury's voice. Mr Paget groped from a dark void of envy to his new joy: no change, no change indeed!

He smiled at Mrs Bambury. He wanted to comfort her about her husband and his arteries but he knew nothing about the stripping of a person's arteries: the resulting nakedness seemed merciless; he was grateful that his wife lay enclosed in sleep, her arteries secret and unyielding.

'I hope everything will be all right with Mr Bambury,' he said at last.

'Oh, there's a risk but a very strong chance of recovery. I do hope there'll be a change in Mrs Paget's condition.'

'Thank you,' Mr Paget said humbly, playing the game. 'So far there has been no change.'

'No change?'

'No change.'

They said goodbye. On his way to the house he stopped to scan the garden. He looked tenderly at the pile of grass and hedge clippings and the succulent golden hedge with the dark pointed roof-shadow eating into it.

Mrs Paget died in late autumn. It is winter now. The berries are gone from the rowan tree, some eaten by birds, some picked by the wind, others scattered by the small boys switching the overhanging branches up and down as they pass in the street. In a luxury of possession rather than deprivation, Mr Bambury, his arteries successfully stripped, rests in a chair on the front porch of his home, looking across the street at Mr Paget in his garden. Mr Bambury and his wife say to each other, 'Mr Paget is tied to his garden.'

Others notice it, too, for Mr Paget seems now to spend all his waking time in the garden. 'Since his wife's death, he's never out of the garden,' they say. 'Why? Nothing grows now but a few late berries. Nothing grows in the garden in winter.'

They wonder why **Mr** Paget stands for so long looking at the dead twigs, the leafless shrubs, the vacant flower beds set like dark eyes in the middle of the lawn, why he potters about day after day in the dead world where nothing seems to change. And sometimes they think perhaps he is going mad when they see him kneel down and put his cheek against the skin of the earth.

O. E. MIDDLETON　　# The Loners

As long as he had been working, all had been well. The other men in the timber-yard had been friendly enough once he had got to know them. They had taught him all the guages, shown him how to tell *rimu* from *matai, totara* from *kauri* and white pine. Once he had grown used to their rough, teasing ways, he had come to like working in the timber-yard.

The day the foreman had told him he was to 'finish-up' he had not at first understood.

'Bad luck, Luke!' one of the gang had growled, clapping him on the shoulder. 'There's seven of us been given our walking tickets today.'

'. . . You too?'

'Yes. Me, my mate Bill here, young Jimmy from the joinery shop and three from one of the other gangs.'

'Bbbut, why?' he had managed to bring out, his eyes searching the man's weathered, unsmiling face.

'Not enough orders. That's why! The country's in a bad way at the moment. The building industry's one of the hardest hit. I've seen it happen before and it'll happen again!' The man had drawn a hand across the grey stubble on his chin, stared past the even stacks of timber at the gleam of sea.

All the next, workless morning, he had sat about, not knowing what to do. There were no labourers' jobs in the paper.

'Why don't you sit on the verandah?' Pine had suggested.

He had gone there meekly enough, glad to be out of the way while the two women made beds and cleaned the house. After a while, though, he had grown uneasy. It seemed to him that the people who strolled past, especially the stiff-faced women with their trundlers and shopping baskets, looked at him disdainfully, as if he had no right to be there. As soon as he had gone back inside, his brother's wife, Rebecca, had begun to scold him.

'Aw, Luke! Can't you give us a chance to get the house straight!'

Ashamed, ill-at-ease, he had gone out again, wandered off alone, not thinking or caring where he went, yet always making for the sea. He had sauntered moodily past the other old wooden houses, all like the one he shared with his brother Matthew, had become aware all at once that this was his first *free* day, his first day to himself since they had got off the ship. From then on, he had wandered through the town, glacing almost furtively into shop-windows. In the window of a fish-shop, something had caught his eye. For some moments he had stared intently, almost affectionately, through the streaming glass at the object; a sizeable squid on a large dish. . . .

He had been on the point of going in to ask the price of the succulent thing, but just in time, realised that he did not know its English name. Besides, he had given Pine all his money the day before, so his pockets were empty.

Moodily, he had turned away. It did not do to go anywhere without money in *this* country. With money in the pocket, there was always something to buy.

At home, he had always gone fishing with friends: either in a boat on the lagoon, or, at night, with torches and spears on the reef. Whatever the catch, there had always been plenty of fun, the warmth of talk and laughter. . . .

Here, everything was different. The people went about singly, many of them with grim, stony faces. Often they passed one another in the street without so much as a greeting.

At last, hardly knowing where he was, he had reached the harbour, walked the length of the old wharf. A solitary fisherman squinting down at a dancing float had glanced at him briefly. In that instant, the two halves of his longing had come together. He would ask Pine for enough to buy a couple of lines and some hooks.

Ever since, he had hardly missed a day. Once he had scanned the job columns, been to see about any work that was offering, his thoughts would turn to the hours stretching ahead. With his gear and a morsel of food in an old basket, he would set out for the wharf.

Though he no longer followed that first, roundabout route, wasted no time gazing into shop-windows, it was still a long way.

Sometimes, another man, or even two, were there before him. One day, when he had been to see about a job, he found four of them perched, intent as gulls, at the end of the wharf.

At weekends and late in the afternoons, small boys sometimes drifted down in twos and threes to fish for sprats.

The old man he had seen that first day came down on his bicycle two or three times a week. He used a homemade rod that he carried tied to the bar of his bicycle, rarely stayed beyond midday and usually went home with a fish. He wore spectacles, moved stiffly and sometimes had trouble taking off and putting on the clips he wore around the bottoms of his trousers. He seldom smiled, spoke little, but usually greeted the other regulars with a nod. Once or twice, Luke thought he saw a gleam, like the sudden sparkle of sun on sea, light up the old man's eyes.

Jock, as the others called him, kept all his tackle in a wooden box strapped to the carrier of his bicycle. Nestling in a honeycomb of small cells were hooks and sinkers, swivels, rod-rings, spare coils of fine wire and nylon, spinners and oddments of all kinds. Once, the old fellow had gone to the box, rummaged a while, and handed Luke a sharp new hook to replace one lost on a snag. He had shown him how to tie a stop-knot, how to 'kinch' it tight so that it would never slip. Another time, Jock had tossed him a piece of fresh mullet, signing to him to exchange it for the bait he had been using without success.

Three other men came down to the wharf almost every day. One rode a motor-bike, another drove a battered car, while a third came on foot. All were married men in their late twenties or early thirties. From the few words they exchanged, Luke guessed that all were out of work and came to the wharf as much to get away from their wives, as in the hope of taking something home for the pot. He would have liked to ask them what work they did; to have told them how strange he found everything after the life he had been used to. But the chance never came.

If one of them spoke to him, it was teasingly, as though he were a child. His halting replies usually brought only shakes of the head, pitying smiles. Their eyes would return to their fishing-lines that seemed to transfix the water like fine spears. He guessed that the three had all been born in the town, had grown up there at about the same time. Yet they were not *real* friends. Perhaps they had gone to different schools, belonged to different churches, worked at different jobs? Often, as he sat brooding on these things, Luke's thoughts would return to his wife. He would stare past the breakwater at the great rock thrusting up through the pale sea like a huge, blunt tooth, his heart swelling with love.

It was natural that she should feel anxious, now that she was again with child. At least Matthew still went to his job at the freezing works every morning. When the wind blew from that quarter, the wail of the works siren would come clearly over the intervening sea. Luke would cock his head, stare uneasily across the water.

There had been a hooter at the timber-yard. The first new words he had learned had been *smoko, knock-off, pay-day:* his workmates had seen to that. Each time he heard the siren, it reminded him of the men he had worked with in the timber-yard, the things they had said. The sound seemed to stir some chord in the others too. They would get up, stretch their limbs, swallow mouthfuls of tea from their flasks, light a cigarette or fill a pipe when the smoko hooter went. Whenever the noon whistle blew, old Jock would get up stiffly, begin reeling-in. Although the old man lived on a pension and none of the others had regular jobs, the mournful call of the hooter seemed to tug at them all, as the sun and moon affect the tide.

Since they were fond of eating their fish raw, Pine had tried to buy limes at the greengrocer's. But even the shops that sold *taro* had only lemons to offer.

Luke was still out of work in May when the mackerel began to come in. He caught a few of the smaller type known locally as 'English mackerel,' found them good bait for larger fish and fine to eat raw when there were enough for a meal.

One day, the other man who also came down on foot, hauled in a fine 'horse-mackerel'. 'Don't often get them like that in the day-time,' he said, holding it up to take out the hook. Shy of the light, the fish quivered and fought, its scutes and nacreous sides catching fire. Adroitly, unmoved by its frenzy, the man held the fish, slipped out the hook. He slid the mackerel into a sack where it went on shivering and vibrating.

There were only the two of them on the wharf that morning and it was the first time the man had ever spoken to Luke. The 'horse mackerel' reminded him of a type of small tuna much prized in the islands for its fine flavour.

'What is the *best* time?' he brought out slowly at last.

'Night-time is best,' the other answered briefly. 'Use a small hook—a treble is best—and no sinker.'

'. . . I used to come down after mackerel a lot at one time,' he went on after a pause. 'It's different now though. My wife doesn't like me coming down here after dark. Says it's too risky for a married man. . . .' He gave a short, scornful laugh, spat between his dangling legs into the sea. 'They're beautiful eating, too,' he finished wistfully.

Luke said nothing and the other soon fell silent. Not long afterwards, he rolled up his lines, slung the sugar-bag over his shoulder. 'So long!' he threw out as he set off home.

As he watched him swing away down the wharf, Luke wondered what Pine would say when he told her he wanted to fish at night.

In the paper next morning, there was an advertisement for men to fill and sew sacks of wheat in a grain store. He was one of the early ones, was given three days' work with some other men in a cold, dimly-lit warehouse.

After that, he came down to the wharf at night two or three times a week, took home several fine horse-mackerel. Even after dark, quite a few people came down to the old wharf to fish. They were mostly men in steady jobs with a sprinkling of boys from the High School. The only daytime fisherman Luke recognised among them was the man who drove the battered car. He offered Luke a lift home one night, on the way, told him that he was an out-of-work carpenter.

Late one night, after he had got back from the wharf, a strong wind sprang up. As he cleaned his fish, the old house started to creak and sigh. Matthew's youngest child began to cry and woke the others. By the time Pine had got their own small daughter back to sleep, he was in bed. When at last she slipped in beside him, hugging his back for warmth, they lay awake for a long time, talking in whispers, awed by the strange howling of the wind.

In the morning, the wind still blew from the mountains. Matthew went off to work swathed like an Eskimo in the warm gear he usually wore only in the freezing-chambers. The wind still prowled about the house, fumbling with a loose sheet of iron on the roof, making the branch of an old tree scrape mournfully against the weatherboards. When the children had been wrapped up and sent off to school, Luke went onto the verandah. The sea was an uneven strip of frosty green under scudding clouds. There would be no fishing that day.

Pine pounced on him the moment he went inside again.

'You can do the shopping for us today, man! Too cold for Rebecca and me to go out. . . !' She handed him a kit, a list and her purse, helped him on with the army greatcoat he had bought at the surplus stores.

At the fruiterer's, he saw two women who came from the same village as his wife. They were buying *taro,* weighing the tubers expertly in their hands, searching for blemishes. They gave the customary polite greetings, which he returned. Yet he was glad when they were gone. It seemed to him that there had been something mocking, sly, in the looks they had darted at the kit. When you did not have a job to go to, everyone, even your own countrymen, began to look at you askance. At home, if a man chose to be idle, no one frowned.

At the butcher's and the baker's, he felt awkward, out of place. In the grocer's shop, he gave up trying to stumble through the list, handed it to the young assistant.

When he came out at last, the kit was bulging. A bell began to clang from a doorway further down the street over which a banner flapped. People came hurrying, jostling one another to get in. Guessing that it must be some kind of entertainment, he went in too. A man with a face as red as the banner outside and a pencil behind his ear, mounted a platform, began to harangue the crowd in a loud, sing-song voice. Two other men in long aprons hunted among piles of furniture, old radios, crockery, lawnmowers, clothes-wringers, books, peering at labels, turning or holding up the goods for the crowd to see.

Although at first, Luke did not follow all that was said, he soon saw that the things were being sold. How stupid he was! Was not this the very place where Pine and Rebecca had bought most of the things for the house?

The kit was heavy. He put it down, could not help smiling at the antics of the red-faced auctioneer. The man grinned at him, caught his eye; Luke gave an answering nod. Only when a chorus of other bids followed and the auctioneer looked at him again, did he realised that he had very nearly bought a large iron double bedstead with brass knobs. Hastily, he gathered up the basket, hurried out, his face burning. How the women would laugh if they knew!

As he came out onto the footpath, he bumped into someone, almost knocking him over. 'Sorry!' he said, putting out his free hand to steady the man who seemed dazed by the blow.

'So you should be!' the man answered unexpectedly. 'Do you always treat your old mates so rough?'

Luke stared at him, saw with surprise that it was one of the men from the timber-yard—the one who had spoken kindly to him that last day. 'I didn't see you,' he said smiling.

'How are things, Luke? Got a job yet?'

'No,' he said. 'Not yet.'

'Nor me either,' said the man. Their eyes met, held.

The same greying stubble stood out on the man's furrowed

cheeks and bony jaws. His breath carried a sweetish reek of alcohol and his pale, blue-grey eyes held a misty, far-off look. 'All on your own?' he asked: then, without waiting for an answer, 'Come and have a drink!'

Luke had been into a pub a couple of times with his brother. Once or twice, he and Matthew had cracked a bottle of beer in the house in the weekend. At home, people had often brewed their own from bananas, oranges, all kinds of things. He had once got very drunk on the stuff when he was still in his teens.

After their third beer, Jack said, 'Oh it's good to have someone to talk to. You get fed-up with your own company and the sight of four walls! . . . I had a missus too, once; and a kiddie. Little girl. I made good wages in those days. Putting up houses for a big builder. . . .' He paused, stared into his glass for a moment before going on. 'Then the Slump came. The builder went broke and for months I was on relief. I started to hit the booze. . . . My wife left me and took the kid. I've never seen them since. I guess the girl will have a family of her own by now.' He raised his glass, tilted his head, closed his eyes as the beer went down.

By the time Luke had swallowed his own drink much of his shyness had gone and he had forgotten his blunder at the auction. He might have forgotten the shopping too, if Jack had not said to him: 'Now, whatever you do, don't leave that basket behind— or your wife will use you for a chopping-block!"

He wanted to bring Jack home, introduce him to Matthew and their wives, give him a meal. But Jack would not hear of it, kept shaking his head. '. . . I'll have a bite to eat somewhere later,' he said vaguely. 'There's a place I know. . . .'

While he was speaking, he must have made a sign to the barman and before Luke could say anything, two more beers had been bought.

Outside, the wind still blew with the same force, plastering the thick stuff of the greatcoat against him, making him lean forward to keep his feet. Where did the others spend their days? he wondered. Some, he knew, came to the pub. Jack had introduced him to a few of them. He was glad he had met Jack. Another time, when it was too rough to fish, he might look in at the pub. It was good for a man to make friends outside his own country-men, his own family. Pine would understand.

He was smiling when he reached their gate. Pine, a blanket about her shoulders, looked anxiously out from the verandah. Her face melted into a smile the instant she saw him, but clouded as he stumbled, almost fell, on his way up the steps.

'Luke! Where have you been?'

'Doing your shopping. . . .' Why was she looking so solemn?

'Man, you've been drinking!'

'I—I met a friend. A man I used to work with. I wanted him to come and eat with us. He's out of work too. . . . We went to a pub, had a few beers.'

'Did you do all the shopping?'

'Yes. See, it's here!' He held out the bulging kit, was astonished at the ease with which she took it from him.

'Where's the purse?'

He began to fumble for it in his pants, fished it out at last from one of the deep pockets in the greatcoat.

'Here it is!' he said cheerfully.

Pine opened the purse, counted out what was left. 'Where is the milk-money?' she asked at length.

'What do you mean?'

'There should have been more than a dollar left after you did the shopping. That money was for our next week's milk!'

He stared into her hot, troubled face and the full import of it smote him, left him aghast. 'It's gone,' he mumbled, hanging his head. 'I used it for beer.'

He stood waiting for an outburst from her. It did not come. She simply stood there, looking at him, her eyes wide, the tears close. Then, without a word, she turned, opened the door and went in.

Dumbly, he followed her, his face burning, his limbs beginning to feel numb.

In the morning, while everyone was still asleep, he slipped out of bed, crept onto the verandah. It was still too dark to make out the sea. The wind had shifted but it was still cold.

Silently, he gathered his gear together, shrugged on the great-coat and went out. A solitary vehicle bumbled about the street. He heard the merry, jingling rattle of bottles in metal crates, hurried his steps as though pursued. Light gleamed from only one or two houses. As though weary from their night-long vigil, even the street lamps seemed to burn with a subdued, worn-out glow.

It was still early when he reached the wharf. The wind was coming straight off the ocean and every so often, breakers boomed against the seaward edge of the breakwater. He baited his small line, turned up the collar of his coat, settled down to wait.

It was the first time he had been out so early. Maybe he should have told Pine? Matthew would not yet be setting out for work.

It was a fine place to live, in spite of everything. When you grew used to it, even the cold had something fine about it. Matthew said it helped you work better. The colder water certainly seemed to make the fish taste sweet.

When the sun began to peer over the ridge of hills beyond the town, the air seemed at first to grow colder. He shrugged deeper into his collar, stared out through slitted eyes at the glittering, grey-green sea.

Footsteps sounded at the far end of the wharf. He turned to see who it was, could not at first recognise the man because of his parka and woollen head-gear.

'You're early!' the newcomer said. 'Any luck?'

Luke shook his head.

'Cunt of a day, yesterday!' the other remarked when he had set his lines.

'No good for fishing!' Luke agreed.

They fell silent. Under them, the sea sucked and gurgled around the piles. Every so often, a comber smashed itself against the breakwater, sending up a smother of white. All at once, the man in the parka got to his feet, began to haul in one of his lines. Luke could tell from the run of the line, the man's movements, that it was something big. He secured his own lines, went to see if he could help.

'Just as well he grabbed my new line!' the other muttered. As he spoke, the water churned and boiled some way out. A red-gold mass flashed for a moment, then beat back out of sight.

'Big snapper!' grunted the man, paying out line.

Luke said nothing. He slipped off his coat, lowered himself over the end of the wharf, began to climb down. By the time the fish came up again, it was close under him. Its great, humped, red-gold back heaved up, glittered an instant, then was gone. Luke glanced up, met the blue eyes staring uneasily down.

'Don't know how long I can hold him!' the man called, gingerly hauling in again.

As the snapper swam up, Luke bent down, steadying the line with his free hand. With a deft movement, he slipped his fingers into the gills, felt the nails rasp the harsh lining of the gullet. As he inched back over the cross-ties, the kicking and jumping of the heavy fish made his arm ache. At last he felt the rough timber of the combing, a hand gripped his shoulder. With a final heave, he swung the heavy fish onto the decking.

They stood for a long while looking down at the snapper as it flapped and gasped at their feet. 'What a beaut!' crowed the man in the parka for the third time. 'He must be all of twenty pounds!'

Luke smiled, flexed his aching muscles.

The man turned to him. 'You don't often get them like that. He's a moocher. A loner.' His plain, colourless face had come to life. His frosty, blue-grey eyes shone with a pale lustre. 'They say they're the survivors of old shoals. . . .'

Luke nodded, went on smiling, though he understood only part of what the man said. He began to shiver, turned away and put on his coat.

The other man pushed back the hood of his parka. Tufts of fair hair stuck out from under his woollen cap.

Luke felt rapid, sharp bites on his small line. He pulled it up, unhooked a plump little fish spotted brown and yellow.

'Do you want him?' the other man called, his eyes on the small fish.

'No! You take him!' Luke got up, glad to have something to give.

The man in the parka stuck one prong of a treble hook through the body of the little fish just below the dorsal fin, carefully lowered it into the water. Just then, the wail of the starting-whistle at the works came faintly to them during a lull in the wind.

They fished in silence for the best part of an hour. All at once, the other man got up, began to haul in the line baited with the live fish. This time he did not pause, kept bringing in the line hand-over-hand, until an ugly greyish fish with a dark blotch on each side lay gasping on the wharf.

Luke went to look at it. 'What do you call that one?' he asked. He had seen a few of these fish caught, had even watched a man casting a murderous-looking weighted jag at one of the slow-swimming creatures on a still day, but had not liked to ask the name.

'Oh that's a johnny: a john-dory. Best eating fish in the sea! My missus will be pleased! Loves them, she does. . . . Only fish she's keen on.' He began to whistle under his breath, rebaited the line with a dead sprat, lapsed into silence once more. Before long, the men's solitary figures became as still as two bollards. The sun slid over the faces of the rocky islands beyond the breakwater, caught the occasional flash of a diving gannet. The wind never ceased to worry at the grey-green sea, making the white under-fur bristle, plucking at the men's lines until they danced and sang.

The sad, peremptory wail of a hooter came faintly again across the water. The man in the parka lifted his head, looked puzzled. 'It's not smoko yet,' he muttered. He glanced uneasily at the tide, which had begun to drop, got up and began to haul in his lines. As he wound them onto their sticks, his elbows wagged in a comical rhythm and he stared fixedly towards the town.

When he was ready to go, he took the snapper from the sack, put it down beside Luke's basket. 'Better take that home with you,' he said.

Luke glanced up with a smile, made a ritual gesture of refusal.

'Look, there's only the two of us. We've got any amount with the johnny. You take the snapper—it's a family-sized feed!' He turned away, his boots thudding dully on the wooden decking, his cowled head turned against the wind.

When the man's footfalls had died away, Luke bent over the fish. The huge tail was dry and stiff where it had stuck out in the wind. But where the sack had covered it, the snapper had kept its moist bloom under the scales, was dappled red-gold, blue-green.

He took out his knife, began to clean the fish. As if by magic, red-legged gulls sprang into the air, began to squall and bicker around him.

Before he set out for home, he slipped a length of cord through the fish's gills, climbed down over the cross-ties once more, rinsed the fish in the sea. All the way back, he had to keep shifting the dead weight from one side to the other, to rest his arm.

As he crossed the railway-tracks near the freezing-works, knots of men carrying lunch-cases passed him in twos and threes. One of them chivvied him, asked if the fish were for sale. Grinning, he shook his head, kept on walking.

He felt suddenly hungry, tried to remember what Jack had said about the place where the out-of-work could get bread and hot soup. Anyway, he was almost home. Yesterday, Pine had been angry, but by now she would be glad to see him. Pine was like that. Still, now that he knew that other world, he could always return there when he felt the need. . . .

He climbed the steps to the verandah, opened the front door and went in. For a moment, he thought he had heard Matthew's voice: then Pine ran to him, threw her arms about his neck.

Next moment, he was in the kitchen. They were all there, talking, admiring the fish.

Soon, it was Matthew's turn. Smiling, he spread his knees, cleared his throat, began once more to explain about the strike. They all listened, watching his face. A couple of times, Rebecca asked him to repeat things she had not understood. When he had finished, everyone began to talk at once.

The brothers looked at one another and laughed. 'Might as well make it a *real* holiday,' Matthew said. 'Let's go into the other room.'

As he watched his brother bring in the bottles, take off the caps, pour out the beer, Luke could not help thinking: 'It's all right now. This is only the first day. Wait till the women begin to scold at him. . . .' Matthew was fond of fish but did not have the patience to sit hour after hour, waiting for bites. Since he had come here, he had learned to play snooker, though, and kelly pool. Perhaps he would fill in the time with some of his mates in one of the billiard saloons in the town. As long as he had something in his pocket, Matthew would be happy. If the strike dragged on and he ran out of money, he would soon grow fretful. . . .

But why worry? The beer warmed him, reminded him he had eaten nothing so far that day. Pine came in, offered him some slices of cold *taro,* drank a little from his glass.

'Such a fish will need careful cooking,' she remarked.

'We will have it this evening, when the children are here and we are all together.'

'How long will the strike last?' Luke asked when the women had gone back to the kitchen.

'Maybe a week, maybe a month. Some of the men say it may last even longer.'

From the kitchen came the sounds of running water and of Pine's singing. It was some new song she had heard on the radio, but her voice had all its old warmth, as though she were helping prepare one of the family feasts back home.

Luke remembered the way the snapper had flashed in the early light as it came up out of the sea, its bony gill-plates gleaming. He saw again the look in the frosty blue eyes of the fair-haired man.

'If the wind is not too strong, I will go down again tomorrow,' he decided. 'As long as things are like this, I might as well be the fisherman of the family.'

O. E. MIDDLETON   # Killers

'I hope the road's not like this all the way,' grumbled the man.

'It can't be much further now,' coaxed the boy.

'Why haven't they widened it and sealed it I wonder,' chimed in the woman.

'We'd be lucky to find any mussels down here *then,*' rejoined the man. 'As it is, no doubt only the locals come down here.'

'Can't say I'd like to live hereabouts anyway,' sniffed the woman. 'Did you see those ramshackle old houses?'

'There are plenty of fine new cowsheds though,' joked the man. 'Where do you think all our city milk comes from?'

'Look! What's that?' asked the girl, suddenly leaning forward.

'It's a hawk!' cried the boy.

'Making a meal off something too,' added the man.

'The beastly thing!' shuddered the woman.

As though it were taking up the slack in a trigger, the man's foot went down on the accelerator. The car surged forward. 'I wonder if I can get him,' he muttered.

As though they were sighting down a rifle, four pairs of eyes became fixed on the shape at the road's edge. Just as it seemed about to be engulfed, the bird raised its head and lifting sudden wings, pulled itself up with uncanny speed. Spinning tyres ground the carcase of the rabbit into the road. The escaping bird skimmed the onrushing bonnet, cartwheeled into a blackberry bush. Three heads craned back, scanning the roadside.

'It got away!' cried the girl, swallowing because her throat had gone dry.

'Oh, the cruel thing!' shrilled the woman. 'Wasn't that a poor little rabbit?'

'You got him I think,' the boy exulted, turning and meeting his father's gaze in the rear-vision mirror.

'Yes I got him—but only just.' The man let out a rush of pent-up breath, slackened his foot on the pedal. 'He thought he had time for another mouthful, but our speed fooled him.'

'Why were such murderous creatures made I wonder?' sighed the woman.

'They're killers all right,' agreed the man. 'Nothing is safe from them.' He fumbled for a cigarette, fed it into his mouth. 'No doubt the hicks around here are too busy milking cows to keep

them down.' He inhaled and blew out some smoke. 'Now look
at that,' he went on, nodding at something that had caught his eye.

Across the paddocks a man in a black singlet was planting a
post, steadying it with one hand while he tamped the earth around
it with short even strokes from a rammer.

'Can you beat that!' gasped the man. 'And on a Sunday morning too! He's never heard of mechanization, that's for sure! He
must be one of the original pioneers.'

'He's more like something out of the Stone Age if you ask me,'
tittered the woman.

'Slow down now,' urged the boy. 'We can't be far now from
that old wharf.'

*   *   *

The harrier awoke to find herself tumbled among dusty leaves.
She smelt blood, remembered the rabbit she had dispatched, the
savour of its warm flesh. She struggled to sit upright, saw the
looped threads spilling from her belly, the useless wing. As
though in a dream, she saw the hurtling car, heard again like the
crackle of ripe gorse pods, the snapping of bones fragile as the
hollow stems of fennel. Sharper than the rabbit's, her own blood-
scent rose in her nostrils. As feeling came back, pain began to
gnaw, to drag at her. From time to time, another vehicle passed,
making the leaves and grass-blades tremble, ruffling her feathers,
scattering a fine dust over everything. The sun crawled up over the
ragged rim of the bush and glared down at her. She twisted and
turned her head, tearing at turf and the tough vine-stems and by
the strength of her jaws and neck, dragged herself into a crouching posture.

The teeming life disturbed by her fall began to venture forth
once more and to explore her promising contours. A column of
ants, excited by the reports of scouts, set out to harvest the
treasure congealed on leaves and grass-blades, but scenting the
richer spoils above, began to swarm over her toes and up her legs.
With deft strokes of her beak, she drove them back, crushed or
dashed down whole companies. But more came on and once safe
in downy hiding-places on her thighs, began their slow, methodical
flensing.

A blowfly, like some bustling land-agent who has got wind of a
choice subdivision, bumbled through the bushes in search of her.
Lesser flies followed, intent on their share. For a time she kept
them at bay, but soon they too had staked their claims.

From inborn habit, not from hope, she scanned the sky, seeking
the soaring cross-shape of her kind. Now that she was cut off
from it, the air called to her with an insistence she had known

only at nesting-time. Whenever the torments of her predators grew more than she could bear, she drove her beak into the turf, tearing up grass-roots with her curved mandibles, laying waste whole commonwealths in the red-brown earth.

Towards evening when she lay hoarding her failing strength, there were other visitors.

'This must be the place!' cried an eager young voice. 'There's the rabbit that chap told us about. The hawk can't be far away.'

'We could hack off the legs with my knife,' said the second voice, 'and go halves in the bounty from the County Office.'

The harrier froze into watchful stillness. The boys put down their bicycles, began to probe the bushes.

'There it is!' cried one, catching sight of her.

'Holy smoke!' gasped the other. 'Look at those flies!' He drove them off with his stick, but came no closer.

'Shivers!' said the one who had seen her first. 'I'm not touching that. Its guts is coming out.'

'Pity we hadn't come sooner,' agreed the other. 'While it was still fresh.' They withdrew. The hum of their tyres, the murmur of their voices grew faint, were drowned at last by the myriad tiny voices close at hand.

Evening brought more heavy-tyred vehicles humming, roaring, rushing by, each leaving its cloud of choking dust. Her head sank once more, the beak agape, the tongue shuttling like a tiny lizard. At first, nightfall brought a lessening of pain. By scraping dew from grass and leaves within the orbit of her beak, she eased her fiery thirst. But soon the full force of the cold felt out the naked nerves. From time to time throughout the night she was roused by yet another rush and roar and the bush was swept by blinding lights. A stoat, hard on the heels of a frog, halted her wavering chase and lifting her delicate nose, weighed the merits of this surprising find. The harrier summoned a harsh cry, clashing her terrible mandibles, and the smouldering eyes sheered off again after the easier prey. A large rat, heavy with young, glided silently from nowhere and began to gnaw the putrifying remnant of the rabbit. She dragged it under the cover of a neighbouring bush and ate voraciously and noisily a long while.

As though to mock her plight, flocks of black swan on their way to water feeding-places, honked to each other high overhead. An opossum, his belly full of fruit from some homestead orchard, squeaked the wires of the roadside boundary fence and, skirting the bush in which she lay, trundled across the road. From their grazing grounds almost a mile away, swamp-hens sent up their piercing earth-bound shrieks.

Near dawn, she was wakened by the lowing of cattle close at hand. A dairy herd straggled past on its way to milking, picking at the dusty herbage, blowing and lowing as it crept along. One old cow, pushing her steaming muzzle between the stalks, caught sight of her. She snorted, tossing her head, but when she had stood a while, looking down, thoughtfully went her way.

Not long after, a young cattle dog padded by. To her alarm he stopped, cocked his leg against the bush, and began to sniff the grass. Instead of finding her, he stumbled on the oppossum's trail and, bounding off joyfully, nose-to-ground, left the herd to wend its own way to the shed.

As the sun began to fleer and grimace at her once more above the bush, the small armies set out again, singing their work-songs. Showers of dust drenched her anew as first a milk tanker, then a school bus, came and went. Swarms of flies, their greed raised to a fine frenzy, returned to gorge on her. A lone questing wasp, the first of countless others hung over her for a time, measuring her bulk with all her glittering eyes.

A pair of sparrows flew down to bathe in the dust at the roadside, filling the air with their shrill chatter. First a plump blackbird, then a thrush, swooped overhead. All she could do was stare up helplessly, like a man trapped in a well.

By late afternoon she lay defeated, neck awry, her carcase racked and twisted. Sharp voices rushed her yet again, while it was still light. She raised her head, struck out blindly as the sounds drew near.

'Holy smoke!' cried out the first boy. 'She's still alive. . . .'

'She *can't* be,' quavered the second. 'She was dead yesterday— or so we thought.'

'The poor thing!' cried the first, closing the knife.

The first stones, flung from too far off, by trembling hands missed altogether. Only when the braver boy, edging close, gave her a well-aimed blow to the head, was she set free. Still unsure, he bent forward, another stone poised. At length he let it fall.

'Imagine going on living all that time, like *that*,' the boy beside him whispered as they turned away.

*   *   *

As he got out of the car that evening the man noticed what seemed to be a leaf, caught in the radiator grille. He plucked it out, saw that it was a feather and, for a lark, stuck it in the band of his hat. As he opened the door, he smelt the mussels they were having for tea and smacked his lips.

'What on earth have you got in your hat?' the woman demanded, hands on hips.

'Just a feather. Doesn't it suit me? I say, those mussels smell good!'

As she took his hat, the girl slipped out the feather. She stood it in a small vase on her dressing-table where the light caught it and brought to life colours that reminded her of earth, blood, and fierce sunlight. When her mother called her for tea, she answered that she was not hungry, and softly closed the door of her room.

'If I were a harrier hawk,' she said to herself as she lay looking at the feather, 'I would stay out of the way in wild places among the hills and swamps.'

Much later, when the others had eaten, the woman was surprised to find the child already asleep, the light on, and that awful feather burning in the vase on the dressing table like some pitiless flame.

PHILIP MINCHER   # The Mace

On the first day of barracks an instructor had made a fool of him over a bren. He had been listening to the band practising on the other side of the field, and this young army chap had shown him up for inattention.

'What's the effective range of this weapon, cadet?'

Fainy had felt his face reddening. He had not actually known until then that he was a cadet, and he was not sure whether or not the soldier could make trouble for him. He had stood dumb with his throat thick and his eyes beginning to sting, and let the soldier bawl him out while everybody snickered.

That had been the first jarring note of his grammar school career: something beyond the initiation things, and the hard, frightening knot of the preliminary exams. What they referred to at the school as the first week's barracks had not turned out so nicely for the new boy. It was a school, he reasoned, like any other school. He wanted to do his best and stay out of trouble.

So that when a Mr Lewis came upon the scene seeking new prospects for the trumpet band, Fainy remembered the nasty glint in the young army instructor's eyes, and put up his hand.

Mr Lewis was a nervous, untidy little man with long dry hair and insipid features. Fainy could tell at once that he would not be one of the popular masters. He was in charge of the trumpet band

because he knew something about music, but he never took any
drill or made a great deal of noise about anything. He had few
volunteers: most were drawn more towards gunnery than to
music. He eyed Fainy hopefully:

'Which interests you, the trumpet or the drum?'

'The trumpet, sir.'

'Can you play?'

'No, sir.'

'But you have the general idea?'

Fainy felt that Mr Lewis wanted him to have the general idea,
wanted it to be all right.

'I think so, sir.' He wanted very badly to be able to play the
trumpet.

'Report to the drum major after lunch,' Mr Lewis said.

'Yes, sir. Thank you, sir.' Fainy thought now that he might have
got himself into something. He remembered the eyes of the army
instructor, and shivered.

The drum major was a stocky, muscular sixth former named
McCall. He was kind to Fainy without really appearing to see him,
and passed him on to the trumpet sergeant, a tall, pouting youth
named Clift who put a trumpet into Fainy's hands and forgot about
him, looking over his head until he went away.

Fainy stood self-consciously among the grouped bandsmen, waiting to fall in. He held the trumpet awkwardly. It was the worse for
wear, dented in the bell, with its braid shredded.

McCall gave the order to fall in. Fainy just found himself in the
ranks, quickly placing the trumpet beneath his arm the way the
others were holding theirs. The bass drummer hooked on his great
bass drum, and they dressed behind the side drummers spacing
with their sticks crossed to either side.

McCall held his mace braided with the school colours. He
walked seriously down the ranks. Fainy stood stiffly to attention
among the motionless bandsmen. The drum major came abreast
of him and stopped.

'Can you play that thing?' he asked.

He looked a good-natured young man and his eyes were smiling.
But in spite of himself Fainy saw in his mind the cutting eyes of
the army instructor, and he heard himself blurting out like a fool,
'No, sir.'

McCall smiled, and a ripple of mirth ran through the ranks.
Fainy knew he had done it again. He wanted to die.

The drum major passed on, then returned to face the band. It
wasn't his fault, Fainy thought, his face red, his eyes stinging once
more. He envied McCall his poise and his self-assurance. He kept

his eyes on the drum major. He had to go through with it now, whatever happened.

The drum major took up his place at the head of the band. Fainy tried to lose himself in what was happening, to be a part of the band and nothing more. Then McCall gave his order and it worked.

'Band—double flam, school tune, by the centre, quick . . . march!'

The drums began to beat and they were marching, and he was in fact a part of the band, feeling at last he was where he wanted to be. He felt himself caught up in the drum music, and he marched as he might well have marched a thousand times before.

The drum major marched with the mace in front of his band. They swung out of the school gates and Fainy could feel everybody watching. McCall signalled with the mace and blew his whistle, and as the bass drummer gave his double flam and the side drums rolled in introduction Fainy knew that the trumpets were going to play. Trumpet sergeant Clift barked out the name of the tune.

They marched up the road away from the school, and Fainy felt himself inside the music, the drums rolling and the trumpets blaring, the whole band one single piece giving out its grand noise to the world. He saw without staring the people on the street stopping to watch. He carried the trumpet proudly beneath his arm, and he knew that he was going to learn to play it, and that he was always going to be a part of this magnificent noise.

It was a grand march. They marched around the block and into one of the back playing fields. Then they drilled for an hour. Towards the end of it Mr Lewis wandered across the field from the main school, a solitary figure crossing the green. They watched him come, and cruel remarks were passed. Fainy was not surprised: they hated him for his meekness.

After some preamble, Mr Lewis and the trumpet sergeant took Fainy aside for an introduction to the instrument. He was nervous, but he put his heart into it. He knew the others were listening, ready to make fun of him, but he could overcome that now. He tried with everything he could muster, as if his life depended on it. Clift played the notes with a casual perfection, then stood by with his constant, disarming pout while Fainy struggled to follow him. Mr Lewis stood willing him to play. Fainy felt that well enough. Mr Lewis wanted him to learn, perhaps he could sense how much it had come to mean to him.

He put his soul into the test, and at last they decided he had the necessary potential. He marched from the field in the centre of the grand noise they made, not yet playing, but a part of it.

That was the start of it. The problems that followed were made to be overcome: the matter of somewhere to practise, for instance.

He had to be far enough away from the house not to activate his mother's migraines, yet a respectable distance from the nearest neighbour. As it was, his best possible site, the woodshed, was well within earshot of the man next door, a retired pork butcher named Sigley, who always managed an ungracious, easily-audible comment at the first blast.

But that could be overcome, too. Mr Sigley had never marched inside the great brass wonder of a trumpet band, or he would have given up before he started.

Surprisingly, it was Mr Sigley's nasty comments that helped to bring Fainy closer to his brother, Tom. One evening Fainy sat down to practise, and with the first note came Mr Sigley's sour remark, and as he closed his mind and redoubled his concentration, there was Tom's voice cutting into the old butcher's with a well-worded counter-blast. Fainy was startled. Tom's sentence was long and furious, and a hair's breadth from libel. There was silence, and then Tom came into the shed:

'You play as long and as loud as you want to, mate.'

He was ten years older than Fainy, and a working man. He had never been much of a one for school, and at Fainy's age had been working out his own destiny in the engineering trade.

'That old pork chop doesn't worry me,' Fainy said, holding the instrument awkwardly.

'Yes he does,' Tom said with authority. 'I've got a better place.'

Fainy followed him in wonder, across the yard to the other building, and into the secret world of the young man, his brother. Tom unlocked the door and switched on the light. The three stripped motorcycles gleamed before them.

Tom cleared pieces of machinery from a chair, and set it clumsily before the boy.

'You'll be able to concentrate better here,' he said.

'Gee, thanks, Tom.'

'I'll give you a key,' Tom said awkwardly. 'You just come in any time you want to get clear of old Porky. . . . And watch out you don't touch anything, or I'll knock your bloody head off.'

'Gee, Tom . . .'

Tom began to make his exit on the gruff note intended, then paused:

'Is it hard to play?'

'Not really. D'you want a try?'

'No,' Tom said flatly. Then, 'What's it feel like in the band—I mean, when everything's playing?'

'It's the best feeling in the world,' Fainy said truthfully. He felt the colour coming to his cheeks, because he had spoken from the heart, but there was no sneer from Tom.

'Well, you do it, then,' Tom said. 'Don't let anybody stop you.' He hestitated again. 'Your braid's pretty well shot.'

Fainy looked, knowing it was so.

'I could make you a new one,' Tom said.

'Boy, could you?'

'Sure. I can do braiding, all right. That's one of the things Grandad taught me when I was younger than you.'

'And you still remember how to do it?'

'I remember, all right. Your grandad had a sail ticket; what he had to say was worth remembering. He taught me every knot in the book, and I could show you them all now.'

'He gave me *The Sea Wolf*,' Fainy said. 'He must have remembered those days. He must have been a young man when Jack London was alive.'

'I read *The Sea Wolf*,' Tom said.

'I've got some Joseph Conrad books,' Fainy said.

'I don't get any time for reading now,' Tom said, and went out

But after that things were different between them. Fainy felt closer to Tom than he had ever been before. He felt how Tom was tolerating him now, respecting him where previously he had been prone to scorn.

He felt himself maturing. The term developed, and he settled into his studies, and there was no fear any more of being caught out of line, or making a fool of himself. And all the while his love was the trumpet, and his secret was the grand, incredible thing that came about when the band played.

And although the other boys were keen eough, he felt that they didn't see it in the same way as he saw it himself. For Fainy it was as though something was brought to life when they played, something martial and magnificent that had come down to him through a thousand years, a spirit evoking the names of Waterloo and Balaclava and a million shows of splendour, and feats of sword and lance he had never even heard of. This was the thing that was there in his head when they played.

And always in front of the band marched McCall, the drum major, with the school mace.

The mace was a magnificent thing of polished wood and chrome, with the school crest moulded into the head of it, and richly braided with the school colours. When you looked closely you knew that it had seen better days, but it was well balanced, and in use it was the focal point for band and spectators alike.

One day Mr Lewis released the news that the band was to appear
in a parade. There was going to be a show in a month or so for
a famous American general, and the band had been given the job
of leading a unit of Waafs on to the field. Everybody was excited,
and they began to drill in earnest. The drum major, too, began to
brush up on his mace work. For the first time Fainy saw him
throw the mace in the air. They were marching across the field,
playing their heads off, with McCall giving the mace everything he
had, and then up it went, at the very peak of the music, up and up
and over and down, and Fainy nearly died with apprehension as it
came down and was taken mechanically, and spun again in the
drum major's hand.

After that McCall threw the mace at least once every time they
trained, and they knew that he was going to throw it in the parade.
In front of thousands, Fainy thought. Thousands!

Then one morning, drilling in the quadrangle, McCall threw the
mace and missed. It hit the asphalt with a crash they could all hear
right through the music, and everybody stopped without the whistle
and stood anxiously watching. It had fallen heavy end first, and
the moulding about the head had been shattered.

It was a blow to the whole band. The mace was its essence, the
kernel of its concord. There was no mending it, although the
tragedy might be disguised. But you couldn't throw an imperfect
thing like that, not in front of thousands and an American general
to boot. The whole act was going to go sour without that big toss
of the mace.

Mr Lewis was most concerned, but offered no immediate hope.
A new one would have to be imported, he said. They didn't make
them here. That was when an idea began to form itself in Fainy's
head. Why couldn't they make them here?

That evening as usual he practised in the private sanctuary. He
had finished a tune, and was draining the instrument of spittle,
when Tom came in with yet more pieces of machinery.

'Carry on, mate,' he said.

Fainy kept on with his draining.

'Needs a vacuum cleaner,' he said.

'Why not?' Tom said, appearing to consider it. He got busy at
his workbench. 'You must be getting pretty good at it by now.'

'I hope so,' Fainy said. 'We've got a big parade next month.'

'Big deal,' Tom said.

'McCall busted the mace today.'

'Oh, how?'

'He threw it up and missed, and busted it on the asphalt.'

'He's the one who should have practised,' Tom said.

'They can't get it fixed,' Fainy said. 'They say they don't make them here.'

'Tell them they don't know what they're talking about,' Tom said. 'And bring it home with you.'

His words rang in Fainy's ears like music.

So next day he was bold enough to approach McCall and tell him that the mace could be saved. It was a proud moment. McCall must well understand and feel the band thing as he himself felt it.

McCall pricked up his ears at the news.

'Does your brother do that kind of thing?'

'He's an engineer,' Fainy said proudly. 'If he can't do it nobody can.'

'All right,' McCall said. 'Take the mace home tonight then, Burridge.'

Fainy's heart swelled with pride. He took the mace reverently. It was all there, locked in the wood and the braid and the damaged metal head of it.

He carried it proudly and delicately home to Tom, who received it with a different kind of interest. Fainy watched with fascination as he tapped it over. Tom measured, weighed and otherwise tested the mace, with all the care and gravity of a surgeon projecting a brain operation. He made a couple of realistic sketches and gave the mace back.

'Give me a week,' he said, and seemed to forget all about it.

'Is that all?' Fainy asked uncertainly. 'Shall I take it back?'

'Oh, yes,' Tom answered indifferently. Fainy felt it might be part of an act. Staking so much on his brother, he carried the mace back to McCall.

'He says about a week,' he passed the message on.

'Can he fix it?'

'Oh, sure as eggs.'

He left McCall, feeling like a man on a tight-rope. It was going to be a long week.

Every day, he could feel all eyes in the band upon him. At home, Tom went on with his 'I have spoken' act. Fainy thought seriously about prayer.

Then one evening Tom came into the sanctuary with a long object wrapped in old newspapers.

'See how this hits you,' he said, and got busy at his bench.

With trembling fingers Fainy stripped away the wrapping. It was a new mace, complete save the braiding, resplendent in its polished wood and gleaming, chrome-plated head and ferrule. Fainy wanted to shout. It all caught in his throat.

'Gee, Tom. . . .'

'What d'you think?' Tom was going through with the act.

'Gee . . . but the whole thing!'

'Thought it was the best way,' Tom said. 'I'll braid it for you after tea.'

'But how'd you do it, the wood and all . . . and the crest of the lions?'

'It was nothing,' Tom indulged himself a little. 'Mate of mine turned the wood. I know a dame at art school and she modelled the lions and stuff and I got them cast. That's a furniture ferrule on the end; I made the dome piece out of a toilet float, screwed the castings on and got it all chrome-plated. You feel the balance, mate. If he drops this one, he doesn't know what he's doing.'

'Gee, Tom. I. . . .'

'Is it okay?' Tom nearly gave himself away.

'Is it ever!' Fainy couldn't find the words. He was lost in the presence of the mace.

After tea Tom was true to his word and got busy with the braiding. He braided the mace with the school colours, naming with authority the various knots, passes and tassels as they appeared. Fainy's head reeled with a myriad of terms such as coach-whipping, Nelson braid, shroud knots and six-pass turk's heads. As the mace grew in beauty there were things in his head as great and as profound as the deep impenetrable thing he had about playing in the band. There were things now about his grandfather, who had sailed in ships as had Jack London and Joseph Conrad, and had lived as they had lived, and whose every word that he could remember would now be as precious as gold to him. And there were things too about his brother Tom, who had known their grandfather better, and had kept his words as sacred things, and was sure of his hands, and was a great craftsman, and had made the school mace for love.

When it was finished, the words wouldn't come; he was silent before its beauty. But he knew that Tom understood.

He all but burst with pride when he took the mace to McCall. He knocked on the band-room door before morning school, and someone from the select hierarchy opened it. When they saw the parcel, they let him in.

He thrust it into McCall's hands and waited as they all gathered around. The paper fell away and there it was.

'My God,' somebody said. Somebody else whistled. McCall held it up to catch the light, and they all gaped. Fainy felt their eyes as one by one they remembered he was there and turned to him.

He drank deep of their praises and fled. Most of all he would remember McCall's grateful acknowledgement, and friendly hand on his shoulder:

'This parade's going to be one out of the box, now, Burridge.'

All that week he was somebody in the band. Mr Lewis thanked him, and asked that his compliments be passed on to Tom for such a fine job. The older boys seemed suddenly to be aware that he existed, and even trumpet sergeant Clift appeared not to look over his head so much when he spoke to him. McCall, who had always been kind, was exceptionally warm about the whole thing.

That was during the first week. Then it began to die off, and Fainy became himself once more—the third-former Burridge, with the oldest, brightest trumpet, and the newest, cleanest braid. All interest focused once more on the mace alone.

It never struck Fainy that it had really been the mace alone that they had seen in the first place. It never occurred to him that the boys had no particular respect for Tom as an artisan, or that, except in this one case, they wouldn't have given twopence for his craftsmanship. When the affair settled down, the mace assumed its rightful proportions, and they trained for the big event as before. But for Fainy there was so much more that came out of the music when they played.

Finally, the big day arrived.

It was a Saturday afternoon. Fainy was ready before time, and sat needlessly polishing the gleaming trumpet. He felt there was something he wanted to say to Tom, but he was not sure about it. Finally, he wandered uncertainly into the sanctuary.

Tom was busy at his work bench, ringing a motorcycle piston.

'All ready then, Tiger?' he said.

'I'm a bit early,' Fainy said.

'Better early than keep the general waiting,' Tom offered.

Fainy answered yes, and started to say what he wanted to tell Tom, how he felt about the mace and what Tom had done for him, and it wouldn't come. He stammered, and stood there like a fool.

Tom bent over his work.

'Never mind about that,' he said, without looking up. 'You just go in there and blow their eyes out.'

'All right,' Fainy said. 'All right, Tom.'

He went out quickly, knowing he was going to blow their eyes out all right.

He arrived early, the first bandsman at the rendezvous. They were to meet and fall in at a small playing field a couple of blocks from the main park, then lead the Waafs down the street and into their place in the show. Fainy stood anxiously waiting for the others.

They came at last, all excited but trying to play it cool. Finally, they were all there except Barrett, one of the senior trumpeters. McCall was there with the mace, discussing the programme with the Waaf officers.

Barrett arrived at last. He had no trumpet. He spoke earnestly with sergeant Clift. It seemed somebody had brought his trumpet into town for him, and there had been a mix-up, and it had been left in a car some place.

There was a hasty council of war. Fainy knew before they spoke to him what they were going to do.

He felt himself handing over his trumpet, hearing Clift's soft, brutal logic: 'Well, it *is* for the good of the band, Burridge. . . .'

'That's all right,' Fainy heard himself saying. 'I don't mind.' He was afraid that his voice might crack, his eyes water and give him away.

Barrett accepted the trumpet apologetically: 'Sorry about that, Burridge. . . .'

'That's all right,' Fainy said. He let go the trumpet, wondering how anybody could care so little. Just because he can play so well, he thought: to think that it ends there! He stood in a vacuum of shock, holding on to himself, coaxing himself to be brave.

It was time. McCall brought his band together and they fell in like professionals, dressing with precision behind the drummers with their crossed sticks. Fainy stood without his trumpet, well in the middle of the middle-most rank. Something came to him, and he tried to drive the idea from his head, but it persisted. He felt that they would have stood him down entirely except for the space to be filled. He remembered Clift's cruel, pouting logic: 'It *is* for the good of the band, Burridge. . . .' Nobody need know, of course. He wondered if he would be able to describe the show to Tom afterwards without actually lying.

They were ready. The Waafs were ready and waiting. As McCall gave his order, the mace shone in his hand.

'Band—double flam, school tune, by the centre, quick . . march!'

They marched out of the little playing field and on to the road. The drums played the school tune and Fainy, truly in the centre of the band, thought of how the Waafs were marching behind him. He saw without moving his head the people lining the streets. Then McCall gave the signal for the trumpet tune, and the bass drummer gave his double flam and the side drums rolled, and as the trumpets began to play he felt himself encased in their music, so close to being a part of the thing they made it didn't really matter that he wasn't playing. He marched proud and erect, his eyes on the mace.

They marched up the road and through the main gates into the park. The field was a vast arena surrounded by a bubbling, vibrant crowd. The distances appeared very great, and the troops already assembled seemed so far away. They marched out on to the field and the people began to applaud.

Fainy was a part of the music. It didn't matter any more about the trumpet. A million visions burst in his brain as they marched, splendid deeds and splendid names like Blenheim and Waterloo and Balaclava, and the march became the ultimate tune of glory, the epitome of a million battle hymns raised to the heavens.

They marched on before the cheering crowd. Then right in front of the grandstand McCall threw the mace.

Fainy saw it from the heart of the music. The mace soared—up and over, and up and over and down—and he heard the roar of the crowd while it was still in the air, as the metal gleamed in the sun and the tassels with the school colours flared, and his ears rang and his eyes stung and the back of his neck tingled with it, and the splendour of it stayed on as the mace returned correctly to McCall's hand, and he saw it still, on and on as they marched, etched into his soul for as long as he might live.

He was fourteen years old, and life was long, and the world was very wide. And the flashing splendour of the mace, flung high with all the joy and flaunted pride of youth, soaring into the afternoon sun while all the world cheered, was the splendour of an instant that would never fade.

NOEL HILLIARD   # Corrective Training

After thinking it over for a week Marcia wrote a note:

Dear Henny, I want to be frends with you. I am so lonely. All the girls in here will not be frends with me. They think I must be someone else frend and they do not want a fight. But I am nobodys I have not been here long enough. And I do not care for that what they do. I have had boyfrends and that is what I like. My boy-frend said he will meet me when I come out. But I need somebody to talk to. Somebody I can trust. I like you Henny you got a kind

face. I want to talk about things to you will you let me?
Your frend if you will have me
Marcia

Henny sat in her room. She was a tall good-looking girl of nineteen with large hands. On the first knuckles of her left hand fingers were the letters E S U K in amateur tattoo and on the right fingers L T F C. She wrote:

Dear Marcia,

I got your illegle note and I have hid it. I liked it when you said you like me. But I did not get that other bit you said about not liking what the girls do. Thats your problem kiddo. You got to sort that one out for yourself. And you never told me how long you are in for. That has a lot to do with it. I have been here on what they call indeteminit sentence but I been a good girl (ha ha,) and they letting me out soon. Want to get rid of me I spose. So you dont have long to make up your mind.
Yours in the meantime
Henny
0 4 1 0 E

Dearest Henny,

This is your kiddo again. I have thought over what you said about *that* and if we can meet you can tell me what you want. Or show me. But take it easy because I am new at this. It is raining now and cold and the wind blows leaves on to my window and the rain water makes them stick to the glass. Then a splash of rain hits the window and the leaves wash away. I always feel sad when its raining and I am inside and nowhere to go and nothing to do. And what is worst is , is nobody to talk to. When we meet we will talk and tell each other about ourselves and make frends before we do that. But I will let you. Thats a promise. You are so sweet I like to look at you. Your a bit like my Aunty Sara in Morrinsville.
Your
Marcia
0 4 1 0 E 2

Dear Kiddo

Your got a cheek to tell me what I can do and I cant do. I dont need you really because I got all the darls I need just now. Your not the only one that wants to be frends with Sweetsie. I will tell you who my darls are and that will make you jelous. They are Cuddles Sister Blanket Noddie Podge Cobra. Hows that now. But I will not tell you who my Special Darl is. That is my secret and

I hope you get even more jelous. But I like you and hope you can get some sense into that sweet sixteen head of yours. You got a lot to learn girl.

So long
Sweetsie
(you can call me that so you are
at first base)

P S Fuck your Aunty Sara

My Dearest Sweetsie Darling,
It was so nice how that happened we never planned it and yet there we were together and nobody else around and at last I had somebody nice and frendly and tender and loving in my arms and nothing else mattered. Nothing else in the world. All the best things seem to happen like that. There was me and this boy once I never even new his name but never mind that. Was worried before but I no now its you I truly love. I am so glad I have met you properly now. This place can never get too bad so long as you are here for me to think about all day long. The sun is shining through the window on to my bed and its nice. It will warm the blankets and that is good this is such a cold place. After I was with you I felt all sort of loose and good and cheerful. Then I got all tight again and grumpy and all I can think about is you and when we can meet again. It cant be soon enough for me. With you close and wanting me I no who I am and I can like myself for a while. Not much but a bit when you want me. I love you Sweetsie and what you said about us that made me feel real good. And that is for the first time since I been in this dump. But it must be all right if a lovely sweet kind darling like you is in here too. I am en-closeing some pictures of flowers I tore from a magazine. Thought you might like them for your wall. So this note is a fat one and I hope it gets to you safely.

Your ever loving Kiddo

X X X O O O X X X

Dear Kiddo,
Dont get too smart now. I seen you talking to Porkchop yesterday. She is not one of my darls but you are. I do not like my darls to talk to any girls that are not my darls. You just remember that or your out. But I do not want to be rough on you. Your such a sweet kid. I am sorry I said that just now. I was in a bad mood and I get jelous. If people are going to like me they have to like ME and not anybody else. That is just the way I am. So glad you

like me Kiddo darling. When you was talking to Porkchop you never had a coat on. You should of else you might have catch cold. That is no good for my sweet Kiddo. Did I tell you I like your new shoes there nice did your parents send them? I wish I had folks would send me things. I am going to see if I can steal a present for you.

> So long for now
> Sweetsie

Dearest Sweetsie,

I love you so much I do not want to share you with your other darls. I hate them. Sweetsie my treasure I want to be your Special Darl. I never asked you who your Special is I never want to no else I might kill her. I would too. You no you like me a lot and we have such fun together and I like you telling me all the mad things you done in your life and we laugh together I never laugh with anyone except you Sweetsie my pet. You make me feel good all over and warm and laughing and kind and loving. You have to *ditch* your special who ever she is and I am going to be your Special Darl from now on. Take me in those cuddly arms of yours and tell me not to worry and that you love me and I am your own Special Darling. I will believe you. I can believe anything you say when you hold me in your warm arms. Gosh you had your hair done nice at church today. Real neat and I never took my eyes off you.

> Yours for ever
> Kiddo
> (Special Darling please?)
> X X X X X O O O O O

My dearly beloved Kiddo,

I ditched Bonkers but not because you told me to. She was only a fucken shop lifter anyway she got no style and she never had any class. She pisses me off and I will be glad when she gets out of here. But you do not get to be my Special as easy as that. When I see you I will tell you what I mean. I do not want to write it down else someone find this note. I do not want them to know about us. You make me happy Kiddo and I want to make you happy to. But you got to let me. Next time I see you I will give you some lollies I pinched from Charmaine's room. She is a dead loss any way just like her fucken mate Bonkers.

> Love
> Sweetsie

P S I thought yesterday you was looking a bit thin are you sure your eating properly? Its not much what they give us here but you should eat it.

My closest darling lovely Sweetsie

I just had a letter from Mummy and my Aunty Sara died. Yes she died in our old house where we use to live before and my uncle Bob (that is Saras husband) he moved there famly in there after. I feel so sad and lonely and awful. I got a brooch my Aunty Sara gave me I use to wear it on my hat when I wore a hat. She was the one to make pikelets. We use to pick lemons from our tree and cut them in four long ways and sqweeze them on her pikelets. Gee they were nice. I thought I would hate it in here and I did at the start but now I dont because it brought us together you and me Sweetsie and I feel safe with you and I would stay in here for ever if it meant being with you. Now without my Aunty Sara nothing is settled for me up there. Sweetsie my darling we will try the other one tonight. I promise. That one you told me about for me to be your Special. The one I would not do. I want to now. But only for you. So please come. I will do it but only with you. Come tonight. I cant stand to be alone. Your been here much longer and will no how to work it. Or see if we can meet. Please Sweetsie. My empty arms are longing to hold you.

> from your Kiddo
> who tonight becomes your
> SPECIAL DARL (please)
> come here for X and O and ?

Dear Kiddo,

No I do not show your notes to anyone else. I might do that with my darls but not with my Special Darl. Thats what special means and you have ernt it. You dont want to get so suspishus. Or jelous because I am nice to all my darls not just you. I am alowd to make other girls happy arnt I? They think a lot of me to you know. And when I was talking with Blanket no we were not talking about you so there. Anyone who hurts any of my darls hurts me to so just you remember that. Or is against them. You better watch out I dont see you talking to girls who are not my darls. Other girls want to be my darls now and other darls want to be my Special. I will not tell you there names. I trust you but dont get smart. You say when I talk to my other darls I hurt you. Sweetheart I know what it is to be hurt. That is why I never go all one way. That is how to get real bad hurt. You trust me and stick to

me and I will look after you and protect you. I told you I love
you and when I say that I mean it. Of course I am not forgetting
you. So stop your fucken moaning. There I go getting wild again.
I get these moods. What it is sweetest is that I am scared you might
stop loving me. Just a bit. That would be awful. I need your love
so much. There is nothing else in here just only our love for
each other. That is the most precious thing in all the world. I
feel good now I have told you that because I know you will believe
me. We should make up a special tattoo for you and me and put it
on ourselves where nobody can see it only us when we are going
to be special. But it might be too sore. I have been worried about
you since I heard you coughing in the bathroom you sure your all
right? Think of a night together just us. Wonder what we would
be like in the morning a sight I bet. Put your hand down there and
swear you will always be true to me. I am doing that now to you
and its good it always is with you and that is why you are my
Special Darling. Must lie down and think about you. Do the same
for me when you get this.

Must rush
Sweetsie

P S Later—I have not sent this yet because I lost my best
    messenger today she has gone outside where we all want
    to be.

I FLY

My dearest darling Sweetsie pet
    Your going today and I will give this note to Miriam to give you
at the door. I feel like killing myself and it is only your promise
that is stopping me. You said you will write and that is what will
keep me going. The thought of a letter from you. Am deeply hurt
to no we are to part. I saw the new girls today that has just come in
and I was wishing it was you and me. That is a mad thing to say I
no but if it was us we could start all over again. I do not no what
I am going to do without you. Sweetsie my Special Darling your the
only one who talks to me and tells me jokes and makes me laugh
and loves me for *real*. I owe every thing to you. The only nice
things that happened to me in this dump was when I was with you.
After I seen you I always lie awake in bed and think over all the
things we said to each other. The ways you have of loving me they
make me feel real close to you. I can not have any secrets from
you after we been doing that. Only just a while. Now your going
away from me. Have nothing left but dreams. I will be a good girl
(true) and try to get out soon with remishon and you will be waiting

for me. I will be true to you and you no I will because I never liked any these other girls here much you no that. Never like I love you. So I will not fall for anyone else and will do any thing you want when I am out there with you. Promise. Sweetsie my darling that Special Darl one you got me to do to you the one on my knees it took some getting use to. I have been thinking we might try that one together you and me. But not any one standing or kneeling you figer it out. And take our time. I will keep out of trouble and if they want me at home after all this I will go but you must come too. You told me you had nowhere. I can easy be faithful when I think of our times together. And the times that are to be. I never seen any one in the new girls as nice as you. Now I am lonely again and now I am crying. Gosh it is hard and cruel them letting you out and not me and yet it is what we all long for and in a way I am glad for you. I have your photo for my treasure. The half with Bonkers in it I tore that half off and put it down the toilet. Good job. You must promise me you will not start going with Bonkers again now you are going out and she is out too. She must think she is smart. She is out there and me in here. I wish you the best of luck and love you more than ever. I am still crying and I cried before when I went past and saw your things gone and new you was in the office and soon you would be gone for ever. And another girl in your room and to sleep in your bed and put her things where all your dear things use to be on the dressing table and the shelf and put up new pictures. It will hurt me every time I look there to no you have gone. God I am feeling awful. Wish I could stop being me and be some body else for a while until this goes away. But I don't think it will ever go away so long as I am in here and you gone. My heart is yours and my body and soul and I can not see the paper any more. I hope you will be very happy. Keep your promise.

For ever and ever YOURS
Marcia (Kiddo S D No. 1)
X X X X X O O O O O
xxxx for you no where)
WAIT FOR ME

Marcia got off the train in Wellington. She walked up the platform and stood in the concourse, her suitcase in her hand, looking for Henny. The mass of people were bewildering. She looked at the women's clothes and particularly the girls'. She put the suitcase at her feet.

Henny came out the women's rest room. She wore a shirt and

jeans and no shoes. They smiled, and put their arms about each
other, and kissed. Henny was a head taller. She nearly lifted
Marcia off her feet. They kissed again. People at the bookstall
turned to look.

They went to a seat. Henny put an arm around Marcia's
shoulders and Marcia put one around Henny's waist and they
gripped hands on their knees. They kissed again.

'Kiddo.'

'Sweetsie.'

Henny gripped Marcia's hand and placed it on her thigh.

'You cold?'

'Not now.'

'You should of borrowed a coat though. You look cold.'

'Not any more.'

'Glad to be here?'

'Glad to be away. Out. At last. With you.'

'Counting the days.'

'Only till I see you again.'

They kissed. Henny licked Marcia's lips.

'I've missed you Kiddo.'

'Me too. You.'

Henny pressed her hand harder. 'You know what I like about you
Kiddo? You're so affectionate.'

'I feel frightened here. All these people.'

'You're with Sweetsie now Kiddo.'

'Where we stay tonight?'

'I don't know.'

'Where you last night?'

'Never mind. Dead loss anyway.'

'Where's your things?'

'Got none.'

Henny went to the bookstall and bought the evening paper.

'Let's see what's all it say here.'

They searched the classified advertisements for the accommod-
ation section. 'You read it,' Henny said.

'I can't read too good. You.'

Henny squinted at the page.

'Nothing here,' she said. 'Nothing here for *us*.'

'You sure?'

Henny screwed up the paper and pushed it under the seat.

'What about Tawa then?' Marcia asked.

'You know anyone in Tawa?'

'One or two.'

'But it's a cold dump, Tawa. Cold and wet and too long to get to.'
'What about Newtown?'
'It's changed a lot. You wouldn't know it now. It's not cheap
up there any more. Same at Aro Street.'
'Where we go then?'
'I don't know.'
'So long as it's just you and me Sweetsie.'
'It will be.'
'Promise?'
'Course.'
'Even if it's just only tonight. Please?'
'Sure.'
'Promise?'
'I said so, Kiddo.'
'Where we go then?'
'We'll find somewhere.'
'Anywhere. Just you and me.'
'That's all there'll be. Nobody else. Promise.'
'Come on then.'
Hand in hand, Henny carrying Marcia's suitcase, they walked out
into the street.

MAURICE SHADBOLT   # The Room

The family kept the room. After all, there was no point in letting
it go; Margaret might be dead, but life persisted no matter how
inscrutably, traffic ran on the highway and seasons changed, and
Sonny would be going up to university, like Margaret before him,
at the end of summer. It would have been foolish indeed to let so
convenient a room—a short distance from the Gothic-spired university—escape simply for the sake of a couple of months' rent. With
the room in mind Mr Hamilton travelled up to the city after the
funeral; at the time everyone was still too preoccupied with grief to
question the point of his journey. For he brought almost none of

Margaret's possessions back with him. All he had done, apparently, was instruct the landlady to keep the room aside for Sonny, pay the rent for the intervening two months, and close the door— nothing, in fact, that could not have been done by letter; except of course that final thing, which someone else might have just as easily done, the closing of the door.

Mr Hamilton's earlier journey to the city, when the news first came, had not been so pointless: for then he travelled, with the undertaker, to bring back Margaret's body, that cold and shrunken thing which Sonny had recognized, with difficulty, as his sister. It was right on Christmas, and they had been expecting Margaret's return at that time anyway; they buried her on Boxing Day, near the sharp-outflung shadow of the steep-roofed wooden church on the hill above the tidal lagoon and mangrove forest. It was a cloudless and perfect summer day, scarcely flawed by the sad dark group among the tangled crosses in the graveyard. Margaret was buried in the last of the Hamilton plots; they occupied a small corner of the graveyard. Now the family would have to take plots in the ugly new cemetery growing near the town. For the grave-yard was filled; most of the graves, many overgrown and anony-mous, went back fifty years at least—some even a hundred or more, to the time when the first settlers in the district, one with the name of Hamilton, walked the pale beaches and forested valleys of a new country. Sonny had often idly wondered who might claim that last plot. He supposed his parents might one day share it. Now Margaret, unlikeliest of all, had taken it first.

At the end of the service he turned with conscious maturity away from the grave, his eyes travelling quickly over his father's sagging face, his mother's swollen features; he saw them as old at the same time as he felt himself older. It seemed, now, they were all castaway on the same shore. He faced the day; the sun was dazzling on the lagoon beyond the glinting mangroves. It did not pain him to see a day so brilliant; he had no wish to project his grief upon it. On such a day it was easier to fix his best memories of Margaret—in tight shorts and light shirt, with clean sunburned limbs—more sharply. Margaret had been a summer girl.

Later, after his father's second visit to the city, he began to wonder about the room. What was it had caused his father to flee the room so suddenly, so inexplicably? And, more to the point, what was it, precisely, that waited for Sonny there? He felt it unfair, suddenly, that it should be left to him to unriddle whatever secret remained; whatever lay behind that quickly-shut door. The burden of discovery might at least have been shared; why should it all fall to him? Then he understood slowly that after the grief and the burial, the shock and shame of the coroner's report, his parents wanted no part of such discovery. They wanted the past buried as simply as Margaret. They escaped quickly, greedily, into the trivia of their lives again; Margaret had already been gone too long a time—there was no discernible vacuum in their lives, no empty place at table. There were simply no longer those rare, cryptic letters from the city; no longer the evenings when his mother, with huge effort, arranged pen and ink and paper on the scrubbed kitchen table and began those long letters, filled with vague warnings, to Margaret. It was quite enough for them to know that Margaret had haemorrhaged to death, in hospital sheets, among strangers, and in circumstances so appalling; the worst had come to pass, after all. And, having come to pass, it was best now forgotten. But there was one thing for which Sonny was grateful: despite all that had happened, they at least did not try to dissuade him from university, from the city. They seemed still to accept, in their stoic way, that he, like Margaret, should flee the nest and take his chance. Perhaps they considered that his sex was more often on the side of safety; that, when all was said and done, there was less risk for Sonny. He didn't know for sure, though; they didn't talk about it with him.

He watched them, with an aching lump of misery in his mind, as they went about their day; his father, with a face as eroded as the upper hills, plodding in gumboots about his dry brown acres; his mother, with pain lightly shadowing her cheerful eyes, busy in the kitchen or gossiping with callers on the back porch. He should have liked, as a gesture, to be able to say he would stay on with them, after all: they would have been relieved, astonished, grateful. But the pull away was still too strong. And they accepted that he should leave just as they had always accepted him as a strange, bookish child. He would go, at the end of summer, as Margaret had gone three years before.

He wandered often into the library which lay to the front of the homestead. Its long windows overlooked the harbour the first Hamilton had travelled on his way to site his shelter in this lonely and perhaps menacing place, to plant his life and learning down where he cleared the kauri forest. The library served, while he battled with the land, as a receptacle for his knowledge and his philosophy of happiness which he had brought to the new country bundled as tightly as the blankets he carried for barter with the brown men. And when his dream of happiness dissolved like smoke upon ravaged hills it became a place of refuge, a place in which to shut himself off from his rebellious sons, intolerant and land-hungry, and where he could assuage his bitterness in his diaries now, ninety years later, crinkling with age. The library had survived like a curiosity through three generations of the family; it was something of wonder to Sonny that the large room was never cleared and put to other use, the books emptied from the shelves, the diaries consigned to the fire. Probably, once past the temptations of the first generation, the library had won its reprieve. No one appeared to have much use for it in the past; there was little time, on a struggling farm, for books. And the interest he and Margaret showed in the library, as children and adolescents, was regarded as something unhealthy by parents and relatives. Perhaps that only drove them more upon themselves, even more hungrily upon the books; looking back, he didn't know, couldn't remember. All he could remember was that so much of their lives had been spent not only on the hills and beaches, but here among dusty shelves. If ever there had been a time to put an end to the library, it should have been then. He and Margaret might have been salvaged, saved from the city, preserved for the less introspective life of their easy-going country cousins. Instead, the inevitable happened and Margaret had shaken free, as easily as a leaf from an autumn tree; first Margaret, now himself.

The day Sonny began packing for the city—he had left it late, and it was the day before he was due to leave—he went into the library for the last time; he intended selecting a few useful books to take along in his suitcases. Here and there, among the ranks of old leather-bound books with gold-lettered spines, stood new bright-covered books; the library had changed and grown since he and Margaret first invaded it. But he found the task of selection too painful; it was like wading upstream, against the current of a dark river lately travelled, seeking something of value lost beneath the opaque, swirling surface; or sorting through a scatter of rock, searching out true gold among fool's gold. After a while he gave up. He had thought he might find something there to help chart his way across new and strange terrain. But there was nothing; nothing, after all, that seemed immediately relevant. He felt naked and vulnerable. He would, depending on his own meagre knowledge, and without even quick-witted Margaret's help, have to chart his way alone. Disquieted, he wandered slowly across the library to the long windows. The more he considered it, the more he felt the direction of these windows marvellously chosen; he was lifted from his bleak mood—he might have been looking out upon some last shimmering vision of the country, preserved intact and framed by the first Hamilton, for it was still almost as it must once all have been, the bush and sea and sky delivered up to the onlooker in a bewildering sweep of beauty. The land, the farm itself, was absent from the picture: the stripped, sunburned acres which had drained all wonder, hope and memory. The land lay behind, on the other side of the homestead, a world away. On one side, the vision; on the other, the truth. Why should he and Margaret have inhabited this divide? What had brought them into the library in the first place? Perhaps boredom, a rainy day; perhaps something waiting to be fed within them. He didn't know; perhaps he would never know. Anyway, whatever it was, it had sent Margaret off to destruction; and now was sending him off—where? He turned from the windows with a gently helpless feeling; he crossed the library and closed the door softly. This act of shutting away the past, made so deliberately, reminded him—if he really needed to be reminded—that in a short time he would be opening a new door.

So it happened that he trod the worn carpet of a gloomy stairway on a late February day in a vague terror of apprehension; his feet struck dully up the stairs, and his suitcases bumped heavily and awkwardly against his legs. He had left, with regret, the warm golden sunshine which poured out of a clear sky upon the pale city and bright harbour. The street in which his new home stood was one of ugly old colonial homes with facades gently peeling, wandering verandahs, elaborately frilled cornices. It was a quiet street, a stale backwater among large white modern buildings; a street neglected, or just forgotten. He found the right place—the number was marked clearly on the gate and, besides, he had called there once before, when on a brief visit to the city, to see Margaret. She wasn't in; and he left disappointed. But he found her by accident, shortly after, wandering with a bearded young man through the park beside the university. This young man pumped Sonny's hand—or so Sonny felt at the time—with a good deal of insincerity. He wore suede shoes, corduroys and a grey roll-neck sweater; he would have looked odd enough, anyway, even without the beard.

Margaret was at once delighted and apologetic. 'But why didn't you say you were coming?' she cried. 'You should have written and told me.' And, turning to the young man, she added, 'Sonny's really such an innocent in the city. I haven't the faintest idea how he'd get on if he hadn't found me.'

It was all so like Margaret: her eyes flashed back and forward from Sonny to the young man, as if she were simultaneously apologizing to the young man for Sonny's presence, and to Sonny for the young man's presence. Margaret always apologized for no reason at all. It seemed her fear for hurting anyone made her apologetic to the world simply for being herself. Taken by surprise that day, she appeared remarkably different, possessed of some new and extraordinary beauty. It wasn't at all the wild outdoor beauty she had at home, when she cantered long-legged beside Sonny about the farm. It was something more suited to the chill of a sunny late-winter day in a city park, with the first thin green leaves sprouting on the bare limbs of deciduous trees above their heads, a beauty of pale skin, dark hair, blue eyes; she wore her hair long and loose, had a bright scarf wound carelessly about her neck, and her hands were thrust deep in the pockets of her warm dufflejacket; her legs were hidden in slender slacks. After they talked a while, uneasily, they went, the three of them, to a coffee-cellar. There, on even more unfamiliar ground—the celler was a dimly-lit place, with Parisian murals—he felt dismayed; he distrusted Margaret's odd, bearded companion and, in a strange way, distrusted Margaret too. They talked across him about theatre, cinema, subjects on which he could express no opinion. And Sonny sat sullenly like someone who had discovered himself, against his will, in a foreign country, who did not understand the language and had no wish to learn it—for they seemed, on the whole, to be talking in an elaborate code. He resisted Margaret's attempts to draw him into the conversation; or into comment on the farm and their parents and his study. His stupid silence, his surliness, must have at last become apparent to the others; for they fell silent too. He wished the young man, whom he now actively disliked, would go away and leave him with Margaret. But the young man didn't go away. He sat idly playing with lumps of sugar, looking up now and then at Margaret, the flicker of a smile on his lips, and his eyes signalling in an even more mysterious code. It was then that Sonny felt altogether an intruder. He was irritated, angry at himself for having hoped for anything from Margaret, appalled by the fiasco of his first trip alone to the city.

Now the landlady shuffled ahead of him up the stairs, across a landing, down a dark passage. He followed her with his suitcases. Halfway along the passage she stopped. In the gloom, her gross face enormous and pale, she clinked two keys from her apron pocket. 'The room,' she said. 'And the keys. Two keys—upstairs and downstairs, your door and the front door.' She seemed, for the moment, more than ever like a gaoler. Then the keys fell into his hand. 'I don't know exactly what happened to that sister of yours,' she said. 'And I don't want to know neither. It's your business. And my business is keeping a decent place here. That's why I usually only let my rooms to girls. They're safer. I'm making an exception for you on account of your father being such a nice man. After all that trouble, and him looking so miserable, I didn't have the heart to say no. It's a wonder I didn't say no. It's the first time I ever had the police call here making inquiries in twenty years, mind you, in twenty years. Still, apart from that, I didn't have no trouble. That's why I made an exception for your father. I hope you appreciate it, that's all.'

'I do,' Sonny insisted. 'I do appreciate it.'

'You clean out your own room,' she continued. 'You do your own cooking in that long kitchen down the end of the passage. You share it with all the other people on this floor. The toilet's up the other end, and the bathroom's next to it. There's hot water, but you pay for the gas—pennies in the meter. And no visitors after eleven. And no parties and no nonsense. And a fortnight's notice either side.'

'Yes,' said Sonny. 'I understand.'

'Good,' she said. 'Then I won't keep you. There's your room.' She clumped off abruptly, along the passage, down the stairs. He was alone; quite alone. He tried to force a key into the lock: it was the wrong one. He had a dry urgent feeling in his throat. He took a deep breath and tried the second key. It fitted with difficulty, as if grown unfamiliar with the stiff lock. He twisted the key sharply and the door fell open. Then he took up his suitcase and, shouldering the door wide, banged into the room. He stopped as suddenly as he entered, overcome by the stillness of the room; he set down his suitcases quietly, turned, and shut the door. Then, with his back to the door, he let himself slowly observe the place.

At first it was neither more nor less than he expected. Everything, already, had a faintly preserved quality. The bed with its faded check cover; the rug with the strange design—it might have been Persian or Indian, a gift from someone—fastened to the wall; the swimming championship pennant tacked near it; the photographs on the bookshelf by the bed, together with the little carved wooden Chinaman, with coolie hat and opium pipe, who gazed deeply into the silence; the neat rows of books—Sonny recognized some of the gold-lettered titles; the sheepskin rug on the varnished floor and, across the room, the compact desk with tidied heaps of paper, pens, and a paua-shell ashtray. On the desk stood a lamp with red rattan tilted jauntily on an odd-shaped raffiaworked bottle on which the word *Ruffino* stood out plainly and, in smaller letters, vino chianti; there was also a clock with the hands stopped at five past midnight. Above the desk, suspended on a triangle of cord, hung an old greenstone tiki. Everything was precise, uncluttered; the simple formality of the room told him little he did not already know. For a moment, though, it seemed odd to him that in three years his sister should have impressed her personality so lightly upon the room. Then he saw that lightness of touch as unmistakably Margaret's. The room was actually small; it could have appeared poky and miserable. Instead she gave it something of her own open, fresh quality. Someone else might have conducted a vain assault upon the cramped, shabby room; she went about it more subtly. Yes, the room was Margaret: he could not have thought otherwise.

Sunlight slanted through the lace of the closed window; stale air was trapped with the lengthening shadows. He went across the room in five, exact paces and lifted the window; there was a rumbling sound of old, worn window-cord as he did it. In the moment the sound died, he was looking at some arthritic fruit-trees in the meagre backyard. Trapped and sunless beneath new-risen office buildings, they seemed survivors of some more mellow, spacious time. Nothing, they seemed to say, was ever quite the same. A mild breeze, off the sea, cooled his face. Through a gap in the new buildings he was given a narrow view of the city crowding down to the harbour, ships and warehouses and great crane-beaks packed along the waterfront, a pale ferry-boat gliding like a seabird, homes sprinkled thickly on a green distant shore.

He half-turned back into the room, pausing as if on the edge of some dizzying height. He would, he supposed, have a long time to get used to the room; certainly he would need a long time to make any impression of his own upon it. At the moment it was altogether alien and forbidding. His eyes fell to the top of the bookshelf, and he was looking at himself: at a photograph of himself, taken years before, when slight and brown in swimshorts. He grinned shyly at Margaret's box-camera; the beach showed between fronds of fern in the background. He remembered, now, when it was taken: the last summer before Margaret left for university. Together they filled warm lengths of time easily, on lonely lagoons and gleaming beaches strewn with bleached driftwood. It was a summer when, for some reason, the unexpected became normal: they ceased being surprised by their own discoveries. They found the spars of some old wrecked sailing ship, uncovered by shifting sand, out near the harbour heads where the sand-bar had taken some of the old voyagers; they dug with sticks and turned up not only an old rusting ship's bell, but some long-buried Maori artifacts. And they found the entrance to an ancient Maori burial-cave, overhung with toi toi, where heaped bones and skulls lay on rock ledges; the sea rang about the cave, but inside there was a queer vibrant silence. They did not touch anything: they peered within and went quietly away, without breaking *tapu*. Only at the end, in the last days of thick February heat, did time grow heavy with Margaret's coming departure: she went about like a last-minute tourist desperate for souvenirs, gathering stones and shells and twisted sticks of sea-worn pohutukawa; that was when she took the picture of Sonny. Finding the photograph in some way reassured him; he was not, after all, entirely a stranger here.

Only the clock, the clock silent on the desk at five minutes past midnight, now disturbed him. He went across to the desk, conscious of his footsteps, of his own slight rustling sound, in the silence. He wound the clock, set it aside, and sat at the desk: the ticking sounded sharply beside him, keeping him company as his hand hovered indecisively over the papers on the desk. He was some time making up his mind. Then he drew all the papers on the desk towards him.

He felt a thin pang of disappointment; there was very little there. A circular from the university literary society. Another circular for a film programme. The titles of the films were in French. Some hasty notes for an essay on the modern novel. Nothing rewarding or revealing. He looked at the notes, at Margaret's large oblique handwriting, seeking something—a clue perhaps, leading to other clues—obscure to himself there. But he was not to find anything so deliberately. As he shuffled the notes together, a scrap of paper, hidden till then, glided to the floor. He picked it up; on it was written a few lines of poetry. The handwriting trailed off in the middle of a stanza. He thought for a moment that the poem, like the notes, had simply been copied from some prescribed book; he might have placed it aside, with the other papers, if the first two lines had not told him something of the lumpy texture of the imagery. He was halted, then surprised: with a lurch of the stomach he saw, in the third line, his own name. He saw also, vividly, the poem as Margaret's own; written, perhaps, in the silence of the university library, when boredom or disquiet had taken her mind from textbooks to sunlight upon a window, and then to a more distant place. Until now he had no suspicion that his sister might have written poetry; his only confirmation of the fact lay lightly in his hand. The poem was not directly relevant to him,

or to his experience; his name just seemed to sit uneasily among
other words. The lines appeared to be written out of some agony
of mind. But the subject of the poem, if a poem so wandering
could be said to have a subject, was their discovery of the Maori
burial cave. She was using their discovery, and their creeping
away, as a parallel for some other thing, investing some other
experience with the same unique, magical significance: it baffled
him for a while until he saw it, at last, as a love poem.

The chair-legs gave a quick cry as he pushed himself out from
the desk, let the poem fall with the other papers. The soft explosion of shock within him, fading as he crossed the room, seemed
suddenly and entirely unreasonable. He stood staring blankly out
into the declining afternoon, his hands fastened on the windowsill.
Why should he feel so betrayed? He sought to unravel the separate
strands of grief and anger within himself: they had, after all, made
no pact, no secret, about the cave; it had simply not occurred to
him that Margaret might, looking back, have seen the discovery in
relation to someone other than himself. And might have used the
experience as if she alone had right to it; as if it had never been
shared. It had simply not occurred to him, in fact, that Margaret
might have loved so tangibly as to make all other love, all other
loves, transparent. And he, apparently, belonged to that transparent
order of things; his was only a name dropped casually, perhaps
just for metre's sake, in an unfinished poem. He was, above all, a
convenient disguise for that other, that faceless and nameless person
whose presence grew behind the scrambled images. And whose
absence, possibly, had dictated the poem in the first place. He could
not have named his feeling, at least not yet: he could not have
named it jealously.

He forced himself back into the room: he had been standing
at the window in some frozen attitude of escape. But there was,
he knew now more surely than he had ever known, to be no
escape. The sun had slid down behind the buildings; the room had
darkened. But it seemed, for one hallucinatory second as he turned
back, that it was his own inner oppression which dimmed his eyes.
Yet it was, after all, only the change in light, the movement of the
world towards evening; it had, until now, escaped him. He crossed
to the desk again and sat slumped, with his head in his hands, for
some time. When he lifted his eyes finally, it was still darker; outside, above the buildings, light drained from the sky. Strips of
cloud held flecks of sunset like a sediment. He felt heavy and tired;
the effort of the long day's journey had overtaken him. Yet he had
to go on; there was no question of his not continuing with the

search until, perhaps, he had nothing left. He had hardly even begun; there was still the inside of the desk to be ransacked. And papers, perhaps letters, to be scavenged through, sorted into heaps of probabilities and possibilities; somewhere there would be one clue, and another. Now he knew a little, he felt impelled to know all. He had to see himself as naked as he felt; he had to shed the last ragged garment of illusion, and see the colour of his loneliness. He needed light; above all, light. He groped in the gloom for the switch of the rattan-shaded desk lamp. Then he was caught, with the desk, in a patch of red light; the rest of the room shaded off into thickening darkness. He raised his eyes to the tiki, swinging gently on the ultimate tip of its triangle of cord: his movement, his clumsy feeling for the lamp-switch, had set it in motion. He did not know how his family had come by the tiki: no one knew, no one remembered; no more than most of the family remembered how or why they came to be in this country. The tiki had lain unwanted, among family trinkets and trivia, for a long time before Margaret claimed it for herself. It was old, probably three hundred years or more; old enough anyway for generations of brown flesh to have worn down the clean lines of the carving. The tiki, he thought: the first man, creation of the devious and incestuous god Tane: or emblem of fertility, the human embryo crushed in the womb, head twisted, tongue lolling: a vision, tantalizing and terrible, of an older, darker, god-begun world. It settled presently, hung still in the pale red glow of the lamp; it settled steadily in his sight as his hands hesitated on the top drawers of the desk. There seemed, before he went further, something he had to say, admit to himself.

He had loved his sister.

But there seemed, after all, nothing terrible in the words. They sounded, in fact, ordinary and usual. Yet that was all there was to say; the words were simply not enough. He was powerless to find others. There was, within himself, a vast void uncovered; he had to beat down the darkness as he might beat down fire, beat it down into the remotest depths of his feverish flesh.

He was still paused in the act of opening the desk. He had a bitter taste in his mouth; and the red of the lamplight burned irritatingly at the corners of his tired eyes. The dark grew enormously around him. It was not all right; it would not be all right for a long time. But it was better, having said it; not much better, but a little.

There was a scraping sound as the first drawer opened. A half-smoked pack of cigarettes lay in it; some paperclips, hairpins. And

the strange harvest of talismans he had half-expected to find somewhere, the stones and shells she had apparently been unable to
discard. He tried another drawer. More notes; and a tidy heap of
typewritten essays. Bundles of letters fastened with rubber-bands.
He took out the letters and placed them on top of the desk. Then
he began to go systematically through all the drawers. There were
more letters, here and there. And a long letter of Margaret's own,
unfinished.

Dear Geoff
   *I have all your letters now. What should I say—that I'm pleased
and happy for you? But you know that wouldn't be true. I know
you think I'm an obstinate creature, but perhaps my obstinacy is
an honesty. Too often the obstinate person is seen as an oddity and
placed in the category of perverse troublemaker. As if he or she
doesn't already suffer enough from the affliction—sickness, even—
of honesty. But probably there is a justice, somewhere, in the
quarantine imposed upon them; such people are, after all, a
menace. Given the chance they might infect others with their
disease. And where would we be without our daily lies, daily
hypocrisy? In the abyss, probably; in the abyss which I seem, at
present, to inhabit. So please don't call me dishonest again. Call
me obstinate if you like—but concede me honesty for the moment.*
   You say you feel

It was typically, painfully Margaret: long-winded, oblique, in an
effort to avoid abrupt hurt. She had written Sonny a letter with
just such a rambling preliminary after his disastrous visit to the
city. *I have all your letters now.* What letters? It was the excuse
he needed, just then, to escape Margaret's own voice.
   Some of the letters on the desk were his; most of those he had
written Margaret from the farm had been kept. He could not have
read them again; they would, with their innocence, have been
embarrassing. There were one or two letters surviving from his
mother: he saw her again labouring to produce the letters on the
kitchen table. He, in turn, would soon be receiving the same letters,
suffering the same reproaches. They, for different reasons, would
also have been painful to read; he eliminated them along with his
own, dropping them back into a drawer. Other letters were less
easy to eliminate. Letters from girl friends, vague and ambiguous.
He scanned a number of these opaque letters before casting them
aside. The pile of letters on the desk diminished quickly. Soon he
was aware of something which linked the few letters remaining.

There was a pattern in the stamps and postmarks. Sydney, Jakarta, Colombo, Aden, Naples: the pattern, and story, of voyage. The handwriting on the envelopes was precise and masculine. Yet there was something missing, like an inexplicably silent note in a phrase of music. Then he found the letter which had slid out from among the others and fallen, unobserved, to the floor. He picked it up and the picture was complete: the envelope was postmarked London; there was the same precise, masculine hand.

Looking at the letters in sequence, Sonny felt they told him just about as much as he was ever likely to know. He didn't need to read them. In a way he didn't even need to know any more about Geoff. To know more might spoil the picture. But Margaret?

You say you feel at home again. Well you are, aren't you? At home, I mean. You came out here to get away from something. I often wonder if I really know all the story. You only ever gave me bits and pieces. A grey childhood, some mean smoky city, a brilliant scholastic career—a break with everything you knew, Oxford, London, an unhappy marriage (What was she really like, I wonder? I always felt she was more important than you'd allow me to know. You only ever let me see a snobbish girl with rather a sulky face). And then a nervous breakdown, a chance for escape, a chance perhaps for happiness—a job in a country twelve thousand miles away, so remote from everything you'd known. You weren't the first to imagine that simply by exchanging one patch of earth for another you might find happiness. It's an old story, and mostly a sad one.

No: it was no use. He had been foolish to imagine he might learn anything about Margaret from a letter anyway. They all seemed so irrelevant, these words which confused him. He was likely to lose Margaret altogether in their thickets and by-ways.

The knock on the door jolted him in his seat, set his body clamouring. He had been locked away with shadows so long now, the least sound would have sparked fright in his body. Then there was the landlady's voice.

'Telephone,' she said. 'Telephone.'

He rose and went bewildered to the door. Who was there, in the city, who might call him by telephone? Perhaps it was a toll call from the country, from his parents. He opened the door. The landlady was dressed in Saturday night finery, in a black dress with silvery trimmings. She smelt of wine and had a cigarette burning in one hand. 'Downstairs,' she said. 'On the right, under the stairs. You'll find it easily.' She tramped down the passage ahead of him.

'For me?' he said, still perplexed.

'No,' she said. 'Not exactly. For your sister. She still gets calls, though they've been dropping off a bit lately. People have been away on holidays and things—I expect they're slow hearing. Anyway I'm tired of explaining. Now it's your turn.'

They were halfway down the stairs now. The landlady stopped, turned off to the door of her apartment.

'You mean—' he began. 'You mean you didn't say.'

'That's right,' she replied. 'I didn't say. Like I told you, I'm tired of explaining. Down that way—on the right, under the stairs. It might be someone you know.'

He doubted that. He knew none of Margaret's friends. This landlady looked at him curiously, almost sympathetically; but only for a moment. She went into her apartment, closing the door. He heard muffled voices beyond the door.

'What happened?' said a man's voice. 'What's the trouble?'

'Nothing,' the landlady said. 'Just the new kid upstairs, the one I was telling you about. The one whose sister died. Nice kid, brown as a berry. Straight from the country, it's written all over him. There was a call for his sister, that's all. I went up to get him.'

'Christ,' said the man. 'Is that all? You looked worried. How's your glass?'

'Empty,' she said. 'Thanks.' Sonny heard a rattle of springs as she fell into a chair. 'Isn't the world a bloody awful place?'

'Cheers,' said the man. 'How do you mean?'

'Christ, don't ask me,' she said. 'Don't ask me. I don't know. It's just I can't sleep nights, sometimes, thinking about it. The world, I mean, and everything.'

No, it was no use delaying; no place to learn anything new. Sonny went on down. There was a feeble light under the stairs, above the place where the telephone receiver dangled from its cradle. He took the receiver and held it to his ear, but remained silent as though paralysed. The sounds of a party, music and voices, pressed violently against his brain.

'Hello,' said someone irritated. 'Are you there? Is that you, Marg?'

He spoke at last. 'Hello?' he said tentatively.

'For Christ's sake,' said the voice. 'Who is it? Where's Marg?'

'She's not here,' he began. 'She's—'

'For crying out loud,' said the drunken voice. 'Who is it? Where's Marg? Who's talking? Is that you, Geoff? I thought you'd gone home to England. Come on, where are you hiding her?'

'It's not Geoff,' Sonny said. I'm—'

But it was no use. Whoever it was, at the other end, wasn't listening. Against the background of party noise, he heard the voice explaining to someone else, 'Some bastard at the other end won't tell me where she is. Says he isn't Geoff. God knows.' The voice came back full into the receiver again. 'Look here, who the hell is it talking?'

'Margaret's brother,' Sonny said.

'Well, for God's sake. What do you know about that? I didn't even know she had one. I'm not even sure about it now—I mean are you sure you're Marg's brother? I mean I've heard this story before. Brothers, cousins—I know the line. You sure about it? You sure you're Marg's brother?'

'Perfectly sure,' Sonny said.

'Well, I'll believe you,' said the voice. 'Thousands wouldn't. Do me a favour, will you? Will you root round and dig Marg out, wherever she is, and tell her Ken's back in town and having a bloody marvellous party. You get the name? Ken. Just tell her Ken—Ken's having a party. Gallons of grog and dozens of people. Tell her, won't you? She's sure to come. Come along too, if you like.'

'Thanks,' Sonny said. 'But Margaret's dead.'

'You're kidding,' the voice said. 'You're—'

'She's dead,' Sonny said quietly.

'Christ,' the voice exploded. 'You're not serious. You mean—'

'Yes,' Sonny said. 'I mean she's dead.' He cried it out this time as if to convince himself. At the other end there was a baffled pause, a confusion of voices against the music, and then he was left with the humming receiver. He dropped it back into its cradle and walked away. Near the foot of the stairs, in the darkness, a nausea overcame him; he trembled, swayed, and held to the bottom stair-post.

Somewhere outside there was a rush of high, clicking heels over pavement; then over the wooden boards of the verandah. The front door banged open. In the brief invasion of streetlight Sonny saw a girl silhouetted for a moment. There was a glitter of hair, and the flash of a silver brooch; he did not have time to see more. Her face remained in shadow. She was small, slight-figured, and had one arm across her front, half-bent as though in pain. The door slammed behind her. She did not see him in the dark, at the foot of the stairs; she fled past him, up the stairs, leaving behind a faint smell of perfume.

The girl was sobbing.

She was gone quickly. Somewhere upstairs, in a remote part of the building, a door opened and closed. Then the place grew silent again. Wonder at the girl, wonder at her tears, for the moment eased his own pain. Slowly he made his way up the stairs, holding to the banister as if old and tired. There was still a faint trail of scent. Who was she, and what was her grief? What caused her to flee a summer evening? He crossed the landing and went down the passage and back to his room. In the room he stood in shadow, before the desk in its patch of red light; he heard, through the slender wall, the fall of a body upon a mattress and renewed sobbing. So the girl, whoever she was, lived in the next room, so close to him. Yet it made no difference: there was nothing, really, he could do; she was trapped as securely in her privacy as he was in his own; she might as well have wept a hundred miles away. He wondered if he might have this helpless feeling often in the city. For this, it seemed, was the condition on which life here was to be lived.

He went to the desk and sat down again. His eyes found Margaret's letter. For some reason he no longer wished to read it. He turned the pages slowly, but they might have been blank for all he saw. Until he came to the last paragraph. The handwriting, with haste, became more and more shapeless, broken up by deletions; Sonny had to read back and forward to decipher the words, follow their meaning.

Nice of you to say you want to rescue me from the healthy squalor of this place. I suppose I should be pleading for rescue. But what if I'm too deep in this squalor, too deep to get out? Of course you wouldn't understand; you wouldn't wish to understand. Anyhow I've seen you get to work like a surgeon on too much I've said. I'm sure you can always reduce everything to the absurd. You see I'm about to join my family on the farm for Xmas. You really ought

Sonny shifted his eyes. Through the window, between the dark buildings, he saw lights glittering on the harbour. In the next room the sobbing had died to a faint whimper. He waited until he was calm again.

to have met my family. My parents, for example—I used to despise them. Then, imagining myself more tolerant, I thought I had the right to pity them. Then I saw that pity was only arrogance in a new disguise. *So I've had to try making sense of it all over again. Then there's my brother. I never told you about him. He's due here next year. In fact I've been hunting for a room for him all this past week. I feel I have to help him. If I don't, no one else will. I've a lot I want to tell him. I'm responsible. I suppose that's what I'm saying. In an odd way you've made me aware of this responsibility. You probably wouldn't understand that either. You say I sound a little distraught, as if there's something wrong. Well, perhaps I am a little distraught. Perhaps there is something wrong. I guess it was too good to be true—that it should end so cleanly, I mean. I knew three weeks after you left, but you were more than half-way to London by then. I didn't want to tell you until I made up my mind, and this letter has been making up my mind. (I wonder if I shall ever post it.) I haven't decided quite what to do yet. I've only a few days before I go off to join the family on the farm for Xmas. Yes, I know someone who knows someone who helps, at a price, with these things. Though I don't know if I'm strong enough—cold blooded enough?—to go through with that. On the other hand I worry about the alternative—getting through next year, when I'll be needed, with all this complication. I hope you're not too shocked. After all you always said it was the wildness in me you liked, and wildness has its consequence. So please don't worry. Because*

Because what? Because she knew someone who knew someone? Anyway that was where the letter ended. Perhaps he had learned all he would ever learn. He folded the pages and, after some hesitation, put them together with the other letters, those of the voyager. Between them there might be an answer; he didn't know what or why. But it seemed the least he could do.

It might have been an hour or year later: he sat at the window and the room was in darkness; the lamp on the desk had been turned out long before. In the next room the girl had lately begun to stir. He heard her slippered feet across the floor, the snip of a radio-switch, soft music. She must have been sitting at her window too, with a cigarette, for he could smell the drift of smoke. He wondered where she came from; had she a family escaped, a farm forsaken? And why should she sprinkle tears upon a city pavement? He might never know; just as he might never know, finally, about Margaret. It was now frightening to believe that he might, after all, have been important to Margaret.

He had suffered this sensation before, once when listening to music he imagined he knew well; everything had been as familiar

as ever, as beautiful as ever, but suddenly strange and terrible too.
It was like contemplating the dark spaces beyond the stars from
the porch steps on the farm at night. He felt the weight of new
questions in his mind. He had been silent too long. He rose and
whispered into the room.

'What is it, Margaret? What is it we never knew, never counted
on? Weren't you strong enough, or were you too strong? Whatever it is, I should know. It's important to me. I only want one
good reason why I should be alive tonight, and not you. What was
it you were going to tell me? How were you going to help me?
Why is it? What is it?' He whispered his last question into the
room, and there was silence.

In a world where uncertainy was the rule, perhaps one thing was
certain: he would have some kind of answer very soon. He was
hungry. And he was tired. He had not eaten; he had not even unpacked. He crossed the room and switched on the desk-lamp. He
had not touched anything in the room yet, but it was as if in the
darkness everything had shifted imperceptibly. Certainly the room
no longer looked so alien. The clock, as he turned back to the desk
again, swung into his vision. He looked at it, baffled. It said five
o'clock; it was surely near eleven, or midnight. Then he remembered that he hadn't, when winding the clock, shifted the hands to
the correct time. His wrist watch said fifteen past eleven. He righted
the clock with a feeling of satisfaction.

He went to his suitcases. There was no urgency about unpack-
ing. It was just that he wanted to deposit a few things of his own
around the room, as if to reinforce his own claim to possession.
Afterwards he would go out into the night and find, perhaps down
near the waterfront, an all-night eating place. There were such
places in the city. There were a great many places, a great many
places to which he might walk, in the city. He unfastened the
straps of his suitcases and began to unpack.

A Retired Life

The white hand pressing the glass made Cliff Poulson think of people hunted. He opened the door and the man on the porch said, 'Excuse me. Would you mind phoning for the police?' He was small and ugly, and in a rage about something. Blotches like strawberry birthmarks stood out on his cheeks and jaw and the lenses of his spectacles were filled with an angry magnified blue. He had forced the woman with him into a corner and was holding her protectively by the arm.

'Is the next-doors' Alsatian loose?' said Cliff. It was all he could think of. The man's expanse of eye was disconcerting; he would have looked blind except for the snapping pupils.

'Nothing to do with Alsatians. It's people. Down on the beach.' His mouth had a rigid movement. 'We want the police before they go.'

'Two people,' the woman quavered. The man jerked her towards him as if he meant to strike her.

'Two. Like animals,' he said. 'Performing indecent acts in a public place.'

Cliff looked at the woman. Her distress embarrassed him less than the man's anger. In spite of its shaping by age her face had an unmade quality. In a play, he thought, she would be cast as the maiden aunt. Innocent and prim. For a woman like this holding hands might be indecent. Yet he was prepared to be angry. Someone might be having a piss, some longhair. It had happened before.

'Are they. . . .' Casting offensive matter? It was too absurd to say.

'It's the children we're thinking of,' the woman said. 'What if children saw them?' Her hands were trembling as she wiped the withered skin under her eyes. Cliff could not believe her distress was for anyone but herself. I've got a couple of baptists, he thought. This was not an exact term—he used it for people whose religion made them uncomfortable. The clothes of these two were Sunday puritan, especially the woman's. She wore black shoes with chunky heels and a black felt hat skewered to her hair with a steel-headed pin. Her dress had a crinkled elastic waist and the hem came down to the middle of her calves. Cliff's mind went back twenty years: the 'new look'. The memory made him sympathetic. They were like the last of the dinosaurs, women like this, and should be allowed to live out their days in peace.

'If you could tell me what they're doing . . . ?'

The man thrust his face forward again. 'Would you be good enough to make that call? Or else they'll get away.' This one called up no sympathy. Cliff said politely, 'I can't ask them to come without knowing. I've got to satisfy myself.'

'I've told you, an indecent act. Do you expect me to describe it in front of my wife?'

'They were touching each other,' the woman said.

Her husband caught her arm with both hands. 'Be quiet,' he said in a vicious tone.

She started to cry and turned away.

'You see. You see what you've done. She's got bad nerves, my wife.'

Then why didn't you take her home? Cliff Poulson almost said. Instead of coming here? He watched the woman go down the steps. She went slowly, bringing both feet on to each step before moving to the next. Her husband passed her and waited at the bottom.

'We'll trouble you for the use of your path.' It was a rebuke and a dismissal. He took his wife's elbow between two fingers and a thumb and turned her towards the gate. For a moment they reminded Cliff of his parents—both dead. People who had known how to live, all the same. These two smelled of mothballs. He went inside and closed the door.

The empty two hours until lunch faced him again. He took a volume of the *Popular Encyclopaedia* from the shelf and sat down in his chair in the living room. Prehistoric monsters, he thought. Should be back in their swamp, not out in the sun. There was a small turmoil in his stomach at the encounter, and he smiled at how well he had come out of it. Poor fools. It was only then that his mind went back to the woman's complaint. Touching each other. He saw at once what this would mean for her. Not in broad daylight, he thought. Although, if the beach was empty. . . . It happened at night, he knew. He'd found the evidence several times, thrown up on his lawn. Collecting these objects on a spade, he'd refused to admit the sensual excitement uncoiling under his disgust. Their burning in the incinerator had become a high-minded affair, and, less openly, an act of exorcism.

He got up and went to the window. The turmoil in his stomach widened—a pre-dentist feeling. There was no one on the beach. God, he thought, here I am, sixty-seven, an old man troubled by dirty thoughts. Exactly where I was at sixteen. He knew that when he went back to his chair he would put the encyclopaedia away and take out *The Carpetbaggers*. For that reason he stayed at the window and watched some men surfing at the south end. There, he decided, was an explanation of the miracle of walking on the water. Jesus had a surf-board. The thought shocked him a little and failed to cheer him up. It was simply a time-gaining tactic, a kind of foul blow, in the struggle he had to put up. But he stood there longer, trying to take an interest. If I was younger I'd be a surfie, he told himself. It was a half-hearted thought. He looked back along the beach. A woman with three black poodles on separate leads had come on to the north end and was striding along in a mannish way at the edge of the water. A group of seagulls flew up as she approached then dropped neatly into place behind her. The dogs yapped, he could tell by their actions. I'm seeing a sound, he thought. In front of his house a black-backed gull was patiently taking up and dropping a pipi to break it on the hard sand by the water. He tried to feel the shellfish's panic, locked in its shell. It wouldn't work. Scenes from *The Carpetbaggers* flickered in his mind. He saw, without interest, a brown foot lying as though cut from its body on the dry sand at the foot of his lawn. One of its toes flicked lazily. He moved a little so the rest of the body slid out from behind the tamarisk tree. There was a dislocation between sight and understanding. He had watched the man for several seconds before it was clear to him that a woman's forearm was lying down the length of his body with its hand resting over the genitals.

He turned away at once. He went back to his chair and found his place in the encyclopaedia, halfway through the article on the Jurassic age. He read a column with almost his full attention, then put the book down and let his mind go calmly back to what he had seen on the beach. It was nothing. Life was cleaner than fiction. He felt refreshed and he stood up and went into the breakfast room where the windows gave him a complete view of the man and woman sunbathing in front of his house. They were touching each other, there was no doubt of that. But not exactly 'touching each other'. They were wearing bathing suits and although the woman's hand was cupped on the placid lump in his thighs it seemed it had simply found this place to rest. Maybe I'm simple-minded, Cliff thought. He could not see this as sexual touching. The man's arm was crossed under hers and his hand sloped up to rest on her thigh. Those baptists, Cliff thought. But he knew he was calmer than he could have expected. Children might misunderstand. He looked along the beach. The woman with the poodles must have gone by without seeing; she had almost reached the place where the men were surfing. No harm done. He watched as the man's hand moved, stroking lazily. It seemed to have black hair on its back. And a ring. Wedding ring? Adultery, he thought, but again without any sensual shock, only with disappointment. He tried to see the woman's left hand. In a moment it came up slowly from her side and settled on the jutting edge of her rib-cage. Feeling guilty, he went to the sitting room and brought back his binoculars. He focussed them on the woman's hand. She wore a wedding ring too. He couldn't believe they were married to each other.

For the next five minutes Cliff Poulson watched the couple on the beach. At first he used binoculars but he soon put them aside. He was no voyeur. (The term, when he remembered it, made him blush.) This was observation. More and more, at last with a kind of breathlessness, he found himself watching the woman's hand. It lay on its side now, like an animal asleep. There was an intimacy in its touching, a matter-of-fact tenderness, he had no experience of. At times he wondered if some subtle act were taking place, too small for him to see. But slowly the hand brought his life into focus: he was old and alone.

He had had these thoughts before, but never without self-pity. The truth about his condition stood sharp before him. He was relieved to see it at last.

The woman's hand moved from her ribs. She had broken a flowering branch from the tamarisk tree on Cliff Poulson's lawn and she tickled the man's face with it. He grappled with her. For a moment they wrestled on the beach, then the woman escaped and ran for the water.

Cliff Poulson saw with disappointment that she had thin legs. For two or three minutes he watched the couple splashing in the waves, throwing water at each other. They were both thirty if a day. He went back to his chair and read about fossilized dinosaurs. It was difficult to understand. He kept thinking of the woman's hand and each time it came back to him the words about himself came with it—old, alone—bringing an image of a stone face, broken, with blind eyes. Greek? Roman? It receded before he could hold it; it sank like a stone in water until its outline was lost. He kept on reading. 'Plesiosaurus was a marine reptile with an immensely long neck adapted to hunting. . . .' But the hand kept coming back, and with it each time the knowledge about himself, the broken face.

At eleven o'clock he mixed a whisky and milk and looked at the beach again. The couple had gone.

'What were those damned baptists moaning about?'

He sat down to read. The next time he thought of the hand he swore. His anger found something to fasten on: that tart had been on his lawn breaking trees. The skinny adulterous bitch. Feeling better, he drank some whisky. He read about Tyranno-saurus Rex. Interesting. He got the sort of excitement from this he had once got from sport. The encyclopaedias had been a good buy, in spite of his son's opinion that anything sold at the door was a pup. He had read first the articles on ancient history, taking up a brief boyhood interest. (The salesman had caught him with Nero's Rome.) Now he was back in Mesozoic times. His pleasure in knowing more than his wife made him unbearable at times. He knew this. A bore. But there was also his pleasure in knowing things, his excitement in discovering new facts. At times he felt tiny, endangered, adventurous. He wanted her to share.

When his wife came home at twelve o'clock he called her into the living room. 'Listen. "And so the era of these great beasts drew to its close. No more would the primeval forest echo to the mating call of Triceratops, the fearsome roar of charging Tyranno-saurus Rex, or the chilling shriek of the diving Pteranodon. The empire of the dinosaur was over. A gentler creature rose to take his place. Small, timid, delicate, unfitted for survival, one would have thought, in this world of swamp and forest and sudden death, this furry creature was to found a dynasty before which even that of the dinosaur would pale into insignificance. . . ." ' He glanced up and saw she was waiting impatiently for him to finish. The mystery went out of the picture, he could no longer hear the roaring of the dinosaurs or the leathery hiss of the pterodactyl's wings. Stubbornly he went on to the end of the paragraph.

'Interesting. I thought you were going to set the table.' She went to the kitchen. Dishes began to clatter. I've got to be back at work by one.'

He sat for a moment fighting off one of the rages that left him cold and sick for hours afterwards. He had slammed the encyclo-paedia shut as his wife left the room. Now he opened it again and closed it quietly. Useless to try and share with people—surely life had taught him that. He put the book in the shelf and went to the breakfast room. His wife had plates and cutlery on the table. She came in with a loaf of bread, and tomatoes, ham and lettuce.

'Hot bread for you. I got one of the girls to buy it.'

'Thanks.' He could smell it, a delicious smell. Hot bread was one of his treats.

He smiled at her. 'Can I help?'

'Too late now.' She went back to the kitchen for another load.

Still in her shop mood, he thought. Treating him like one of the juniors. Well—he had promised to have the table set.

He watched the beach. There was the usual lunchtime crowd from the town, getting in a quick swim. Some good-looking kids in bikinis. His wife told him to sit down and he started to tell her about the 'baptists' and the 'adulterers'. He hadn't got the second half clear and knew he wasn't making a good story of it. He couldn't say where the woman's hand had been. After forty years married to her. It upset him. He told her about the branch of the tamarisk tree.

'Some people,' she said, without real indignation, and he watched her retreat from his 'woolliness' to the shop—Windle's Pharmacy. The name was embroidered in pink on her smock. Just where her left breast used to be.

'It's been a hectic morning. Susan Johnson didn't come in. She got her mother to ring and say she was sick.'

'Is she the one who pinches—' Another word he couldn't say—had they really got this far apart?—'thingummybobs?'

'Durex? She's given that up. Changed her boyfriend. I'll bet she's off with him now somewhere.'

Good luck to her then, Cliff Poulson thought. Good luck Susan Johnson. There's more to life than lipstick and indigestion powder. And pile ointment, for God's sake. Have fun while you can.

It almost became a rhapsody, but his wife interrupted.

'I'm going to tell Mr Windle to fire her. I knew that girl was no good the day she started.'

'And will he? Fire her? Because you say so?'

'That's what he hired me for. Someone mature to keep the junior staff in order. This bread's not as hot as you like it.'

He made himself a thick sandwich and went back to the window.

'Are you going to stand there and eat?'

'I like to watch the people.'

She said nothing for a moment. 'Are there many down there?'

'Many what?' he said angrily. He knew she meant girls.

'People, dear.'

'Quite a few.' He meant girls.

'I think it would be more polite if you sat down with me.' It was almost impossible for him to get under her skin and he looked at her with a feeling of gratitude. He sat down and said he was sorry. They ate in silence, then he made another sandwich and said he was enjoying the bread. 'He's a good baker, George Rainy.—You know, those people this morning, they really were pretty cheeky.'

'Which people?'

'The adulterous ones. They were lying there in the middle of the beach and she had her hand on his —' He had meant to say 'cock', but found he couldn't bring the word out.

'On his?' his wife grinned.

'Penis.'

'But they had their bathing suits on?'

'Yes.'

'What are you getting upset about then?'

'I'm not upset. It's the baptists who were upset.'

'Baptists? Really Cliff, you are hard to follow.'

'The ones who came to the door. I told you.'

'Oh. Those.' She lost interest.

'She had her hand on his cock.'

'There's no need to be crude.'

'Working in a chemist's shop gives you a broad mind. That's what you said.'

They finished their lunch in silence. Then she escaped into her clattering efficiency: clear table, wash up, put away. He timed her. Eight minutes. A record. Windle had got a good woman.

She came back before leaving and searched for a peace-making remark. 'Is Peter calling for you?'

'Half past one.'

'Well—it's a hot day. Don't over do it.'

'I won't.'

She went out. That, he thought, was my wife. My darling blue-haired wife. He thought of her sadly. Theirs had been a good marriage. No doubt about it. Successful. And still was of course, of course. If only she could have retired with him ('I'd go mad,' she had said), gone mad with him.

At half past one when his son arrived to take him for a game of golf he said, 'Have a talk with your mother some time. See if you can get her to give up her job.'

'Why? What's gone wrong?'

'Nothing's gone wrong. I think she needs a rest, that's all.'

'She'd go mad stuck in the house all day.'

'I'm stuck in the house all day.'

Peter began to sulk and kept it up after his father's mood had lightened. They drove to the golf course. Cliff was pleased to be out of the house. The busy main street of the town excited him and he thought, By God, I made my mark here, a lot of these people would be broke if it wasn't for me. He had been a good accountant—an advisor more than a book-keeper. He doubted if Peter could ever be that, although of course the business had grown. But that was the times. He looked at his son and was sorry to see him still sulking. It was good of the boy (at forty?) to ask him out to golf. And stupid of him to let the day be spoilt.

'Hey, there's Harry Bell. Look at him go. After a sale.' He grinned. 'Tyrannosaurus Rex. Pity the poor customer.'

'What? What are you talking about?'

'Seventeen tons of implacable bloodlust.'

'Have you been reading those encyclopaedias again?'

'The Jurassic age, when the dinosaur was king.'

'Why don't you read the useful articles?'

'Cheer up, son.'

'Nothing wrong with me.'

'No. Who are we playing with?'

'Friends of mine. No one you know.'

Implacable, thought Cliff Poulson. If he doesn't come right it's going to be a lousy afternoon. He set himself to improve his son's mood. It's like trying to get him to eat his vegetables, he thought. That had been the only difficult thing about Peter—an easy-going child who had wanted to be a pilot, then a scientist. Cliff couldn't remember how these enthusiasms had passed. He remembered the boy being sent out to dig a root of potatoes and blowing them out of the ground with home-made explosives. 'Mashed potatoes, Dad.' The only thing to do had been laugh. How had he decided to be an accountant? My God, it was me, Cliff remembered, I pressured him. But accountancy was a good life, nothing wrong with it.

'Remember the time you blew the potatoes out of the ground?'

Peter didn't remember and this shocked Cliff. It was as if his son had admitted some part of him was dead.

At the course they went to the locker room to change. Cliff put on shorts, long white socks and two-tone golfing shoes with tasselled flaps. He looked down at himself approvingly. Part of the modern world, as much as Enid with her blue hair. The men they were playing with came in and Peter introduced them. Lionel

Broadhead. Alan Rope. When everyone was changed they went out to the tee.

Cliff enjoyed the round. He had been a careful golfer until his retirement and had got his handicap down to thirteen. These days he really went for his shots and had slipped back to twenty-four. But he enjoyed himself more. There had been some pleasure in lobbing the ball down the middle and scoring steady pars or one overs. Accuracy had pleased him. He could not understand at first the wildness that came into his game. Concentration, he decided, must have depended on the mental exercise of his work. Now he did not worry. His shots sprayed all over the course, he lost on the average three balls a round, but he also scored an occasional birdie. It was much more fun. Peter meanwhile kept the Poulson tradition alive, poking his shots down a dead straight line.

The first hole was an easy par four. Cliff scored a birdie.

'I think there's something fishy about your handicap,' Lionel Broadhead joked. Cliff picked him for a bad loser. He played well after that. For the first time in months he went round in less than a hundred. He and Peter won easily.

Lionel Broadhead was a good loser. His plump face glowed with friendliness as he brought the first round of drinks to the table. Alan Rope was the one who seemed sour.

'Alan's a real office man,' Lionel Broadhead cried. 'I had to talk hard to get him out here today.'

'I had work to do.'

'Work. You can work any day. Nothing like a round of golf to get the old juices flowing.'

Alan Rope looked pained at the word. He sipped his glass of beer and said nothing. The others talked about the game. Peter was in a good humour now and Cliff felt happier than he had for a long time. When the conversation changed he told them about the couple on the beach. As he went on he realised that again he was not telling the story well. It was too simple to make much out of it. He coarsened the thing to make it funnier. A sense of shame overtook him and he tried not to look at his son. At the end, while Lionel Broadhead laughed, he thought of the brown curled hand and the statue with the broken face but the images had no meaning.

'And you had a grandstand view?'

'Yes.'

'You retired blokes have all the fun. What do you say Alan, shall we retire?'

'Not while there's money left to make.'

'See? See what I mean? He carries the office with him. Get that monkey off your back, boy. Be like old Cliff here, having fun.'

They were like a pair of cheap comedians, Cliff thought. He began to dislike them.

Peter tapped his glass nervously. 'Lionel and Alan are the directors of Amalgamated Properties.' The name meant nothing to Cliff. He saw the two men looking at him expectantly. Alan Rope was managing to smile. Cliff tried to guess what they wanted him to say; something complimentary.

'They're the ones who are putting up those flats.'

Cliff Poulson understood. The afternoon was a set-up. He wondered if they had let him win.

'I thought you asked me out to play golf,' he said to Peter.

'I did. But still, Lionel and Alan wanted to meet you. . . . They've got a proposition to make.'

'If they want to buy my land the answer's no.' He felt sick at the deception; and sorry for his son who was being used. His anger at the two men across the table was so intense he could not bring himself to look at them.

'Listen Cliff,' Lionel Broadhead said, 'we've got a great little scheme on the boards. All we need is your place, then we'll have the two hundred feet of frontage we need. Now we've talked it over and we can see our way to offering twenty-four thousand dollars.'

'I'm not interested.'

'Perhaps you'd rather discuss it at the office,' Alan Rope said. He turned to Lionel Broadhead, smiling. 'Lionel, I told you it wasn't a good thing to mix business and pleasure.'

'Nonsense Alan. If a couple of friends can't work out a deal over a pint of beer then things have come to a pretty low ebb.'

Comedians, thought Cliff Poulson. Except that they were dangerous. His son was glaring at him. There must be something in it for him, he must have been bought.

'Peter's told us what you paid for that place,' Lionel Broadhead went on.

'Has he?'

'And what we're offering represents a gain for you of almost one hundred per cent.'

Cliff made no answer. He looked at his son with pity.

'Just try seeing it this way.' Lionel Broadhead held up his hand and started to count off points on his fingers. 'Firstly —'

'Lionel, Lionel, we'll leave it at that,' Alan Rope broke in. He looked at Peter coolly. 'Perhaps you'll arrange a more suitable time

—and place.' The words carried an insult and Cliff saw his son go red. Poor fool, he was out of his class. As much for Peter as for himself he said, 'There'll be no other time and place. My property's not for sale.' Stick with me boy, he tried to signal Peter.

Alan Rope smiled tightly. 'We might see our way to raising the offer.'

And Peter said, 'You can't hold back progress Dad. That beach is ready for a scheme like this.'

Cliff said nothing. He felt lonely, and felt Peter's loneliness. He wished there were some way he could help his son up to the level of Broadhead and Rope, if that was what he wanted. But selling the house wasn't it. He knew now that he loved that place, he wanted to end his days there; and he blamed Peter for not understanding this.

'I don't want to talk about it.' He tapped his watch to show Peter it was time to leave. There was a long silence while the others drank more beer. Then Lionel Broadhead said heartily, 'Tell me Cliff, what does a retired gent do with his time?' He had not the skill to hide the dislike in his eyes.

'I read encyclopaedias.'

'Dad bought a set at the door. A real con job,' Peter tried to joke.

'The best buy I ever made,' Cliff said shortly.

Alan Rope smiled. 'What kind of article do you read?' He was smooth Cliff thought, a dangerous man. It was typical of Peter to think that Broadhead was boss.

'All sorts.'

'Nero and his pals. Suchlike,' Peter said.

'Interesting. What are you going on to next?'

Cliff grew more angry: they were humouring him. 'Astronomy.'

'Ah, the stars.'

'I'd like to get to the stars,' said Lionel Broadhead. 'Think of the opportunities. All that real estate.'

Cliff could not control his anger. 'There's life out there.'

'Eh?'

'There's life out there. Intelligent life. They'll keep your sort out.' He stood up and went to sit in Peter's car.

Peter came five minutes later—like a third former from the headmaster's office. They were halfway home before Cliff trusted himself to speak.

'Next time you take me out to golf make sure it's only for golf.'

'There won't be any next time,' Peter said.

He threw Cliff's clubs into the garage and drove away. Cliff went

inside. It was after six o'clock. His wife was eating her dinner in
front of the television set. She served his in the breakfast room,
then went back to watch. Cliff ate slowly. Poor Peter—he was
such a boy, living in a romantic world of big deals. The office
boy trying to go with the bosses. Cliff knew there was no way
he could help. Twenty-five years ago he could have helped but
not now.

He went into the living-room to talk to his wife.

'Did you know Peter was mixed up with the crowd that's trying
to buy this house?'

He saw she did—and guessed the meeting today had been her
idea.

'You know I'm not selling?'

'Why not? You keep saying this place is too big.' She was
impatient and kept looking back at the television set. 'Neither of
us uses the beach.'

'I do. . . . I like to watch the people.'

'Yes. I'd forgotten.'

He ignored this—a feminine reflex. 'Those blokes are out of
Peter's class. They'll take every penny he's got.'

'Nonsense.'

'I know the type. They're con men.'

'Nonsense. They're respectable businessmen. Lionel Broadhead
comes into the shop.'

'I see. It was your idea.'

'Cliff, do let me watch. This is funny.'

He turned and went out of the house. A light rain had started
to fall but he walked to the end of the path before turning back
for his raincoat and hat. Then he went down to the water. The tide
was three quarters in; each new wave pushed its rim of froth
further up the partly dry sand. The water looked warm. He began
to feel calmer watching its easy advance and retreat and he decided
to take his shoes off and paddle. He sat down on the sand near the
spot where he had seen the couple in the morning. The limp
branch of the tamarisk tree was lying just off the edge of the lawn.
He picked it up. At once he was overcome by a longing to have
a woman with him. The feeling surprised him by not being sensual.
The image of the statue floated up in his mind. He stood up
impatiently. He did not like this, it was too dramatic, he did not
like the self-pity that came with it. He put his shoes and socks
on the lawn. The statue was going to haunt him; he wondered
how to get rid of it.

At the edge of the water he rolled up his trouser legs. He

supposed he must look odd barefooted, in his plastic coat and fishing hat. No matter. No one in sight. They were all crouched over their television sets, like his wife. He wondered if she had really helped Peter set Broadhead and Rope on to him. It seemed likely. She wanted to sell the place and move into something newer. And she liked the idea of all that money in the bank. He couldn't blame her. They had neither of them got over the depression—bread pudding days, she called them. And she had had some bad knocks in her life. A stillborn daughter, an operation that took off one of her breasts. (He shuddered.) And now a bad-tempered husband and a son who seemed stuck in a sour adolescence. He began to feel tender towards his wife. Good on her, he thought; she was getting by, with her job and blue hair and her television set, and her grim pride in looking after him well.

He started to walk towards the south end of the beach. Several times the waves touched the roll of his trousers but this made him feel reckless and boyish. He wondered why, in spite of everything, he could not regret retiring. Things had been easier then. Forty years of juggling pieces of paper, manipulating, balancing. Necessary work, and he had been good at it. He had saved some of his clients from bankruptcy—and helped others through it like a kind of operation and back to financial health again. But it was only now he could see this as exciting. If he were back in that sort of life the dullness beneath the fiction would be exposed. Now, at least, things happened in colour—even the past happened in colour.

Through the thin mist of rain he saw the last sunlight of the day reflected off the windows of houses on the cliffs across the harbour: orange lights as bright as flares set in the dark-blue bush. As he watched they began to go out. Everything seemed to turn several shades darker. He sat down on a rock at the southern headland and looked at the sky. The stars would soon be coming out. He laughed when he remembered what he had said to Lionel Broadhead—then looked around quickly to see if anyone had heard. He smiled. Where had he got that idea, life out there? But he hoped it was true, and that people like Broadhead would be kept out.

His legs were sore from the round of golf and he rested for several minutes. Then he began to walk towards home. Cars came roaring down a road to the edge of the beach, like dinosaurs he thought, and U-turned with a blaring of horns. A dozen young people in bathing suits got out and ran down the beach towards him. For a moment he thought they were after him. But they broke and ran by on either side. He watched as they plunged into

the water and started swimming. Some of the girls shrieked at
the coldness.

Cliff Poulson watched. They had gone round him as if he were
some natural object—something inanimate. An old man. Cliff
smiled. He welcomed the statue this time. He saw its stone face
dripping with rain. He wondered if he had seen it in the encyclopaedia, but thought that probably it came from further back, from
his boyhood.

He kept on walking. The noise of the young people in the sea
became fainter. The rain was so light it was almost a vapour. Low
down in the sky several tiny white stars had appeared. If he
watched, he thought, he would see them grow large and coloured.
He stood still and watched. A small very old man went past him
towards the north end of the beach. His crooked arms and straining face showed he was trying to run, but he went at no more
than a slow walking pace. He was wearing slippers and yellow
pyjamas. Cliff started after him.

'Mr Webb,' he called. The old man was running away. It happened every two or three weeks and the people living at the beach
had learned to walk beside him until his daughters came to take
him home. Cliff looked back. A hundred yards away the two Miss
Webbs were coming at a middle-aged run. They would catch the
old man before he reached the end of the beach. Cliff wondered
what he thought was round the headland. The women should let
him get that far. 'Mr Webb,' he said.

The old man kept up his wooden progress, looking straight
ahead. He came to a place where a trickle from a storm-water
drain had cut a shallow channel in the beach. It was only a couple
of feet wide but Mr Webb went back and forth at its edge like
a bird at the bars of a cage. He looked back and started to
moan with fright.

I could hide him, Cliff thought. Or tell the women to let him
go. He touched the old man's arm.

'Mr Webb, wait here. Your daughters are coming.'

The old man ran through the water. One of his slippers came
off. Cliff saw that he had prepared himself for this escape by
tucking his pyjama legs into his socks. He picked up the slipper.
It smelled strongly of urine. He held it out as the daughters came
up and the older, taller woman took it on the run like a relay
baton. She gave a hoarse cry of thanks. Poor bitches, he thought,
watching them catch Mr Webb. They brought him back past Cliff;
sturdy figures, supporting the old man so that his feet only touched
the sand lightly. The tender sounds they made died away.

'Naughty boy. Running away from the ones who love him.'

The old man must be wet, Cliff thought. He'd catch pneumonia. In a couple of days he would probably be dead.

He went on towards home. At the edge of the sand he saw the branch of the tamarisk tree. He picked it up and put it on the lawn, then took his shoes and socks into the wash-house. He hung up his coat and hat.

When he opened the door he heard his wife laughing. She was watching the Dick Van Dyke Show. He put on his slippers in the bedroom and came back to tell her about Mr Webb.

She laughed again with the television set. 'Rob wanted to buy his wife a fur coat and Buddy said he could get it wholesale. Now they've got a coat that's ten sizes too big.'

Cliff Poulson thought he was going to cry. It surprised him because he was not unhappy. He sat down and stared at the television set until he knew it was safe for him to talk. No quaver, he managed it well.

'I'll get you a cup of tea later on.'

'Thanks,' said his wife, staring and laughing.

Cliff got the volume A-Bi from the shelf. He took it into the breakfast room and started to read about the stars.

MAURICE GEE   # Right-hand Man

For the first time in twenty-four years Vincent Brown was without a chairmanship. It should not have made him angry or even surprised him. Seventy-three votes were all that stood between him and what he had jokingly called 'the axe' when others got it. Seventy-three was his age.

The mayor could have spared them his record. (Ambitious to be an autocrat, the mayor, but still needing to soften the blows he dealt.) The record was in the minds of the people who mattered. One term before the war and seven after it. He had had no chairmanship in that first term; but after the war had moved straight into the big stuff. No library committees for him. Traffic, Parks and Reserves; and three terms as chairman of Works. He was deputy mayor for six years under Frank Olsen. (Sir Frank; dead now, with a street and a park and a wharf named after him.) That was when he had really made his mark. But even later he had got things done, when he had slipped to sixth on the list and Bright, fresh in the mayoral chair, had fobbed him off with Special Purposes. Special Purposes could be made to cover just about anything. It only needed a bit of political know-how.

Bright had learned. He had taken the committee for one of his new boys.

'Councillor Brown is our Grand Old Man,' Bright said. 'I don't want him to think he's been down-graded. There's still important work he can do—although heaven knows he's earned a rest. I hope at seventy-three I'll be wanting to lead a less strenuous life. But Councillor Fulton on Library and Councillor Pearce on Parks and Reserves—don't overlook this man. You've got him on your committees. Use him. You'll find him a tower of strength and a mine of information. And Vince—' he smiled—'if by any sad chance this should be your last term—we all know how funny the voter can be —well, maybe at last we can name that street after you. Vincent Brown Street. Think about it. Now. Our new councillors. . . .'

Vincent Brown had never left a meeting early. He sat to the end of this one. His face felt like wood. The mayoral chain he had once expected to wear rose and fell with Bright's middle-aged breathing. Beside him Olga Fulton doodled on her blotter. He had seen obscenities in her doodles once: a penis and a bush of pubic hair. Under his eyes her biro had changed them to trees and she had smiled at him and whispered, 'You see what you want to see, Vincent.' Now her disease had made her monstrously fat; but she had answered it by dyeing her hair a lilac colour and painting her eyes a green he found atrocious—another obscenity. At times he had suffered the vision of a blade slicing her throat and exposing not flesh but red wet plastic foam. He was a practical man, who kept his feelings out in the open (except the domestic ones that were nobody's business) and the political ones. It was unfair that he should be troubled in this way. He looked sideways at her blotter; and saw—flowers and butterflies. She smiled at him sympathetically.

Bright laid down a set of hard instructions; and softened them with his incurable smile. After Frank Olsen he was pathetic, Vincent thought. Frank had needed neither ambition nor popularity. His was a hardness Bright's would have broken to pieces on.

Olga Fulton seemed to have the same thought. 'He'll never be an Olsen,' she said as they walked to the door: the two senior councillors, keeping up their show of amiability. 'But oh Vincent, I really am pleased to have you on my committee. There are so many things you can help me with.'

'You've never needed help, Olga. And don't feel sorry for me. I'm not finished yet. I can branch out without a committee. There's a few things I've got my eye on.'

As he drove home his anger fastened on her rather than Bright. In spite of her disease—she had dismissed him tonight with the girlish smile that served to call attention to her courage—and of her God-damned female laziness, the woman had kept her committee. She had even had Social Services tacked on. Yet what had she done in her twenty years on council? Look at the parking metres he'd installed, and his and Frank Olsen's new abattoir; and the sewage outfall. He'd piped the stuff two miles out to sea to save it polluting the beaches. That was the sort of thing that changed people's lives. All she'd done was fill the library up with arty books. And even there he'd beaten her, with the sunken garden. That was arty, and useful at the same time. He'd had it built as chairman of Parks and Reserves. She'd ruined it later, of course, with the statue her big-city sculptor had dreamed up—or nightmared. A tub of amputated legs: he'd said as much in council, and the paper had quoted him. But Olga, in her pommie voice—and pretty then and plump, with half of them eating out of her hand—Olga had said she found it aesthetically pleasing. 'Just in case Councillor Brown doesn't know the word I've brought my dictionary along.' She had slid a book on to his blotter. Frank Olsen had laughed along with the rest of them.

It was the unhappiest memory Vincent had. In those days he had been Frank's right-hand man; his hatchet-man according to some. Together they made the decisions that mattered. Council was simply a rubber stamp. One or two people said that Vincent was boss, that Frank Olsen was only a figure-head. But Vincent put a stop to that sort of talk. It did not hurt him to be second to Frank. Frank had been a great man: a hard-driver, who let nothing stand in his way, but a schemer too who could break a man on the quiet or get a policy off the ground before people knew it was even being talked about. A politician, a down-to-earth practical man. And the only friend Vincent Brown had ever had. But Frank had laughed and voted for the statue.

Vincent had found means of forgiving him. Frank was under pressure. He was sick. His wife was in a mental home, and his son's failure preyed all the time on his mind. He was able to give Vincent less of his time.

In the next year as Frank began to talk about retiring, Vincent's career had shown signs of levelling out. People were used to thinking of him as part of Frank—as an extra limb, Olga had said (grinning), a kind of executive member. By himself they seemed not to see him. So in the years that followed he could do nothing as Bright moved past him; nothing as Olga moved past. Her M.B.E. had come in the year of Frank's knighthood. And Vincent had slid from number one to six, and now to twelve; down to Special Purposes; and at last to no committee at all.

When he reached home he went into the sitting-room. He kept it as his wife had kept it, not out of sentimentality but because he had little use for the place. He lived in the kitchen. When forced to remember his marriage he tried to think of it as happy. He was troubled at these times by the quietness, the air almost of relief, with which his wife had died. He glanced at her photograph on the mantelpiece. She looked talkative. Olga had made a friend of her and taken her to concerts and talked her into trying things like yoghurt. It had all been feminine, beneath his notice. Tonight it seemed a betrayal equal to Frank's. He felt no need to forgive her.

On the wall, with their shoulders touching, were the glassed photographs of the eight councils he'd served on. He had two more than Olga, who made her first appearance in 1950. Bright, with his face like a third-former's, didn't show up till 1956. But it was Olga he followed, always on his left. In 1950 she looked like —he struggled for the name—Olivia de Havilland. Even Frank, who was cold and moral and if anything, over-religious, even Frank seemed to have a cast in his eye. But by 1962 she'd lost it. She was porky. She had a kind of dead look in her eye. It took her till 1968, growing huge, to find a new style. And there, in '68, she had it: her smile—light and rubbery at once, gross and flirtatious. It seemed unrighteous to him—and he thought with disgust of her claim to be, what was it?—a Rosicrucian?

In the morning he examined his own face in his shaving mirror. He didn't look seventy-three, he decided; he looked not much more than fifty. He had hair a boy would be proud of, and eyes that wouldn't look out of place on a sniper, even though he'd ruined them with paper work. He felt sharp and ready to go. But that other seventy-three came to his mind. Seventy-three from the axe. This term would be his last. He knew it. The smart thing would be not to stand again. But he made up his mind to use the term—remind people who he was. He would get something done, something they'd talk about along with the sewage outfall and the sunken garden—and, by God (he polished his face with a towel) he'd chop Olga Fulton down while he was about it.

Later in the morning Vincent called at the library. He knew he would not find what he needed there, but he wanted to show his face, make the librarian jump. He had not been in the place since its opening five years before. He grew angry at the sight of the books. There were thousands of them. The cost must have been huge. So must the cost of the furnishings—the steel shelving and carpet and easy chairs. The place was like a luxury hotel. All this for people who had nothing better to do than read. He found it useful to claim that he had not read a book since *The Cruel Sea,* and even that he hadn't been able to finish. He'd said as much in council when he'd argued against changing the place over from a subscription library to a free one. Reading was a luxury. What was more it got people into bad habits, told them more than they needed to know. If they wanted it let them pay. But Olga had won. He'd been alone in that fight.

For several minutes he wandered about; then said quietly to the girl at the information desk, 'There's a book on the floor over there.'

She turned pink and ran to pick it up.

'We have to look after council property, don't we? What's your name?'

'June Partridge.'

'Where can I find your boss, June?'

But Liversedge was bearing down on him: a tall young man with a boxer's broken nose and sideburns that ran into a bushy moustache.

'Can I help you, Councillor?'

'Come and look at this.' Vincent turned on his heel and walked to a stand marked *Additions to Stock.* 'Do you usually put this sort of thing on display?' The book had a naked woman on its cover. A bunch of flowers hid her private parts.

'What's the objection?'

'It's dirty.'

'I find it rather charming.'

It was not a man's word. Vincent eyed him suspiciously. 'How many people have complained?'

'They've been putting their names down for it,' Liversedge said.

'You make it your business to supply dirty books? I've heard about the ones in the office.'

Liversedge began to look angry. 'Restricted books, not dirty, Councillor.'

'People copulating. I've heard. Photographs of it. Tell me that's not dirty.'

'Vincent, it's all in the mind,' Olga's voice said.

He turned with a show of anger. 'It's all in a book, Councillor Fulton. And the librarian keeps it in his office. Tell me what you think about that.'

She leaned on her stick, breathing with a quick shallow wheeze. 'I think he's very lucky.'

Liversedge said easily, 'It's a book recommended by the National Library and passed by the Indecent Publications Tribunal for people over the age of eighteen. It's an instructional book on the sexual positions and it's done with a great deal of taste.'

'There Vincent, you see, it's educational.'

'How about this then? I suppose this is educational?' He waved at the book on the stand.

'Ooh Paul,' Olga said to Liversedge, 'that looks really yummy. I think I'll put my name down for that.'

'I'll be asking questions, Olga,' Vincent said. 'I'm taking notes. There's other things I don't like.'

'The main thing Vincent is to keep you occupied.'

'Why aren't the staff in uniform?'

'Because we're not a girls' school, dear. Now do go away and let me talk to Mr Liversedge. We're both very busy people.'

He was not dissatisfied. He had not expected to score off her on her own ground. He was simply exercising.

He made another tour through the stacks and began to feel some pleasure in their neat appearance. He would take Olga on over something else. She was bound to have a pet scheme—was famous for pet schemes, in fact—expensive ones. Bright had probably put him on the library committee in the hope of keeping her occupied there. So—he smiled—he would let her run. Watch Bright get jumpy. And then chop her down. She was on Parks and Reserves. He would get her there.

As he came back towards the display stand he saw Mark Olsen examining the illustration of the naked woman. The bent and furtive stance he held was in a way a family characteristic—a genetic inversion of his father's front-facing style. The boy— Vincent thought of him as boy although he was now in his fifties —was the campaign Frank had lost. Frank had made him study law, but the course had turned into an endless chapter of crises and failures. Mark seemed to have no strength—of mind or character or even body. He had not even had the strength to keep his failure hidden in another town, but sprang back to Hardinge after each fiasco as though on the end of a rubber band. After the war he took a clerical post in a wool-scouring firm; a job he still held although Frank had left him well-off. He had no children, and his wife was an invalid—which seemed in character to Vincent.

He took with Mark by habit the tone Frank Olsen had used in the hope of jolting the boy into some sort of action.

'No work today?'

Mark put the book back on the stand with a guilty thrust of his arm. 'No, Mr Brown. I'm on leave. Compassionate, you know. Er, Melody's sick. I'm choosing some books for her.'

It had always seemed appropriate to Vincent that Mark's wife should have this foolish name. 'She doesn't read that sort of stuff, does she?'

'Oh, I was just looking you know. He's a new author to me. They choose lurid covers, don't they? It detracts a bit.'

The strength of Frank's features had turned to weakness in Mark. The large nose was simply fat, the blue eyes washed out, and the narrow mouth here gave the impression of something that had failed to grow. Vincent had an affection for the boy that had its rational base—he would admit nothing irrational—in his affection for Frank; and he had Frank's mastery of him too. Keep silent, hold Mark under your eye, and he started to babble in an effort to keep himself from fading away.

'Oh no, I don't read this type of thing at all. I read books of good quality. Biographies mostly. Lives of great men. And women. I don't like fiction any more. It's all so unpleasant. Since Indian stories. You know, I used to feed on Indian stories. It's strange— that's the only time reading really meant anything in me. A sort of perfect matching. Can you imagine—with me here in Hardinge? I was Red Cloud, the lost white boy. Ha, ha. I was the best tracker in the tribe. Really. I mean literally. I could flit through the trees up there in the park so no one would ever see me. I used to sneak up on the other kids. And lovers, ha, ha. The things I used to see.'

Twelve years ago Mark had worked up the nerve to write to the paper attacking the plan for a sewage outfall. 'The sea does not belong to Hardinge. It is part of man's priceless heritage.' The rest was a sort of essay on nature—poetic stuff. It threw

Frank into a roaring fist-thumping rage unlike his usual anger. Vincent was frightened for his heart; and had a momentary belief that he could be this man's master. He was never sure Frank's decision that Councillor Brown must be left to make his own way was not a punishment for his having seen too much. With Frank control was everything.

'I hope you voted for me, Mark.'

Mark averted his eyes. His face grew pink. But he looked back smiling and said, 'You were a friend of my father. Oh, by the way, congratulations. A lot of people said you'd get beaten. But I guess you're too well known. And you're on two committees too. I heard it on the news. Congratulations.'

At times Mark's simplicity was unconvincing. Vincent watched him with suspicion. Chairmanship was what mattered. A son of Frank's should understand, no matter how dim he was. But Mark was beaming.

'You'll do great things. I was always sorry you missed out on being mayor.'

'You'd better get Melody's books.'

'Yes, I will. It's difficult though. You can't recommend something, can you?'

'I haven't read a book since *The Cruel Sea.*'

'No? Well—I suppose that's why you're on the library committee.'

Vincent pointed slowly. 'You're laughing at me, Mark.'

'Oh no, truly. I mean, you'll bring a fresh mind. No pre-conceived ideas. There's so much tired thinking, isn't there? But a mind that's sort of—blank, you know, uncluttered, it could do great things.'

'You're laughing at me.' He was so shocked he could say nothing more. He made his way out of the library and along the street to his car in the council yard. Mark Olsen laughing at him: in no other way could his loss of stature in Hardinge have been so firmly underlined. For a while he thought of leaving. He would find a place where nobody knew him. He surrendered to pity for himself: an old man scorned, who had worked his heart out for this town; exiled now to some northern beach, where the children threw stones on his roof and the neighbours thought he was nobody. Or playing draughts in an old men's home. He made an exclamation of anger, and grinned in disgust at himself. Self-pity! Pity of all sorts he despised, but this was the worst. It sucked a man's blood out and got him ready for the garbage heap. He climbed out of his car. He would find a way of making Mark

Olsen pay. In the meantime he was a person of importance, twelfth or not. Five thousand people had voted for him—for twenty years. He rode in the lift up to the council cafeteria and sat down unasked between the town clerk and the city engineer. He was Councillor Brown, by God. This was where he belonged.

He began to fret. Olga did not seem to have any schemes. He heckled her in council and Bright called him to order. On her own committee she ignored him, doodling little men and dinosaurs; or briskly put him down by calling a vote. And in Parks and Reserves she had no opinion. Even her biro was still.

He waited, chewing his lips. He walked about town. He stared in land agents' windows, thinking he might buy a smaller house. In April he wrote to his daughter in Invercargill and his son in Adelaide complaining that they never wrote to him. And they sent him a letter each, saying how busy they'd been. The weather in both cities was almost too good to be true.

His business had been printing. He called twice at the works and spent time chatting with Spurdle, the man he'd sold out to. Spurdle eyed him, wondering what he was after. He had kept going four years on goodwill, on the Brown reputation; but Vincent saw signs that the place was starting to fail. There seemed to be no order. Things were piled in corners. And Mrs Spurdle was doing the accounts. That told a tale.

On his third visit she came out of the office and faced him bitterly.

'I've got a bone to pick with the Hardinge City Council.'

'Fire away.' He was used to this sort of thing. He welcomed it.

'I'm trying to bring my girls up decently.'

'I'm sure you are—'

'But I get no help from the people in authority. I've written to the paper. That was my letter. "Perturbed." And I've spoken to three city councillors. But nothing's going to be done. You don't have to tell me. It's the old story, isn't it? You pinch all our money for rates but when we want something done we might just as well be talking to thin air.'

He remembered the letter. 'Perturbed' was the mother of girls who had seen a man exposing himself at the edge of the Olsen Park pine plantation.

'It's a matter for the police, Mrs Spurdle. You should make your complaints to them.'

'I have. But they're useless. Three times this has happened. Three times in less than a year. In a balaclava—that should be a clue. But they haven't even questioned anybody. What's the use of that? When our daughters are being debauched. I'm telling you, Mr Brown, our patience is running out. Us Olsen Park parents. We're going to take some action. This town has got to get rid of its dirty old men. And its homosexuals. That's another matter. We know they're here. Running fancy shops.'

'What do you suggest we do, Mrs Spurdle?'

'We want those trees cut down. And the scrub. We want it levelled flat. We had a meeting last night and that's what we decided. He won't have anywhere to hide then. We can keep our daughters safe. Asphalt. That's what we want. You'd think a woman would understand.'

'You've talked to Councillor Fulton?'

'I rang her up. And I can tell you this, I won't be voting for her again. I told her. I told her she needed kids of her own if she thinks trees are that important. Things of beauty. I ask you. When my girls have seen what they've seen.'

He listened for another quarter hour, watching her stiff curls tremble. She was sharp and silly and bitter. He would find a role for her.

'I'm sympathetic, Mrs Spurdle. It's a serious problem you've got. Young lives can be ruined. But we'll see. I might be able to do something. Let me have a couple of hours. I'll think it over and call back later on.'

When he called back he said, 'You've got the machines here. Why don't you run a petition off? They might even put it in the public library.'

'What good will a petition do?'

'Let me worry about that. Just run a hundred or so forms off and get as many names as you can. I'll draft it. And tell the paper what you're doing. But keep my name out of it.'

'I don't know—'

'You want something done, Mrs Spurdle. You brought the matter up. I'll get council behind it if you get public opinion worked up. Tell your friends to write to the paper too.'

'I'm not sure they'll want to—'

'Are you interested, Mrs Spurdle? If not, we'll drop the whole matter.'

'Oh, I'm interested.'

He worked with enjoyment and cunning. He kept very quiet. At the May meeting of the Library Commitee he passed around a copy of the petition and asked if it was library policy to display matter of that sort.

'Of course,' Olga Fulton said.

'Have you signed it, Councillor?'

'No. It's misguided. But that's not our business. It's done in good faith.'

'Is it misguided? This man's showed himself off three times. To innocent children. I'm inclined to agree with the Olsen Park parents. There'll be a murder next.'

'Oh come now, Councillor. Any text book of elementary psychology will tell you that that sort of person gets his kicks simply from display. Why should we deny him his simple pleasures?'

Only Liversedge was amused. Olga tried to repair the damage by talking about conservation. She was fanatical about it, of course, in the way that people who thought they were intellectuals had to be. He wouldn't have been surprised to see her wearing a badge. But the more high faluting she got the more she would lose ground with council, especially with Bright. Bright was a realist for all his smarmy ways.

Yet her passion made Vincent curious. She was no fool whatever else she might be. He began to be troubled by a suspicion that there was something he had failed to understand. To overcome it he visited Olsen Park. He sat in his car and looked across the hockey fields and the adventure playground. The shadow of the pines lay over the climbing frames and the miniature fort. The trees themselves were secretive and ragged. He could see how they would attract a pervert. Or—he felt it with a start of emotion—a sentimentalist like Olga Fulton. Like his wife.

He was angry. He threw himself into a businesslike frame of mind. Those trees were coming down. He would see to it. They were a menace. He drove out of the park and along the unsealed access road to the back of the plantation. He parked in the firebreak between the scrub and the pines. It astonished him that an area like this should exist in the middle of a city—a city like Hardinge that had heated swimming pools and traffic lights and sunken gardens and a two mile sewage pipe that dumped the waste of fifty thousand people into a current that carried it clear across to South America. He could not understand how he had overlooked it. He could feel the threat of the place—a stirring in his blood—and knew as he climbed out of his car and stood in the presence of the trees that he was facing something dark and untamed that must be brought under control.

Again he forced a flatness on to his mind. He walked in the trees—it required no courage—and soon lost sight of the world beyond the plantation edge. He drove a straight line; exclaiming angrily as his leather soles slid on the needles that coated the ground. He ploughed across patches of pig-fern and once tore up some plants of deadly nightshade—another menace to children, though he doubted that children came this far. Only toughs—he saw broken bottles—and illicit lovers. He approached the park. Beyond the jagged shadow-line the grass showed like water: crossed by the calling of names and the sounds of laughter. He stood a dozen trees back and watched. A group of high school girls walked by, wheeling bicycles. They were the ones the pervert aimed at—old enough to know what they were seeing. The man must stop here, hidden, and pull his khaki balaclava on. . . .

Darkness seemed to enclose Vincent. The trees moved close by his sides. His knowledge of how the pervert must feel was a kind of sympathy. The red uniforms of the schoolgirls beckoned, and the sunlit grass. For a moment he saw how the act would explode one into light and power. Then he turned and walked back through the trees, brushing past scurfy trunks and sores of gum. He had been crazy to come here. If he were seen he would be under suspicion.

As he walked he thought he saw someone ahead of him, a grey shadow always turning behind the farthest tree. He thought he heard the whisper of feet on needles. But when he came into the sunlight he knew that they had had no real existence.

In his car, in traffic, held in place by white and yellow lines, he made a vow that he would push his plan through. He would have the trees down. They had no place in a modern well-run city. They were a kind of call into dark places, away from reason. It was easy to see how people with weak minds could be led astray if he, Vincent Brown, could glimpse a depravity not impossible. . . .

There were four letters in the paper that night and he read them with satisfaction; with a solid and happy feeling of gathered strength. The radio news said that more than seven hundred people had signed Mrs Spurdle's petition. A deputation was being formed to carry it to council. Vincent had not bothered to sound out his fellow councillors. He had no high opinion of most of them: amiable nincompoops or incompetent pushers. Most would go whichever way the wind blew—the wind being Bright, and Orringe the deputy mayor, and Parkinson the chairman of works. Realists: they would not ignore a thousand signatures. And Parkinson was a bulldozer man. He loved knocking things down. Orringe on the other hand was a neat little Presbyterian grocer who seemed to find it difficult to be in the same room as Olga Fulton. Her disease, he believed, disqualified her from public life; and his opposition to her had taken the firmness of a principle.

So the letter Mark Olsen published in the paper had little importance. Vincent was annoyed by the boy's ridiculous claim that his father would have opposed this 'slaughter of trees'. He was pleased by the accusation that certain councillors 'more at home with sewage and traffic lights' had engineered the petition. But then the letter turned into a sort of poem in praise of trees. Female stuff. Nobody would take it seriously. Vincent was pleased to be getting back at Mark. But it amazed him, this passion for greenery. There was a grieving tone in the letter he could not find a cause for. He could only put it down to some failure to get a firm hold on the facts that brought a man to usefulness in the world. Mark remained a child; a friend of women. The sort of man who got emotional over polluted water and found himself with a wife named Melody. It was as well, Vincent thought, that Frank Olsen had not survived to read this letter.

The following night he was quiet. Beside him Olga wheezed, clasping a damp handkerchief in her hand. The deputation filed out, led by its spokesman, a Baptist minister named Pye—who had shown an impressive gift for moral outrage. Olga, Vincent saw, had written *Pye in the sky*? on her blotter. He had not often known her use words instead of pictures.

Bright moved the meeting into committee. He asked for opinion. 'Councillor Fulton? You've been active in this.'

Olga sneezed. She wiped her nose, stuffed her handkerchief into her purse, and took a fresh one from her bosom.

'I think this is a put-up job, Mr Mayor. And I say now that in my opinion that grove of trees is worth any number of offended virgins—though I find it hard to believe that most of those girls are either the one or the other.'

She had conceded defeat to be using this sort of language. Vincent enjoyed her bitterness.

'Councillor Brown is responsible for this. It's no secret that he's behind this petition. I don't think he'll be happy until every last piece of grass in Hardinge is covered over with concrete.'

Bright called her to order. She rambled after that, in the manner of Mark Olsen. When she moved Vincent caught from her body a faint vegetable smell that lay somewhere between ripeness and decay. 'The aesthetic—my apologies, councillor—the aesthetic pleasure given by those trees cannot be measured. I realise that most of you are interested only in things that can be measured —counted up, like votes and money. But consider this: those pines stand in the middle of a desert of suburban houses. And women go mad in houses. I'm serious. They go mad. They beat their children and start hiding bottles of sherry. But if they can look out their kitchen windows and see something green, or even go walking there once in a while—'

Parkinson said, 'If they do go walking there councillor they're likely to meet a man with his fly buttons open.'

And when it came his time to speak, Vincent said, 'I'd like to point out to Councillor Fulton that the people who've put their names on this petition are mostly the suburban housewives she talks about. But I don't want to argue. I think opinion is plain. And it's plain what we have to do.'

Orringe agreed, and Bright, more wordily; enunciating his platitudes in a barbed tone unusual for him. When the vote was taken Olga found herself alone.

After the meeting she sat in her chair as the others filed out, and Vincent, looking back from the door, had a feeling of pity for her. But he had no regret—he was pleased to have brought her down. Cleverness was all she had. Her ugliness—her sickness—seemed to emphasise her lack of standards. Sitting there, seeming to squat, with her chin embedded in swollen jowls, she had the appearance of a toad.

She turned her head and looked at him. 'Vincent.'

He went back to her side. 'Are you feeling all right, Olga?' He saw that she had drawn a small uneven box and blacked it in.

'Will you help me down?'

He took her arm. The dampness of her skin came through the cloth of her jacket. He tried not to shrink from it.

'I'm not very well tonight. I shouldn't have come.'

'Why did you? You must have known how it would go.'

'I'm concerned for your salvation, Vincent.'

In the lift her smell and the sugary smell of the cosmetics she wore turned in the air like sewer gas and incense. He understood that her illness was killing her, and knew by a premonition not open to question that she would be dead very soon and that he had a long time to live. He would be an old dry man, all bones— his death at the other extreme from her death of smell and corruption.

Her husband came from their car and took her away. Vincent drove home. He drank a glass of whisky—for recovery more than celebration. His victory seemed to have been put back to an earlier time. He was frightened by an old age in which he would not have his seat on council.

But in the following days he was troubled only by the memory of a counter-blow to his that now seemed intentional: Olga was tricky. But he had won. That was the fact. If his pleasure in having defeated her was obscured, if he could find no place beyond the vote on which to stand and enjoy what he had done, it must be, he decided, because the part not done over the table had importance. There was the danger in politics of coming to believe that decisions completed events.

So on a Monday morning several weeks later he returned to Olsen Park to watch the felling of the first of the trees. (Parkinson's men had already crushed the scrub.) The scream of the chainsaws drove him back to his car. He sat with the windows wound up and watched the trees fall with a heavy hanging motion that mixed clumsiness and grace. (Until he identified it he felt uneasy.) In the wintry light their foliage was more grey than green. The trees themselves seemed ancient, twisted into knots. And as they crashed down one by one he began to feel an inexplicable sorrow. The men had the busy-ness of beavers. They seemed to worry at the trunks, undermine them with their saws. As the shock of the final cut ran up the frames of the trees they seemed to make themselves harder, their boughs seemed to grow rigid, straining to hold on to life.

Vincent rescued himself by an act of will that was becoming too familiar for his liking. He read the newspaper he had bought on his way to the park. Later he listened to the radio weather forecast. Rain was on the way. The contractor would be working in a quagmire before the job was done. He looked at the southern sky where the clouds had gathered a brown colour as though from the tiled roofs of the houses that stretched away up the rising ground. Olga's suburban desert: he saw what she had meant, but grunted angrily at the mental betrayal. With relief he saw Mark Olsen's car—the silver-grey Austin Princess Frank had owned—creeping round the perimeter of the park. It passed his own and stopped at the entrance of the access road. Mark got out. He walked along the edge of the flattened scrub, approaching the pines, but the sound of the saws slowed him; turned him finally, propelled him back to his car.

Vincent's contempt was from the ordinary world. He ran his car close behind Mark's. Mark had no doubt come to grieve—perhaps to write a poem. He watched the boy, enjoying the sad inclination of his head; but in a moment saw Frank in the attitude, who had never indulged in sadness in his life. He got out of the car, walked along to Mark's, and let himself into the front passenger's seat.

'That was a cheeky letter you wrote.'

Mark glanced at him and looked back at the pine trees. 'I thought I'd allow him a decent sentiment.'

'Hold on, Mark. That's your father you're talking about.'

'I didn't have a father.'

For Vincent people had a simple shape. He was not often troubled by people for his idea of them held them in a vice. But when he was forced to admit a change there was a painful moment in which his idea of himself seemed to be lost. He saw Mark crack a second time and felt himself fade away.

'I had some kind of jailer, not a father. He put me on bread and water, you know—literally, for weeks on end. My mother used to smuggle me cake in bed. He would have put her on it too if he could have. But he just broke her spirit instead.'

'Frank Olsen was my friend.'

Mark smiled. 'Oh no, Mr Brown. He never had a friend in his life. The word wasn't in his vocabulary.'

'He called me his friend.'

'That was just politics. Little Brown, that was his name for you. Or the Messenger Boy. When he didn't have any use for you any more he tossed you away. Didn't you see it? I'll tell you Mr Brown, he had no sense of humour but there was always one thing that could make him laugh. That was the thought of you expecting to be mayor.'

Mark had taken his father's features. The fat nose had gone, and the weak eyes; and from his narrow stony mouth the voice that came was Frank's. But behind it all was a grief Frank could never have known. 'I'm not trying to hurt you, Mr Brown. But it's no good believing what isn't true. You should have known all this years ago. You could have worked out ways of getting by. I did. There are things I do—that I have to do—that keep me in one piece. I'm not ashamed of them. They do no harm. But they're over now.'

Another tree crashed down. A fractured branch pierced its foliage and stood yellow and bleeding in the light. Mark opened the glovebox of his car. He took out a khaki balaclava. 'It will be a dreadful scandal. Sir Frank Olsen's son.' He looked at Vincent with his own sad eyes. 'But I cared for those pines in a way you'll never know. They were part of me.'

Vincent's understanding was lost in an envy released in him like a flush of blood. He lost all the sense of his past that remained to him, all sense of his worth. He held the balaclava in his hands, turned it over, as though it were some magical device that he must learn mastery of before a door would be opened to him—leading to that light, that power, he had glimpsed as he stood in the pines looking out over the sunny park where the high school girls wheeled their bicycles.

'I want you to tell the police,' Mark said. 'It's the only way to end it properly.'

'They'll put you in prison.'

'Yes. Melody doesn't need me. She'll get well when I'm gone.'

Rain started to fall and the contractor's men ran from among the fallen pines into the shelter of the standing ones. Mark Olsen took off his glasses and wiped them with his handkerchief. He closed his eyes, making himself look naked. 'I'm not a bad man, Vincent. I'm foolish, that's all—childish. I still believe in magic. Maybe prison will get me out of that.'

Vincent heard only the use of his Christian name. He began to come to himself; but could not fully return, for what Mark had told him about Frank Olsen waited. And he brought with him the knowledge that possibilities once his, for adventure, for love, for a place in the minds of other people, were lost, and now could be identified only in the light of a criminal desire. His wife had said to him once that his life must be a disappointment to him: this when he was deputy mayor, Frank Olsen's right-hand man. He understood her now. He had done none of the things that once—fifty years ago—he had dreamed that he might do.

The rain stopped and the saws began to scream again. Vincent put the balaclava on the seat. He got out of the car.

'Are you going to wait?'

'Yes. Don't be too long.'

He carried with him the image of an acre of desolated pines. In the main street he stopped at traffic lights that until now he had seen as his contribution to the town. Today he knew they were Frank's. The outfall too was Frank's. Only the leg-work had been his own. The mental stratagems by which he had avoided know-ledge of this and swollen the importance of his part even while performing it—these were clear to him now. Even the sunken garden had been Frank's: he remembered for the first time in fifteen years that he had not wanted it. But Frank, with a word, had given him a new opinion. He saw too that Frank had preferred Olga to him—saw the steps by which he had raised her up. He could find no comfort in the knowledge that Frank was dead; that Olga would soon be dead. It could not be brought to touch upon what was left of his life; any more than could Mark Olsen, who might have presented him with part of a victory.

The lights turned green. He drove on. There was nothing he wanted to do; nothing from his old life to carry on with. He knew he could save himself only by growing old. He must turn away from a public life that now seemed only a game played on a board—from a lifetime of snakes and ladders. He must choose proper cares—about what went on inside his skin. He must read books, and watch the television, and grow things in his garden. And be finicky and slow, and not give a damn beyond the edge of his section. He began to be pleased with himself—pleased in a way he recognized as minor and fussy and old—at the quickness with which he had understood. There was nothing wrong with his mind.

But one thing from his old life remained for him to complete. He put his car in the garage and walked up to the house. He felt imposed upon as he dialed the police station number.

BARRY MITCALFE # Black Cat

I have eliminated six men, or should I say, four men, a woman and a child. There may have been others that I don't know about but those I do know because, for once in our lousy lives, we had time to stop and count.

A body is just a thing, not very nice to look at.

The first was perhaps the worst, because I didn't know what to expect and it had no hardware, but then who's to say it's not Charlie? In the bush they're all Charlie, otherwise they wouldn't be there.

Turning it over and finding just that small hole in the forehead—unlike the back which was pretty messy—I got quite a bad feeling to see it was just a young boy, perhaps twelve, though I couldn't tell their ages too well. Not then.

That one was not too good, because I kept wondering, was he, wasn't he? Trouble was Charlie could be anybody.

So what if I'd made a mistake? It was V.C. country, wasn't it? He'd been told to get out and he hadn't gone.

He had a sort of soft look about him, for Charlie. But that didn't mean a thing, their women would skin and tan a living man, no trouble. Some of the pictures we saw in Orientation would turn your guts over. But this one didn't even have the old Charlie Chang look that most of the dead ones got, he was just a skinny kid, much the same dead as alive, apart from the mess where the back of his head had been.

He reminded me of another mistake—or was it a mistake—back at Matamau, which is south of Norsewood, which is in the North Island of New Zealand, which is and was my home. Got me placed now?

That was the time I killed the kitten. I'd been after the mother cat for months, she was a wild one, black with a white patch. Bloody townies, haven't got enough guts to get rid of their own cats, put them out to live or die. She'd lived, because she was smart and there was—or had been when she first started—a hell of a lot of birds.

Funny thing, though I was only fourteen or fifteen at the time and hadn't heard of 'Nam, I'd called that little kitty 'Charlie' and I was out to catch him because soon he'd be getting too wild.

So I was going to bowl the mother and tame old Charlie. I could have sneaked the gun and skittled the mother, no sweat, but trouble was the old black cat would only show up when I was bringing the cows in for morning milking and I didn't want to send our daily bread and butter stampeding back into the bush or half way through the boundary fence. Dad'd have me guts for garters. Anyway, it seemed more of a sporting proposition to 'have a go' with the quarry rocks off the race. I was a pretty deadly shot. Too deadly. Zang, zowie and I got the wrong one, little kitty jumping and kicking and going no place, with a piece of his head hanging over one ear and the blood thick as gravy on his fur. I stomped him with my boots, stuffed him down an old rabbit hole and crumbled the bank over the top so that he was out of sight, but not out of mind. Poor old Charlie.

I can still see him, he would have been a mighty cat, much better than the two kittens I'd already more or less tamed. Only thing was, he'd been left with his mother a bit too long and his face and shoulders were all patchy with ringworms. Like that kid. Couldn't help noticing down his arms and legs, the scabs and scars of what we used to call 'Maori sores'.

Both cases I went to the nearest water to wash. With the kitten it was a long way, with the kid it was a well, just beyond the row of huts. I was leaning over beginning to haul up the bucket when

bhwam! if you've ever heard a gun fired in a well you'd know
how loud it was. We'd been warned never to drink the stuff but
hell, nobody said anything about snipers in it! I'd gone back a
few paces, just enough to drop him a pineapple, which I did. The
whole well rose up and fell in on itself. Instant grave, much tidier
that way, sergeant said. Hell of a sense of humour, that fellow. I
felt a lot better about what had happened to that kid and somehow
forgot all about any handwashing. Lucky to have hands.

It was a funny war, that one. There weren't too many of us from
the S.A.S., but I know us and the R.T. (artillery that is) were
getting stuck in. Don't ask me what the Yanks were doing,
the place was lousy with Air-Cav and Cal-tex and Tam-pacs,
bloody useless and bloody everywhere, noisy as a fart in a
nunnery. It was almost a relief to be given bivvies next to the
R.O.K.s at Quang Ngai. Well named, those bloody Koreans
weren't nothing but head hunters—those babies didn't care whose
so long as it wasn't theirs. Bit like some Aucklanders I know. So
apart from a few of the Aussies, there was only ourselves we could
really trust—especially after our R.T. plastered an Aussie platoon.
It weren't our fault, the R.T.'d been given the wrong co-ordinates,
could just as easy been us on the end of the bread-run.

But we did our job and it was just a job, what we'd been trained
to do, only this was for real.

Like the 'Christmas pudding,' that's what the Maoris called it
—boy, they've got a sense of humour, I'd sooner serve with Maoris
than with white men, but God help the man who rubbed them
the wrong way—Christmas in 'Nam is just a little more and less
than usual, a little less of this and more of that, but Tet is
Charlie's big time, not Christmas, they never heard of it, though
why we should observe their Tet and they should ignore our
Christmas never seemed right to me. Anyway, this Christmas finds
us a damn long way from home, air-dropped into Hill 840 which
is just a bare, bloody piece of dirt with a bunch of Montagnards,
real head hunters who'd even put the bloody R.O.K.s to shame,
and a black American sergeant who claimed Charlie squeezed
'em so tight last night he woke up to find one in bed with him.
Anyway, that was Christmas, calling in air-strikes all round, watching the scrub go up in smoke and flame, 'palm and phosphorous,
some of it so thick we had to wear gas masks on the clean-up.
That was Christmas, easing the squeeze on Hill 840 .

Like I said, call came on the radio, that Christmas morning,
'Gotta little Christmas surprise for you Kiwis, just keep your
heads down, we're coming right over.'

And it surely was the most god-awful Christmas present any-body ever had, they'd developed these screamers that would go deep into the earth, then blow, whoomp! which was the only way to dig Charlie out. After them came the usual incendiary stuff—they had this new napalm that really stuck, you could jump under a creek and it would still sizzle the skin off your bones. Well, they did that whole goddam ridge until the gravy ran out of the clay. It was a good few hours before it was cool enough for us to go out and mop up. That was when we saw their 'Christmas pudding.' Must've been a good twenty or thirty of them, all joined together, burnt and blackened, so at first a man didn't know what his eyes were seeing. That was the only time I was sick, I mean, really spewing, a lot of us were, otherwise I'd've never heard the last of it.

Reminded me of the time before. There was this hillside up the back where the wild cats used to give me the slip every time, it was all gorse and manuka. Having bowled little Charlie, I reckon I'll have his ma, one way or another. So I ask my Dad about a burn-off, and we take the kerosine and matches and set the whole hillside alight. I waited up the top end, well armed with rocks, while Dad worked below, stopping the fire from burning back into the grass. But no sign of that cat, only a few half-cooked hedgehogs and that was that. All we did was give that bloody black cat the kind of cover she needed in amongst the black stumps, so that she was able to get stuck into the birds that came in to feed on the grubs and beetles.

Hill 840 was the same. Charlie came in unseen, dusk not dawn, which was unusual, so much so that we took half our casualties of the whole bloody war, right there.

So it was back to base for the unit, the nearest to R&R we ever got. Not like the Yanks, it was all laid on for them, every six months out to HK or Tokyo, but we had our compensations. You might think it funny after what happened at the Hill, but there were these two laundry boys, we called them Rin and Tin Tin, that the unit sort of adopted. We tried to take them with us when we were ordered out on stand-by outside Duc Tho, where there were the usual so-called 'disturbances'. All we saw was smoke by day and a little more small arms fire than usual each night, other-wise nothing. After a week of it we were ordered back to Qui Nhon, back to Rin but not to Tin Tin. 'Where's Tin Tin?' It took a lot of pressure to make Rin tell what had happened—the A.R.V.N. had used the Tet disturbances as an excuse to clamp down hard on the shanty towns, the huts of cardboard and tin on the sand

flats between the airbase and the sea. They'd found all sorts of
military gear we'd given Tin Tin and that was that.

We went to see the A.R.V.N. District Commander and he
called in an interpreter, and in the end we got the story—or rather
their story. Tin Tin had tried to make a run for it, they'd fired,
'only to wound, you understand,' but one shot had gone too high.
I don't think even they knew what had really happened and they
certainly couldn't understand why we should carry on like this all
for the sake of one lousy little kid. But they'd been thoughtful
enough to call out what looked like a whole regiment of A.R.V.N.
—we found them waiting as we came out, so we didn't wreck the
joint, which had been our original intention.

Again, the cat, or rather its kittens came to mind. The two
kittens I'd caught early on, before I'd bowled poor old Charlie—
were getting pretty tame and cheeky, in fact too cheeky, because
one came up to old Tip's meat. One snap and it was flipping and
somersaulting all over the lawn. Old Tip had broken its back. It
was really my fault. I shouldn't have given Tip his meat with the
kitten around, I mean, Tip is naturally a gentle dog, but a bit
bad tempered where food is concerned—what dog isn't? But at
the time I blamed Tip. Two down and one to go, the runt of the
litter, a scrawny, frightened female that never tamed down enough
to come except when food was laid down.

Well, I came home. And what do I see, rubbing round Dad's
slippers? that same kitten, black with a little patch of white, just
like its mother, but purring fit to burst. 'Hi, kitten.'

'Kitten,' said Dad, 'that mangey thing died of rickets a month
or two after you left. This one's the mother.'

I couldn't get over it. How the hell had he done it. After all
the time I'd spent trying to get it tame, hunting it over hill and
bloody dale, feeling bad about it, saying to myself it was the
best thing, couldn't afford any more wild cats cleaning out the
quail.

'The mother! What did you do?'

'Do? Nothing. Started comin' in for feeds. Now she's in for
keeps.'

Now, every time some smart ass comes up to me and says
Vietnam this and Vietnam that, as if he's got all the answers, I
tell him about my little old black cat. Only I never get time to
finish me tale before they're off somewhere else on their own
track.

But I dunno. Guess everyone's gotta find out for themselves.
The hard way.

OWEN LEEMING   # Wet Season

Pretty soon I shall have to be getting back to work, not a moment
I particularly relish. I can't say I particularly relish siesta-time
either—not with my air-conditioner. It's full of sound and fury,
cooling and drying nothing. Rather, that's only a sign that
siesta-time itself is totally inadequate. It doesn't in any way act
as a rest-cure.

I tried to sleep, I always try, but I can't make the room dark
enough. I stared at the mosquito net, in focus to begin with, its
round meshes, glazed cotton. . . . I'm sure if a mosquito had the
wit to clap its wings and legs close to its body it could squirm
through. Then the meshes began to blur and they became . . .
water, water I was sinking down through. It was at this season
last year, during a rainstorm, that the ferryboat capsized. An old
landing-craft with planks missing everywhere and a bridge of
boards and roofing-iron, it was caught in the cross-current where
the river hits the tide and just heeled over. I could see it, the
woman screaming, all the bicycles sliding down the deck, all the
chaps scrambling up the side that hadn't gone under yet. The rain
whipped up the river-water and the wind turned it into small
white waves. Then everything was below. I could see the black
arms and legs sliding down past me and the bright cloths of the
woman fading. The water was grey. It was warm, and I was
swallowing mouthfuls of the stuff. Since last night I haven't been
able to clear my mind of this.

Now I must try to find my notes on a survey I collected figures
for two years ago but never had time to write up. The Minister
wants to make a speech in the Assembly on the subject and he
needs them.

There's a view of the ferry terminal through my window. The
rain has stopped. It probably won't rain again today. The passengers have taken the calabashes off their heads. They're jumping
off the catwalk on to the ferry. Some of them wheel bicycles, some
of them hold chickens by the claws upside down, or have armfuls
of bread. The trailing edge of the storm is out over the river
mouth. The clouds are piled up so high in the sky they look as
though they're going to topple back on the town. It's horribly

humid. You can't get rid of that bunched feeling at the armpits, and at the crotch.

Only a fortnight ago, it rained almost continuously every day. It's the season the French call 'wintering', although in reality it's summer . . . rather like England. Anyway it makes the rice-growers happy. I suppose there *is* a certain exhilaration in the sensation of deluge. On this particular evening, there was a purple glow everywhere. With the rain sheeting down and the spray dancing up, it was like being in the centre of a loom.

I dashed from my car to the hotel lounge entrance with the water cascading on all sides off my umbrella, but my trouser cuffs still got thoroughly soaked. The hotel is a regular call. After a day of work, the work I have to do, you need a drink. The work has a way of demanding more energy than you can give it and that makes it slip out of your control. My colleagues tend not even to make the effort. Or to put it differently, there's little to show for the energy you do expend.

I gave the boy my umbrella to be shaken out and dried and sat down. I was first there. I ordered my whisky and looked through a bound volume of tabloid newspapers, three weeks old. In the early days, there had been a certain interest in wondering who would come in next and join me—a doctor, a lawyer, a politician, one of the ones who had thrown over the Koran's ban on drink, or one of the Lebanese importers. But when it rained, it wasn't certain that anyone at all would come. I looked at incomprehensible strip comics and read accounts of county cricket matches. Meanwhile the rain outside was making an incredible amount of noise.

Eventually, during my third glass of whisky, Fuad came in, unashamedly drenched. He had obviously come from his emporium on foot, about a hundred and fifty yards up the street. Fuad is a man who has always troubled me . . . I suspect he resembles me too much, in spite of notable external differences. He's rich beyond the dreams of avarice from selling wire netting and alarm clocks and transistor radios to the local inhabitants. Not only that, but he has a wife, a girl so beautiful that I'm ill when I see her. She's only half his age, well, two-thirds at the most. But Fuad, despite the fact that he can escape—he goes on amazing voyages, Japan, Western Germany, *Liverpool,* and once a year to his birthplace in the Lebanon— Fuad is what I term a perturbed spirit. It's something you can see in his eyes. They're never quite on you when he talks to you. He's one of these people who feel they've failed in respect to some aspiration they probably couldn't define. When he speaks, it's his own thoughts that he's looking at. The other Lebanese nicknamed his wife Sophia Loren, because of her face.

Fuad sat by me, smelling of wet cotton. Drops of water were running from his curly hair down behind his ears. He smiled towards me with his mouth. I put down the tabloids. When he had his drink, he spoke.

'Did you know, I suppose you did, that Greta Liston is back?'

Gossip—ah well—no, I didn't know. Greta Liston was the community's best property, a planter's daughter who had gone away, gone 'home', and become a great actress.

'That ought to give our little pond a stir,' said Fuad. All the tired old tritons, newts, axolotls creeping and peering about at each other . . . now, plop, a new face.

Almost as soon as Fuad had made his remark, father and mother Liston, along with daughter Greta, came into the lounge. Once they had taken off their plastic anklets, they hardly looked splashed. I found myself goggling. My first impression was of how big and bony she was. She had the matt skin and the glossy hair of a new arrival. She was a dark redhead. Fuad turned back.

'A pity there are only us two here. Because they want to show her off. I know the Listons. They never come into town when it's raining. Within a week, she'll be bored dead. A new land bill's being drafted—did you know that? It's a fact, because I know who's in charge of the drafting. But keep it to yourself. The Listons are going to be hit very hard. It's African socialism.'

Not because of me but because of Fuad, the Listons wouldn't sit with us. They sipped their drinks with their heads turned towards the door. Greta surprised me while I was looking at them. She rocked her head and opened her eyes wide in rather an inane way and grinned at me. I suppose I was meant to grin back but I looked down instead to where the Tiger Balm mosquito coils were smoking away by our ankles.

In only a few minutes I must leave for work. The ferry's pulling out. The other one's waiting to run in on the sand with a load of hump-backed Brahma cattle. The steam's rising off them, I can see it from here. In this climate . . . desire, libido . . . it's another thing entirely, a little like the rainstorms. There's plenty of it, even when it's Highland night at the British Club, but everyone waits for everyone else—there's no initiative. You never see anything going on, only hear the gossip afterwards. X sleeps with Y, and then with Z, but she never dances with anyone except her husband, A. You feel terribly wan and out of it when you first arrive. But now I have to think of work. I'd do anything not to have to go. There'll be more of that passive obstinate opposition. I wish I knew the answer to it. I've tried being cheerful, being inspiring . . . I've even tried being a tyrant like in the colonial days. It's shaming not being able to obtain results without play-acting. You're in a false position. On the face of it, it's simply a question of passing on information, of implanting an organization, transmitting things one knows to those who don't know. But they're so different in every way. Then there's the post-colonial fact. The simplest instruction becomes fraught with tension and emotion. *They* can't help it, nor can I. I'm not insulting their intelligence, or their tradition. It's because I respect both that I seem to upset everybody. Perhaps they need a thorough-going racist so that they can relax. I've been over all this a thousand times. I have that feeling of cold still on my mouth.

After the night in the lounge bar, I made Greta Liston's acquaintance quite rapidly. It was merely a matter of going to the British Club the following Saturday night and asking her to dance. I was one of many who had the same idea. Some of the Lebanese boys had braved the hostility, and most of the unmarried technicians were there. With its First Division football pennants and piled-up crates of Scottish beer, what everyone calls the 'BC' has the atmosphere of a working-men's pub or even a Naafi, but it considers itself to be Maxim's and the Ritz combined. You need references to join and the Lebanese find these hard to come by. The only black member is the Prime Minister who knows much better than to turn up. The band, of course, is black and schooled in the Gay Gordons, the Lancers and the Highland Schottische, beside the more usual Madisons and twists. I admit the Club has a swimming-pool, plus a patio with trellis for dancing under the tropical stars. I danced with Greta, whose style was as angular as mine. I asked to take her back in my car and she agreed—somehow, miraculously, I'd cut out the massed competition. She told her parents, introduced me, and at about half-past eleven they left by themselves.

The Listons live up-river twelve miles out of town. About half way there, there's a beach. This was where I decided to pull off the road. The car headlights shone out over the sand where the giant crabs had been moving about undisturbed. Greta liked the way they stopped when the light shone on them, with their eyes standing straight up on stalks . . . she thought they looked shocked. When I turned the headlights off, we could see the lightning flickering and flashing inside a storm out at sea which seemed to be moving towards us. All these things reminded Greta of her childhood. She spoke with a deep voice, laughing a good deal, and putting much stress on certain words in her sentences. What about your acting, Greta, I asked.

'What about my acting *indeed,*' she said. 'You can hardly have any idea living here, darling, of the *change* that's come over theatre. Have you heard of Grotowski, total projection? You have to be a mystic, you have to be an athlete, all in one, it's *exhausting*. Just rehearsing changes you as a *person,* leaves you quite collapsed. Poor Mummy and Daddy, they have no idea, but *they're* happy doing what they're doing, aren't they.'

No need to ask Greta whether *she* was happy doing what she was doing. While we were embracing, the thunder became audible and soon the rain started lashing down. I switched the headlights on and backed out on to the road again. I like the effect of the streaking silver of the rain which mixes with the white cloud bouncing back from the asphalt. Then as I drove off with Greta's arm around my neck, the frogs started jumping all over the road. It really is very comical the way they jump in the headlight beams, hundreds of them, a good four or five feet in the air. The trouble is you can't help killing them, and pulling them out of the radiator grill the next day is unpleasant.

From then on, my nights were all Greta—in thought, that is. I systematically refused to admit that in a few weeks' time she'd be going back to her work.

I had a strange encounter about this time with Fuad's wife. We found ourselves together on the ferry. There's a small village on the other side of the river mouth. One of her relations runs the store. Fuad's wife looks very sophisticated in the way she makes up and dresses, but she's really a very shy person. She has a calm smile and a soft voice. I never can make out whether she's deeply under-standing and mature or deeply ignorant. She left convent school at the age of fifteen to marry Fuad. That is the way these things seem to be done in their country. Fuad himself never talks about her, except to say that he has a taste for beautiful things. I have a mad wish to tear her away from Fuad, to run away with her from this heat, this damp, the utter *tininess* of this place, and set her up where she can blossom forth, where she can breathe. I've always felt there to be a bond between us. On the ferry, I inexplicably found myself *telling* her all this, close to her ear. She wasn't visibly shocked. She looked up at me with her large wide eyes, then looked down. That was all. When the ferry came to the wharf, she left me, still without looking up.

After that, I had to put in a couple of days' field work a hundred miles up-river. Up there your main thought is malaria. The children die like flies from it. We have an anti-malaria campaign running in the up-river villages and I was doing some inspecting. Spray, mosquito netting, and pills, that's the prescription, but putting it across is the problem. We work through the local state midwives. In spite of the conditions, I rather like field work. I have the impression I get on well with village people. They seem to be so much more direct. It rained without a let-up. Mould formed on everything. I didn't have much sleep, due to a combination of heat, the noise of the rain and the uproar of the frogs—by comparison, the mosquitoes were inaudible. I should have liked at night to have kept my mind blank, but I kept thinking of my work and of the enemies my work makes me. They never appear to understand that I *volunteered* to come to this inhospitable place . . . in order to give a hand, to improve conditions. They think it was for the money, or because I couldn't succeed at home. Obviously you can't explain. The effect is that these years don't exist as part of my life, while they age me twice as fast. And what if I catch something?

Greta called on me after I came back and suggested we go to the beach. At this time of the year, the sand's damp, the sea's rough and it's full of jellyfish. None of that would stop Greta from swimming. I warned her too about the sun on her skin, infra-red, it burns without browning. Greta's skin was so white it almost looked green. She stretched straight out on the sand.

'It all seems so far away,' she said, 'the rat-race—I'm not at all sure I want to go back.'

On an impulse, I came very near asking Greta to marry me. But before I was able to get it out, she jumped up and ran into the sea again. Marry Greta Liston—stark staring madness, but there are times when you don't think.

The cold on my lips. The cattle are stumbling off the ferry. The way *they* go about it, walloping and yelling and arguing, its a slow process. Under the water where the ferry went down, I see pointed outlines, grey, slipping firmly towards the coloured cloths and the back limbs. I see this very vividly.

Fuad had me to his home for lunch the day before yesterday. Lebanese food is good, it suits the climate. His sister and brother-in-law, his father and mother were all there, as well as his wife. I sat opposite her, positively aching. She smiled at me from time to time, quietly. The conversation at the table was nearly all in Arabic, but after the meal Fuad and I talked together.

'I should have liked to have been a professor of medicine,' he said. 'I began, you know, to study in Beirut. Then my father needed me here. And what is there here? I'm wasting myself, and so are you. What do you think of Greta Liston? You should marry her and go away. I have an idea of offering the government to construct a medical school, if they will call it by my name. What do you think of that idea? I can feel I'm going to have an attack of malaria. It's lucky that I have you to talk to.'

That was the day before yesterday. Five minutes at the most and I shall have to be at my desk. I have to set the example for punctuality. Moral authority is everything. The clouds have moved right out to sea. But the sharks have started to slash through the cloths and the limbs. Red veils sink in the water after them. Where to God are those papers?

After dinner last night, I was working, it was my semi-annual report. I usually *do* have to work after dinner, so I'm careful not to drink too much. It's important to conserve your mental energy, a precious commodity here. There was a moon up outside. It was quiet—well, apart from my loud-mouthed air-conditioner and the odd mosquito which had survived my spraying. A flying cockroach would crack against the window from time to time. I was transcribing some statistics from a government report into mine, when I heard a car pulling up outside, and shortly after there was a banging at my door. I opened it, and it was Fuad. His hair was plastered over his face. His suit was wet through and clinging to his skin. He was in a bad way.

'Help me,' he said. 'Help me. I don't know what to do. Help me to bring her inside.'

Fuad went out in front of me and opened the rear door of his car. Greta was lying on the back seat. I noticed Fuad was holding her clothes in one hand. The water was trickling off her skin on to the seat. After looking both ways up and down the street, we lugged her into my place and laid her on the divan. I tried to make out whether or not she was alive. Meanwhile, Fuad was telling me what had happened.

'We went out in my boat. It wasn't my idea. Ever since she came, she's been chasing me. What could I do? I needed her. I need somebody who understands me. But the stupid girl moved so much we capsized. There was a current and I lost hold of her . . . I nearly drowned as well.'

Greta didn't seem to be breathing. Her eyes were slightly open. There was mucus on her upper lip. I packed cushions under her shoulders and set myself astride her.

'I came to you,' Fuad said, 'because I knew you'd know what to do, and because you'll be discreet. My family are old-fashioned, they would condemn me because of my wife. My wife is a nothing. Except by me, she doesn't exist. That's the truth, and Greta understood that. I told Greta everything about myself, I told her everything I wished for and which has no chance of happening.'

While Fuad talked, I bent down to Greta's lips. It was strange, it was a perversion. My own were so hot by contrast. I puffed my air into her, tasting the salt. Her chest filled up. I pushed it empty, then filled it again.

'When Greta heard about me,' Fuad was saying, 'she cried. And then she said she would tell me about her. I made myself listen because, you'll understand, I needed her. She couldn't find work as an actress. Greta is no good as an actress. She's exactly what you'd expect to come from here. This is no surprise to you. Nor to me. She came back because there was no other possibility.'

Greta was beginning to breathe. I was both proud of myself, and nauseated.

'If the boat hadn't turned over,' Fuad said, 'I should have told her about the land bill. That would have been interesting. Please don't say anything to my father or my mother about Greta, or to my wife even. *You* should have married my wife, she likes you. I shall have to go to Tokyo next month, and then to Liverpool.' Fuad let out a long sigh.

The cattle are off the ferry, mooing and steaming. The chaps are hosing down the deck, making it ready for the passengers. I really must get up this time, I really must go.

WARREN DIBBLE   **A Way of Love**

Dust kicked up by the ewes settled all along the margin of the road, on grass, blackberry, manuka.

Dust and sweat smeared the face of the spectacled farmer.

It was a listless, burning afternoon, with a pulsating drone of cicadas in the air. The sheep were tired and hot. Paddocks away could be heard the distant throb of a baler.

The farmer walked his horse behind the mob.

Once he stopped to break himself a switch from an osier willow and a green and gold ladybird glinted up into the sun and alighted on his singlet. He flicked it off.

He had two work dogs with him. One was a pup in training, the other a big black thing that seemed to be always grinning.

A car, an old model Morris, rolling huge clouds of pumice dust behind it turned a bend and slowed down as it came upon the sheep. Some of them scrambled wildly against each other and tried climbing up the bank. The pup went leaping and barking excitedly after them.

In low gear the car began to nose very slowly through the sheep. The older dog trotted after it, sprung up and onto the running board and carefully began to work himself, slithering and scratching, in between the headlamp and mudguard. The manoeuvre successful he stretched himself comfortably and began barking at the sheep, clearing a way for the car through the mob. His tail thumped madly against the body of the car and despite his barking he seemed to be grinning more than ever.

As soon as the car had got through he wriggled forward and floundering a little, sprang down to the road some three yards ahead of it and then trotted back through the sheep.

The car drove on a short distance and pulled up. A middle-aged couple got out and waited till the farmer came up to them.

'I guess he'll have to take us through again now. But I've never seen a dog do that before. My wife wants to take a photo of it.'

'Where did he learn to do that trick?' smiled the woman.

'Eh?'

'He's a great dog,' she said to the farmer.

'Buck? He's o.k.'

'Here boy!' called the man. 'Here boy!'

The dog made no response. It haunched down for a moment, panting; and snapped half heartedly at a fly.

'Here boy!' called the woman.

The farmer took out a tin of tobacco from his khaki shorts.

'He don't answer no one but me. He's trained for it.'

He rolled a cigarette, lit it, and then called: 'Buck'.

The dog crossed to them.

'Sit.'

'You lovely old fellow,' said the woman stooping down and patting his sides with both hands. 'You nice old boy.'

As she straightened, the dog jumped up with his forepaws against her dress.

'Down boy!' she said, laughing.

'Buck!' called the farmer sharply. 'I said sit! Sit!'

The dog squatted again.

The farmer removed his spectacles and wiped them against his singlet. Then he stepped forward a couple of paces to the dog, drew back his boot and slammed it hard and savagely into the dog's stomach.

The dog screamed and backed painfully.

While her husband watched amazed the woman gave a little cry and ran towards the dog.

'Poor boy! Poor fellow! Poor old chap!'

She bent down to pat him but the dog uttered a low snarl and snapped at her hand. She pulled it away hastily.

'He won't hurt you,' drawled the farmer. 'He don't hurt anyone.'

The woman and the farmer stared into each other's eyes.

WARREN DIBBLE   # In It

'Put one up the spout and shoot the bastard!'

He hung up. His wife asked:

'Who was that?'

'Mick. That big black dog of Wilson's been hanging round the ewes again.'

'You'd better go. You're late.'

He grunted.

'Is your uncle going to stay with us?'

'Don't know.'

'I expect he'll want to.'

'He can please himself.'

'When's he go into hospital?'

'Tomorrow I think.'

She took his gumboots outside to the porch, saying:

'Why's he coming all the way down here to the reception? If he goes into hospital tomorrow?'

'Reception my ass. He's come down to put the bite on me for a few thousand.'

'Do you think so?'

'He sent me thirty typed pages on his affairs. He's been diddling the tax men for years.'

'Are you going to give it to him?'

'Don't know.'

He drove fast, nonchalantly, to the pub. His uncle, a farmer from up north, had not yet arrived. He joined a few farmers in the private bar.

He was young, of big build, especially powerful in the legs, and worth a couple of hundred thousand. Nobody's fool. He ran three farms, two dairy and one sheep. He didn't put on airs but had nevertheless a natural authority. At boarding school he had been head prefect. Up to a few years ago he'd represented the province as a rugby lock. Older farmers listening to one of his forthright, contrary pronouncements might say dubiously, 'Well, I don't know . . .' but in discussing him critically among themselves one of them was sure to add, 'Mind you, he's got brains. Once he's made up his mind he won't mess around.' There were one or two rumours about other women but no one knew anything definite. All the same it was certain that women found his curt, take-it-or-leave-it style and his faint aloofness intriguing.

He had fairish brown hair that sometimes needed cutting on the neck. Well over six foot, he slouched rather than slumped. When not in working gear he dressed casually. At the moment he was wearing a white open shirt, expensive herringbone sportscoat, crumpled grey flannels and sneakers.

One of the farmers greeted him.

'Gooday Jess. What are you having?'

'Gin.'

'Right.'

'Been to the saleyard?'

'Yes. Very iffy market.'

It was twenty minutes or so before his uncle showed up; a bulky man with high colouring, grizzled tufts of eyebrows and a nose that ballooned out like a spinnaker. He was dressed in an ageing but well cut suit of some cinnamon coloured material, with matching waistcoat.

'How are you?' his nephew asked, stretching himself from the barstool and shaking hands.

'Not bad, Jess, not bad.' He had a deep, almost fruity voice.

'First time I've seen you wearing a hat.'

'It's a new one, too,' said the uncle.

'Well you must be doing well. Dough in the wool, eh?'

'Hah!'

'Yes, well: what are you going to have? I'd better introduce you. Henry. Bill. Mac.' He indicated his uncle. 'This is Jim Burton. My uncle. Silly old bugger, really.'

'Your face is familiar,' said one of the men.

'Yes,' said the nephew, 'I think you've met the old boy before. I try to keep him away—but you know—!'

'Last year, wasn't it?'

'That's right.'

'Whisky, uncle?'

'Yes. And lots of water.'

'Right.'

The uncle placed a pound on the bar. His nephew shoved it back at him.

'Put it away. I'll shout.'

'Hah! Nothing like having a wealthy nephew.'

'Nothing like having a destitute uncle.'

The uncle made a grimace and asked seriously:

'You got the typed packet I sent you?'

'Yeah.'

'Yes, well then, you've got my finances at your fingertips.'

'And I don't think much of them. That enough water?'

'Good.'

'Cheers.'

'Cheers.'

The uncle said doubtfully:

'I suppose I'd better book in.'

But his nephew instead of extending the expected invitation merely replied:

'It's not a bad pub. Good table, they tell me.'

The uncle swallowed his whisky and said, with a troubled expression:

'Well, I don't know what's going to happen to me tomorrow.'

'Why?'

'They may have to amputate my leg.'

'That bad, eh?'

His uncle launched into a long and detailed account of X-rays and the opinions of his specialist. 'Still, no use worrying,' he concluded.

'If they cut it off,' commented his nephew, 'You'll really have one foot in the grave then, eh?'

The young man turned and drew the others into conversation and the talk became general.

His nephew's bantering tone threw the uncle off balance a little. Understandably he was worried. He needed several thousand to clear his tax arrears and of late had found himself unable to make decisions. He didn't know whether to sell up his farm or not. If he did, where would he go? All his friends and associations were in the district. City life had few attractions. He was hoping that Jess would lend him some ten thousand. In fact, if he didn't. . . . But it was a delicate subject to broach. The boy seemed almost flippant about things. And he knew he'd have to put it delicately to his nephew, mention at least ten per cent, because if Jess once made up his mind to pass the deal, nothing would change it. But whenever I try to get him on the subject, he thought, he dances away from it; surely he's aware that I need to know before I go into hospital?

He felt dispirited and began to brood. His nephew, a little boisterous with gin, jabbed him on the arm.

'Come on you silly old bankrupt bastard. You'd better have a few more drinks before they amputate you. You won't be playing much golf after tomorrow, either.'

'By the way, Jess. I didn't tell you. I had a hole in one. It was on—'

'Oh shut up. No one believes you.'

'No, truly. I did. Cost me a packet, too.'

'Drink up. You talk like a bloody politician.'

A little while later the uncle thought: I feel drunk, and I've got to get in a serious talk with Jess, damn it.

But his nephew had swung away into a kind of larky, facetious mood. The uncle looked around for the Gents.

'Where are you off to now?'

'For a long spit.'

'Well don't stand there all day looking at it.'

But the truth was, he wanted to be alone for a moment. He was rather dazed by all this downrightness from his nephew. It was so far from his own mood. When he returned, Jess, who was smoking a cigarette and chewing his empty pipe at the same time, had just begun a description of some calves he'd sold.

'. . . to Harrop. I said I'd deliver 'em, so I drove them to the Patai bridge, half way, where this bloke met me. Do you think I could get 'em across that bridge? I'll be damned if I could. We tried everything. Forcing them, leading them. We even put hay on the bridge.'

'Were they weaners?'

'Yeah. In the end we had to get some milk from a cocky down the road. That brought 'em. Well, we just about had them all across when two of the buggers broke. Those two cows! Do you think we could get them to come back? In the end I had to bring the whole bloody herd back to them. Then they all came across like lambs.' He said suddenly to his uncle:

'That's not your gin. That's yours on the ledge.'

'Oh yes. I didn't notice.'

'You wouldn't notice if I had a horse with me.'

'I shouldn't be into the top shelf, you know.'

'If you conk out I'll put you to bed.'

'No you won't. I don't need to be picked up and nursed.'

'Don't you, you old bugger. I should pick you up and bounce you on your head to give your brain a shakeup.'

Desperately, the uncle said:

'I'm worried, Jess.'

'So you ought to be.'

'Can't we have a talk?'

'What do you want to talk about?'

I thought you might be able to give me—some advice. I mean I may have to lose the farm. Sell up to pay the tax people.'

His nephew frowned slightly.

'And you know. It's a good farm, Jess.'

'Then what the hell are you going round buying new hats for?'

'Christ, it's not funny.'

'Sell out then.'

'But I've got that farm up to peak production. It's showing good returns.'

'You don't want a lot of money, you'll only spend the stuff. But if you're going to spend it, spend it.'

'But I don't want to give up the farm.'

'Look, you're going to die soon. Sell out and spend it. If they slice your leg off you won't be able to work, anyway.'

'I suppose I could sell half, or lease it. But it's the tax I'm worried about.'

'Get on the right side of your bank.'

'I'm on the wrong side of my overdraft already.'

'You'll just have to push on regardless.'

'Yes, but it's critical Jess. I've just had another letter from the tax people. A nasty one.' He took a deep breath and said slowly:

'I'm liable for nine thousand.'

There was a pause.

'W-e-ll, I'll tell you what,' said the nephew in his slurred, nasal and not unattractive voice. He gave his empty pipe a suck. 'I think you're in the shit.'

And from the settled, almost malevolent tone in which it was said, the uncle knew that he was.

ALEXANDER GUYAN   **Summer Story**

It was one of the best parts of the day.

'How are you this morning Johnny?' Mrs Branston said.

'Very well this morning', John said.

They were always the same, the initial words of greeting, even on special days. They were unnecessary of course; he knew that she had already enquired from his mother. But he liked it just the same.

'It's a beautiful day out. Such a shame for you to have to be lying there.'

She practically always said that too. She was very sorry for him and had no qualms about showing it. And John liked it, the pity he received, not just from her, but from everyone. He had often read of men who resented being pitied, and he was never able to understand that. To him it was something to be savoured and enjoyed. He had even managed to break the pity he received into different degrees, and he believed that his deductions were always correct.

'I don't mind. I'm used to it,' he said.

'Yes, I suppose you are. You're a good patient for a boy of fifteen, I'll say that for you.'

They smiled at each other, and John again thought she was one of the few persons, perhaps even the only one, who was sincere and absolutely honest with him.

'Cheeky though,' she added, and then hearing the grandfather clock downstairs chime nine, 'but I can't stand here gassing to you all day.'

Moments later the bedroom was filled with the howl of the vacuum cleaner, and partly because the noise made it impossible to concentrate on anything, and partly because he enjoyed doing it, he sat up against the pillows and watched her.

No one knew how important she was to John, that was one of their friendship's most endearing features in fact. It was a secret that was precious to him, as all secrets were, especially those that were kept under the very nose of his mother. Mrs Branston came to the house every day to do the cleaning, and she always started with John's room. It was then that John's mother usually did the shopping so that they had the house to themselves, although he wasn't sure if Mrs Branston realized this.

She was forty-eight, but didn't look it, something she credited to a life of hard work. Certainly there was nothing faded about her; to John she radiated a kind of healthy attractiveness that was caused not so much by her appearance, but rather by her bubbling vitality.

And she loved to talk, that was another reason why John enjoyed her presence. She talked about her family which was large and, to John, an only child, amazingly complex and interesting. She told him of her husband's illnesses, her children's report cards, her sister who lived in Canada, her oldest daughter's boy friends. He learnt everything of their past and present history, and of what she predicted for their future. He was able to comprehend the web of characters that made up her family, but what he particularly enjoyed and appreciated was the knowledge that what she was telling him was absolutely true. He believed, utterly, that everything she told him was told honestly, and this was something that he felt with no one else.

And there was another thing. A few weeks before he had made her weep by reading a poem to her. She hadn't wept much of course, but she had been upset, and not by the poem itself either, he was sure that she didn't understand it—he didn't himself—but by the way he had read it.

This thrilled him, especially when he realized that the tears were not the kind he was familiar with, and that actually she had enjoyed the reading. It was like having control over her. It *was* having control over her. And if there seemed to be something reprehensible about this, a vindication of it might be that it had helped him spend the long summer months in bed.

His name was John Freman, and he was fifteen. He had been ill with glandular fever, and his recovery, hampered by a weak constitution, had been slow. Since late spring he had lain in his room, not feeling ill, but almost always tired, his skin white, except around his eyes where it was dark. Yet except for the tiredness he was hardly conscious that he was ill. He had begun to think of his illness as something he owned, and which others had an interest in too, yet also as something that was only tangible when he felt the doctor's stethoscope against his chest, or at medicine time.

He was enjoying his illness; and that was another precious secret. The sadness that his visitors showed when they saw him lying in bed, with the sun throwing shadows of light on the bedroom walls, this an accentuation of the room's 'insideness', their sadness was mistaken.

For John the wonderful feature of being ill was the world he was able to create during these months. It was a world where he was all-powerful, where he ruled absolutely and without fear. Outside it was different: people snapped at him, or ignored him, or frightened him. Outside he came upon situations—or they were thrust upon him—which he was unable to comprehend or deal with. Yes, he *knew* that outside it was different. But here in his room, within the shelter of the walls he felt safe and, paradoxically perhaps, truly free.

Mrs Branston switched off the vacuum and said: 'It'll soon be medicine time.'

'Yes.'

'And I don't want any performance today.'

'But it *is* horrible.'

'The worse it tastes the better it's for you,' she said, and left the room.

Later he heard her foot on the creak. No one coming up the stairs could avoid standing on it, and John used it as a warning signal. Once or twice a visitor had attempted to surprise him, and he had had to simulate shock. This had amused him greatly, and made it even more obvious to him that no one could violate the security of his room.

'You know,' Mrs Branston said when she came back into the room, 'you remind me of my Elsie, as far as taking medicine is concerned that is.'

'How?'

'Well she hates taking it too. The others they don't mind, but she hates it. Just like you.'

She poured some of the medicine into a spoon. 'Now quick and you won't taste it.'

He swallowed the medicine and made a face. 'It's horrible,' he said.

'Just like Elsie,' Mrs Branston said. 'Now wipe your mouth. That's it.'

She sat down on the bed and watched him.

'The taste lasts so long,' he said.

'Then have a piece of chocolate. That'll take the taste away.'

He broke off a piece and put it in his mouth.

'Better?' she asked, standing up.

'A little', he said, hoping she wasn't going.

'I have to hurry,' she said, 'because I've got a lot to do this morning.'

The medicine *was* awful. The taste lingered in his mouth long after it had gone down his throat. But even this ordeal was not without one compensation. Mrs Branston often wore low-cut dresses, so that when she bent forward to give him the medicine, and while she waited for him to take the spoon into his mouth and swallow, he was able to look down her dress, and see the start of her breasts.

After she left the room he wrote in his diary. The diary was a large exercise book and he kept it under his pillow. John thought it was wonderful, much better than any other book he had ever read. In it he recorded everything that happened to him and around him, his thoughts and opinions, his aspirations. He did not recognize the diary for what it partly was, an escape valve, but only saw it as something very precious, very clever, and—this not fully realized either—important to him.

Today he entered his thoughts about the vacuum cleaner. He enlarged and developed them, for this was another feature of the diary: a great many of the entries started as actual happenings and gradually became fiction. Still another feature was that some of it was in code. At the top of today's page for instance, precisely in the right hand corner, were the letters LDMRSBD, which meant, *to no one else in the world but him*: Looked down Mrs Branston's dress.

With this system of capital letters, and the others he used, he felt secure from the fear of anyone understanding certain entries.

He closed the book and put it back under the pillow. He could still taste the medicine so he ate another piece of chocolate. He lay back and closed his eyes. He could hear Mrs Branston moving around downstairs as she prepared lunch. That was a pleasing sensation: sounds coming from downstairs, muffled and suppressed, yet familiar and reassuring in their modulation and character. He wondered if anyone else felt like that. Probably not. Yet he couldn't be sure. That was something that lately he had thought and puzzled over a great deal. Did others have these sensations too? Until lately he had presumed, unconsciously, that they had. But now he wasn't so sure.

They were not, as the noises downstairs were, always sensations of reassurance. Sometimes they were of fear.

Once he had been passing a large building, a factory of some sort, and the huge doors were open. Inside it was empty, and the roof seemed to be miles from the floor. The whole place was still, and in semi-darkness, so that it was some time before he noticed three men standing in a corner, standing huddled together as if they were conspirators of some sort. And at the precise moment he had seen them they had seen him, and one of the men had yelled something at him, something that was lost in distance and echo. It was then that John had been frightened, for in his mind and in his senses, clearly, the three men came forward and began to drag him into the place. No more, he did not visualize them doing anything else to him. But the experience of them dragging him in was so real that for a moment he actually *was* in the place, the dreadfully still, empty place, and the street, seen through the doorway, was a distant, receding square.

Then he had started to run, his legs moving as they never did on the playing field, propelled by a desire to get as far away from the building as possible, and because the sight, sound and feel of the street comforted him, and finally, when he was a great distance from the place, because the whole happening seemed funny and exciting.

But afterwards when he thought of how actual it had all been, he became uneasy, especially when he decided that no one else he knew, none of the boys at school for instance, would have felt and acted the way he had; he was quite sure of that.

He heard the creak on the stairs again, and he sat up. A moment later Mrs Branstan came in.

'I've made an orange drink for you,' she said sitting down on the bed. 'I put plenty of sugar in it, but don't tell your mother.'

John grinned, took the drink from her, and sipped it. 'It's very nice', he said. 'What are we having for lunch?'

She laughed. 'You men! All you worry about is your stomachs. It's stewed chops.'

'I don't like stewed chops', he said.

'There's rice pudding. You like that. I'll see you get an extra big helping. You need something. You're so thin.'

'I can't help it if I haven't got muscles.'

'It's not muscles. I'm sure you don't weigh much more than six stone. It certainly takes it out of you, that glandular fever. Of course you're the type, like my Elsie. She don't weigh nearly enough either. It's a worry for the mothers though.'

'I don't think mother is worried about how much I weigh.'

'Of course she is. All mothers worry. My brother Bertram, he's the same. That's who Elsie got it off, I'm sure. Thin as a rake he is, and always has been. But strong just the same. So you don't have to worry about not having muscles.'

'I'm not worried about it,' he snapped.

She laughed again, causing the bed to shake.

They both heard the front door slam, and Mrs Branston stood up.

'That'll be your mother', she said.

They waited in silence, and after a while there was the creak on the stairs, and then John's mother came in.

'Hello Mrs Branston,' she said. 'I hope John hasn't been bothering you?'

'No, not at all. I came up with a drink for him.'

John was always intrigued by the change that came over Mrs Branston when she was confronted with his mother. She was always polite and respectful, and always enthusiastic about any chore that Mrs Freman might suggest. She was the perfect help in the home, and yet John knew that it was an act. The real Mrs Branston was the one who joked with him, and told him stories about her relations.

'I'll go down and see how lunch is getting on', she said now.

When she had gone his mother sat down on the bed and said: 'Has it been a long morning for you darling?'

'No. I've been writing in my diary.'

'You've really taken to the idea of keeping a diary haven't you?'

'It's lots of fun,' he said. 'Did you get some books for me?'

'I did, but I've left them downstairs. Never mind, Mrs Branston can bring them up with your lunch. Has she been boring you with her relations again?'

'It doesn't bore me mother. I like hearing about them.'

'Everyone to his own tastes I suppose,' she laughed. 'The lady at the library asked for you. Oh yes, and I met Bill Cozzens's mother. She said that he is going to come and see you this afternoon.'

Bill Cozzens was John's best friend. He had called regularly since John had been ill, especially since the holidays had begun.

'So you have something to look forward to', his mother added.

John guessed that she wasn't really pleased about it. His mother didn't altogether approve of his friendship with Bill, in fact she didn't like the Cozzens family at all. That was because they were modern, and although he knew what that meant he couldn't understand how it could be a reason for not liking them.

Recently John had found it hard to understand a great deal of what his mother said and did. The realization had come slowly that she was not only his mother, but a person as well, and the combination of these two things seemed somehow to be dangerous, and his manner towards her since then had been guarded.

'I wonder what time he'll come', he said.

'If he comes late he can stay for tea—if you want him to that is.'

'Yes, I'd like that.'

Bill Cozzens had played an important part in John's life three months previously. Bill had been the cause of a discovery John had made that deeply affected him: No one, no one, no one could be trusted.

Bill Cozzens had a sister who was the same age as John. She was a tall, slim girl, whom he considered to be incredibly beautiful, and with whom he was in love. He hadn't admitted this to himself at first, he had simply thought and wondered about her continuously, and when the word love had entered his mind he had been amazed and excited, and not a little proud of the fact that he had fallen in love with such a beautiful girl.

Then, during one of their discussions that occurred after school, which John enjoyed so much because of their personal nature, and because of the bond they seemed to create between the two of them, during one of these discussions he had told Bill of his love for his sister. Bill hadn't seemed very interested at the time, but later John discovered that he had told Barbara. She, it seemed, had thought it a wonderful joke, so wonderful that she had shared it with all her friends, and before long everybody knew about it. *Everybody.*

John had felt sick with a mixture of rage and humiliation. But what was even worse was the thought that his best friend, his only confidant, had done a thing like that. It had been completely shattering. He had argued with Bill about it, but rather than apologize for what he had done Bill had made matters worse by treating the whole affair as a joke.

They hadn't spoken to each other for a long time, not until the start of John's illness when Bill had visited him, and that had been at his mother's instigation. Neither had mentioned the argument or its cause again, but it had not been forgotten, certainly not by John. His relationship with the other boy was never the deep, per-

sonal thing he had imagined it to be before. Bill was again his
closest friend, but now it was with reservations, for he never
allowed himself to be caught off guard again, and everything he
said had first to go through a mental censorship before it was
uttered.

John, always a suspicious, frightened boy, had decided that if his
best friend could behave in such a way then his suspicions that
others could too were surely correct. And he had gone further
inside himself, until now he believed that he had never been so
happy, could never be happier, than he was within the security of
the four bedroom walls.

Bill arrived a little after three. John, practised at observing his
numerous visitors, had found Bill to be the only one who seemed
unmoved by his illness. They might just as well have been out on a
hillside on the edge of town, or in the classroom, for all the difference it made to Bill.

They talked for a while on subjects that Bill obviously felt his
friend should know about. They worked on a jig-saw puzzle that
had been given to John. It bored John as intensely as it amused
Bill. Then John decided that it wasn't just the puzzle that was
boring him, but Bill himself, and this revelation was exceedingly
pleasant; it seemed to dispel the hurt that Bill had caused him, yet
leave the valuable knowledge that he had gained from it.

Bill didn't stay for tea, and before he went he said: 'Barbara
said that she would like to come and see you, now that it's holidays
you see.'

He didn't look at John when he said this. John didn't know what
to say. He felt a little embarrassed.

'I'll come back on Wednesday to see you', Bill said.

When he had gone John brought out his diary and made an
entry:

*Bill came to see me. He bores me intensly. I didn't say anything
queer, or anything that he might laugh at, or make something
of. I was very careful. He says B. wants to come and see me, but
I bet she doesn't.*

He misspelt intensely, but he didn't notice.

II

Since John had been confined to bed his father had made it a habit
to carry his son's breakfast tray up to him. John wished he
wouldn't. There was something about the sight of his father carry-

ing the tray, with a wide, good-morning grin on his face, that John found distasteful.

John had long since decided that he didn't like his father. He knew that he was a disappointment to him: both his school work and his ability at games were mediocre, and his shy, dreamy quality irritated him. Yet his father never showed it. Always on his face there was a cheerful grin, as if he had accepted his son for what he was, and was trying to like it. John wouldn't have been surprised if his father had asked him how his dreaming had gone today, much as other fathers asked about the football game.

And it wasn't just towards his son that this mien of cheerful acceptance was directed. Had it been so John would not have minded so much. But his father was like that with everyone; agreeable, considerate, smiling, and especially so with his wife. John was sure that these were sufficient reasons for disliking his father. If only, he thought, he would show some sign of displeasure at something. Just once.

'How do you feel this morning?' he asked. 'You look perky enough.'

'I feel fine', John said.

His father laid the tray on his lap. 'The sooner you get well the better. I'm tired of playing butlers.'

This was GOODNATURED BANTER. John grinned out of pity, and because he was unexpected to.

'Actually,' his father went on, 'it shouldn't be long should it?'

John looked at his father quizzically.

'Your return to the fold. Your getting up I mean. From the way you seem to have improved lately. I'd say that you will be up and about before long.'

John felt himself flush. 'The doctor said it would be another few weeks.'

'Yes, I know, but at least it isn't months. But you had better eat your breakfast before it gets cold. That's another thing, you've been eating much better lately.'

After his father left—with a mock military salute—John began to eat his breakfast, but without enthusiasm. What his father had said had sharply upset him. In a few weeks' time this will all end he thought. I'll have to go downstairs, and become part of everything and everybody! The world of safety that he had created during his illness would be gone, and he would again be an inhabitant of the outside, the disgusting, alarming outside.

No, he couldn't!

Remember what Hunter the maths teacher had said at the beginning of last term? *Don't tell me I'm going to be inflicted with you
again this term Freman?* In front of everyone! Not that that mattered; everyone hated Hunter. But he had so obviously *meant* it.
Remember how that had hurt, knowing that he meant it, and
remember the panic-stricken thought at the vision of endless maths
periods supervised by someone who hated me?

Could he return to that? No. No.

He lifted the breakfast tray off his legs and sat it down on the
floor. Then he slipped down in the bed, and pulled the blankets
over his head. He drew his legs up until he was curled into a ball,
and then made sure with his hands that he was completely covered
except for a tiny hole which was for fresh air. This position was
his shell within his shell, his last resort against everything.

And there was the way he was never sure if he was like the
other boys, and how he wondered all the time whether the other
boys guessed that he was different. Did they know that he didn't
feel the same way about things as they seemed to?

And those long afternoon periods when time seemed to stand
still, yet every second standing by itself, and filled with dread for
fear he should be snapped at, or asked a question that he couldn't
answer.

Or going downstairs and listening to his father joke uncomfort-
ably with his mother.

Or being with his mother and not liking it very much.

Or being in a place that should have been familiar, but suddenly
wasn't any more.

Or—everything.

No, he couldn't.

He felt sick, and he wondered if he should call for someone. But
he couldn't bring himself to. He wanted. . . . He didn't know what
he wanted. Through the air-hole in the blankets he could see a
corner of a picture on the wall. It was a picture of snow-capped
mountains. If only I was there now he thought, and no one knew
me, and I didn't know anyone else. . . .

He wondered if he should pray. But that wasn't any use. The
only time he ever did that was when he wanted something, and He
must know that. Still He must also know how much this means
to me.

'John?'

He hadn't heard the creak on the stairs. He felt the blankets
being drawn away from his head.

It was his mother. 'Were you asleep?' she asked.

'No.'

'What on earth were you doing under the blankets?'

'I don't feel well.'

She sat down on the bed, and put her hand on his forehead. 'Where don't you feel well darling?'

'I don't know', he said, and then he was crying in her arms.

Afterwards he felt better. He fell asleep, and when he awoke Mrs Branston was there, and his mother was saying '—be a long time yet before he really recovers properly.'

When his mother left, and he sat up fully awake Mrs Branston said: 'How are you this morning Johnny?'

'Very well this morning', he answered.

'Naughty boy, frightening your mother like that.' She said this with a grin, making it obvious that she was only joking. 'Mind you I do think you have been over-taxing yourself lately. Too much reading and the like. How do you really feel now?'

'A little better.'

'Well enough for a change of pyjamas?'

'Yes, I think so.'

'Your mother said there were clean ones here.' She went over to the chest of drawers. 'Yes, here they are. Now I'll be through in your mother's bedroom if you want me. Take your time.'

She laid the pyjamas down beside him and left the room.

For a while he sat there looking at the empty doorway, and then he threw the blankets back and stood up shakily. He pulled off his pyjamas, and stood there looking down at himself. He was startled to see how thin he was. Surely he hadn't always been like that, surely it was just since his illness. He walked unsteadily over to the mirror on the wall. He stared at his reflection, and was shocked. His face was so white and drawn, and the skin over the bridge of his nose was almost transparent. It was someone else's face, not his. I really am ill he thought with wonderment. How can *he* say I'll be getting up soon when I look like this?

'Are you changed yet?'

It was Mrs Branston calling from the other room.

'Won't be a moment', he called back.

He hurried to the bed, his legs starting to ache. He put on the clean pyjamas and slipped back into bed. It was a relief to be lying down again.

'All right now', he called.

'My, but you took a long time', she said.

He didn't say anything about having looked at himself in the mirror. 'Aren't you going to use the vacuum cleaner today?' he asked instead.

'No, not today,' she said. 'Just a quick brush up today. There isn't time for anything else. I've got to help your mother prepare for tonight.'

'What's happening tonight?'

'The party.'

He remembered. His mother had mentioned it to him. 'I'd forgotten', he said.

John hated when his parents held parties. The laughter, and the often coarse voices intruded into his room and frightened him. They only happened occasionally, and perhaps it was their alien quality, the unusual, sudden disruption they caused that made him dislike them so much. Yet if they had happened often—as they did at Bill Cozzens's house—he doubted if even then he could have grown accustomed to the offensive, drunken clamour, and the thought that his parents were part of it.

'I'm staying to help out tonight', Mrs Branston was saying.

'Do you drink?' he asked her.

'No. Well a glass of beer sometimes. But Eddie, that's my sister's husband, he does the family's share.'

'Is he a drunkard?'

'Well, not all the time,' she laughed. 'But when he drinks, he drinks!'

While she tidied the room she talked about Eddie. John listened intently. He marvelled at Mrs Branston for knowing so much about something, especially a family. To John, a family, and being part of one, were mysterious circumstances, almost incomprehensible, yet not quite enough so for him not to feel that—perhaps—he had missed something.

Mrs Branston went on talking about her brother-in-law right up until medicine time. She was wearing a frock that John hadn't seen before. It had a high neckline, and he didn't like it at all.

The party was in progress, Although his light had been out for an hour—his father's breath had stunk of alcohol—John was awake, staring up at the ceiling which was quite visible because of the moonlight. But it wasn't the moonlight that was keeping him awake. From downstairs came the noise of the party, a continual buzz of talk, broken occasionally by deep male laughter and high-pitched female laughter. John didn't know which he hated most. Once he heard a loud crash, someone had knocked over a tray of glasses, and everyone had laughed. To John it was as if they had all gone mad.

He was very frightened. He wished they would go home. He wished, until he sweated, that they would go home. *Why* didn't they? His fear was tinged slightly with annoyance. They must know that I'm up here—sick. At least *they* know (his mother and father), but then they are drunk.

Suddenly he felt terribly sad, and unhappy, and lonely. He didn't think he had ever felt so miserable in his life before. It must stop he decided. This thought was answered by a shrill scream from downstairs. He turned on his side completely dejected.

It was then that he saw the shadow on the window, and the moment he saw it he realized the unbelievable fact that there was someone outside, and then he heard the tapping.

He sat up slowly and craned his neck. Yes, there was someone there. He didn't know what to do, but the tapping was insistent, so he slid out of bed and walked to the window. He wasn't the least bit frightened. He stopped some distance away, but even from there he recognized the face that was grinning at him. It was Barbara Cozzens.

'I thought you were never going to hear me', she said when he opened the window.

'What are you doing out there,' he whispered.

'I've come to visit you. Can't I come in?'

He didn't answer, but stepped aside, and she clambered into the room.

'You'd better go back to bed if you're sick', she said.

He went back to bed. She sat down beside him.

'Can we put on the light?' she asked.

'Better not', he said.

'Why are you whispering? No one could possibly hear us with that noise going on. Just listen to them! They're worse than juvenile deliquents.'

John felt embarrassed. 'It is pretty terrible isn't it?'

'You should hear at our house when Mum and Dad have a party. Bill and I crawl downstairs and watch.'

The audacity of doing a thing like that startled John, but he didn't show it. 'Won't your parents find out about you coming here?'

'How can they when they are downstairs?'

'Did you climb up the drain-pipe?'

'Yes. It's quite easy with gym boots.'

This is wonderful he thought. Imagine doing a thing like that!

For me! Of course she knows that I love her. He blushed and wondered if she noticed. The bedroom was quite light.

'How are you feeling now?' she asked.

'All right.'

There was a pause, and then she said: 'Do you smoke, ever?'

Careful, he thought. 'Sometimes I have.' He had too, but not very successfully.

'I've got one in my pocket, and a box of matches. Move over a bit.'

At first he didn't understand what she meant, and then when she moved to lie down he felt the shock warm inside him, and then spread over his body.

The bed creaked a little, and he could feel her against him although they weren't touching. He heard her light the cigarette and then draw on it. He stared at the ceiling, too excited to speak.

'Here', she said.

She was offering him the cigarette. He took it, and drew on it carefully.

'This is fun', he said.

'Mmm. Is it true what Bill said?'

'What?' he said, although he knew what she meant.

'That you told him you were in love with me?'

'Yes', he said feeling foolish.

'It's all right. Everyone thinks it's a joke, but it isn't. I like you too.'

He felt incredibly happy. He gave her the cigarette back. He turned his head and watched the glow descend, then brighten, and then travel up through the semi-darkness again.

'Will you be better soon?'

'Yes. In a few weeks.' Those words which had held so much dreadful meaning before, were merely words now that answered her question.

'That's good. We could go swimming together.'

She passed the cigarette back, and he took two draws, and he knew that if he took any more he would be sick. He gave it back to her.

'It's nearly finished,' she said. 'I'll squash it out on the match box and then take it with me. Better not leave evidence.'

John laughed. The cigarette was a secret—shared.

'Can I kiss you?' he asked, and the words were out before he realized it, and he was at once apprehensive. Had he gone too far again, as he had done when he had told Bill that he loved her?

'Is it catching—what you've got?'

'No.'

'All right then.'

They turned only their heads towards each other, and then moved them forward. John could see her face close to his, and then there was the sensation of their lips touching, hers cold, yet so positively there.

'Is that the first time you have kissed anyone?' she asked.

Before he could answer—he was going to say yes—she sat up and spoke again. 'It must be quite late. It took me such a long time to get here. You see if Dad gets very drunk then Mum is sure to take him home early. You'd better come to the window with me, and close it afterwards.'

He followed her to the window. He didn't mind that she was going. He was too happy to mind. He was in love, and he wished he had put the lights on.

'I'll come and see you again,' she said. 'During the day though. This has been good fun hasn't it?'

'Oh yes.' He wondered if she would kiss him before she went. She didn't. She went over the window-sill, grinned, and then was gone. When she reached the garden he saw her look up and wave. He waved back, and then closed the window and returned to bed.

The noise was still going on downstairs, and because of that, and the excitement of the last half hour, he didn't think he would be able to sleep. Yet within three minutes, minutes devoted entirely to the remembrance of her lips touching his, within three minutes he was asleep.

And he slept soundly, and when he awoke it was as if he hadn't been asleep at all, he remembered everything of the previous night so clearly. How gratified he was for her coming. That would show everyone. Wouldn't *they* be full of envy. And the kiss! She had lain down beside him on the bed and he had kissed her. What a girl to be in love with.

When Mrs Branston came in he had difficulty in not telling her about it all. The moment she entered the room he realized that she was the only person he could tell. But he didn't. He decided that for the time being Barbara would be a secret among his many others.

'It was a lovely party', Mrs Branston said.

'Did you get drunk?'

'Don't be silly,' she laughed. 'I wasn't a guest.' She grinned at John. 'But if you promise not to tell your mother—'

'I promise.'

'Well I did have two drinks. One of the men gave them to me.

Some sort of cocktail they were. Quite delicious. Don't tell anyone though.'

'I won't', he said laughing now. He enjoyed and appreciated other people's secrets as much as he did his own.

She began to assemble the vacuum cleaner. John stared at it. Today it was merely a vacuum cleaner. He shifted his gaze to Mrs Branston. She was wearing *that* frock.

How stupid I was yesterday morning he thought. But I didn't know about Barbara then. She must be keen on me to have done what she did. She let me kiss her! I wonder if she was wearing lipstick. She does sometimes, or so Bill says. But probably she wasn't. Lipstick looks so warm, and her lips were so cold. I must enter everything in my diary. I will after medicine time. In code.

The sound of the vacuum cleaner had stopped.

'I'll be back with your medicine in a minute', Mrs Branston said.

He wondered when Barbara would come back to see him. Soon he was sure. It would be fun for her to come in the afternoon, but not so much fun as it had been last night. In the afternoon his mother would be around—Mrs Branston didn't count—but last night they had been so alone, and secret.

'Here we are,' Mrs Branston said. She poured the medicine carefully into the spoon. 'Now no performance.'

She sat down beside him, and leaning forward guided the spoon towards his mouth. It went into his mouth, and he swallowed.

'There now', she said smiling.

John was smiling too. Then, because he was smiling at her, and she at him, and because of a sudden need to communicate with her, and *perhaps* because of other reasons that were obscure, obvious, complicated, simple, and because it was that precise moment of his life, he lifted his hand from the bed covers, and put it forward onto her breast.

She jumped up, the spoon falling to the floor.

'You bad boy! You filthy boy!' She repeated this again, at a loss for better words to explain how she felt.

She stood towering over him, and he thought she was going to hit him. He knew with painful certainty that he would never forget these moments, no never.

'Don't tell,' he said. 'I'll tell about you drinking at the party if you do.'

'You dirty boy', was all she said.

Where can I go, he wondered frantically. Where can I go to be safe?

III

Nothing happened.

He waited for three days, and on the third day he decided that everything was going to be all right, Mrs Branston wasn't going to tell his parents.

He couldn't understand it. Mrs Branston didn't talk to him much now, and only when his mother was present. It was obvious therefore that she was still angry, yet equally obvious that she had no desire for his mother to know what had happened.

Those three days were the most unpleasant he had ever known. He lay there waiting for his parents to come to his room—they would come together of course—and start to question him. There would be no direct punishment, John knew that, but it would be there just the same: in their hurt, shocked expressions; in the way their kindness towards him would be just a little reserved, and their preoccupation with him not so intense, because they would be unable to accept him quite as they had before. They would question him, and the questions too would be a punishment, for he knew what they would do to him: they would strip away his secret life, pull apart the walls of his bedroom, probe and discover, upset him, and frighten him.

But nothing happened.

On the fourth day he grew resentful towards the whole thing. He felt safe now, and his resentment showed in his manner towards his parents. He treated them coldly, as if they did have knowledge of what had happened, but instead of their questions frightening him, he had managed to withstand them, and prove their attitude to be erroneous. He spent a great deal of the fourth day pursuing this idea. He composed alibis which were unlikely, although they didn't seem so. They were reassuring, but only because he was now convinced that they would not be necessary.

Eventually he even managed to discover to his satisfaction exactly why Mrs Branston hadn't told his mother. She obviously hadn't given the occurrence much thought afterwards; she had probably forgotten it the moment she left the room; he had made too much of the whole affair; she probably wished now that she hadn't called him all those horrible things. Really, nothing had happened.

The fact that this reasoning was not compatible with his knowledge that Mrs Branston no longer behaved in the same way towards him, and that he did not feel the same towards her—he hated her now—did not occur to him. And no amount of self-deception could lessen the misery of those three days, nor the horror he felt when he thought of them afterwards.

A few days later his mother suggested that, as he seemed to have improved so much lately—how he wondered at that!—perhaps he would like to spend at least the afternoons downstairs, and later perhaps, to sit in the garden. He said yes, he would like to, and it was true. Because of what had happened (sometimes it had happened, and sometimes it hadn't) his room had lost a little of its aura of safety. He had begun to spend some of his time looking down at the garden from his window, hurrying back to bed whenever he heard the creak on the stairs. He saw the high, honeysuckle-covered walls as enclosing another outpost of security in the country of ever-present danger that his mind inhabited.

On John's first afternoon outside Barbara Cozzens visited him. His mother had settled him in a canvas chair at the far end of the lawn, and he had two books and his dairy of course. It was warm, and the garden seemed crowded and close to him. He was about to begin one of the books when he heard footsteps on the concrete path.

'Your mother said you were here', the girl said, and then, 'You're up.'

'Yes,' he said. 'I've been up for a few days, although this is the first time I've been outside.'

She sat down on the grass near his feet, but not quite facing him. Her long hair was tied tightly at the back of her head. It made the bones of her face more pronounced and fragile. He suddenly remembered that he had kissed her, he looked at her lips. They seemed pale and dry, and he wondered if his mother would bring out a fruit drink.

'Wasn't it a lark the other night?' she said.

'Yes, wasn't it. You didn't get caught?'

'Nope. Although I only just got home.' She laughed. 'Bill heard me coming in, and said that he was going to tell Mum and Dad.'

John looked down at her. How could anyone be so cruel, he wondered, especially someone fortunate enough to be related to her.

'Did he tell?'

'No, but only because I gave him two shillings to keep quiet.'

'That was a bit awful of him wasn't it?' John said with genuine anger.

'It didn't matter', she said lightly. 'That's a sort of arrangement with us.'

It all seemed very strange to John. Not just that her brother should treat her like this, but that she should be almost a party to it. The intricacies of family life were a mystery to him.

'I'll give you two shillings', he offered.

'Don't be silly. I've got lots of holiday pocket money left.'

'So have I.'

'You're not quite well yet, are you?' she asked.

'Not quite.'

'I thought so. Your mother said that I mustn't over excite you.'

'Oh?' He felt annoyed. 'You mustn't mind anything she says.'

'I didn't, but she's right of course.'

He wished he could think of something to do. It didn't seem to be enough to sit there and talk to her like this. He wanted to suggest something that would please her, and make her glad that she had visited him. He longed for the informality that the darkness in his room had induced the other night.

'I'm playing tennis this evening,' she said. 'I've been playing a lot lately. Do you play?'

'No, but I'd like to.'

She began to talk about the game, and John listened intently. After a while his mother came out carrying a tray of fruit drinks. He noticed with displeasure that there were three glasses on the tray.

'It's warm,' his mother said, 'and I thought you would both appreciate this.'

'It's very nice', Barbara said, sipping her drink.

'It takes a lot of sugar to make.'

John looked at Barbara. He knew that she wasn't interested in the amount of sugar it took to make the lemon drink. A girl who climbed drain-pipes, who kissed, and who had smoked and shared a cigarette with him *couldn't* be interested in such mundane things.

And does mother have to be such a bore he thought.

'Do you think John looks better?' his mother asked.

'Much better. He'll be able to come swimming with us soon.'

'Well. . . .'

John listened to his mother tell Barbara about his illness. She had done this before to other people, in his presence, and he had on those occasions enjoyed it. But now he was embarrassed, and wished his mother would go away. He emptied his glass quickly, hoping that she would do the same and then leave. But she sipped her drink slowly and talked, while Barbara listened with—John believed—a quite transparent show of interest, so much so that after a while he became frightened that his mother would notice, and by the time she did leave them he was convinced that she had.

'Thank goodness she's gone', he said.

'You're not supposed to say things like that,' Barbara said primly, 'at least not to me.'

'I didn't actually mean it', he said hurriedly. He was completely puzzled. How could he have known that she would take that attitude? But it was always like that: he never knew when he was going to fall into a trap.

Somehow he wasn't enjoying himself as much as he wanted to. Everyone is so queer he thought.

'My mother is just the same though,' Barbara said. 'She is always over-friendly with all my friends who come to the house. It's a sort of roundabout way of being nice to me; of getting through to me.'

She giggled and fell back on the grass. Her head touched one of the books, and she pulled it out from underneath, and looked at the title on the spine. 'The Coll-ected Po-ems of Ru-pert B-rooke,' she said in a voice of recitation. 'I didn't know anyone read that sort of thing for fun.'

'It isn't very good,' he said. Careful he thought. 'Mother suggested that I read it', he added defensively.

She groped for the other book, and gave it a quick glance. 'Have you ever read *Ulysses?* You know the one I mean.'

John, who didn't, said—'No, is it good?'

'Not worth the bother really. There's a girl in my form—she's very, very clever—who punctuated all the end part. What's this?'

She was holding the diary.

He was about to say 'My diary', but after a moment's hesitation said—'Just a diary.'

'You keep a diary!' she exclaimed. She sat up quickly. 'I won't look at it. I know that's not done. Imagine you keeping a diary!'

'What's so strange about that?' He had the familiar feeling of nervous alarm. Something dreadful was going to happen, something over which he had no control.

'Well, nothing ever happens to you, does it? Did you put in the bit about me coming to see you the other night?'

'Yes.'

'I say,' she laughed, 'I'm in a book!'

Nothing ever happens to me John said. That is what she thinks. I don't climb drain-pipes, or smoke cigarettes, or kiss. Nothing ever *does* happen to me. Except terrible things like Mrs Branston, or being laughed at like now. I'm different, yes, but in a horrible way. Oh, I hate, I hate, I hate. . . .

'You're not annoyed because I said that are you?' the girl said.

'Of course not.'

'It's just that I think it's a bit funny.'

She laid the diary down on top of the two books.

'It's very nice to keep a diary, I suppose,' she said. 'I always mean to, but I never seem to be able to get round to it. Bill would probably do something mad with it anyway.'

'Yes,' John said, 'probably he would.'

They'll have a laugh about this he thought. He looked at the girl. She was staring across the garden. Everything turns out rotten he thought. Why doesn't she go away and laugh.

'The sun has gone', he said.

'I suppose I'd better go too if I'm to be in time for tea.'

He walked with her into the house. They didn't speak, although for John the silence was not uncomfortable. Self-pity had swamped every other emotion he was capable of feeling.

'There is something about that girl I don't like', his mother said soon afterwards.

You shut up he thought. Just you *shut up*. You were *nice* to her —but you don't like her. And she was nice to you, and you bore her. Everybody *shut up*. Especially you.

'I think I'll go back to bed', he said.

'Yes, do. You look a little tired dear. You may have overdone it a little. And with that girl coming. . . .'

John stood by his bedroom window looking down at the garden It looked dismal now, the canvas chair solitary and pitiful, so that he had a ridiculous urge to rush out and bring it in.

The diary was so much fun he thought. But not now. Not any more. Of course not. Not any more. Everything becomes rotten. She laughed and spoiled it all. Something spoils everything. Something fearful happens. I never mean it to happen, but it does. Mrs Branston, and Hunter the maths teacher, and the diary being laughed at—they're laughing now, and those men dragging me into the factory. It can't be avoided. Everything traps me.

He looked down at the concrete path below and thought—I wish I could die.

And there he was: and there he was falling, falling, falling—the vision was so clear that he had the actual physical sensation—falling; and now he was staring at himself on the path below, dying, and inexplicably, Mrs Branston was kneeling beside him, holding his bleeding head in her lap. And there he was—dead, dead and away, away from the dilemma of being alive; escape and away. The question that had no answer had been answered, and at last he was safe. . . .

Oh yes he thought. I'm not at all frightened.

JOY COWLEY   # The Silk

When Mr Blackie took bad again that autumn both he and Mrs Blackie knew that it was for the last time. For many weeks neither spoke of it; but the understanding was in their eyes as they watched each other through the days and nights. It was a look, not of sadness or despair, but of quiet resignation tempered with something else, an unnamed expression that is seen only in the old and the very young.

Their acceptance was apparent in other ways, too. Mrs Blackie no longer complained to the neighbours that the old lazy-bones was running her off her feet. Instead she waited on him tirelessly, stretching their pension over chicken and out-of-season fruits to tempt his appetite; and she guarded him so possessively that she even resented the twice-weekly visits from the District Nurse. Mr Blackie, on the other hand, settled into bed as gently as dust. He had never been a man to dwell in the past, but now he spoke a great deal of their earlier days and surprised Mrs Blackie by recalling things which she, who claimed the better memory, had forgotten. Seldom did he talk of the present, and never in these weeks did he mention the future.

Then, on the morning of the first frost of winter, while Mrs Blackie was filling his hot water bottle, he sat up in bed, unaided, to see out the window. The inside of the glass was streaked with tears of condensation. Outside, the frost had made an oval frame of crystals through which he could see a row of houses and lawns laid out in front of them, like white carpets.

'The ground will be hard,' he said at last. 'Hard as nails.'

Mrs Blackie looked up quickly. "Not yet," she said.

'Pretty soon, I think.' His smile was apologetic.

She slapped the hot water bottle into its cover and tested it against her cheek. 'Lie down or you'll get a chill.' she said.

Obediently, he dropped back against the pillow, but as she moved about him, putting the hot water bottle at his feet, straightening the quilt, he stared at the frozen patch of window.

'Amy, you'll get a double plot, won't you?' he said. 'I wouldn't rest easy thinking you were going to sleep by someone else.'

'What a thing to say!' The corner of her mouth twitched. 'As if I would.'

'It was your idea to buy single beds,' he said accusingly.

'Oh Herb—' She looked at the window, away again. 'We'll have a double plot,' she said. For a second or two she hesitated by his bed, then she sat beside his feet, her hands placed one on top of the other in her lap, in a pose that she always adopted when she had something important to say. She cleared her throat.

'You know, I've been thinking on and off about the silk.'

'The silk?' He turned his head towards her.

'I want to use it for your laying out pyjamas.'

'No Amy,' he said. 'Not the silk. That was your wedding present, the only thing I brought back with me."

'What would I do with it now?' she said. When he didn't answer, she got up, opened the wardrobe door and took the camphorwood box from the shelf where she kept her hats. 'All these years and us not daring to take a scissors to it. We should use it sometime.'

'Not on me,' he said.

'I've been thinking about your pyjamas.' She fitted a key into the brass box. 'It'd be just right.'

'A right waste, you mean,' he said. But there was no protest in his voice. In fact, it had lifted with a childish eagerness. He watched her hands as she opened the box and folded back layers of white tissue paper. Beneath them lay the blue of the silk. There was a reverent silence as she took it out and spread it under the light.

'Makes the whole room look different, doesn't it?' he said. 'I nearly forgot it looked like this.' His hands struggled free of the sheet and moved across the quilt. Gently, she picked up the blue material and poured it over his fingers.

'Aah,' he breathed, bringing it closer to his eyes. 'All the way from China.' He smiled. 'Not once did I let it out of me sight. You know that, Amy? There were those on board as would have pinched it quick as that. I kept it pinned round me middle.'

'You told me,' she said.

He rubbed the silk against the stubble of his chin. 'It's the birds that take your eye,' he said.

'At first,' said Mrs Blackie. She ran her finger over one of the peacocks that strutted in the foreground of a continuous landscape. They were proud birds, irridescent blue, with silver threads in their tails. 'I used to like them best, but after a while you see much more, just as fine only smaller.' She pushed her glasses on to the bridge of her nose and leaned over the silk, her finger guiding her eyes over islands where waterfalls hung, eternally suspended, between pagodas and dark blue conifers, over flat lakes and tiny fishing boats, over mountains where the mists never lifted, and back again to a haughty peacock caught with one foot suspended over a rock. 'It's a work of art like you never see in this country,' she said.

Mr Blackie inhaled the scent of camphorwood. 'Don't cut it, Amy. It's too good for an old blighter like me.' He was begging her to contradict him.

'I'll get the pattern tomorrow,' she said.

The next day, while the District Nurse was giving him his injection, she went down to the store and looked through a pile of pattern books. Appropriately, she chose a mandarin style with a high collar and piped cuffs and pockets. But Mr Blackie, who had all his life worn striped flannel in the conventional design, looked with suspicion at the pyjama pattern and the young man who posed so easily and shamelessly on the front of the packet.

'It's the sort them teddy bear boys have,' he said.

'Nonsense,' said Mrs Blackie.

'That's exactly what they are,' he growled. 'You're not laying me out in a lot of new-fangled nonsense.'

Mrs Blackie put her hands on her hips. 'You'll not have any say in the matter,' she said.

'Won't I just? I'll get up and fight—see if I don't.'

The muscles at the corner of her mouth twitched uncontrollably. 'All right, Herb, if you're so set against it—'

But now, having won the argument, he was happy. 'Get away with you, Amy. I'll get used to the idea.' He threw his lips back against his gums. 'Matter of fact, I like them fine. It's that nurse that done it. Blunt needle again.' He looked at the pattern. 'When d'you start?'

'Well—'

'This afternoon?'

'I suppose I could pin the pattern out after lunch.'

'Do it in here,' he said. 'Bring in your machine and pins and things and set them up so I can watch.'

She stood taller and tucked in her chin. 'I'm not using the machine,' she said with pride. 'Every stitch is going to be done by hand. My eyes mightn't be as good as they were once, mark you, but there's not a person on this earth can say I've lost my touch with a needle.'

His eyes closed in thought. 'How long?'

'Eh?'

'Till it's finished.'

She turned the pattern over in her hands. 'Oh—about three or four weeks. That is—if I keep it.'

'No,' he said. 'Too long.'

'Oh Herb, you'd want a good job done, wouldn't you?' she pleaded.

'Amy—' Almost imperceptibly, he shook his head on the pillow. pillow.

'I can do the main seams on the machine,' she said, lowering her voice.

'How long?'

'A week,' she whispered.

When she took down the silk that afternoon, he insisted on an extra pillow in spite of the warning he'd had from the doctor about lying flat with his legs propped higher than his head and shoulders.

She plumped up the pillow from her own bed and put it behind his neck; then she unrolled her tape measure along his body, legs, arms, around his chest.

'I'll have to take them in a bit,' she said, making inch-high black figures on a piece of cardboard. She took the tissue-paper pattern into the kitchen to iron it flat. When she came back, he was waiting, wide-eyed with anticipation and brighter, she thought, that he'd been for many weeks.

As she laid the silk out on her bed and started pinning down the first of the pattern pieces, he described, with painstaking attempts at accuracy, the boat trip home, the stop at Hong Kong, and the merchant who had sold him the silk. 'Most of his stuff was rubbish,' he said. 'You wouldn't look twice at it. This was the only decent thing he had and even then he done me. You got to argue with these devils. Beat him down, they told me. But there was others as wanted that silk and if I hadn't made up me mind there and then I'd have lost it.' He squinted at her hands. 'What are you doing now? You just put that bit down.'

'It wasn't right,' she said, through lips closed on pins. 'I have to match it—like wallpaper.'

She lifted the pattern pieces many times before she was satisfied. Then it was evening and he was so tired that his breathing had become laboured. He no longer talked. His eyes were watering from hours of concentration; the drops spilled over his red lids and soaked into the pillow.

'Go to sleep,' she said. 'Enough's enough for one day.'

'I'll see you cut it out first,' he said.

'Let's leave it till the morning,' she said, and they both sensed her reluctance to put the scissors to the silk.

'Tonight,' he said.

'I'll make the tea first.'

'After,' he said.

She took the scissors from her sewing drawer and wiped them on her apron. Together they felt the pain as the blades met cleanly, almost without resistance, in that first cut. The silk would never again be the same. They were changing it, rearranging the pattern of fifty-odd years to form something new and unfamiliar. When she had cut out the first piece, she held it up, still pinned to the paper, and said, 'The back of the top.' Then she laid it on the dressing table and went on as quickly as she dared, for she knew that he would not rest until she had finished.

One by one the garment pieces left the body of silk. With each touch of the blades, threads sprang apart; mountains were divided, peacocks split from head to tail; waterfalls fell on either side of fraying edges. Eventually, there was nothing on the bed but a few shining snippets. Mrs Blackie picked them up and put them back in the camphorwood box, and covered the pyjama pieces on the dressing table with a cloth. Then she removed the extra pillow from Mr Blackie's bed and laid his head back in a comfortable position before she went into the kitchen to make the tea.

He was very tired the next morning but refused to sleep while she was working with the silk. She invented a number of excuses for putting it aside and leaving the room. He would sleep then, but never for long. No more than half an hour would pass and he would be calling her. She would find him lying awake and impatient for her to resume sewing.

In that day and the next, she did all the machine work. It was a tedious task, for first she tacked each seam by hand, matching the patterns in the weave so that the join was barely noticeable. Mr Blackie silently supervised every stitch. At times she would see him studying the silk with an expression that she still held in her memory. It was the look he'd given her in their courting days. She felt a prick of jealousy, not because she thought that he cared more for the silk than he did for her, but because he saw something in it that she didn't share. She never asked him what it was. At her age a body did not question these things or demand explanations. She would bend her head lower and concentrate her energy and attention into the narrow seam beneath the needle.

On the Friday afternoon, four days after she'd started the pyjamas, she finished the buttonholes and sewed on the buttons. She'd deliberately hurried the last of the hand sewing. In the four

days, Mr Blackie had become weaker, and she knew that the
sooner the pyjamas were completed and put back in the camphorwood box out of sight, the sooner he would take an interest in food
and have the rest he needed.

She snipped the last thread and put the needle in its case.

'That's it, Herb,' she said, showing him her work.

He tried to raise his head. 'Bring them over here,' he said.

'Well—what do you think?' As she brought the pyjamas closer,
his eyes relaxed and he smiled.

'Try them on?' he said.

She shook her head. 'I got the measurements,' she said. 'They'll
be the right fit.'

'Better make sure,' he said.

She hesitated but could find no reason for her reluctance. 'All
right,' she said, switching on both bars of the electric heater and
drawing it closer to his bed. 'Just to make sure I've got the buttons
right.'

She peeled back the bedclothes, took off his thick pyjamas and
put on the silk. She stepped back to look at him.

'Well, even if I do say so myself, there's no one could have done
a better job. I could move the top button over a fraction, but apart
from that they're a perfect fit.'

He grinned. 'Light, aren't they?' He looked down the length of
his body and wriggled his toes. 'All the way from China. Never let
it out of me sight. Know that, Amy?'

'Do you like them?' she said.

He sucked his lips in over his gums to hide his pleasure. 'All
right. A bit on the tight side.'

'They are not, and you know it,' Mrs Blackie snapped. 'Never
give a body a bit of credit, would you? Here, put your hands
down and I'll change you before you get a chill.'

He tightened his arms across his chest. 'You made a right good
job, Amy. Think I'll keep them on a bit.'

'No.' She picked up his thick pyjamas.

'Why not?'

'Because you can't,' she said. 'It—it's disrespectful. And the
nurse will be here soon.'

'Oh, get away with you, Amy.' He was too weak to resist
further but as she changed him, he still possessed the silk with his
eyes. 'Wonder who made it?'

Although she shrugged his question away, it brought to her a
definite picture of a Chinese woman seated in front of a loom
surrounded by blue and silver silkworms. The woman was dressed

from a page in a geographic magazine, and except for the Oriental line of her eyelids, she looked like Mrs Blackie.

'D'you suppose there's places like that?' Mr Blackie asked.

She snatched up the pyjamas and put them in the box. 'You're the one that's been there,' she said briskly. 'Now settle down and rest or you'll be bad when the nurse arrives.'

The District Nurse did not come that afternoon. Nor in the evening. It was at half-past three the following morning that her footsteps, echoed by the doctor's sounded along the gravel path.

Mrs Blackie was in the kitchen, waiting. She sat straight-backed and dry-eyed, her hands placed one on top of the other in the lap of her dressing gown.

'Mrs Blackie. I'm sorry—'

She ignored the nurse and turned to the doctor. 'He didn't say goodbye,' she said with an accusing look. 'Just before I phoned. His hand was over the side of the bed. I touched it. It was cold.'

The doctor nodded.

'No sound of any kind,' she said. 'He was good as gold last night.'

Again, the doctor nodded. He put his hand, briefly, on her shoulder, then went into the bedroom. Within a minute he returned, fastening his leather bag and murmuring sympathy.

Mrs Blackie sat still, catching isolated words. Expected. Peacefully. Brave. They dropped upon her—neat, geometrical shapes that had no meaning.

'He didn't say goodbye.' She shook her head. 'Not a word.'

'But look, Mrs Blackie,' soothed the nurse. 'It was inevitable. You knew that. He couldn't have gone on—'

'I know, I know.' She turned away, irritated by their lack of understanding. 'He just might have said goodbye. That's all.'

The doctor took a white tablet from a phial and tried to persuade her to swallow it. She pushed it away; refused, too, the cup of tea that the district nurse poured and set in front of her. When they picked up their bags and went towards the bedroom, she followed them.

'In a few minutes,' the doctor said. 'If you'll leave us—'

'I'm getting his pyjamas,' she said. 'There's a button needs changing. I can do it now.'

As soon as she entered the room, she glanced at Mr Blackie's bed and noted that the doctor had pulled up the sheet. Quickly, she lifted the camphorwood box, took a needle, cotton, scissors, her spectacle case, and went back to the kitchen. Through the half-closed door she heard the nurse's voice, "Poor old thing," and she knew, instinctively, that they were not talking about her.

She sat down at the table to thread the needle. Her eyes were clear but her hands were so numb that for a long time they refused to work together. At last, the thread knotted, she opened the camphorwood box. The beauty of the silk was always unexpected. As she spread the pyjamas out on the table, it warmed her, caught her up and comforted her with the first positive feeling she'd had that morning. The silk was real. It was brought to life by the electric light above the table, so that every fold of the woven landscape moved. Trees swayed towards rippling water and peacocks danced with white fire in their tails. Even the tiny bridges—

Mrs Blackie took off her glasses, wiped them, put them on again. She leaned forward and traced her thumbnail over one bridge, then another. And another. She turned over the pyjama coat and closely examined the back. It was there, on every bridge; something she hadn't noticed before. She got up, and from the drawer where she kept her tablecloths, she took out a magnifying glass.

As the bridge in the pattern of the silk grew, the figure which had been no larger than an ant, became a man.

Mrs Blackie forgot about the button and the murmur of voices in the bedroom. She brought the magnifying glass nearer her eyes.

It was a man and he was standing with one arm outstretched, on the highest span between two islands. Mrs Blackie studied him for a long time, then she straightened up and smiled. Yes, he was waving. Or perhaps, she thought, he was beckoning to her.

PATRICIA GRACE   # A Way of Talking

Rose came back yesterday, we went down to the bus to meet her. She's just the same as ever Rose. Talks all the time flat out and makes us laugh with her way of talking. On the way home we kept saying, 'E Rohe you're just the same as ever.' It's good having my sister back and knowing she hasn't changed. Rose is the hard case one in the family, the kamakama one and the one with the brains.

Last night we stayed up talking till all hours even Dad and Nanny who usually go to bed after tea. Rose made us laugh telling about the people she knows, and taking off professor this and professor that from varsity. Nanny Mum and I had tears running down from laughing, e ta Rose we laughed all night.

At last Nanny got out of her chair and said, 'Time for sleeping. The mouths steal the time of the eyes.' That's the lovely way she has of talking Nanny, when she speaks in English. So we went to bed and Rose and I kept our mouths going for another hour or so before falling asleep.

This morning I said to Rose that we'd better go and get her measured for the dress up at Mrs Frazer's. Rose wanted to wait a day or two but I reminded her the wedding was only two weeks away and that Mrs Frazer had three frocks to finish.

'Who's Mrs Frazer anyway,' she asked. Then I remembered Rose hadn't met these neighbours though they'd been in the district a few years. Rose had been away at school.

'She's a dressmaker,' I looked for words. 'She's nice.'

'What sort of nice?' asked Rose.

'Rose don't you say anything funny when we go up there,' I said. I know Rose she's smart. 'Don't you get smart.' I'm older than Rose but she's the one that speaks out when something doesn't please her. Mum used to say Rohe you've got the brains but you look to your sister for the sense. I started to feel funny about taking Rose up to Jane Frazer's because Jane often says the wrong thing without knowing.

We got our work done had a bath and changed, and when Dad came back from the shed we took the station wagon to drive over to Jane's. Before we left we called out to Mum, 'Don't forget to make us a Maori bread for when we get back.'

'What's wrong with your own hands' Mum said but she was only joking. Always when one of us comes home one of the first things she does is make a big Maori bread.

Rose made a good impression with her kamakama ways and Jane's two nuisance kids took a liking to her straight away. They kept jumping up and down on the sofa to get Rose's attention and I kept thinking what a waste of a good sofa it was, what a waste of a good house for those two nuisance things. I hope when I have kids they won't be so hoha.

I was pleased about Jane and Rose. Jane was asking Rose all sorts of questions about her life in Auckland. About varsity and did Rose join in the marches and demonstrations. Then they went on to talking about fashions and social life in the city and Jane seemed deeply interested. Almost as though she was jealous of Rose and the way she lived, as though she felt Rose had something better than a lovely house and clothes and everything she needed to make life good for her. I was pleased to see that Jane liked my sister so much and proud of my sister and her entertaining and friendly ways.

Jane made a cup of coffee when she'd finished measuring Rose for the frock then packed the two kids outside with a piece of chocolate cake each. We were sitting having coffee when we heard a truck turn in at the bottom of Frazer's drive.

Jane said, 'That's Alan. He's been down the road getting the Maoris for scrub cutting.'

I felt my face get hot. I was angry. At the same time I was hoping Rose would let the remark pass. I tried hard to think of something to say to cover Jane's words though I'd hardly said a thing all morning. But my tongue seemed to thicken and all I could think of was Rohe don't.

Rose was calm. Not all red and flustered like me. She took a big pull on the cigarette she had lit, squinted her eyes up and blew the smoke out gently, I knew something was coming.

'Don't they have names?'

'What. Who?' Jane was surprised and her face was getting pink.

'The people from down the road who your husband is employing to cut scrub.' Rose the stink thing, she was talking all Pakehafied.

'I don't know any of their names.'

I was glaring at Rose because I wanted her to stop but she was avoiding my looks and pretending to concentrate on her cigarette.

'Do they know yours?'

'Mine?'

'Your name.'

'Well. Yes.'

'Yet you have never bothered to find out their names or to wonder whether or not they have any.'

The silence seemed to bang around in my head for ages and ages. Then I think Jane muttered something about difficulty, but that touchy sister of mine stood up and said, 'Come on Hera'. And I with my red face and shut mouth followed her out to the station wagon without a goodbye or anything.

I was so wild with Rose. I was wild. I was determined to blow her up about what she had done, I was determined. But now that we were alone together I couldn't think what to say. Instead I felt an awful big sulk coming on. It has always been my trouble sulking. Whenever I don't feel sure about something I go into a big fat sulk. We had a teacher at school who used to say to some of us girls, 'Speak, don't sulk'. She'd say, 'You only sulk because you haven't learned how and when to say your minds.'

She was right that teacher, yet here I am a young woman about to be married and haven't learned yet how to get the words out. Dad used to say to me, 'Look out girlie you'll stand on your lip.'

At last I said, 'Rose you're a stink thing.' Tears were on the way. 'Gee Rohe you made me embarrassed.' Then Rose said, 'Don't worry Honey she's got a thick hide.'

These words of Rose's took me by surprise and I realized something about Rose then. What she said made all my anger go away and I felt very sad because it's not our way of talking to each other. Usually we'd say, 'Never mind Sis,' if we wanted something to be forgotten. But when Rose said 'Don't worry Honey she's got a thick hide,' it made her seem a lot older than me and tougher, and as though she knew much more than me about the world. It made me realize too that underneath her jolly and forthright ways Rose is very hurt. I remembered back to when we were both little and Rose used to play up at school if she didn't like the teacher. She'd get smart and I used to be ashamed and tell Mum on her when we got home, because although she had the brains I was always the well behaved one.

Rose was speaking to me in a new way now. It made me feel sorry for her and for myself. All my life I had been sitting back and letting her do the objecting. Not only me, but Mum and Dad and the rest of the family too. All of us too scared to make known when we had been hurt or slighted. And how can the likes of Jane know when we go round pretending all is well. How can Jane know us?

But then I tried to put another thought into words. I said to Rose, 'We do it too. We say, "the Pakeha at the post office," or "the Pakeha doctor," and sometimes we mean it in a bad way.'

'Except that we talk like this to each other only. It's not so much *what* is said but *when* and *where* and in whose presence. Besides, you and I do not speak in this way now, not since we were little. It is the older ones. Mum, Dad, Nanny who have this habit.'

Then Rose said something else. 'Jane Frazer will still want to be your friend and mine in spite of my embarrassing her today, we're in the fashion.'

'What do you mean?'

'It's fashionable for a Pakeha to have a Maori for a friend.'

Suddenly Rose grinned. Then I heard Jane's voice coming out of that Rohe's mouth and felt a grin of my own coming. 'I have friends who are Maoris. They're lovely people. The eldest girl was married recently and I did the frocks. The other girl is at varsity. They're all so *friendly* and so *natural* and their house is absolutely *spotless.*'

I stopped the wagon in the drive and when we'd got out Rose started strutting up the path. I saw Jane's way of walking and felt a giggle coming on. Rose walked up Mum's scrubbed steps, 'Absolutely spotless.' She left her shoes in the porch and bounced into the kitchen. 'What did I tell you. Absolutely spotless. And a friendly natural woman taking new bread from the oven.'

Mum looked at Rose then at me. 'What have you two been up to? Rohe I hope you behaved yourself at that Pakeha place?'

But Rose was setting the table. At the sight of Mum's bread she'd forgotten all about Jane and the events of the morning.

When Dad, Heke and Matiu came in for lunch, Rose, Mum, Nanny and I were already into the bread and big bowl of hot corn.

'E ta,' Dad said. 'Let your hard working father and your two hard working brothers starve. Eat up.'

'The bread's terrible. You men better go down to the shop and get you a shop bread.' Rose.

'Be the day,' said Heke.

'Come on my fat Rohe. Move over and make room for your Daddy. Come on my baby shift over.'

Dad squeezed himself round behind the table next to Rose. He picked up the bread Rose had buttered for herself and started eating. 'The bread's terrible all right,' he said. Then Mat and Heke started going on about how awful the corn was and who cooked it and who grew it, who watered it all summer and who pulled out the weeds.

So I joined in the carryings on and forgot about Rose and Jane for the meantime. But I'm not leaving it at that. I'll find some way of letting Rose know I understand and I know it will be difficult for me because I'm not clever the way she is. I can't say things the same and I've never learned to stick up for myself.

But my sister won't have to be alone again. I'll let her know that.

PATRICIA GRACE

Between Earth and Sky

I walked out of the house this morning and stretched my arms out wide. Look, I said to myself. Because I was alone except for you. I don't think you heard me.

Look at the sky, I said.

Look at the green earth.

How could it be that I felt so good? So free? So full of the sort of day it was? How?

And at that moment, when I stepped from my house, there was no sound. No sound at all. No bird call, or tractor grind. No fire crackle or twig snap. As though the moment had been held quiet, for me only, as I stepped out into the morning. Why the good feeling, with a lightness in me causing my arms to stretch out and out? How blue, how green, I said into the quiet of the moment. But why, with the sharp nick of bone deep in my back and the band of flesh tightening across my belly?

All alone. Julie and Tamati behind me in the house, asleep and the others over at the swamp catching eels. Riki two paddocks away cutting up a tree he'd felled last autumn.

I started over the paddocks towards him then, slowly, on these heavy knotted legs. Hugely across the paddocks I went almost singing. Not singing because of needing every breath, but with the feeling of singing. Why, with the deep twist and pull far down in my back and cramping between the legs. Why the feeling of singing?

How strong and well he looked. How alive and strong, stooping over the trunk steadying the saw. I'd hated him for days, and now suddenly I loved him again but didn't know why. The saw cracked through the tree setting little splinters of warm wood hopping. Balls of mauve smoke lifted into the air. When he looked up I put my hands to my back and saw him understand me over the skirl of the saw. He switched off, the sound fluttered away.

—I'll get them, he said it quietly.

We could see them from there, leaning into the swamp, feeling for eel holes. Three long whistles and they looked up and started towards us, wondering why, walking reluctantly.

—Mummy's going, he said.

—We nearly got one, Turei said.—Ay Jimmy, ay Patsy, ay Reuben?

—Yes, they said.

—Where? said Danny.

I began to tell him again, but he skipped away after the others. It was good to watch them running and shouting through the grass. Yesterday their activity and noise had angered me, but today I was happy to see them leaping and shouting through the long grass with the swamp mud drying and caking on their legs and arms.

—Let Dad get it out, Reuben turned, was calling. —He can get the lambs out. Bang! Ay Mum, ay?

Julie and Tamati had woken. They were coming to meet us, dragging a rug.

—Not you again, they said taking my bag from his hand.

—Not you two again, I said. Rawhiti and Jones.

—Don't you have it at two o'clock.

—We go off at two.

—Your boyfriends can wait.

—Our sleep can't.

I put my cheek to his and felt his arm about my shoulders.

—Look after my wife, he was grinning at them.

—Course, what else.

—Go on. Get home and milk your cows, next time you see her she'll be in two pieces.

I kissed all the faces poking from the car windows then stood back on the step waving. Waving till they'd gone. Then turning felt the rush of water.

—Quick, I said. —The water.

—Water my foot, that's piddle.

—What you want to piddle in our neat corridor for? Sit down. Have a ride.

Helped into a wheelchair and away, careering over the brown lino.

—Stop. I'll be good. Stop I'll tell sister.

—Sister's busy.

—No wonder you two are getting smart. Stop. . . .

—That's it Mrs, you'll be back in your bikini by summer. Dr McIndoe.

—And we'll go water-skiing together. Me.

—Right you are. Well, see you both in the morning.

The doors bump and swing.

Sister follows. —Finish off girls. Maitland'll be over soon.

—All right sister.

—Yes sister. Reverently.

The doors bump and swing.

You are at the end of the table, wet and grey. Blood stains your pulsing head. Your arms flail in these new dimensions and your mouth is a circle that opens and closes as you scream for air. All head and shoulders and wide mouth screaming. They have clamped the few inches of cord which is all that is left of your old life now. They draw mucous and bathe your head.

—Leave it alone and give it here, I say.

—What for? Haven't you got enough kids already?

—Course. Doesn't mean you can boss that one around.

—We should let you clean your own kid up.

—Think she'd be pleased after that neat ride we gave her. Look at the little hoha. God he can scream.

They wrap you in linen and put you here with me.

—Well anyway, here you are. He's all fixed, you're all done. We'll blow. And we'll get them to bring you a cuppa. Be good. The doors swing open. —She's ready for a cuppa Freeman.

The doors bump shut.

Now. You and I. I'll tell you. I went out this morning. Look, I said, but didn't know why. Why the good feeling. Why, with the nick and press of bone deep inside. But now I know. Now I'll tell you and I don't think you'll mind. It wasn't the thought of knowing you, and having you here close to me that gave me this glad feeling, that made me look upwards and all about as I stepped out this morning. The gladness was because at last I was to be free. Free from that great hump that was you, free from the aching limbs and swelling that was you. That was why this morning each stretching of flesh made me glad.

And freedom from the envy I'd felt, watching him these past days, stepping over the paddocks whole and strong. Unable to match his step. Envying this bright striding. But I could love him again this morning.

These were the reasons each gnarling of flesh made me glad as I came out into that cradled moment. Look at the sky, look at the earth, I said. See how blue, how green. But I gave no thought to you.

And now. You sleep. How quickly you have learned this quiet and rhythmic breathing. Soon they'll come and put a cup in my hand and take you away.

You sleep, and I too am tired, after our work. We worked hard you and I and now we'll sleep. Be close. We'll sleep a little while ay, you and I.

VINCENT O'SULLIVAN **Mavvy Phoenix**

David opens the door as Tucker said he would and Tucker it seems has written to him, to tell him there's this friend coming, man, put out more flags. Once I'm inside his room he says, 'I knew you were on the way,' takes my bag from me, prances before me. There are posters on every wall and over the fireplace a strip of dung-coloured paper and across it and half mixed with the brown, white writing that says *Bartleby is Ahab with the Whale in his Pocket*. 'What it's all about,' David tells me, seeing me looking at it, 'that's the whole scene.' He puts his lips for a second to the corner of the brown. Then he says, 'Out here,' out on to the verandah at the back, clinking glasses as he steps behind me and where the shag is the bottle-opener, while I look over red tin and houses like matchboxes, the grass in the yard green as if I've never seen grass growing before.

That night we're still on the verandah. Several people come in, shake my hand. David unrolls each friend, a kind of scroll, *sotto voce*: 'Tony, now. Saw through it all, Tony,' his fingers for a moment on his friend's shoulder. His other hand circles a girl's wrist, pulls her closer to say hello to me properly. 'Maureen. She's Tony's, you know how it is, Mavros.' His black sleeves rolled up, a medal fallen out from the thick hairs inside his shirt, he is almost nose to my ear, telling me, 'Kathy, there. Like to give that a try?'

Two or three or four hours later when I put my hand flat over my half-filled glass he tells me, 'This'll help you then,' uncorking a bottle of dark red. Before or maybe after that bottle Francis arrives, Francis called Frank, O.K.? Frank's Coral, yes, friends of

Frank and Coral. Near the end of it all, Angelica, like a visitation.
David is saying that she lives here in the flat, not his bird or
anything, just a room she rents, no strings, Mavros, just friends.
'Works like a Trojan,' he finishes up, tells that to me, the Greek.
The beer and the red turn mean inside me and I'm dancing with
Frank's Coral, with Coral while there's still a very bad Mouskouri
song played over and over and hands clapping until David's bed
comes up like a small white beach on the other side of my breaker,
then Angelica seen as through water, not a foot from my head.
'For Christ's sake!' says the medal swinging into my half eyes,
'not there, eh? Don't chunder there, boy.' And David has hold of
me by one arm, Angelica by the other. And I'm thinking, last thing,
the walls a top humming about me, Oh Tucker, where have you
sent me?

Tucker and I worked the same shift, shared the same cabin. We
were the youngest stewards and because I am short and dark and
my English too precise, and Tucker has a hare-lip, we were men
alone. The others at first said like to play cards? or have a drink?
But we stayed outside because there was nothing inside worth
belonging to, a lot of pommie talk and a few fights and once a
knife-cut two inches long, the attacked man in sick-bay and a quiet
man who read the Bible locked out of our sight for the rest of the
voyage. Whenever Tucker talked it was about home, and he didn't
mind if I lay quiet, smoking while he told me night after night,
Parnell Herne Bay Ponsonby Mt Eden, his lovely places. He wore
a moustache that attracted more attention to his lip, and he talked
me into growing one. In a week mine was thicker and blacker, my
teeth very white beneath it when I smiled.

'You want to keep that,' Tucker said, 'they'll go for that sort of
thing.' Then two nights before we sailed into Sydney he gave me
more advice, my protector now his side of the world received us.
'Don't,' he advised me, 'don't make your English all that hot.
That's another thing they'll go for— not the way you talk good if
you want to.' It was ten o'clock and we leaned over the rail, the
night warm enough for Tucker to take off his shirt and let the
breeze move under his thin arms. He'd started the habit of drawing
his bottom teeth over the fringe of his moustache, so half of it
looked dipped in water when he talked. 'Man,' he said, 'that's some
town you'll be in next week.' As though to assure it, he handed me
a piece of folded paper. 'Look, this is a mate of mine. First thing
you do, you see him. He'll see you right.' Then a few minutes later,
straining to remember it all before he changed ships at Sydney,
'Now you won't forget what I told you about your accent, like?'

'O.K., Tucker,' I nodded, it's your town.'

'That, and the moustache bit. My mate'll do the rest for you.' And among the last instructions the next night, in his hare-lip voice and handing me one of the beer-cans he'd carried on deck, 'There's one more thing, you know.'

'What's that?'

'This Nick bit they call you on board.'

'What about it?'

'It'll have to go.'

'Change it, you mean?' I said to him. 'But it's only what they call me. It's not my real name.'

'But that's no good either. You can't be Joseph.'

'What would you recommend?'

'Something pretty way out,' he said. So I joked and asked him what he thought of Ephialtes, say. 'Oh yes,' he said, smiling down at the sea. 'Further out you make it the better, man.'

Next morning they bring coffee for me to drink in bed, and a piece of toast. Angelica stands next to David and she asks me if he's been lying to her. '*You* tell me what your name is, will you?' So I give them the ambience they long for, I am no mere Joseph. 'Call me Mavros,' I tell her.

'There,' David says, 'didn't I say he was Mavros?' For a second I am maybe ten years old and brand new from Ankara, my father (who is half-English, and partner in a company that exports olives and raisins and figs) returned to open a branch in my mother's country. It is my first day at a school near Nea Smyrna, a suburb that seems nothing but the smell of cement and the heavy move-ment of trucks in narrow streets. My accent is uncouth, I am fresh with the stink of Turks still on me, I am darker than the children of Athenian doctors and lawyers who ring me in. Accidentally I have crossed the path of their game, at once I am the thick-tongued, half-black centre of their shouting. One girl whose hand has veins like small blue tracks, under parchment skin, puts her finger to my face. Little black, she laughs, and her chorus takes it up, black, black. Mavros from Ankara, Mavros the accent. I would like time to let the memory hurt me more, or at the least make me angry, but AG (which is what David calls Angelica) asks me, for the second time, 'What's it mean? Does it mean anything?'

'No, just a name.'

'Like Greek for Maurice,' David tells her.

'Something like that, yes.'

She is content to accept that, and the household begins. Because I am Mavros the Greek from revolutions, I do not pay rent. From time to time I cook badly with much garlic and paprika, and David invites people specially to eat my meals. In front of visitors, David, and those who honour suffering, my accent labours at English. The greater my emotion, the heavier the demands upon my listeners. (Am I not in exile, unable to return to my country? To the city where my aged mother still sits in the evenings, her balcony towards the purple-blue range, once famous for honey?) Only with AG is the game already up. In private we speak a similar tongue, my English even, perhaps, a little better than hers. But she does not reprimand me—my little pretences she calls my social lies. This means they do not seep from the depths of a flawed character. I can help them, I could stop them, and so they are not to be regarded as me, but merely mine. And as for David my host, AG concedes that what I give him for my keep is far more than rent. I have added substance to his world, I have carried the barricades to his doorstep.

'Don't think I'm all talk,' David often says. He has a map of the city opened on the table, parts of it circled in red crayon. 'Planning anything like this takes time, you'd be the first one to know that.' He will light a cigarette, then again attend to his map. 'Action,' he says, 'that's what's going to come from it, Mavros.' His fist closes on the chain that holds his medal. 'How do you say that?'

'Say what?'

'Action.'

'In Greek you mean?' I tell him, and he holds the word for several repetitions, turns and turns its flavour. There is much coming and going of friends who talk about action. The word is written on the bricks around the fireplace in seven languages. One day David introduces me to a heavy Lithuanian, who added an eighth. The Lithuanian says nothing not suggested to him by a young political scientist, all hedgehog hair, all glasses. After several hours, made up of cool exposition interspersed with the grunts of experience, David confides in me, 'You probably wouldn't guess this, Mavros, *They're the key men.*'

Five out of every ten I met in the pub, at parties, or in David's flat, wanted me to tell them about the *coup,* or any torture stories I knew about the police, or songs I might know that had been smuggled out of prison. A fact which I found politic to keep to myself was that I had been with my father in Alexandria when the army took over. But at least I knew the names of streets and

squares. (I had stayed in Athens two months the year before, with
a friend from school in England who now earned his bread in the
Royal Gardens, snaring the anxious blonde males from the north
with his promises of the whole classical hog, although as a rule
he provided no more than the quick hand of friendship, or what
cognoscenti might call the oral tradition). These squares and streets,
where we had idled an entire spring, and early summer, were
where I set my adventures, the escapades and risks of a man for
whom fear was merely an incentive. So I'd say to David's friends
(trying to sound like a fish-shop Greek, to load each bad vowel with
pathos), 'The tunks, you know. That's when it was for real, friends.
Tunks from NATO ready to blow the arse'—carefully, I pronounce
it 'aahz'—'right off anyone who don't like Yunks or tunks or—'
and I grope for the word.

'Kernals. Say it like that, Mav.'

Thus I learned to say colonels like kernals, as David told me.
Then back at the flat he liked me to tell it again, as if we were
talking of a woman who demented him. He'd be on the verandah
with his knee under his chin and his fingers mining in the side of
his shoe. His eyes when anywhere were right beyond what he called
the big titty island, past the dull blue harbour, and when I'm
talking I know it's like when he's lying back with mary jane with
the match in the end and his special records playing. 'Special, this
one, Mav,' he'd say. There were no red tin roofs, no quiet streets
once the specials started. It was poster time and revolution time
and when he lay flat on the floor his fist was folded on top of his
head, as if only that kept it on. 'Mav, Mav,' he might say. And
he'd make me tell him again the Greek word for Freedom. He'd
say it between his teeth while Hendrix the special rolled his lovely
black feet in his sad guilty whiteman's face.

'I don't ever want you to talk to me about politics, Mavros.' I
have my eyes shut but she says, 'I know you're awake and I never
want politics.'

'O.K.' I keep my eyes closed.

'They're trivial.'

'O.K.'

'They presume virtue is on one side.'

I feel up for her breast shading a few inches above me. 'Like,'
she goes on, 'I don't care for talking about violence.' I lose her
next sentence. My head is on her lap and I turn my nose to truffle
in her generous belly, the pearl-smooth belly of AG my mistress of
three days or rather three nights standing, AG for Angelica Grace

or (what is David's joke) for Avant Garde. She is fattish and clever and in bed is a dogfight made from silkiest putty. 'She is a country that never hates its army,' I say to David, when I talk about her. 'She is a noose necks yearn for.'

'Too much, Mavvy,' he shouts. When I speak like this his eyes screw up and his flattened palms press against the sides of his head. My words delight him like coloured birds in front of a child. He is at once effusive when I tell him that AG has taken to me, has deserted her Canadian lover for—as he seriously says—an older continong. So to show my host some gratitude I say bits to him that I remember from the litany, scraps from when my mother stood on the other side of the church with the blackveiled women and I was waiting only to be out, to meet once the praying's over my uncle who played draughts with me, and drank coffee thick as treacle. I speak of Gold and Ivory, Tower and Ark, until AG shimmers like an enamel angel, and David, almost sobbing 'That's it, Mavvy, that's loving for you!' has to sit down and stamp his feet, 'Too much, too much.'

Her hand touches my head, her little finger an insect in my ear. My tongue skims her skin and my nose nests in her plump thighs. *I am dove returned* (I think for David later on), *I am Mavvy Phoenix.*

'Like I don't care for talk about torture, which distinguishes too sharply between principle, and vanity. Or religion, which is always comparative.'

'O.K.' I filter.

'What are you saying?'

Swimmer-like I mouth sideways for air. 'I said O.K.' Then AG takes a firmer grip on my skull. She mutters above me like a cleric behind a screen.

'My uncle,' AG informs me one afternoon, 'he's dying to meet you.'

'Meet me?'

'Meet the Greek you're inside of,' she says. 'Or vice versa.'

Her uncle is Strevens, one time Labour M.P., collector of coins and medals, bachelor. His niece claims for him a youthful senility. In two days time we are standing in his livingroom, the windows closed although the tar at the side of his path is melting in the heat. The man is redolent of cats and yellowing papers. Delphi, he accosts me as soon as we shake hands, summer of '30, his first year down. Clouds over Europe blank and frightening as a wall. Yet for all that Delphi still the navel. The uncontaminated source . . . His

speech is staccato, his hands here, there, one fingernail on the edge
of a coin, or index finger smoothing the side of a wax-yellow nose
Fortunately my father's dubious Ankara moneys had overpaid the
English to teach me classics. Homer in consequence remains what
makes a tall man with a limp and almost no hair lick his finger
before he turns a page; Virgil a vision more in focus for the eyes
of a near albino than for boys (I the only foreigner) troubled (if
like me) by tumescence in heavy serge, in every season.

'Why on earth,' asks Strevens, 'why on earth leave there? Leave
all that?' The back of his hand flicks along his shelves. 'And for
this,' a finger to the double window opposite the bookshelves, out
to the slope of a hill partly converted to a children's playground.
AG saves my having to answer with her talk of experience and
new horizons. 'Romantic, Romantic,' he smiles at his clever niece,
at his niece's Old World lover.

'Once the chance,' he informs me, 'once we had our chance.'
With one finger kept in a book as if only that will preserve it, he
narrates that golden hour. 'Before you were born,' he says, 'before
Angelica.' And after a moment's nostalgia, 'On the verge of something big, you must take my word for it. For three years, maybe
four.' Another silence. 'Oh,' he laughs, 'then the people clamoured
against those who led them.'

'What happened?' AG prompts.

'Thersites was returned,' he says. We leave it at that, until later
his niece tells me, 'It's always of politics, his party out, another in.
Or something like that. The details get confusing, but it's the same
grief.' That was why in disappointment (he enjoys confessing) he
took to coins. 'Swam from the sea of public abuse to a more pacific
pontos,' I say, to cheer him up. His smile lingers several minutes
and AG, her fingers immoderate while he is out fetching glasses,
says in admiration, 'He's eating out of your palm, Mavros. You old
wog.'

'She is absolute,' David had told me. And she was his clenched
fist, clenched teeth, the rough side of his jeans punched four, five
times. Then he began to chant a poem he calls *All Time Rides
One Outflowering*, which begins with Time like an exploding
firework, jet on jet from centre, and ends

> If I close my eyes
> That jet behind my eyes
> On the velvet inside my eyes
>   Is fresh, Is ever.

'That's hers, Mavvy,' he says.

'Hers?'

'AG's. Wrote it herself.'

So I said, 'AG, tell me about your poems,' and she says, 'Mavros, what the hell?' and then laughs when I say, 'Fireworks outflowering.' It's all the poetry she's ever written, but David had thought Too much, and had it by heart. She insisted the poem was nothing, but kindles to her thesis which is about Time. Time (AG explained what now I summarize) time is not circular not tending towards the eternal not part of the eternal not even an unfolding ribbon. It is none of these things, she instructs me. So next thing I say is, 'Then tell me what it is, my love.' Instead I am told that an epic from 2000 or 200 years ago is not so relevant as one hair on her arm held up to sunlight. (She lifts her arm—again she is sitting up and my head again in her lap—and her left breast raises a slow balloon because it is her left arm raised. Then it swings back from argument, across my face like cargo to its hold.) Everything is not just relative but *so* relative nothing exists which is not and what is is *Absolute*.

'You make all that up?' I ask her.

'I Am Who Am and Berkeley crossed,' she smiles.

'O.K., O.K.,' I say. And I cram my mouth chocker with Alpha and Gamma.

My life thus became a rich triangle. Tickled or rubbed or struck squarely centre, it was resonant and full. Its apices of course were David-AG-Strevens. In that line between David and AG, grass and pubs and revolution; between AG and her uncle, intellect and body drew parallel joy; between Strevens and David (to return whence I began) I swam the social spectrum like a fish through multi-coloured streams. And on one occasion at least I felt the full triangle, splendidly complete. AG was meditating, her head against the wall, her accoutrements untrussed. I lay as customary in her lap, my lips from time to time engrossed in small devotions. At AG's feet, and parallel to myself, David in Che-beret and chewing a butt, observed not in the least my mild venery, but rode the tracks of Cuban folklorico, a special. And in my hand the telephone through which Uncle Strevens invites me to dinner with the dean of the Law School, and a schismatic bishop. (All my own year, Strevens assures me, our sort of chaps.) Carefully I say to myself, no, Mavros, there is still more to life than this, yet AG, who listened as she meditated, whispered *consummatum est* as she took the receiver from my hand, and reached it up to its cradle.

When David says 'Key Men' he means in the S.F.P. This is Strike For the People, each capital in a third of a round badge, the letters anti-clockwise ('nothing is done except against the current'), the divisions red, yellow, black. The key men met at David's two nights a week. Always there is the Lithunian, although I never hear speak. His young friend from political science presents his earnestness for him. Once I say mockingly to AG, 'That fellow's glasses steam up before he's been talking half a minute.' 'He generates fervour,' she corrects. I begin to suspect that once he was her lover. Similarly, I suspect a great Zambian called Havelock was not, and that he cherishes intentions. Havelock came first with Frank, whose Coral I danced myself sick with on my very first night. He taps the fingers of both hands on the edge of whatever solid surface is closest to him. Several times I have spoken to him, without courtesy, or even marked distaste, in return. His eyes eat AG.

If I am at home when the key men call, I prefer to sit in AG's room, fondling her feet while she reads, or if she works at her desk, I pass from time to time to kiss the crown of her head, or sit by myself, threading worry-beads I have made from a rosary I found under her bed. And one week I read a small blue-covered history which purports to be of a country I cannot believe is this.

I have been in the flat perhaps eight weeks when the bronze plate is blown from the Brazilian Consulate. The newspapers show a businessman standing near a small hole in a large expanse of wall. His hand has disappeared to the other side, through the hole. The headlines, in the language of bomb-wreck and panic, speak of diplomacy outraged. When I walk home from taking drycleaning down town for AG, David is lying on the floor, a special turning within inches of his ear. The morning paper is over his face, although there is no strong light, no flies. Another page of the paper is opened double, covering him from chest to knees. As the record ends David throws the paper from him, sits up to smile.

'Jeeza Christ!' I say. David is wearing *a suit and a polka dot tie.* There is also a watch dangling from his waistcoat, a carnation set in his jacket. I think he is married, that this is his surprise. I take the hand he stretches towards me, unsure must I congratulate him, simply help him to his feet. He kisses me on both cheeks, looks me in the eyes.

'We're eating big, Mavvy. On me.' We are David, AG, the political scientist, Frank and Coral, Havelock, myself. (The Lithuanian has left town, but sends his wishes.) Eating big it is, as David promised, eating eight or ten storeys high, candles on the table, bows from the waiters. We are all dressed fine. AG wears virgin white, her dress scooping her to erotic bunches, that Havelock is never so immersed in oysters, in steak, in champagne, to remove his eyes. And why all this, says David, because he loves us all, loves me Mavvy and her AG and them the other four. The world is beautiful you have only to look down there and see it, black satin water, pearls on the harbour. We are love and youth and comrades, we soar above the city. By champagne eight or maybe nine AG is the eel of paradise slipping my nets, Havelock is treading the shores of my domain. But (as God willed it) Havelock must be put into a taxi, his head lolled, a sweet chain of saliva from mouth to lapel, the car shared with Frank and Coral. The political scientist walks off, alone, brave with his ideals, into Auckland night. Hand in hand, David, AG, myself, sing and dance the road from the hotel to Grafton, down the sloping trees to David's flat. Then I am singing perhaps too loud the praises of my divesting eel, shouting allelulia to one liberated hemisphere, enjoining Rejoice, ye peoples, as I uncup the other. For once AG exists unclever, no more (once I have pulled the looped cord above her bed) than white and silver woman, shoulders and hair against her moonstruck window. She chants antiphonal to her own bright praises. David is on the other side of the thin wall, drumming naked feet about level with my right ear, my consort's left, 'Too much, Mavvy, too much,' above the drumming.

Next day I was not well enough for Strevens's dinner. It is a week later when I sit facing the wax nose, the uneasy hands, the lines from Homer. Of course I was generous with my smiles, I ladled out my accent. Twice he closed his eyes, and asked me to read out bits he had underlined in very light pencil. I had taken him a bottle of ouzo, not the Australian crap but the real thing, mine that very day from a steward on the *Patris,* in return for Parnell addresses that did not exist. 'For you,' I told him.

'Extremely large of you, Mavros,' he said. His mouth puckered with feeling. As if in return for *his* hospitality, I gave him the lines from Book One that I had learned at school. 'Again?' he asked, his head tilted, eyes closed. So I came again, with Athena being taken into the big hall before Telemachus clicks to who she is, with her grey eyes and wanting to sit away from the others, just herself and him and the big gold bowls and the roasted meat. 'That's very beautiful,' he said. 'I must thank you for that, too, Mavros.' We drank the ouzo, slowly, as I thought, but too quickly for my Philhellene. We eat nuts and I piled the best part of 2 doz.

olive pips on the little dish he had provided for them. Then he told
me for the third time about that day at Delphi as a young man,
before he realized where the omphalos was, and he'd heard this
noise that he'd not heard before (a kind of heavy sibilance not
unlike skis on snow, he said to make it plainer), and next thing
there was the first snake he had ever seen, flickering between the
dry stalks, behind *the* rock. 'Pure coincidence,' he smiled. 'But it
elated, Mavros. Elated.'

'I can understand that, sir,' I said. Another ouzo, and he confessed more. Before he knew it himself, I could see how the drink
was hitting him. Twice he dropped his cigarette, and then he was
away talking about Sappho the lesy and on about the loveliness of
the *Symposium,* and when he was out of his chair as I thought to
make for the toilet (that still is not an impossible thought) he was
stumbling against me, his stiff fingers against my black shirt. I put
him back in his chair, gave him what was left of the bottle like
feeding a sick child, my hand behind his head, glass tipped to his
lips. David took it more seriously than I did. When I told him later
he said I should have given him the old knee-in-the-cods' routine.
'That'd bring him up short,' he said. And at him too, at my friend
David I smile, and remind him of this, how we have managed
Strevens for three millenia.

I leave Streven's quiet street to meet AG at the S.F.P. party.
There is a light in only one room and there are too many people
for the house. Havelock the Zambian (whose uncle Strevens said is
a diplomat in Canberra) tells a girl that he is a political refugee. He
is more than six feet tall in his darkglasses and I am Mediterranean
obsequious not to provoke him. I stand pressed against him saving
nothing and AG kneels between our feet. Europa between the West
and pagan lust. Then policemen are in the room, more lights
turned on, a sergeant saying (as people say policemen say), Orlright,
whose party's this?

'Jeeza Christ,' I venture, 'bad news, Havelock.'

'You shut up,' Havelock tells me. 'You shut up when you see
fuzz.'

At once I regret my Greek liberator moustache, which draws the
sergeant like a magnet. He touches my arm and asks me my name.
'Name?' I say, and he shouts back to me, yes, don't I understand
name? I smile and say masturbator and mother-defiler to him in a
foreign tongue. He attempts to take down these words when David
forces himself between us, ready to fight them all for my sake.

'You don't know what a man can go through,' he says to them.
'You're too bloody thick to know a man when you see one!'

Inevitably they drag him out and he kicks one in the shin and
screams 'Elevtheria! Elevtheria!' until his arm twisted up his back
squeaks him breathless. I think what am I to do now, now my
friend, my host, is manhandled by police? But the policeman I had
accused of vileness comes back with a superior. One on either side
of me, I am taken to a police car, to a grey tomb-like building, a
gleaming desk.

An officer faces me across the desk. 'Your writing?' he asks me.
I look down and see the Greek letters for 'Freedom' on a piece of
scorched paper. I tell them, 'The third letter from the end is back
to front.' The officer says, 'Cut being smart, son,' so I say nothing
until David kicks and shouts, shouts even louder in this room than
he did at the party. 'He's innocent, you bloody swine!'

It is not enough that David confessed, that the Brazilian consul
requested the police not to press charges, or that I am now set
free. AG has shifted from the flat. She left no message, there is no
sign of flight, yet she does not return. Havelock I cannot raise
through friends or enquiries at his hostel, and I fear for my ring-
dove, my double-dyed slut. Her uncle, pederast and sybarite, has
sent me a note: he is pained at my want of finesse, and asks me to
return a rare and rotten translation of a dirty Latin book, which of
course I have torn to pieces, and burned. The ashes, mixed with
facecream, I have thrown into a drawer of his niece's clothes. And
now for two days I have sat on David's verandah, in this time
eating no more than half a pound of bacon, and drinking only tea.
None of David's friends have approached me, and half a dozen
times an hour I pray May the True God curse them, yet I feel no
relief. Am I to be treated like a pig, because I know an alphabet?

Also I have been saying to myself simple sentences of Arabic I
remember from when my father was posted in Alexandria (grills on
the window of my white-washed, black-beamed room, my learning
to count on an abacus, prayermats rolled in the corner). I do not
recall a great deal, but enough. Enough which includes a maimed
cat the servants called 'The much-persecuted one'—now an appropriate name for a man who is fleeing war. David's carefully stacked
piles of *Time* have given me ample background, and twice I have
heard him deplore the Australians for their hardness of heart
towards the Jews. Today I am on the verandah for the last time,
sewing what was once a private garment of Angelica's into the
likeness of an Arab headpiece, And this afternoon I shall book a
plane to Sydney, where I have the address of Tucker's friends.

MICHAEL HENDERSON

Freedom's Ramparts

January 1 1954. This is the First day I have had a diary to enlist in. This diary was given me by the kindness of Granpa, Dr Ernest Happenstance. It is a special doctor's diary, so each day has a medicine. Now for my recordings. Nice day at beach. Had 3 swims. Dad accompnied us in one. Had big bonfire last night to celebrate New Year. Water was phosferescent.
                                      CALCIUM-S: *Allergic states*

Once bronze fists called Victoria—*long to reign over us!*—annexed the toilet fixture tight at the level of his upcrouched eyes, the virginal scroll ever giving cause to sing with heart and voice *God Save the Queen!* And he, holding fast to the high cold throne while parental steps patrolled the linoleum court, learned too soon the joys of monarchy; he was an infant despot wielding a septic sceptre, leaning victorious on the ancient plunge flush in that inaugural dike and disposing the common law of his people's principality. No such thing as a wet bed, plague and dearth, no fowls to be fed, aeroplanes could not find him. He launched his dream raft and turned all his woes to mirth.

January 15, 1954. 11.20 a.m. Amazing sight rendered us from the heavens. In the midst of reading, excited cackling from the ducks roused me and upon looking out the window I saw large vapour trails headed by some object, beyond explanation, at an amazing speed. Three objects were seen. Newspaper report: 'Royal Air Force Vampires flying at 400 m.p.h. at 35,000 feet.' MESANTOIN: *Psychomotor seizures. January 16. Went to Nelson to see Queen. After a very interesting proccession of floats we had lunch with my Granpa, Dr Ernest Happenstance. Shortly after 2 o'clock the Queen drove past allowing a quick glimpse.* CALCIBRONAT: *Rhume des foins. Notes. We must remember the 16th was the day of the Queen's visit to Nelson. It was a typical Nelson day, on the 16th, hot sunny and cloudless. On the way to Nelson all cars were held behind an endless stream of cars. I did not get a medal because I did not go with my old school class (Std. 4). All the school got a medal a flag and a QE2 ice block.*

Neither at school could they get him there. Not the masters smelling of chalk, strange blunted men with their pencils in their pockets. Not Jerp nor Straight nor Piles nor Sack. Not one of those blackboard dusters. Nor Scrooge nor Greasy nor Hori nor Fungus. No not one of those dry-cleaned gaffers could enter his dike *built by Nature for herself* and say Now Look Here Young Man When I Was Your Age I Read The Dictionary. Reassuring us on our spiteful behinds. *Vivant professores!* Vivant Scobie, Shag and Moon! Let sense be dumb, let flesh retire—he who would valiant be 'gainst all disaster, let him incontinently wallow the master!

Nor the boys smelling of morning milk, blobs who clotted together. They could not get him there though they might knee-see his feet and lob water overtop. There he sat divining the patterns in the concrete, praying he was in The Team for Saturday. *February 27. In morning play cricket for C team. Go in last man score 0 not out. Did not bowl. Clubs in morning as usual.* PURSENNID: *Atonic constipation.* There after lights out the chocolate-chippie read unconfiscated books. *Notes. Books read during April Man Alone worth 4/5 Down in the Drink 3/5 Merchant of Venice (School) 4/5. Notes. Every night pranks in dorm are numberless: Pillow fighting, throwing slippers, stripping beds, fighting, arguing, throwing property outside etc.* While there on his dike—*Sanctify our every pleasure!*—he read The Perfumed Garden and waterlogged his dream raft, O balsa balsam, balm of Mecca, Hercules' inceptive labour, flowering *Impatiens Balsamina!*—for when golden youth is wed, and in marriage our joys are dead, *nos habebit humus, nos habebit humus.*

Pavilioned in splendour, he let the name calling assembly rant on. Father Son and Holy Ghost. Pilate's voice called your name and Dangle Smith's and Smoothie Gascoyne's and Hangman Harper's and Corkscrew Coney's and Dropsy Duncan's and Glorious God's. These People Report. Do Shall Did Not. Onn Up. Stand Up. Hands Up. Line Up. Speak Up. Shut Up. Socks Up. *Ad Alta.* Fear Not The Heights. With Three Times Three Shout Lustily. World Without Amen. Follow Up. On Your Balls! *Adeste Fideles.* Sing Up. *Alleluia.* Once More Boys. On Our Balls! On Our Balls! We'll Shout As We Roll On Our Balls! Send Forth A Proud Rajah! Never The Battle Raged Hottest But In It! Lest We Forget Uprightness. Lest We Forget *Probitas.* Lest We Forget. They turned the calendar of his teens with dippoldic digits until the days stuck; with paraphiliac prohibition inspissated tongues saccharined the moth of youth until be sank twinkle twinkle little star while they sang god defend new zealand *in the nations' Butcher van selling beef and* Truth *to man,* until on his dike he— O still the small voice of alarm—sang *Set down my name, Sir. Sitfast. I'll fear not what men say. They do but themselves. My strength the more is.*

February 18. Every morning we have a cold shower and then practise clubs, which you have to swing like a bag-pipes dumb major. METHERGIN: *Post-partum period.* Dumb-bells, clubs, hakas, military parade, church parade, fagging, fatigues, hard labour, fives, showers, prep, first bell, cross country, second bell, boxing, prayers, preparing young men, roll call, preparing young men to be Old Boys, bend over, face the wall, bending young men to be Upright old boys. *March 20. Schedled to play for C's against Old Boys, who did not arrive, so had pick up game between ourselves.* DIGILANID: *Paroxysmal tachycardia.* Reading under the blankets with a Woolworth's torch; talking after lights out. *February 16. Caned in pyjamas by Mr Algernon, commonly known as 'Fungus Face' or 'Fungus Bum'.* OPTALIDON: *Antalgique non stupéfiant.* Talking in prep, talking in assembly, talking in church, talking in English. Gated. *March 23. We, the new boys, are suffering count- less amounts of shoes, cricket boots, shirts, socks, jockstraps, foot- ball jerseys, etc. to clean* for Great Seniors! *Ha! Ha! They send us to shops for whitebait hooks and left-handed pocket knifes. By end of this month we have to know by heart College Song, Board of Governors, Cowdeamus, School motto, God Defend NZ, 1st XI, House XI, and what is on the sundial. If you do not know, the old boys cane you. They make you put your head in a tuck locker. Or go in the Drying Room or boiler room. If you stay on the dike you can not be tested.* PLEXONAL: *Terreur nocturne.* Report in, report out. *March 22. School parades in cadet companies to see film on Royal Coming at Majestic Theatre. Am in F Company.* HYDERGINE: *Arteriosclerosis obliterans.* No crew-cuts, no Yul Brynners. *Notes. Every morning now we have clubs in squads. Clubs—at which hopeless. March 2. Clubs. Usual school work. Cadets. Practise clubs murderously during day. Have been at Col- lege 4 weeks today.* BELLADENAL: *Peptic ulcer. March 4. Fine day with shifty breeze. Clubs. Ordinary school day. Caned by Algernon. Practise for C's in nets. Violin practise. Bible-class.* CALCIUM-S OINTMENT: *Dermatitis. March 31. Clubs. School. Military parade. Violin Practise. Caned twice by Mr Sawney-Beane for playing with ruler and not saying sir.* BELLERGAL: *Acrodynie infantile.* Squads.

Quad. Physical reject. Shooting. Life saving. Debating. *April 3.
Sports Day. Dad comes in morn. In afternoon I run in 100yds
under 12. Governor General presents prices. After dinner Dad
leaves for home. I cryed profusely. Caned by Buttons for not
cleaning his sports gear enough.* HYDERGINE: *Dead fingers* One
man had one talent, another had two. Pull your talons out. *April
25. Holiday, but we have to parade in Anzac Day parade. Headmaster saluted as College Band played God defends NZ. Buttons
and other seniors attacked demonstrators.* CALCIUM-S: *États
allergiques. Notes.* The Headmaster said this fight for the War
Memorial was in our War Record. He made Buttons R.S.M. At
the mowing down of our sons and in the mourning we shall
remember Buttons. *May 6. Home for Holidays:—Hooray!!!! Catch
8.45 Newmans bus, arrive home safely. Been away 93 days in all.
Bevan sick in bed with German meals. Beaut to be home.* ALLI-
SATIN: *Infectious intestinal catarrh.* Report in. Roll call. First bell.
Second bell. Second term. Lights out. *May 25. Back at College.
Military parade for resumtion. Two new boys arrived from Chch.
Moved to dorm 6 so as 2 new boys can stay together.* HYDERGINE:
*Intermittent claudication. June 2. First Dancing class for me
(Alright).* STROPHOSID: *Paroxysmal nocturnal dyspnoea. June 3.
Gym:—hurt wrist, pissed off. There is now alot of mumps going
round, & we think that if theres a few more we might be able to
go home! Mr Algernon confiscated my book.* HYDANTAL-S:
Jacksonian seizures. Boaters, waistcoats, collar and studs to
church: do not buy Sports Post and do not go by Crouse. *June 6.
1st XV play Wellington Old Boys. (Am Ballboy). Buttons gave
me all his gear to wash after the game. School sees 'D-day, sixth
of June'. We have to know School haka, house haka, 1st XV,
house XV, forty years on and all the prefects by heart. The only
way not to be reached is to stay in the dike. Three chaps in San.
in our dorm. Kerr, Jack, Pahar. Who will be next? Quite alot of
sickness. Join Drama Club, hope it will be worthwhile. Campbell's
Kingdom 4/5.* BELLERGAL: *Anxiété.* Dumb-bells. Hakas. Preparing
young men to be old boys. *Tempus fugit. Pietas probitas et
sapientia. July 3. Brown I was 4 wrong in Pick the All Blacks:—
Bowers Elsom Hill Pryor diffed out. Mr. Norman McKenzie says 5
fundamentalls of Rugby are:—1. Tackle balls and all. 2. Kick balls
with both feet. 3. Dribble. 4. Fall on balls. 5. Catch all types and
pass. (Buttons says to learn well all these).* CALCIBRONAT: *Post-
concussional disorders.* Clean shoes clean mind. Sixpence in the
church plate. *August 9. Junior Speaking, have quite a crap. After
school have kicks with football. Dancing. Go up rifle range in drill*

*period for 1st. time. Don't do to bad, get 52/100. (Experience will
tell.) Do Hard labour for Algernon, shovelling coke and grubbing
gorse on Grampians. Bible-class.* HYDERGINE: *Troubles circula-
toires cérébraux. August 15, Sunday. Church. Drama Club
rehearsal. Go off alright. First time I've had make up on.* CALCIUM-
S: *Exudative conditions.* Dotheboys' Balls. *September 20. Royal
Air Force Vampire came over at about 1.40 p.m. School stayed
out to watch. Had super views of it has it came over us three
times. Supposed to be very powerful plane. Headmaster saluted
under school flag. Military parade instead of cross-country run, to
celebrate. Afterwards play Brown I and King II in fives. Then
bible-class.* HYDERGINE: *Insuffisance coronarienne.* Dining-room
maids out of bounds. Fifteen minutes after the dance. Fifteen
inches between partners. *Vivant omnes virgines!* Hands off. Hands
up. Bend over. Uprightness. *Vivat Alma Mater! September 25.
Cold showers in morning supervised by Mr Algernon. Buttons
caught me walking on seniors path. Massed choir practise after
tea. New headmaster announced. A Mr Bercich. He will move in
next Feb. All we know is he has a good war record and was a
colonel and is in Territorialls. Mr Marfell fainted during tea. At
lights out Jerp told us Mr Marfell had been a batchelor to long.*
PARTERGINE: *Induction de l'accouchement. Note. Jerp is our
housemaster. He said we do not now how the Nelson mother's
scheme for their daughters. Only Prefects may walk past Crouse.
Note. Crouse is the Girls' College.* The Power of The Badge.
Respect all badges: Prefect R.S.A. Boy Scout Rotary Rosicrucians
Round Table M.R.A. Lions Royal Overseas League Y.M.C.A.
Salvation Army Royal NZ Vampire Force Navy League L.M.V.D.
P.P.T.A. *October 9, Saturday. Muck around all day. Had book
confiscated. That night 'Cantate Domino' in concert with National
Orchestra in Assembly Hall. Have pretty bad cold, my nose bled
alot.* FERRONICUM: *Essential hypochromic anaemia. October 15.
During morning, rehearsal for tomorrow nights' Music Festival.
Have still got pretty bad cold, can't seem to get rid of it.* CEDI-
LANID: *Auricular fibrillation. October 16, Saturday. Fine to wet.
That night Music Festival. (Was in 4 items.) (Of the prefects—
Blundle is pissing me off now.)* CALCIBRONAT: *Sédatif et neuro-
équilibrant. October 20. Finals of boxing: Brown I did well out of
our house. After tea, house music competitions. We sang 'Rule
Britannia' and we were second.* MESANTOINE: *Epilepsie—Grand
mal. October 30, Saturday. Wet day. The weather has pissed me
off lately—. In morning wash clothes. Meet Brown II's father,
General Brown, who is Chief of N.Z. scouts. In afternoon (too wet*

Michael Henderson

for cricket) others go to pictures but I Do preparation of form magazine. A bit off a piss off of a day. CALCIUM-S: *Piqûres et morsures d'insectes. November 20, Saturday. Only 27 days to end of first year! Buttons caned me for not knowing clubs. MEM:— Write to Gran, home. SWOT. (Write to:—Secretary French Consul French legation, Wellington, for Facts on france.* OPTALIDON: *Céphalées. November 22. School certificate begins for fifth formers. Just think, in four years I'll have to sit . . . ! What a crap! Jerp tore up book I was reading. Past-Present cricket match. The whole house has been gated on General Principle. Hard labour for me: wash quad with scrubbing brush.* BELLAFOLINE: *Spastic constipation. November 28, Sunday. Bloody piss off of a day. Nobody in the House is aloud out after College Service. Just muck around. Today Brown II learnt he didn't have a father and through a wobbly. Brown I isn't really his brother either. He wasn't meant to learn but he saw one of Jerp's papers.* PARTERGINE: *Uterine inertia. December 6. Annual Physical measurements—which are, unfortunately, a bit of an embarrassment to me. I seem to be a naturally light and thin boy—but I am becoming increasingly unheeding and unworrying over physical appearance: anything anyone says etc. I got 5/- from the Quiz Kids for having a question selected—it was answered. Then I was sent some french material and had a letter from Uncle Thrumbull. MEM—Write letter one prep night to Uncle Thrumbull telling all news.* MESANTOIN: *Electro-shock therapy. December 10. Caned for being out of bounds, also for not wearing cap, by Algernon. Find out I have won a prize for drawing. I was very pleased and surprised.* SCILLAREN: *Portal cirrhosis with ascites.* One man had five, another ten, another one. To every man according to his.

All This Free To The Age Of Nineteen!

June 6, 1956 Buttons caned me for not knowing God defends New Zealand. Am considering writing book. HYDERGINE: *Labile hypertension.*

MICHAEL HENDERSON   # The Dead Bush

'Keep the dogs in.'

The man went around the cattle. Then he was indistinct in the dark.

The boy listened to the birds. Then the wires snapped one by one.

'Come on,' called the man.

The boy felt his way over the logs and through the fern and rocks. He came up behind the cattle and drove them through the gap in the fence. The man tapped their backs with his crook as he counted them. They took a long time to go through. The man shouted for the dogs to shut up and stay behind.

'Hear the morepork?' asked the boy.

'Laughing owl,' said the man.

'Owl?'

'They live in the Park. Everything lives in the Park.'

They lugged the fence back across the opening.

An invisible owl laughed overhead.

On the other side of the fence the cattle were eating already.

'Will we have to pay?' asked the boy.

'Just listen to those birds,' said the man.

'Will we get the cattle back?' asked the boy.

'Twice as many again.'

'They won't die out there?'

'Die out there? In the Park? Goodness me, they're in seventh heaven!'

The boy stood with his hands between the barbs on the fence. Matai, miro and totara made a second storey of bush, while the tallest rimus were skyscrapers with smudgy balconies of orchid and fern. Supplejack hung like licorice.

'Listen to the woodhens,' said the boy.

'Yes,' said the man, 'those are woodhens.'

Several invisible owls flew and laughed high overhead.

'They're spooky,' said the boy.

'They like the dark,' said the man. 'That's all. Now help me with the fence.'

The boy bent down feeling about for the wire. He bumped against the man.

'Owls like dark nights,' said the man.

Together in the dark they could have been the same person.

A long-drawn cry, plaintive and clear, came from near or far.

'What's that?' cried the boy.

'A cuckoo,' said the man. 'It should have gone.'

'Gone?' said the boy.

'They come for summer,' said the man.

'Where do they go?' asked the boy.

'New Guinea,' said the man.

A woodhen drummed and then shrilled three times. Another bird went *chop-chop-chop*. The wire twanged and raunched.

'It's a concrete post,' said the boy.

'The Park's got everything! Roads. Water, Deer. Birds. Everything!'

The man tested the seven wires.

'Now they've got cattle!' He shook the fence. 'Let's go.'

Together they started back. The cattle went on tearing at the trees in the Park.

'They get rain when we never see a drop,' said the man.

'Those concrete posts must last a long time,' said the boy.

'At first there was no fence. For a long time there was no boundary fence. Now they've built a bloody fort!'

'Those concrete posts must be good for burning-off.'

'—we were part of that Park once, by Christ!'

'Our posts are all burnt.'

'Our posts are all right.'

The land fell away and it was downhill going with the ridges on either side. Now back over their shoulders in the west there was no moon.

'Follow the dogs,' said the man.

The boy felt his way along the track. The dislodged stones rolled a long time.

'This land isn't fit for goats!' The man swung the crook in his left hand and slashed the scalloped limestone.

'Tell me about that stick—' said the boy.

'Shepherd's crook.'

'—your shepherd's crook.'

'It was your grandfather's.'

'I know—'

'One day it will be yours.'

The boy did not lift his boots high and he kept his weight on his back foot until his front foot was safely down.

Possum paws scrabbled uselessly on limestone.

'Damn the dogs!'

'They're not even hungry,' said the boy.

'Those dogs are full as ticks! Stuffed full on heifers dead of starvation!' The man slashed the pup with the crook. 'Keep that cur behind you!'

The boy watched for the dogs and for the man's crook and he waited for the lightning.

'I should be able to follow the bloody track,' said the man. 'My first year out of school I rode out here every day. But the horse knew the way, and the path is not so good now.'

'Was it a bridle path?'

'It was madness. My father should never have bought this land.'

'I know.'

'He bought this godforsaken place to please my mother. That's why he bought it, and he never got rid of it.'

'Because of Gran?'

'He did what she wanted and that was that. Do you know, I got up at daylight every morning to ride out here. My first year out of school. I used to ride out with a married man who lived in the cottage—the hayshed was a cottage in those days. A single man camped out here and when we got here we had breakfast.'

'Did he have a tent?'

'One of us would go ahead scrubbing. Slashing the undergrowth. The others cut the trees. We cut them up to three feet in diameter. We felled them all one way. When they were dry we burned the bush.'

'I know,' said the boy, and watched the man's crook.

'Nothing would stop the fires. They went up the bluffs and burnt the sky. Ash blew to Australia. Sparks landed on the house like brimstone. I spent whole nights on the roof. The woman went to the city. They should never have come back. Not for this! None of us should ever have come back—'

The man stopped walking.

'—to a damn volcano!' he cried.

The pup's tail tapped the boy's leg. The boy's heart thudded like a dislodged stone. The bluffs walled up the dark.

'Aren't you had it?' said the man.

'No. Just hungry.'

'All for this!'

The man's hobnails struck fire in the dried-up creekbeds. Dead fuchsias lined the dried-up creeks like empty webs. The man's boots struck fire from the stones in the creekbeds. Woeful sheep jerked away.

The boy listened to how his grandfather should never have bought their land.

The boy listened to how his grandmother wanted to be queen of the mountains.

'She says she's the queen of the mountains,' he said.

'Damn her!'

'Is she dippy?'

'She's old—'

'—her hands shake a lot.'

'She used to be clever with her hands. She spun a very old-fashioned way. She wound wool around a staff. She even spun flax from that staff.'

'When Mum was here, she had a spinning wheel.'

'She did.'

'It was spooky.'

'Women have always had those things.'

'I won't let my wife spin,' said the boy. 'If I have a wife.'

'You have no say,' said the man.

'I'll be a single man.'

'Yes, but someday you'll want a son.'

'You don't know.'

'Someone will want a son and you'll be the father.'

'If I have a son,' said the boy, and felt for the path behind his father.

'Don't ever be out here alone. There are enough bones in these holes. It's all right for me,' said the man. 'I know the way the gullies lie. I know the rocks and the pot-holes.'

The lightning lit the stumps and burnt them black again.

'Damn the pot-holes!' cried the man, and slashed the limestone with his crook.

They came out on a spur and saw the glow of the city to the north-east but in between was a great pitblack pot-hole and the rest of the farm fell in the pit and they walked down into it and the night lay over the land like ash.

'You'd be nix if you were out here by yourself,' said the man.

'I'd find my way.'

'You'd wander around till kingdom come.'

'I've been this way before.'

'What way?'

'I've come this way in the dark before.'

'You must have dreamt it.'

White stumps populated the dark as though the man mustered them with his curses.

'I left school to fell this bush. She said I was a man while the rest stayed boys.'

'How old were you?'

'We burned the bush and underneath it was stone. This land is all stone. Just listen—'

'I can't hear anything.'

'Not a bloody bird! Nothing!' said the man. He snorted. 'We are rich in rock!' He spat. 'Rich as Pluto!'

'That shepherd's crook—'

'It was my father's. It's going to be yours.'

'Yes, I know—'

'Well?'

'It's a wonder it wasn't burnt too—'

'Damn the crook!'

The boy kept the pup behind him and followed his father home. Their boots kicked the sides of the narrow sheeptracks cut into the granite between the stumps and the logs.

'How are you?' said the man.

'I'm all right.'

'You don't want a rest?'

'No. I'm all right.'

'How are your feet?'

'They're all right.'

'Give me the pack.'

'I can manage.'

The man's hobnails struck sparks. Each footfall was a furious description of sound.

They pushed through biddy-bid and briar and smelled the burning carcasses in the holding paddock at the bottom of the valley.

'When did you stop burning the bush?' asked the boy.

'When my father died.'

'I know how he died.'

'Damn you all!'

'Was he going to sell?'

'Was he damn well what?'

'Going to sell—'

'You can't sell land like this!'

The boy felt the night pressing on them. He thought of his grandfather's body charred and impenitent as the stumps as he rode his father's horse on the bridle path. The horse knew the way and its shoes struck sparks from the stones in the dark. Under the iron horseshoes the land shone like priceless moonstone and he thought of his missing mother and his grandmother and a woman who was all the women he knew put together, a daughter unavoidable as the night in which he followed the man and the memory of a man through the dark.

They had got the cattle out of their parched paddocks and he could smell the man's sweat and he wanted to say to his father that he liked being with him and following him and helping him but he didn't say anything.

The dogs they had left chained up were barking. They went through the iron gates. The poplars stood black over shucked leaves. They passed the old hayshed. The hydraulic ram creaked and clanked. They smelled the carbon from the gas-house.

The boy poked the unburned hooves and shins into the smouldering fires. The hair sparkled and died. The hides burned pungently. The man dragged palings from the cattle-yards. The boy raked the earth around the fires. The flames lit the man's beard like a libation of blood spilt and congealed on his chin.

'Don't get morbid!' he cried. 'Think of those cattle in the Park! Standing in water with leaves on their heads!' A decrescent moon of sparks hung from his flaying crook. 'Tantalizing, isn't it?' He booted the fire into the air. 'Damn the Park! Tie the dogs!'

The dogs strained at their chains and the boy felt their flying slaver.

The man's hobnails were lost and soundless on the lawn.

The boy smelled the mint and the rosemary outside the wash-house door.

The man sat on the form and dropped his boots on to the floor.

He splashed his face with water. The water was loud and then soft as the soap lathered. He left soap behind his ears.

He left the water for the boy.

He took the food out of the oven and they ate quietly.

From his bedroom the boy heard the pup howling. Then he heard the man belting mosquitoes.

The dark was a blanket of fire and mint and rosemary.

He heard voices.

Then gaslight from the hall fell across the boy's bed and he smelled the old woman in her white nightgown. Her shadow swaddled him, ran into the corner behind his head and rose up like black wings.

'You can't leave land like this,' she said. 'If you leave it the bush comes back and you might as well never have been born. Now turn your pillow over and go to sleep.'

MARGARET SUTHERLAND

A Servant of the People

A black jersey seemed appropriate. I wore little lipstick. It was still not time when I parked. A few faces looked out from nearby cars. I did not want to intrude so I waited until the service was underway. Someone handed me a hymn book as I went in. The usher beckoned me up to sit with the others, but I went into the back row of seats and sat close to the wall. It was a very small gathering.

I had found Edgar Adams in the Deaths column. I knew nothing about him, but I did not think he would mind me looking on at his funeral. The coffin was on a black marble slab raised like an altar. There was a bunch of home-picked flowers and one wreath. It was a Salvation Army service and several men and women in the customary uniform were there. The relatives of Edgar Adams were seated on four chairs in the front row. Three were elderly; there was one boy, perhaps fourteen.

They began with 'I Am the Resurrection and the Life'. The boy cried a great deal. I cried too; not for Edgar Adams who certainly had no use for tears, but for the boy and the rain and the downcast proteas. It was not a real mourning. It would hardly have made any difference if there had been no Edgar Adams inside the closed coffin. The tears were something apart, born of nothing, like the organ music which bellowed out on cue when there was no organ there. The prayers that were offered were of hope, life, eternal reward.

Once, coming up from my snifflings, I saw that the coffin had vanished and primitive fears sprang to life until I saw the relatives file up and drop, each of them, a white carnation into the void that had appeared, magically, in the centre of the catafalque. I went up last, and let the last carnation fall down, and tried to believe in Edgar Adams. It was hard, though a woman sobbed, and the boy's face was terribly swollen and puffed. He looked, in his unhappiness, epileptic. As I went out I saw one of the women in Army bonnet put her arm around him. Her face was calm. 'He is not dead,' I heard her say. 'He is not DEAD.' I went away quickly.

Half a mile down the road I stopped at a milk bar and bought a chocolate milk shake and a sausage roll. As I ate I remembered that I had not offered a single prayer for Edgar Adams who was dead and in a coffin scattered with white carnations. I sat in the dairy and said a guilt-prayer and brushed the pastry crumbs from my lap. When I thought my eyes were less red I drove back to the crematorium. There was no one about now. The mourners had left. The place seemed quite deserted. I found another chapel, larger than the first. It was empty.

In the gardens there were small apertures let into the wall like private boxes at a Post Office. In the halls and corridors I could not find anyone. I went back to the gardens. A man came down the path. He was dressed neatly and walked purposefully, and I did not think he was a visitor. He was a Maori, with an old scar twisting his mouth into a curiously wry expression. He said he worked there. I explained that I needed to know about cremation for a book I was writing. He did not think that odd.

It only cost $12 to be cremated, he told me. At the other place it would cost me double that amount. We're government, he said; for the people.

I said it sounded very cheap. It must cost at least that, surely, for the fuel.

Diesel, he said.

I mean, I said, it would have to be so hot.

Hot all right, he said.

About how long, I wondered, did it take?

About an hour.

Coffins and all? Or did they . . ?

No, they didn't. People said they did, but they didn't. Coffins and all.

And what about the ashes, I asked, and wondered what I would do with the ashes of someone I had loved. Nothing came to mind. He pointed to the wall spaces I had already seen.

Seven dollars sixty, he said. For maintenance and so on.

A year, did he mean?

That was it, he said. The lot. He looked pleased that I was impressed.

All the time we were moving through the gardens as though the buildings were drawing us in. We went through the main door, and he led me into the empty chapel, and showed me the button which controlled the lowering of the centre part of the marble slab. The heat of your hand was enough to set it off, he said. It had to be unobtrusive. He pointed down into the space.

They pull it through there, he said.

There was a drape covering the end where the head of the coffin would lie.

In the side room he pointed out the tape-recorder.

For the music, he told me. People think I'm a funny guy, he said. Working here.

He'd gone off to the war at seventeen. His job had been to get rid of the dead. Sometimes they'd had to use bulldozers. He'd been sick in the nights.

But you get used to it after a while, he said.

I believed him.

So that, he said, this job seemed pretty clean, if I saw his point.

They weren't really supposed to, he said. But after all there was nothing to hide. He held the door open for me. The room was tidy and clean, and centred around the three black cylinders. It was a little like entering a ship's engine room, except that the throb and the smell of oil and grease were missing. It had something of the same practical and cheerful atmosphere all the same. There wasn't any smell, apart from the Maori's hair oil.

The other man there, a closed-up fellow with small eyes, noticed me and came towards us. Was it all right if he . . . ? He glanced away to the two coffins set on biers at the end of the room. Yes, said my friend. It was all right. And he went on explaining about the gratings through which the parts that did not burn fell down, and were ground up afterwards. He indicated an object like an outsize mincer.

Did he mean bones?

Yes, he said. That's right. Bones, mainly. Screws, nails, they had to pick those out, naturally. You can see, he said, it's pretty hot in there.

The other man had wheeled a coffin across, and left the trolley and went to open the furnace door. The light inside was golden and fiery. He had to stand back a little and take a run up, to give the coffin a push. It slid through the door perfectly. I had been half-afraid that the momentum of his run might take him in after it. He fixed the door shut, and dusted off his hands.

People say we take the handles off, my friend said, but you can see for yourself.

I asked what happened to them.

They melt, he said.

We went behind the furnace so that he could show me the ashwell. It was empty. A faint roaring sound came out of the ashwell, and, now and then, smoke.

It's only the varnish, the other man told me.

And after a few minutes the smoke did not billow out any more.

You can see, said my friend as we walked back outside, that we haven't anything to hide. I wouldn't mind going that way when the time comes.

I said I wouldn't mind either.

Of course, he said, Maoris were superstitious. They weren't supposed to go in for cremation. But times were changing. Like with the Catholics. They weren't supposed to either. But times changed. He was a Catholic, he said.

I said he must have problems. Being a Catholic Maori.

He grinned back and said not really. The only thing that bothered him about the job was the way people came and blamed him when vandals got into the nearby cemetery and broke the vases and moved the angels about and tipped out the flowers. They got upset, he said, so they blamed him. How could he tell them the truth, that vandals had been in and broken the vases and moved the angels about and tipped out the flowers. He didn't want to upset them more. So he was a sitting duck. They wouldn't believe him sometimes. He had to say well go on and look under the hedge and you'll find the pieces where I tidied them away. He'd gone after the vandals some nights, but he hadn't caught them.

It's like the flowers, he said, and pointed to them, banks of colour rising from a kind of platform at the front of the building. Might be a couple of hundred dollars worth there after a big do. They had to lie there and rot. Otherwise people came along and accused him of selling them. Once they'd phoned from that institu- down the road . . . the mad-house . . . and asked for flowers to put in the wards, and he'd had to refuse because they weren't his flowers to give. He was only a public servant if I saw his point.

So they just lie there, he said; and we shovel them up when they die.

I was thanking him when the other man came outside. He walked over, treading round the puddles. He smiled and looked less closed-in. He said his lunch hour was at twelve, if I liked to wait. He had a little room down the back. We could have a cup of tea together.

I told him thanks, but I'd really found all I needed to know. I thought he winked at me as he went back inside.

I caught up with the Maori again.

Would he mind explaining to his friend? I had to take the children to the doctor, I'd just remembered . . .

He grinned. Don't you worry about him, he said. He fancies himself as a bit of a Romeo, like.

I was sorry to say goodbye to him, but I felt all right, leaving the second time. Anyway, I thought, Edgar Adams was in good hands now. My friend stopped me as I was backing the car from the parking area.

By the way, he said. If you're writing that book. Tell them we don't sell the flowers, will you?

I said I would.

The Healing Springs

RACHEL BUSH

Before each guest arrives at Deep Waters' Inn, a housemaid in white cleans the room thoroughly, to remove any trace or sign someone else has slept there. She lays the hotel notepaper and the Tourist Bureau pamphlet on the table. For women guests she provides the human touch, arranges a bowl of flowers.

When Kathryn came, she smelled the flowers and read the pamphlet carefully. 'The community of Deep Waters is situated in one of the smaller basins in the great chain of mountains. Although during the winter months many parties flock from the city to enjoy the unexcelled opportunities for ski-ing on the Western slopes of Mt Lawrence, the township of Deep Waters has only a small residential population. The community centres on the Queen Victoria Convalescent Hospital for women with the Deep Waters' Pool and the luxury Government hotel, Deep Waters' Inn. Geologists tell us that earth movements as recent as the time of William the Conqueror caused the hot waters to break through the crust of the earth.' 'And 1066,' said Kathryn, 'that is important.' 'Although the hospital has been established for fifty years, the healing properties of these famous waters and the benefits of this rarified atmosphere were not unknown to the Maori people of New Zealand. There is a legend . . .'

'And I am Kathryn,' she thought when it was dark. 'For it is important to remember I have been sick and must rest in this hotel and be plump as gourds or swelling fruit, for I touch my shoulders, arms crossed over my breast and I am thin. My bed is straight and narrow. Straight and narrow is my bed beneath these decent sheets. I open my eyes and objects thrust on me. The light is trapped within the looking glass and stares. There is a door to the bathroom and a door to the wardrobe. There is a chest of drawers and all my clothes are trapped within its chest. But I shall remember that I am not far from the city, shall not drown in the darkness. Beyond the mountain basin, through the mountains is the city not far from me. There is a city with tall buildings and bus drivers and men swing on scaffolding.'

When she woke she saw how the mountains enclosed Deep Waters. Except to the west where there was still native bush, the pine forests grew almost to the town, and above it were the stony slopes and a few peaks so high they were covered with snow in November. A white-uniformed housemaid brought Kathryn her breakfast and pulled back the curtains. She had the day to spend in writing letters to people beyond the mountains, but she must lie by the pool and get brown and sink in the waters there.

Within the village, at each corner signposts directed her to the convalescent hospital and within its grounds, most paths and alleys led to the pool. The public bath has no roof. It is surrounded by a high wood fence. Inside there are changing sheds and a strip of concrete that encircles the actual bath. An attendant is there to take the money and towels from the women who use it. Kathryn saw women everywhere. Within the pool they floated or made gentle arcs of breaststroke. As many lay on the concrete, hot from the sun. Some sat knitting. They talked in twos or threes, like a sorority. It was important to establish connection with them, not to avoid stretching towards their sisterhood, for she would be here for a week. 'I am in the privacy of a closed shed,' she thought 'And here I take off each of my clothes, fold everything separately with care and want to linger here and dally and fold my clothes again on the wood bench before I encounter their sororal love. For they are brown in the sun and I wrap my towel around my paleness. I could dress and leave, but walk out, and without looking at them, I read the notices with care. It is comforting to read 'It is compulsory to use the lavatory before entering the pool' and '2s. extra for towels'. I shall surrender my towel to the pretty Maori girl and enter naked.'

It stung, was hot at first, a consuming heat until only her head was visible and her body hidden in the deep warmth of the bath. One becomes accustomed to the heat quickly. For much time the water must lull and hold her hidden limbs. Kathryn could no longer sense the peculiar odour of the chemical vapour that floated about the pool. For much time she would move her arms cautiously, finding her senses were not oblivious here, but conscious differently. 'I do not care about their fellowship, am not different, but only a head in the pool moving myself secretly beneath the water,' thought Kathryn. When the water tired her, she was not afraid to sit by the edge of the pool.

The Maori girl gave Kathryn her towel. 'Did you enjoy it?' she asked.

'It was marvellous,' she said. She chose a place alone in the sun where she could watch the others. She would spend much time in this strange enclosure. The woman sat idle as they shall sit for ever at Deep Waters' Pool. Not all of them are beautiful and brown. There are thick pallid women with purple scars from operations, and women so emaciated the skin must stretch to reach between the bones. Kathryn listened. Near her a middle-aged woman, plump and serene, embroidered a strip of linen with birds of paradise and rich exotic flowers. A stout woman left the pool and limped over to her. The woman looked up from her work.

'Well, Audrey. And what did Dr Orange have to say?'

The stout woman puffed as she replied with a severity and resentment that seemed incongruous and like an angry woman in the city. 'I was quite furious. Do you know, he had the impertinence to tell me. . . .' She lowered her voice. 'I could have smacked his face. "Dr Orange," I said, "I'm a married woman and I will not tolerate such rudeness."' Marriage, like anger, seemed something incompatible with Deep Waters; the prerogative of people in all places but this basin.

On the other side Kathryn heard a soft complaint. 'Such pain I've been through. O such pain. Last night I thought, "I just can't bear this any longer."' The voice lapsed, exhausted, dominated by the persistent sympathy of the woman's companions.

'You're new here, aren't you?' Kathryn had not been aware that anyone had joined her. So this is what it was to be a novice in the sisterhood.

'Yes, I only arrived last night. But how did you know?'

'One gets to recognize the faces here pretty quickly. I always notice anyone else who's relatively young. There are always thousands more middle-aged women.'

'You've been coming here for some time?'

'Mm. I've got a little cottage and I teach at the hospital. There's always a few kids there.'

'That must be interesting.'

'O, the work's a hell of a bore, but I like the pool and the way of life here.'

Kathryn wanted to keep her, hold on to the first person who had made an overture, but what is there one can say. 'It's certainly very different from the city.'

'Mm. You'll find it slightly bloody at first. The awful cut-offness. And one feels frightfully shy. You were when you got into the pool. Do you smoke?'

Kathryn shook her head. She noticed the woman wore a wedding ring. There was marriage here, too. Still holding the lit match the woman said, 'By the way, I'm Sydney Priest. Bloody name, but I'm only responsible for half of it.'

'I'm Kathryn, Kathryn Lancelot.'

'Exquisitely medieval. Names mean such a lot. I do care for them. And what you you think of Deep Waters, Kathryn?'

'It's hard to say.' She seemed a sophisticated person, talked cleverly. Kathryn must say what was right. 'There seem so few men.'

'Lord, you wouldn't want both sexes bathing here, back to nature or something.'

'No, no.' She blushed, but laughing with her. 'I must say her name,' she thought, 'and it will sound awful and forced.' 'No, Sydney, but I think I've seen about one man since I came.'

'It's perfectly true to a point. There's a frightfully high percentage of women here, but you'll find that has a charm of its own. After a while one finds how little one really does depend on men. How long are you here for, anyway?'

'Only a week.'

'Too short. Lord, you must spend at least a month. I do hope you will manage to stay longer. It would be marvellous for selfish me to have someone my own age.'

In an instant, Kathryn planned her letters, how she had found a new friend, how lucky she was, and that her name was Sydney Priest.

'You see, you can't possibly learn to relax in a week. There's a real art in our leisure. The city makes life so damn tense. Cares become quite habitual, and the bloody thing is one clings to them.'

'I'll see how I get on here.'

'Well you must meet some of the others before you go. And

Miria, of course.' Kathryn looked at her. 'Miria's the attendant. She's a real pet.'

That night, Kathryn thought, 'I have met a friend and if I open my eyes, though the objects in my room are apart and unidentifiable, tomorrow I shall meet my friend, Sydney Priest. She has a bloody name, but only half is her fault. Tomorrow I shall write letters to my mother and father and I shall tell them what I have done, although they will not know from what I write what difference there is here with only women around the pool, half slumbering. For my parents are in the city where there are buses and men swing on scaffolding round tall buildings.'

Next morning she went to the pool. It was the hour when the hospital patients strolled in the gardens, paused by the beds of roses or on the seats sheltered by hedges. Within the pool, the woman were the same, but now some faces seemed familiar and their tranquillity as soothing as the waters themselves. Sydney lay face down on her towel, a novel open beside her. One may join one's friends and Kathryn went over to her. 'Hullo,' said Sydney. 'So you weren't an illusion. I half expected you wouldn't reappear. you haven't met Mrs Bowes, have you, Kathryn?'

'No, I don't think so,' and Kathryn smiled at the second of the sorority.

'This is Kathryn Lancelot. She's just up from the city for a week if you please.'

Mrs Bowes was what is commonly called a well-preserved woman, who kept her hands and fingernails immaculate, her greying hair softly bouffant and rinsed with blue. Her overweight had not advanced so much that it was beyond the control of modern underwear. She was varnishing her nails at the moment. 'I can't possibly shake hands,' she said, 'but I'm pleased to meet you. I do like to see young faces. You must be pleased, Sydney, to have someone apart from old hags like me.' This was obviously a joke and Kathryn joined their laughter and Sydney's protestations. 'Did Sydney say you'll only be here a week? You really ought to stay longer.'

'I think I might stay on a bit.'

'Lucky girl. I wish I could,' said Mrs Bowes. 'I'm so ridiculously well looking that I don't think Dr Orange will hear of my being at Deep Waters till Christmas. I still get so tired though. I don't really think I could cope with the house and meals for my poor neglected husband.'

'What does he do in the meantime?' Sydney asked.

'Eats at the club, poor dear. And there's a woman two days who does the house.'

'My poor husband is surrounded by thousands of little black girls, all at his beck and call. Gauguin-type little girls.'

'It always sounds delightful to me,' said Mrs Bowes.

'Samoa?' Sydney shrugged slightly. 'All those natives. Anyway, my health just wouldn't stand up to the climate. No, I'll be here till his year's up.' So there was no marriage here, thought Kathryn, only sororal love.

She met Miria, too. Sydney mentioned it before they went up to her. 'She's hardly like a Maori, so clean. A real pet. She's engaged though to the most bloody creature. He comes up here deer stalking at weekends. Totally uncouth.' However, she asked Miria how was her fiancé.

'Fine, thanks, Mrs Priest. And we've bought the section. Jim's seeing them about plans next week. He'll be up in about ten days.' She showed Kathryn her engagement ring which she wore on a string round her neck at work. 'Jim wanted to buy me a chain, but I said we'd have to watch every penny. Anyhow I'll be going at Christmas.'

An old lady, hair bound up beneath a plastic shower cap handed her towel to Miria. 'The Lord be with you,' she said. 'And with you, too, Sydney. And I think that's a new face.'

'Yes, this is Kathryn Lancelot, Miss St John.'

'The Lord be with you, too, dear.' She walked into the pool and swam in a strangely archaic breaststroke.

'She always does five widths,' said Sydney. 'She's frightfully eccentric and religious.'

Miss St John joined them later. She had put on her spectacles. After a few routine inquiries into the health of Kathryn and Sydney, she turned the conversation on to her faith. 'You see, my dear,' she said, touching Kathryn's knee apologetically, 'where we are here, Deep Waters, it seems we are more able to be in contact with our Lord. I hope you don't mind my speaking like this. Sometimes we old people feel things more strongly than the young. Here we are less trapped in our worldly cares.'

'No one could be worried here,' said Kathryn cautiously.

Miss St John seized on this. 'Not worried about the world, my dear. But we have time to think of the more spiritual side to our nature.'

When Miss St John left, Sydney grinned. 'She's a batty old thing, but she's right in a way. One is more in touch with God or Nature. They come to the same in the end, don't they?'

Before her week was finished, Kathryn received a letter from her mother. She read the solicitations for her health, the instructions to get plenty of sleep and to eat a good breakfast. The news of the city bored her slightly. A neighbour's daughter was engaged. Daddy had begun painting the house. Did Kathryn think yellow doors would be nice? These things seemed irrelevant. They had no bearing on what she was doing at the time. Sydney understood. 'I know exactly. One loves the people in the city, but differently here. It's like my husband. I adore him, but everything he writes on what he's doing seems so terribly petty.'

'Yes, it does seem petty,' said Kathryn.

'It's a question of perspective,' said Sydney. 'That's what changes really. You know, Kathryn, when you say things like that, you really seem one of us.' This last remark made Kathryn so happy she could not bear to sit still, but went into the pool and swam till she was tired.

The next day was her last. Everything must go beautifully. It began to go wrong as soon as she got to the pool. She heard shouting and loud laughter. 'I'm afraid it's the students again,' said Mrs Bowes. 'They were here last night, too. A party of them are studying the geology of the basin.' There were about a dozen of them, all shrieking contentedly, laughing at their nakedness. They chased each other round the concrete, swam vigorously in the pool. One of them even produced a camera and Miria had to explain this was not allowed. They formed a starfish in the water, floating on their backs. They splashed each other joyfully. 'What bloody imbeciles,' said Sydney. 'On your last day, too. You just can't take this away as your last memory.'

Miss St John was upset. 'They destroy,' she said. 'It's the sense of place. They override everything here. I'll have to leave the pool till they go.'

Finally Kathryn agreed to stay a little longer. Sydney was delighted, insisted on going to the bus depot with her. The seat was cancelled. Did Miss Lancelot want to make another booking? 'No, thank you,' said Kathryn. 'I'm not sure when I shall leave.'

The students left two days later. The pool assumed again its own ordered tranquillity. Miria said they weren't bad kids and laughed over the camera incident. Miss St John resumed her daily five widths. For almost a week nothing occurred to disturb the lapsing time, the days that evaded count or recapitulation.

On the Thursday the pool was to be cleaned in the afternoon and the women left together at midday. As they came from the lawns and hedges of the hospital, they heard a siren. An ambulance came speeding, passed them, its red light flashed. The dust rose from the country road behind it. There was an urgency in the moaning siren that Kathryn had never heard here. Everyone stopped, followed the ambulance with their eyes, silent as it turned into the hospital. "Well, whatever next?" said Mrs Bowes. It was distressing. No one knew what had happened. Kathryn felt alarm, almost panic rising in her, wanted to run somewhere very fast. 'I suppose it's some tramper,' said Mrs Bowes.

'That reminds me,' said Sydney. 'I want you and Kathryn to come to dinner with me tomorrow night. I've something special I want you two to try.'

On Friday, Miria was not at the pool. Sydney said, "The poor child. It was that boy of hers. Some frightfully ghastly accident up on the mountains."

'Is he dead?' said Kathryn. She remembered the ring about the girl's neck, the section in the city.

'No, I don't think so, but it's all fearfully touch and go.' She looked at Kathryn. 'You're white as a sheet. You mustn't take it to heart too much. He was rather a bloody little man.'

'I think I'll go for a swim,' said Kathryn. 'I'll feel better then.'

The evening, Kathryn had to dress for the dinner party. She took a long time, lost her stockings, sponged a mark from her frock. It would be great fun, of course. Sydney was such a good companion. She was a bit tired, that was all, and she ought to write to her parents. She couldn't bear to do anything that might offend Sydney, for she was her friend. Anyway she mustn't take Maria's troubles to heart too much. It made her white as a sheet.

It was easy to admire Sydney's cottage with its polished wood walls and wide windows that opened to the north mountains. "Such tasteful drapings,' said Mrs Bowes.

'Neither of you have half an idea what we're going to have for dinner,' said Sydney. 'Venison steaks! Not all those ghastly little deerstalkers fall over precipices.'

'They have their uses,' said Mrs Bowes.

'Very useful,' said Kathryn. They were useful, while Miria cried out and beat the ground.

The dinner was well cooked. 'I adore continental cooking,' said Mrs Bowes. 'So few New Zealanders understand cooking is an art. You really are clever Sydney.' The wine they drank made Mrs Bowes affectionate and Kathryn dazed and heavy.

'I'm so glad you're still here, Kathryn. You really seem one of us. And you look so well now. She's put on weight, hasn't she, Sydney?'

'Half a stone,' said Kathryn. 'I'm nearly well now.' She wanted to mention Miria. 'Have you heard any more about that deer-stalker?'

'So it is worrying you,' said Sydney. 'Lord knows what's happened to the boy. I don't suppose he's dead, but it's not our worry if he is.'

Then in a parody of maternal tenderness, the childless Mrs Bowes took Kathryn's hand in hers. Her voice had the simple sweet tone that women use on erring infants. 'My dear. We all feel sad about it. You're too sensitive. Our job is to get well here, not to fuss about other people's troubles. Your being upset isn't going to help Miria, now is it dear?' Mrs Bowes leaned back and patted her hair.

Sydney was more excited. 'She's right, you know, Kathryn. That's the whole thing about living here. It may be only an illusion, but we just have to keep up the pretence that there's no disaster and no tragedy. We couldn't bear it otherwise. The whole thing would fall to pieces, this whole bloody paradise.'

The rest of the evening passed pleasantly. They listened to records of Mozart and Haydn. Mrs Bowes murmured phrases like 'artistic sense' or 'cultured women'. Kathryn wept within herself and planned her return to the city.

That night she thought, 'I am Kathryn who was sick and is made well. I shall leave this paradise. I touch my shoulders, arms across my breast and am not thin, but wide and empty is my bed. My bed is wide and empty. The objects in my room contain my clothes, but I shall empty them. I shall go beyond the mountain basin. Through the mountains is the city where there are tall buildings and bus drivers. For I am well. I have eaten steak brought by a deerstalker who did not fall. He was useful to me, useful as Miria was useful, as the hotel was useful and the Deep Waters' pool. I shall go back to the city where there are tall buildings and men swing on scaffolding.'

She packed her bags before the maid brought her breakfast. She paid her hotel bill. She found it hard to do things like this again and was slow and fumbling. A taxi was rung for her. The manageress shook hands with Kathryn and regretted her departure. When Kathryn had gone she told a housemaid, for when a guest leaves Deep Waters' Inn, the room is stripped of sheets and flowers, all traces removed that anyone has slept there.

At the bus depot, Kathryn was told the minibus was full. It just wasn't possible to take another passenger. The woman was apologetic. They could take her luggage. She really was sorry. A man standing at the counter said, 'Look, excuse me. Is it important you go today?'

'Well, I should like to, very much,' she said.

'I don't know if it's possible for this lady to arrange for your luggage, but if you can fix that up, I'm flying back and there's room for a passenger.'

'That's terribly kind of you,' said Kathryn. 'I really do want to leave.' She left no note for Sydney or Mrs Bowes. She could write to them from the city.

As she walked to the airstrip, the man introduced himself. He had come up to see his son who had been injured deer culling. Kathryn might have heard of the accident. The whole village seemed to know.

'I think I did,' said Kathryn. 'Is he all right?'

'Should be, he's as strong as an ox. It was the exposure to cold as much as the fracture that's laid him up.'

He showed her where she must step to climb into the frail small plane. 'They're mainly paper, these things,' he said. When the propeller turned and the whole plane shuddered, he climbed in beside her. Over the noise of the vibration he bellowed, 'Sorry to be leaving?' She smiled and shook her head. Later he told her to look back. There was a fine view of Deep Waters. There was too, but from a perspective so different she hardly recognized it. The village had become infinitely smaller, insignificant in the mountains. The pool itself was merely a splinter, like glass that caught the sun. He shouted, 'Still glad you left?' and when she nodded he said, 'Gets you down, that place, after a while. Too many chattering women with not enough to do.' Kathryn nodded. He looked at his watch. 'Should be in time for the pub,' he said.

WITI IHIMAERA   # A Game of Cards

The train pulled into the station. For a moment there was
confusion: a voice blaring over the loudspeaker system, people
getting off the train, the bustling and shoving of the crowd on the
platform.

And there was Dad, waiting for me. We hugged each other. We
hadn't seen each other for a long time. Then we kissed. But I could
tell something was wrong.

— Your Nanny Miro, he said. She's very sick.

Nanny Miro . . . among all my nannies, she was the one I loved
most. Everybody used to say I was her favourite mokopuna, and
that she loved me more than her own children who'd grown up
and had kids of their own.

She lived down the road from us, right next to the meeting house
in the big old homestead which everybody in the village called
'The Museum' because it housed the prized possessions of the
whanau, the village family. Because she was rich and had a lot of
land, we all used to wonder why Nanny Miro didn't buy a newer,
more modern house. But Nanny didn't want to move. She liked her
own house just as it was.

— Anyway, she used to say, what with all my haddit kids and their
haddit kids and all this haddit whanau being broke all the time and
coming to ask me for some money, how can I afford to buy a new
house?

Nanny didn't really care about money though. Who needs it? she
used to say. What you think I had all these kids for, ay? To look
after me, I'm not dumb!

Then she would cackle to herself. But it wasn't true really,
because her family would send all their kids to her place when they
were broke and she looked after them! She liked her mokopunas,
but not for too long. She'd ring up their parents and say:

— Hey! When you coming to pick up your hoha kids! They're
wrecking the place!

Yet, always, when they left, she would have a little weep, and give
them some money. . . .

I used to like going to Nanny's place. For me it was a big
treasure house, glistening with sports trophies and photographs,

pieces of carvings and greenstone, and feather cloaks hanging from the walls.

Most times, a lot of women would be there playing cards with Nanny. Nanny loved all card games—five hundred, poker, canasta, pontoon, whist, euchre—you name it, she could play it.

The sitting room would be crowded with the kuias, all puffing clouds of smoke, dressed in their old clothes, laughing and cackling and gossiping about who was pregnant—and relishing all the juicy bits too!

I liked sitting and watching them. Mrs Heta would always be there, and when it came to cards she was both Nanny's best friend and worst enemy. And the two of them were the biggest cheats I ever saw.

Mrs Heta would cough and reach for a hanky while slyly slipping a card from beneath her dress. And she was always reneging in five hundred! But her greatest asset was her eyes, which were big and googly. One eye would look straight ahead, while the other swivelled around, having a look at the cards in the hands of the women sitting next to her.

— Eeee! You cheat! Nanny would say. You just keep your eyes to yourself, Maka tiko bum!

Mrs Heta would look at Nanny as if she were offended. Then she would sniff and say:

— You cheat yourself, Miro Mananui. I saw you sneaking that ace from the bottom of the pack.

— How do you know I got an ace Maka? Nanny would say. I know you! You dealt this hand, and you stuck that ace down there for yourself, you cheat! Well, ana! I got it now! So take that!

And she would slap down her hand.

— Sweet, ay? she would laugh. Good? Kapai lalelale? And she would sometimes wiggle her hips, making her victory sweeter.

— Eeee! Miro! Mrs Heta would say. Well, I got a good hand too!

And she would slap her hand down and bellow with laughter.

— Take that!

And always, they would squabble. I often wondered how they ever remained friends. The names they called each other!

Sometimes, I would go and see Nanny and she would be all alone, playing patience. If there was nobody to play with her, she'd always play patience. And still she cheated! I'd see her hands fumbling across the cards, turning up a jack or queen she needed, and then she'd laugh and say:

— I'm too good for this game!

She used to try to teach me some of the games, but I wasn't very interested, and I didn't yell and shout at her like the women did. She liked the bickering.

— Aue . . . she would sigh. Then she'd look at me and begin dealing out the cards in the only game I ever knew how to play.

And we would yell snap! all the afternoon. . . .

Now, Nanny was sick.

I went to see her that afternoon after I'd dropped my suitcases at home. Nanny Tama, her husband, opened the door. We embraced and he began to weep on my shoulder.

— Your Nanny Miro, he whispered, She's . . . she's. . . .

He couldn't say the words. He motioned me to her bedroom.

Nanny Miro was lying in bed. And she was so old looking. Her face was very grey, and she looked like a tiny wrinkled doll in that big bed. She was so thin now, and seemed all bones.

I walked into the room. She was asleep. I sat down on the bed beside her, and looked at her lovingly.

Even when I was a child, she must have been old. But I'd never realised it. She must have been over seventy now. Why do people you love grow old so suddenly?

The room had a strange, antiseptic smell. Underneath the bed was a big chamber pot, yellow with urine . . . And the pillow was flecked with small spots of blood where she had been coughing.

I shook her gently.

— Nanny . . . Nanny, wake up.

She moaned. A long, hoarse sigh grew on her lips. Her eyelids fluttered, and she looked at me with blank eyes . . . and then tears began to roll down her cheeks.

— Don't cry, Nanny, I said. Don't cry. I'm here.

But she wouldn't stop.

So I sat beside her on the bed and she lifted her hands to me.

— Haere mai, mokopuna. Haere mai. Mmm. Mmm.

And I bent within her arms and we pressed noses.

After a while, she calmed down. She seemed to be her own self.

— What a haddit mokopuna you are, she wept. It's only when I'm just about in my grave that you come to see me.

— I couldn't see you last time I was home, I explained. I was too busy.

— Yes, I know you fullas, she grumbled. It's only when I'm almost dead that you come for some money.

— I don't want your money, Nanny.

— What's wrong with my money! she said. Nothing's wrong with it! Don't you want any?

— Of course I do, I laughed. But I know you! I bet you lost it all
on poker!

She giggled. Then she was my Nanny again. The Nanny I knew.

We talked for a long time. I told her about what I was doing in
Wellington and all the neat girls who were after me.

— You teka! she giggled. Who'd want to have you!

And she showed me all her injection needles and pills and told
me how she wanted to come home from the hospital, so they'd let
her.

— You know why I wanted to come home? she asked. I didn't like
all those strange nurses looking at my bum when they gave me
those injections. I was so sick, mokopuna, I couldn't even go to the
lav, and I'd rather wet my own bed not their neat bed. That's why
I come home.

Afterwards, I played the piano for Nanny. She used to like *Me
He Manuere* so I played it for her, and I could hear her quavering
voice singing in her room.

                    Me he manurere aue . . . .

When I finally left Nanny I told her I would come back in the
morning.

But that night, Nanny Tama rang up.

— Your Nanny Miro, she's dying.

We all rushed to Nanny's house. It was already crowded. All the
old woman were there. Nanny was lying very still. Then she looked
up and whispered to Mrs Heta:

— Maka . . . Maka tiko bum . . . I want a game of cards. . . .

A pack of cards was found. The old ladies sat around the bed,
playing. Everybody else decided to play cards too, to keep Nanny
company. The men played poker in the kitchen and sitting room.
The kids played snap in the other bedrooms. The house overflowed
with card players, even onto the lawn outside Nanny's window,
where she could see. . . .

The woman laid the cards out on the bed. They dealt the first
hand. They cackled and joked with Nanny, trying not to cry. And
Mrs Heta kept saying to Nanny:

— Eee! You cheat Miro. You cheat! And she made her googly eye
reach far over to see Nanny's cards.

— You think you can see, ay, Maka tiko bum? Nanny coughed.
You think you're going to win this hand, ay? Well, take that!

She slammed down a full house.

The other woman goggled at the cards. Mrs Heta looked at her
own cards. Then she smiled through her tears and yelled:

— Eee! You cheat Miro! I got two aces in my hand already! Only four in the pack. So how come you got three aces in your hand?

Everybody laughed. Nanny and Mrs Heta started squabbling as they always did, pointing at each other and saying: You the cheat, not me! And Nanny Miro said: I saw you, Maka tiko bum, I saw you sneaking that card from under the blanket.

She began to laugh. Quietly. Her eyes streaming with tears.

And while she was laughing, she died.

Everybody was silent. Then Mrs Heta took the cards from Nanny's hands and kissed her.

— You the cheat, Miro, she whispered. You the cheat yourself. . . .

We buried Nanny on the hill with the rest of her family. During her tangi, Mrs Heta played patience with Nanny, spreading the cards across the casket.

Later in the year, Mrs Heta, she died too. She was buried right next to Nanny, so that they could keep on playing cards. . . .

And I bet you they're still squabbling up there. . . .

— Eee! You cheat Miro. . . .

— You the cheat, Maka tiko bum. You, you the cheat. . . .